By Lisa Scottoline

Daddy's Girl
Dirty Blonde
Devil's Corner
Killer Smile
Dead Ringer
Courting Trouble
The Vendetta Defense
Moment of Truth
Mistaken Identity
Rough Justice
Legal Tender
Running From the Law
Final Appeal
Everywhere That Mary Went

LISA SCOTTOLINE

DEVIL'S CORNER

HARPER

An Imprint of HarperCollinsPublishers

This is a work of fiction. Names, characters, places, and incidents are products of the author's imagination or are used fictitiously and are not to be construed as real. Any resemblance to actual events, locales, organizations, or persons, living or dead, is entirely coincidental.

HARPER

An Imprint of HarperCollins*Publishers*
10 East 53rd Street
New York, New York 10022-5299

Copyright © 2005 by Lisa Scottoline
Excerpt from *Dirty Blonde* copyright © 2006 by Lisa Scottoline
ISBN: 978-0-06-137935-2
ISBN-10: 0-06-137935-2

First Harper paperback special printing: June 2007
First HarperTorch paperback printing: April 2006
First HarperCollins hardcover printing: June 2005

HarperCollins® and Harper® are trademarks of HarperCollins Publishers.

Printed in the United States of America

Visit Harper paperbacks on the World Wide Web at
www.harpercollins.com

10 9 8 7 6 5 4 3 2

to my daughter,
my favorite heroine of all time

PART ONE

I do call the city to be laid out by the name of Philadelphia. Let every house be placed, if the person pleases, in the middle of its plat, so there may be ground on each side for gardens or orchards or fields, that it may be a green country town, which will never be burnt, and always be wholesome.

—WILLIAM PENN,
Instructions to His Commissioners, 1681

Q: What type of drugs did you deal?
A: I started out dealing small quantities, then over the years I grew to bigger quantities of drugs.
Q: And what type of drug was it that you specialized in?
A: I started out dealing crack cocaine, and I started dealing cocaine, powder cocaine.
Q: About when was it that you started dealing crack cocaine, about how old were you?
A: About 13 years old.
Q: And can you tell me where it was that you got started?
A: I got started on the block of Ithan Street, 50th and Market, around West Philadelphia area.

—JAMAL MORRIS,
United States v. Williams,
United States District Court,
Eastern District of Pennsylvania,
Criminal Docket No. 02–172, February 19, 2004,
Notes of Testimony at 242–243

ONE

VICKI ALLEGRETTI ALWAYS WONDERED WHAT it would feel like to look into the barrel of a loaded gun, and now she knew. The gun was a black Glock, nine millimeter, and it was aimed at her right eye. Vicki observed the scene out-of-body, as if it were happening to a girl with a better sense of humor. *Wonder if black guns make you look thinner*, she thought.

Holding her point-blank was an African-American teenager with cornrows, who looked as terrified as she was. He looked about fourteen years old, showing just a shadow of a mustache, and his brown eyes were jittery with fear. He kept shifting his weight in his big Iversons, standing tall in baggy jeans and a red satin Sixers jacket. He'd frozen in place when he'd come downstairs and found Vicki standing there, his shocked expression suggesting that he hadn't shot many lawyers. *At least not his share.*

"You don't want to do this, pal," she said, only apparently calmly. The kid's long fingers trembled on the gun's cross-hatched grip, and his other hand cradled a bulge underneath his jacket, as if he were hiding something. She had evidently interrupted a burglary by a rookie. Unfortunately, the Glock was an all-star. "I'm an assistant U.S. Attorney."

"Wha?" The teenager swallowed hard, his eyes flickering with confusion.

"I work for the Justice Department. Killing me is like killing a cop." *Okay, it wasn't technically true, but it should have been.* "If you shoot me, they'll try you as an adult. They'll go for the death penalty."

"Get your hands up!" The teenager's eyes flared, and he wet his lips with a large, dry tongue.

"Okay, sure. Relax." Vicki raised her hands slowly, fighting the instinct to run. He'd shoot her in the back if she did; the living room was so small, she'd never make it to the front door. Maybe she could talk her way out of it. "Listen, you don't want to upgrade a burglary charge to murder. The stuff that's under your jacket is yours now. Take it and run."

"Shut up!"

So Vicki did, holding her hands up, her thoughts racing ahead. None of this was supposed to be happening. She had come to the row house tonight to meet a confidential informant in a minor straw purchase case. The meeting was to be so routine that Bob Morton, an ATF case agent, was finishing his cigarette outside by the car. Could she stall until Morty got here? And where was her CI now?

"Jay-Boy!" the kid yelled up the stairwell, panicky. "*Jay!*"

Vicki noted the nickname. She could identify every zit on the kid's face. She wasn't getting out of this alive. She couldn't wait for Morty. She had to do something.

"Jay! Where you at?" the teenager shouted, half turning away, and Vicki seized her only chance. She grabbed the barrel of the Glock and twisted it upward. At the same instant, Morty walked through the screen door and the whole world exploded.

"Morty, watch out!" Vicki shouted. The Glock fired, jerking convulsively. The barrel seared her palms. The shot split her eardrums. The teenager wrenched the gun back, yanking her off her feet. Simultaneously, another shot rang out. Not from the Glock. Too close to be from Morty's gun. Vicki's throat caught and she looked past the teenager. A man in a goatee and a black coat was shooting at Morty from the stairs.

"No!" Vicki screamed, grappling for the Glock. She glimpsed Morty as he fell backward, grimacing with pain. His arms flew open like a marionette's, throwing the gun from his hand.

"NO!" Vicki screamed louder, as the shooter on the stairs kept firing. A second gunshot, then a third and fourth burst into Morty's chest, exploding the blue ripstop of his down jacket, jerking his fallen body on impact.

Vicki's heart hiccupped with fear and she yanked harder on the gun. The teenager punched her in the stomach, and she doubled over, gasping for breath. She released the Glock and hit back. She connected with his Sixers jacket and held on for dear life.

"Let go!" the teenager shouted, punching Vicki again and again. She flailed and after a solid body blow, crumpled to the floor, the wind sucked out of her. As she fell, she heard the faraway scream of a police siren and the kid shouting, scared, "Jay, we gotta go! Jay!"

Vicki lay doubled over on her side, her body paralyzed with pain. Tears blurred her vision. She couldn't collect her thoughts. She heard footsteps and panting, then a chamber being ratcheted back. She opened wet eyes into the two bottomless black wells of a sawed-off gun. Hot smoke curled from the barrels, filling her nose with a burning smell. Aiming the weapon was the shooter with the goatee.

My God, no. Vicki rolled over in a last effort to save herself.

"Don't do it, Jay, she's a cop!" the teenager screamed. Then, "No! Get it! Hurry!" Suddenly they were scrambling to pick things up off the floor. Whatever they'd stolen must have fallen out of the Sixers coat.

"Leave it go, Teeg! We gotta go!" The shooter was already sprinting away, his hands full. The teenager bolted after him, jumping over Morty and out the front door, leaving the row house suddenly quiet.

Morty. Vicki rolled back over and struggled to her feet, stumbling across the living room to him.

"Morty!" she called, anguished, when she reached his side. He was lying on his back, his arms still flung wide, his blue eyes fluttering. "Morty, can you hear me? Morty?"

He didn't answer, his gaze barely focused. His neat features had gone slack and a sheen of perspiration coated his forehead and wet his sandy hair. Fresh blood gurgled from his chest and drenched his jacket, soaking its bright blue to slick black, spattering its exposed white stuffing with red flecks.

No, please, God. Vicki choked back tears. She covered the wound with her palm to stanch the flow and reached into her raincoat pocket, grabbed her cell phone, flipped it open, and pressed speed dial for 911. When the dispatcher picked up, she said, "I'm at 483 Maron Street, off of Roosevelt Boulevard! I have an officer down! Officer shot!"

"Excuse me?" the dispatcher answered. "Miss, what did you say your name was?"

"Allegretti! Hurry, I have an ATF agent shot! Send an ambulance! Now!" Vicki tucked the slippery cell phone under an ear and pressed against Morty's wound with all her might. "What do I do? He's shot in the chest! I'm trying to stop the blood!"

"Keep it up and don't move him," the dispatcher answered. "Stay calm and I'll get you an ambulance."

"Thank you! Hurry!" Vicki pressed harder on the wound. Blood pulsed hot and wet between her fingers. Morty's lips were parting. He was trying to say something.

"Vick?" Morty's forehead creased. "That . . . you?"

"Yes, I'm here, it's me!" Vicki felt her heart lift. She kept her palm over the horrific wound. If anybody could survive this, Morty could. He was a fit forty-five-year-old, he worked out religiously, and he'd even run a marathon.

"What the hell . . . happened?" A watery red-pink bubble formed in the corner of Morty's mouth, and Vicki fought to maintain emotional control.

"Two kids were here when I came in, it was a burglary. The door was open, and I thought I heard somebody say come in—"

"How's . . . the CI?"

"I don't know. She may not be home."

"You're okay . . . right?"

"I'm fine. You're gonna be fine, too." The blood bubble popped, and Vicki watched in horror. If only she'd let him smoke in the car. If only she'd grabbed the gun sooner. The shooter hadn't killed her because he thought she was a cop, but Morty was the cop. On the cell phone, the emergency dispatcher was saying that an ambulance was ten minutes from the house. Vicki said, "The ambulance is on the way. Just hang in, please, hang in."

"Funny. You always said . . . cigarettes will . . . kill me." Morty managed an agonized smile.

"You're gonna be fine, Morty. You'll see, you'll be fine. You have to be fine."

"You're bossy for . . . a midget," Morty whispered, then his smile suddenly relaxed.

And he stopped breathing.

Vicki heard herself scream his name, then dropped the cell phone and tried to resuscitate him until police showed up at the door.

And things got even worse.

T W O

BY MIDNIGHT, THE SMALL ROW HOUSE WAS crammed to bursting with uniformed cops and homicide detectives from the Philadelphia Police Department; crime scene technicians from the city's Mobile Crime Unit; Vicki's chief, Howard Bale, from the U.S. Attorney's Office; and bosses from the FBI and Alcohol, Tobacco, Firearms, and Explosives. The only person missing was Morty, whose body had been photographed, placed inside a black nylon bag, and taken away, officially pronounced dead. It left Vicki feeling more alone than was reasonable in such a crowd, as she sat on a patterned couch across from a homicide detective.

"Okay, that's it for now," the detective said, flipping his notebook closed and rising from the ottoman.

"Good." Vicki stayed put on the couch, emotionally numb. She had washed her hands but hadn't taken off her trench coat. Dried blood stained its lapels, which she realized only when the detective started looking at her funny. "I forget, did I give you my business card?"

"Yes, you did. Thanks."

"Sure." Vicki would have used his name but she had forgotten that, too. Her body ached and her heart had gone hollow. She'd given a long statement to ATF, FBI, and finally the homicide detectives, with every detail poured out like murder-scene stream of consciousness. All the time she was thinking of Morty and the CI, who lay upstairs, shot to death. Vicki hadn't seen the body yet because the cops had wanted her statement first, in order to get the flash on the radio.

She rose from the couch on weak knees and threaded her way through the crowd to the stairs. The house was January cold from the front door being opened so often, and she avoided the curious glances and tuned out the ambient conversation. She wanted to stay mentally within, insulated by her stained Burberry. She had to figure out how tonight had gone so wrong, and why.

She made her way to the stairs, past the numbered yellow cards used to mark where shells had fallen. Her thoughts circled in confusion. This was only a routine straw purchase case; the indictment charged that a woman had bought two Colt .45s at a local gun shop and illegally resold them to someone else, the violent equivalent to buying scotch for a minor. The CI had called to inform on the defendant before Vicki had joined the office, and she had inherited the case because straw cases were dumped on newbies to cut their teeth. One of the most dedicated agents from the Bureau of Alcohol, Tobacco, Firearms, and Explosives had been assigned to partner with her.

Morty. Please forgive me.

Something brushed Vicki's shoulder and she jumped. Her boss, Howard Bale, was standing there, all five feet nine of his African-American pin-striped, well-tailored, tassel-loafered self. A cashmere camel-hair coat topped his characteristically *GQ* look. Bale always joked that he wasn't black, he was a peacock.

"Oh, Chief." Bale's eyes, the rich hue of espresso, were tilted down with strain, and his lips, buried under a mustache that hid an overbite, curved into a fatigued but sympathetic smile.

"You all right?"

"Fine." Vicki held on to the banister as a crime scene tech wedged by, a quilted vest worn under his navy jumpsuit.

"You drink that water I got you?"

"I forgot."

"I'm the chief, kid. You're not allowed to forget."

"Sorry." Vicki faked a smile. When Bale first arrived at the scene, he had given her a big hug and a cup of water. The gesture wasn't lost on anybody; he was saying, *I don't blame the kid, so don't you.* Nor did he yell about what a screw-up this must have been, though she guessed that would come. Not that it mattered any longer. Vicki had wanted to be a federal prosecutor since law school, and now she didn't care if she got fired.

"Where you going?" Bale asked.

"To see my CI."

"Wait. Got something I want to show you." Bale gentled her from the stairs by her elbow and guided her back through the living room. Uniforms and detectives actually parted for him; Bale, as section chief of Major Crimes, was next in line for U.S. Attorney. He led her near the front door of the row house, and Vicki stiffened as she got close to the spot where Morty had been killed. "S'all right," Bale said softly, but Vicki shook her head.

"No, it isn't."

"Look down. Here." Bale pointed, and Vicki looked. A ring of cops who had been kneeling around something on the rug rose and edged away. On the rug lay a white object the size of a brick, covered several times in clear Saran Wrap and closed with duct tape. A kilogram of cocaine.

"How'd I miss that?" Vicki asked, surprised. She'd practically had to trip over it, but she'd been focused on Morty.

"You said they dropped something from the Sixers coat." Bale had listened to her statement. "It musta been upstairs, from what you described, with them running down."

"Yes." Vicki had assumed the teenagers had stolen normal things, like jewelry or cash. "Cocaine? A kilogram?"

"That's weight," Bale said significantly, and Vicki understood. A kilogram of coke was supplier-level weight. It would have a street value of $30,000, called "weight money" as opposed to "headache money," the money that street dealers made. Bale leaned close. "Obviously, we won't be releasing this detail to the press. You'll keep this to yourself."

"Got it." Focusing on the cocaine was clearing Vicki's head. "So my CI was a coke dealer? Why would a dealer volunteer to talk to us?"

"After you look around, tell me what you think. I have a theory and everybody agrees. That tells me I'm in trouble."

Vicki couldn't manage a smile because she kept looking at the brick. *Morty died for coke.*

"No, he didn't," Bale said sharply.

Vicki looked up, surprised she had said anything aloud.

"Morty died for his job, and that's the way he would have wanted it."

"Maybe," Vicki said, though she didn't know if he was right. She couldn't wrap her mind around it just now.

"Notice anything special about this cocaine, little girl?"

"No. Do I flunk?"

"Look again, in the light." Bale snagged a Maglite from a uniformed cop, eased onto his haunches, and turned on the flashlight. He aimed it at the cocaine, and Vicki, crouching beside him, saw what he meant. There was a telltale shimmer to the cocaine, like a deadly rainbow.

"Fish-scale cocaine?" Vicki asked, surprised. She'd thought it was urban drug myth, yet here it was; a rainbow shine that looked like fish scales, if only in the vernacular of people who didn't fish.

"Right. It's so pure, it increases in volume when they cook it."

Vicki had learned this somewhere along the line, too. Most cocaine decreased when it was cooked, by mixing it with water, baking soda, and a cutting agent like mannitol, and stirring until oil formed on the water's surface. The oil would be cooled on ice, so it crystallized to form rocks. The crackling sound the mixture made when it was boiled gave the drug its name. *Crack.*

"This is quality coke, it's worth forty grand, maybe more," Bale added.

"Really?" Vicki couldn't help but feel a little wide-eyed. It was the reason she had wanted this job, after two years at the D.A.'s office; the chance to prosecute big-time, high-stakes drug trafficking. Only now it had gotten Morty killed. She rose, biting her lip not to lose control, and Bale switched off the Maglite, rising beside her.

"You guys couldn't have known," Bale said, an uncharacteristic softness to his tone, and Vicki felt a tear arrive without warning. He pretended not to notice, and she blinked it away.

"I should go see my CI."

"Name was Jackson, right?"

"Yes. Shayla Jackson."

"Did you meet with her before tonight?"

"No." Vicki felt her cheeks grow hot. "I talked to her on the phone to schedule the meeting. I waited to talk to her because I thought she'd speak more freely in person. Obviously, I made a terrible mistake."

"No, you didn't. It wasn't a bad call."

"Yes, it was. None of this would have happened. I should have known."

"Stop. Hindsight is twenty-twenty, you know that. I'd have done the same." Bale put a hand on her shoulder. "What'd Jackson say before the grand jury? That'll tell you something."

"I don't know. The transcript wasn't in the file."

Bale frowned. "Now, that shouldn't be. You gotta keep your files better."

"I got the file as is, remember? The only background info in the file is a memo from the old AUSA, saying that Shayla Jackson called the office and offered to testify that the defendant bought the guns for resale."

Vicki felt another wave of regret that she'd waited to meet with Jackson. If she had known more, the CI would be alive tonight. And Morty. She pressed the thought away, but she knew it would return. "The coke confuses me. Jackson didn't sound like the type. I wonder if this has anything to do with the straw case."

"How?"

"Well, Jackson knew I was coming over tonight. It was risky for her to meet with me here, if she had coke in the house. It doesn't make sense." Vicki was thinking out loud, a bad habit in front of a boss. "What if she was killed to prevent her from talking to me tonight? Or from testifying?"

"In a straw purchase case, it's unlikely. How many counts is it?"

"One."

"So, five years at most. It's penny-ante. Who's the straw?"

"Her name is Reheema Bristow. No priors, held two jobs."

"So, nothing special. They pick straws who have valid ID, no record, and a steady employment history, in case the gun dealer checks. Straws don't have the juice to get anybody killed."

"Maybe whoever she resold the guns to does." Vicki couldn't dismiss it so easily. "And the timing's funny. Bristow's trial comes up next week, or would have."

"What's this do to your case?"

"It's over."

"No corroboration for Jackson's testimony?"

"No."

Bale frowned again, this time puckering his pinkish lower lip. "Okay, go on up, but you know the drill, don't touch anything. The locals don't like you walking over the scene, but they already sketched and took pictures. Just be careful; the techs haven't finished upstairs. You want company?"

"No thanks," Vicki answered. Bale was already nodding to a uniformed cop, trying to commandeer him to baby-sit, but turned away before he could see the cop hadn't budged an inch. No city cop was doing anything for the feds, other than lending him a Maglite.

"We'll talk later, at the office." Bale squeezed her shoulder again. "Don't stay long upstairs. Go home and rest yourself."

"Sure. Thanks for the water." Vicki turned to go.

Not knowing what she'd find.

THREE

VICKI LINGERED AT THE THRESHOLD OF THE upstairs bedroom. A team of crime techs clustered at the foot of the bed, working around Jackson's body, obscuring it from view. One tech vacuumed the light blue rug for hair and fiber samples, and another bagged Jackson's hands to preserve evidence under her fingernails. A police photographer bundled in a dark coat videotaped the crime scene, and another took photographs. Flashes of white strobe rhythmically seared the bedroom.

Vicki told herself that she was waiting for the police personnel to finish their job, but she was getting used to the primal odor of fresh blood and fighting to keep her emotions in check. She had seen three murder scenes at the D.A.'s office, but she had never experienced anything like tonight, in which a federal agent and a witness had been killed. The crime struck at the justice system itself, and Vicki wasn't the only one feeling its gravity. The crime techs seemed unusually subdued, absorbed in their tasks. Nobody was going to screw this one up.

The police photographer, an older man with bifocals, turned and asked, "Excuse me, am I in your way?"

"No, the investigation comes first," Vicki answered, and hoped she sounded convincing.

She glanced around the bedroom, sizing it up. Even by city standards, it was small; typical of the two-bedroom brick row houses that lined the blocks around Roosevelt Boulevard. Vicki could see the other bedroom down the hall, at the back of the house and figured she'd use the time to check it out.

She walked down the hall, and the lights were on inside, revealing a spare bedroom full of stacked boxes, gathered evidently from a liquor store. Two crime techs in latex gloves were slitting the neat brown packing tape with boxcutters and searching the boxes. Handwritten in black Sharpie next to the Smirnoff and Tanqueray labels, they read CDS and SUMMER CLOTHES.

"Looks like she was moving," Vicki said to the techs, then heard herself. "Duh."

"You must be a detective," the red-haired tech joked.

"No, an AUSA."

"Worse." The tech laughed.

"So what are you finding?"

"It's fascinating. Inside the box that's labeled summer clothes, there are summer clothes, and the box that says CDs has CDs."

"I'll leave now," Vicki said with a tight smile, and pondered the discovery as she returned to the master bedroom and stood again at the threshold. The techs were still at work over the body, and she made a mental note that the bedroom hadn't been packed up yet. If Jackson was leaving, it wasn't imminent.

Vicki looked around the bedroom. The oak dresser and night table had been ransacked and drawers hung open, and the bed, a king-size, sat opposite the two front windows. It had been covered with a quilted comforter of blue forget-me-nots, which had been yanked off, and even the mattress was off-kilter.

One of the techs muttered, "Sheee. Whole lotta blood."

"Whaddaya expect?" another asked.

Vicki eyed the messed-up bed. Stuffed plush animals tumbled on the pillows: a pink teddy bear, a fuzzy puppy clutching a white heart, and a greenish snake with black diamonds. There hadn't been any toys downstairs, so the stuffed animals had to be Jackson's. Vicki felt a twinge.

Her attention was drawn to the other messy areas in the bedroom; to the left was a closet whose white louvered doors hung open, with clothing spilling out. She walked over, giving the body and the techs wide berth. A stack of sweaters and sweatshirts had been pulled out and onto the rug. Empty Nine West shoe boxes lay scattered and open on the bedroom floor, as if they had been pulled from the closet in haste. The burglars hadn't stolen Nine West sandals. Had the cocaine been in the shoe boxes?

Vicki turned and scanned the bedroom again. Next to the closet, the dresser, a modern oak one, sat ransacked against the wall. She went over and caught sight of herself in the large attached mirror. Her blue eyes were red-rimmed and puffy, her small nose pink at the tip from crying, and her hair, jet-black and shoulder-length, looked unprofessionally messy. And Morty's blood was still on her coat lapel. She looked away.

The corners of the mirror were festooned with plastic leis, a multicolored array of Mardi Gras necklaces, and a black foamy cap that read Taj Mahal. Photographs had been stuck inside the mirror's frame, and Vicki eyed them. There were five pictures, and everybody in them was dressed up. The venues were tony, if the prominent advertising backdrops were any indication: the NBA All-Star game, the BET awards. Three of the photos were of the same young man: an African American about thirty years old, with a broad smile and largish eyes. He had a muscular, compact form, a heavy gold chain around his neck, and his hair was shorn into a close fade, revealing a script tattoo on the side of his neck, indecipherable.

The other photos were also of the young man, but this time he was standing on the boardwalk, the ocean behind him, being hugged by a young woman with an equally broad smile. She looked to be about twenty-something and wore heavy makeup, a white halter top, jeans shorts, and platforms. Lots of gold jewelry but no wedding ring. A sea breeze blew through her straightened hair, and in the last photo she wore a foamy black cap, turned sideways. Taj Mahal. The same hat as on the mirror.

Vicki felt a pang. The woman must be Shayla Jackson. The man must be her boyfriend.

Her gaze fell under the lamplight on the bureau, where an open jewelry box gleamed like a cartoon treasure chest. The trays overflowed with hoop earrings, gold bangles, diamond-studded tennis bracelets, gold chain necklaces; it was several thousand dollars' worth of jewelry, and amazingly, none of it had been disturbed, much less stolen, by the teenagers. Obviously, Teeg and Jay-Boy were no ordinary burglars.

Clutter around the jewelry box hadn't been touched either. Bottles of expensive perfume—First, Chanel, Shalimar—lay next to a pen, a pair of Gucci sunglasses, and a few scattered bills for Philadelphia Electric, Verizon, and Philadelphia Gas. Vicki looked closer. They were utilities bills for this house, and the postmark was last month. The bills were addressed to Jackson, but she hadn't opened them. She had crossed out her own name and address and written in its place "Jamal Browning, 3635 Aspinall Street."

Assuming it was Jackson's handwriting, which seemed likely, even Vicki could connect these dots. Jackson was sending Browning the bills for the house. He was keeping her. He had to be the boyfriend in the photos. Vicki hadn't seen drug paraphernalia anywhere downstairs, much less money counters or digital scales used by big-time dealers. Jackson probably wasn't a coke dealer, especially of fish-scale coke; more likely, hers was a stash house and she was keeping the drugs for someone else. Someone she would risk her neck for by keeping it on her premises; someone who trusted her with such valuable merchandise. Jamal Browning, her boyfriend. But why was she moving?

"It's a goddamn shame," one of the techs said, behind Vicki. She braced herself and turned on her heel. Even so, she was completely unprepared for the awful sight.

Shayla Jackson lay on her back on the blue rug, between her periwinkle-flowered bed and the wall, her slim arms apart and her pink palms skyward. Her brown eyes, the same lovely ones in the photo, lay wide open and staring fixedly at the ceiling. Her legs, slim and long in jeans, lay horribly twisted, and she was barefoot. She was wearing a dark, loose V-neck sweater, now soaked with black blood. Bullet holes strafed the front of her chest, cutting a blood-drenched swath between her breasts. The blasts exposed red muscle and white sternum, and the skin unfurled like common cloth to expose the cruelest blow of all: Jackson's bloodied midsection puffed high and round.

"She was *pregnant*?" Vicki asked, appalled, and one of the kneeling techs looked up.

"Eight months," answered an Indian doctor working on Jackson's body, his glossy head bent over her chest wounds.

"My God." Vicki shook her head. Her stomach flipped over. She gritted her teeth to keep queasiness at bay.

"Who are you?" The doctor looked up, his round eyes flickering with annoyance. He wore a maroon sweater vest under his lab coat, which had a black nameplate that read Dr. Mehar Soresh.

Vicki introduced herself and said, "This is my case."

An African-American tech added: "She's the AUSA almost got shot with the ATF agent."

Dr. Soresh returned to his examination. "Then you're one lucky lady tonight."

Vicki didn't reply. She couldn't. She wouldn't know where to start. She had gotten her partner killed.

Dr. Soresh continued, "In answer to the question you were about to ask, the child could not have been saved. Mother and child were dead when they hit the floor."

Vicki wasn't about to ask.

"Furthermore, my theory is that the first bullet was to the uterine area, so the baby died first." Dr. Soresh extracted a long silvery probe from his black bag. "Somebody wanted this baby dead, that's for sure."

Vicki's thoughts raced ahead. Was it Browning's baby? Was it somebody else's? Who would want a baby killed? And what, if anything, did it have to do with the straw case? The questions forced her to think clearly. "Dr. Soresh, do you know who's going to identify the body? Who's next-of-kin, do you know?"

Soresh didn't look up. "Mom's coming in from Florida. Tampa, I think. She'll come to the morgue, look on the TV screen. We make it easy on 'em, not like on *CSI*. Big dramatic thing, undraping the body, ta-da."

"No boyfriend is coming?"

"Not that I know of."

"A baby mama drama," the black tech said, and Dr. Soresh shot him a dirty look.

"I don't know, that's not my bailiwick. I have Mom coming in at noon tomorrow. She's next-of-kin, and that's good enough for me."

"Will you send me a copy of your report, when you're finished?"

"Sure. What's your name again?"

"Allegretti. I'm an AUSA."

"Got it."

"Thanks," Vicki said, getting her bearings. Morty was dead and so was a pregnant woman. And a baby, gone. She didn't know how or whether any of this connected to her straw purchase case, but she intended to find out.

Starting now.

FOUR

DOWNSTAIRS, THE CROWD IN THE HOUSE HAD grown, and Vicki made a beeline through the badges for Bale, who was shooting his French cuffs, revealing a flash of gold cuff link as he stood talking to the U.S. Attorney, Ben Strauss. Strauss, a blond six footer gone gray, towered over Bale in a dark blue suit and no topcoat. The first and last time Vicki had seen Strauss was when he addressed her as one of five new assistant U.S. Attorneys, after they'd returned from orientation. Strauss had impressive credentials, almost twenty-five years working for Justice, even if he came off a trifle Aryan, as compared with Bale; standing together, the two men were a twin cone of soft-serve chocolate and vanilla.

Bale spotted Vicki first, as she reached them. "How's my girl?" he asked, looping an arm around her, pulling her into their circle.

"Hanging in," Vicki answered, and Strauss nodded somberly.

"I'm sorry about Morty. I know you two were friends."

"Thanks."

"He was a great agent, one of the best. I had been meaning to drop you an e-mail about the nice result you two got in Edwards. Good job."

"Thanks."

"You were a good pair. I'm sure he taught you everything you know, right?"

"And then some."

"Morty never liked me, you must know that."

Maybe he's not so bland. "He never said anything like that to me," Vicki said, though it wasn't true. Morty had disliked the U.S. Attorney for his grandstanding and headline grabbing. Strauss churned out initiatives all the time, press-released and posted on the DOJ website; Project Clean Sweep, Project Clean Schools, Project Clean Block. Morty had nicknamed him, predictably, Mr. Clean.

"Good. Well. Maybe I'm wrong. I'd like to think that." Strauss patted Vicki's arm stiffly, his eyes a razor-sharp blue.

"Vicki's had a rough night," Bale said, drumming up positive reinforcement.

"She sure has, a rough night," Strauss repeated, properly cued. "I'd say this is trial by fire, isn't it? Maybe you should take some time off. Tomorrow, and the weekend."

"Actually, I'm wondering if this is connected to my straw case. I know we found the coke, but I think this was a stash house. Jackson wasn't the dealer, not for that kind of weight. I think she was just keeping it for—"

"I drew the same conclusion and so did ATF," Bale interrupted. Strauss's pale eyebrows lifted.

"Her boyfriend's name is Jamal Browning." Vicki knew she was talking out of turn, but it had never stopped her before. "I think he keeps her, and he may be the father of her baby, because there's bills on her dresser with his address. Her moving puzzles me, though. They weren't moving in together or she wouldn't be forwarding bills to him by mail. If they were breaking up—"

"You did some detective work, huh?" Bale smiled in a way that said shut up, which Vicki ignored.

"I don't think there was another man in the picture, not yet. First off, she was pregnant, and it's hard enough to meet anybody. Second, there's still her boyfriend's photos on her mirror and—"

"Vick, let's finish this discussion later," Bale said, his voice low. He shifted from one fancy loafer to the other. "This isn't the time or the place."

"Agreed." Strauss glanced around to see if anybody had been listening. "We don't need leaks."

"But time matters." Vicki lowered her voice, even though no one was snooping. "Tonight, everything's fresh, and at bottom, this is a murder case. In the D.A.'s office, we would always—"

"You're in the bigs now." Bale frowned. "We're lawyers, not cops. Morty's in very good hands, the very best. Philly Homicide's on it, and the FBI and ATF are breathin' down their neck. They'll collect the evidence and run it down."

"The Mayor's Office has shown a special interest, too." Strauss checked his watch. "I'm on my way to see him right now. We'll press-conference in the morning." He turned to look out the open front door of the row house. Klieglights shone outside, from the TVs and other press. "They're swarming out there. A triple homicide, a cop murdered." He glanced back at Vicki. "I don't have to tell you, no statements to the press."

"Of course not."

"Good." Strauss clapped her on the shoulder, then nodded to Bale. "How, we'll talk tomorrow."

"Whenever you're ready." Bale nodded. He and Vicki watched Strauss leave, his silhouette tall and lean in the klieglights, framed by the threshold of the front door. His breath made a puff of smoke in the frigid air, and he didn't even pause in the spot where Morty had been cut down.

"You like him, Chief?" Vicki asked, watching Strauss go.

"I got a uniform out there, to take you home," Bale replied, his dark eyes reflecting the white glare of the TV lights, and the moving shadows.

As soon as Vicki reached the pavement, reporters hit her like a blast of cold air. "Vicki, any comment?" "Vicki, can you describe the killer?" "Ms. Allegretti, what were you doing here tonight?" "Where were you when Special Agent Morton got shot?" "Vicki, did the ATF agent have any last words?"

Morty. Vicki kept her head down as she barreled through the crowd, holding up a no-comment hand. She'd run this gauntlet once in the D.A.'s office, but Strauss had been right, this was the bigs. The police presence was double the usual, including dogs and horses, and the media was national, evidently including jackasses.

"Is it true the woman was pregnant?" "Was this a drug bust?" "Why weren't the Philly cops there?" "Why were you involved?" "Victoria, look this way! Just one picture, please!"

Reporters thronged so close that Vicki almost tripped on a black electrical cable powering the bright klieglights, foam-covered microphones, black cameras with rubbery collapsible shades, and whirring video-cameras. She caught sight of herself in a monitor, her head floating, oddly disembodied, in the wintry black sky. On the screen, she looked even shorter than five two, which she hadn't known was physically possible.

A uniformed cop signaled to her from in front of an idling cruiser. Traffic on the usually busy boulevard had been rerouted to the inner lanes, and behind the cruiser sat a ring of police sawhorses, holding back neighbors and onlookers who were talking, smoking, and calling out questions, despite the frigid temperature. Vicki wished she could find out what they knew about Jackson, Jamal Browning, or comings and goings at the house, but she wasn't about to canvass the neighborhood within earshot of the media.

She sprinted for the police car, introduced herself to the cop, and slipped into the warmed-up backseat. The car took off, edging through the crowd until they reached open road. Vicki didn't say anything as the cruiser sped through the darkened streets. She tried not to feel the ache in her ribs. Or, worse, in her heart.

In time, the cruiser took a right onto the drive that snaked along the Wissahickon River: they passed lovely old Tudor homes, and in the next few minutes they arrived at her development, East Falls Mews, which was supposed to blend in, but didn't. Attached town homes of faux stone with ersatz Tudor touches lined the winding streets, newly paved; it was a lame place to live, but the rent was low and it sat just inside the Philly limits, a job requirement for D.A.'s. Lately

Vicki had been talking about moving into Center City, so she had a hope of Meeting Somebody, but her social life was the last thing on her mind tonight. That is, until the squad car pulled up in front of her house.

Because, to her surprise, shivering as he sat on her front step was just the man she wanted to see.

FIVE

ONCE THEY WERE INSIDE, VICKI FELL INTO Dan's embrace, realizing when she was enveloped how much she needed him. She burrowed into the chilled puffiness of his North Face jacket, feeling underneath the hard contours of his chest and the comfort of his strong arms. His open neck smelled of cold air and hard soap, and he was tall and lean, even in the down jacket. She held him as close as was permissible, then pulled away. Theirs was a relationship that drove Vicki crazy, even if it would make Plato himself proud.

Because Dan Malloy was married.

Vicki knew the rules: a hug was allowable, if the duration was brief and there was no contact below the waist. A kiss was kosher, if it was on the forehead and she had won a felony conviction. The word that began with L and rhymed with *glove* was forbidden, unless they were talking about Sicilian pizza, which they both loved. Of course, explosive sex, hot sex, combustible

I-have-denied-myself-for-too-long sex, I've-been-think-ing-about-this-forever sex had never happened. And it wasn't ever going to, outside of Vicki's imagination, where it occurred with great frequency and mutual satisfaction.

"I wanted to make sure you were okay." Dan held Vicki at arm's length, searching her face with sky-blue eyes, slightly watery from the cold. His gingery hair, layered with longish sideburns, was a sexy rumple. "You must be dying inside. I always thought Morty was like a father to you."

Exactly. Vicki had never felt so completely understood by someone who was so completely married.

"Jesus, he's dead. I can't believe it."

"How did you find out?"

"From TV. It's impossible that he's gone." Dan's eyes went dazed and his voice husky. His eyes clouded with sadness, and the corners of his flattish lips turned unhappily down, his frown so deep that the freckles dotting his forehead clustered together. "He was such a great guy. A hardworking guy, and fun. He could always make me laugh."

Vicki felt a twinge of fresh grief. Dan had really liked Morty, and Morty liked him, too. Of course, everybody liked Dan; he was the Golden Boy of the office. He'd racked up more convictions than anybody in his class, quarterbacked the AUSA football game against the federal marshals, and bought the vanilla sheet cake for the receptionist's birthday. At thirty-five years old, Dan Malloy had been anointed, and everybody knew it but him.

"Morty didn't deserve to die that way," he said.

"Nobody does. Neither did she." Vicki blinked her tears back, postponing them. She didn't know when

she'd feel safe enough to cry. She kept getting exten-
sions of time, a lawyer's habit.

"Mariella says she's really sorry. She'd be here if
she could but she's on call."

"Tell her I said thanks." Vicki hoped this sounded
convincing. Dan's wife, the exotic Dr. Mariella Suarez,
was a resident at Hahnemann Hospital; beautiful, wil-
lowy, fake-blonde, and constantly on call. She spoke
three languages, including her native Portuguese, and
was remote even for a surgeon. She was married to the
most wonderful man on the planet, to whom she paid
no attention, which was why, in the incomprehensible
logic of the cosmos, she had him.

Dan was saying, "You must be beat. I brought wine.
Come on, it's medicinal." He turned and went into the
kitchen, sliding out of his jacket on the way, revealing
a gray T-shirt in which he'd undoubtedly been playing
basketball. He set the coat on a dining room chair, releasing a subtle odor that gave credence to the
pheromone thing.

Vicki breathed deeply and followed him into the
kitchen. She stopped before she got there, taking off
her stained trenchcoat and laying it over another dining
room chair. She couldn't bear to look at it again, much
less wear it. She entered the kitchen, flopped into the
wooden chair at the round table, and kicked off her
pumps. "I hate high heels."

"Me, too." Dan set the wine on the tile counter and
went into her silverware drawer for the corkscrew. He
knew exactly where it was, because he was over so
often. They had met a year ago, when she'd become an
AUSA and got the office next to him, and they'd
become close, sharing gossip at lunch and war stories

whenever possible. They had dinner after work, too, when Dr. Bitchy was on call; Dan had probably cooked more meals in this kitchen than Vicki had, which made her feel oddly ashamed. She eyed the room in case there was a pop quiz.

The kitchen measured about twenty feet long and was just wide enough to qualify as a galley. Authentically distressed oak covered the floor, and matching cabinets lined the wall. A halogen light of tangerine Murano glass hung down from the ceiling, casting a soft, if concentrated, glow on the round kitchen table. Dan stood at the indefinite edge of the lamplight in jeans that were too big, which Vicki found secretly charming.

She watched him pour the wine into two glasses, and it washed bubbling against the side. It was a Chardonnay, which Dan knew was her favorite, and his thoughtfulness triggered a wave of longing so powerful that she had to swallow, physically forcing it back down her throat. She wished that she could lose herself in him for just one night, but he didn't think of her that way. *Not that it mattered, for those purposes. He could just lie still.*

"Here's what the doctor ordered." Dan turned, glasses in hand, and brought them to the table, where he put them down and sat in the other chair. They both lifted their glasses without saying a word, tacitly toasting Morty. Their eyes met, but Vicki broke contact first and took a sip. The cold Chardonnay tingled on her tongue. Cold comfort, but comfort.

"Thanks for doing this," Vicki said.

"What a guy."

"Really, it was nice of you. I know you hate Chardonnay."

"Not true." Dan took another sip and rallied, putting the moment behind them. "Chardonnay is classy. Even the word is classy. Chardonnay makes me feel almost as classy as you."

"Don't start." Vicki smiled. It was a running joke between them. Her parents were prominent lawyers who ran a prosperous firm in Center City, and Dan had grown up in a working-class city neighborhood, Juniata, and his father was a ne'er-do-well who had served time for petty forgery. Dan had a chip on his shoulder about his family, but it didn't matter to Vicki, except that it reminded her of her parents. She fleetingly considered calling to tell them she was okay, but they generally went to bed by ten o'clock.

"So, you want to talk about what happened?" Dan looked at her so intensely, it could qualify as foreplay in most jurisdictions. Just not the Platonic jurisdiction.

"In a minute."

"Fair enough. I was worried about you."

"You'd better." Vicki always shrugged off any nice thing Dan said, even borderline flirting. He would never have cheated, and she wouldn't want an affair with him; frankly, not only because of her morals, which went out the window when he wore those jeans, but because she wanted to be number one. What trial lawyer would settle for number two? The name for number two is loser.

"They said on the TV news that you 'narrowly escaped with your life.'" Dan made quote marks in the air, but didn't smile. "Is that true?"

Vicki flashed on the guns. It struck her that she had faced two tonight, which should count as narrowly, if not miraculously. "Yes."

"Were you scared?"

"My underwear is clean."

Dan laughed. "That was an overshare."

"I'm proud of that. It wasn't easy."

"I try not to think about your underwear."

Don't try so hard. Vicki watched him drink his wine, which was almost half gone, and a silence fell between them. She fought her customary urge to entertain him by filling in the conversational gap, but she didn't want to turn Morty's death into another war story. And she knew it was a bad habit, her jumping up and down for him. Always reaching for him, inside. Unrequited didn't begin to describe her feelings for him. Unrequited wasn't even the warm-up act.

"I switched around the channels, to get the story." Dan drained his wineglass. "They had video from outside the house, and interviews. Strauss was on, too, before he went in."

Vicki didn't comment. Dan liked Strauss.

"Did you see him?"

"The cheese? Yes. Bale was there, too, and he didn't fire me."

"How could he? It wasn't your fault."

Vicki couldn't say as much. She took a sip of wine, but it didn't help.

"On TV, they showed your picture. The one from orientation. You looked great. One of the anchors said you were 'attractive' and 'a rising star.'"

"Did they mention I was single?"

"They must have forgotten," Dan said, slurring his words slightly, and Vicki eyed him, amused.

"Hey, did you have dinner tonight?"

"No. I shot hoops and we went out for a beer after. Why?"

"Your mouth stopped working a few words ago." Vicki smiled. It was another running joke. "Face it, Malloy. You're a girl."

"No! I had a few beers is all. Then I saw the TV, I didn't wait for the burger." Dan's freckled skin flushed pink. "I suck at being Irish."

"It's the Jesuit in you."

"No, it's all *your* fault, Vick."

"Mine?"

"I spend too much time with you."

"Not possible," Vicki said, then caught herself. It was the wine talking and it had accidentally said something true. She felt like her slip was showing and she didn't even wear slips.

Dan looked down for a moment, into his empty glass. Then he looked up, taking her in, but saying nothing.

"What?" Vicki asked.

"I went to the house tonight, but the FBI wouldn't let me in. That was one mother crime scene. They didn't honor my ID, the scene was so restricted."

Dan had been there? "You were at my CI's house tonight? How'd you know where it was?"

"The street name was on the TV, and you mentioned where you were going, remember? You tell me everything."

Not everything, handsome.

"I waited outside at the scene for a while. I figured they were taking your statement, so I came here. I knew you had to come home. I picked up the wine on the way. Anyway, I had a lot of time to think about, well, how it would be if you had been killed tonight. I mean, you could have been murdered."

But Morty was. Morty was the cop.

"It made me think about what my life would be like." Dan paused, his lips pursed and his gaze unfailingly blue and steady. "If you had, you know. It made me think about some things. Like how I feel about you."

Huh? Vicki told herself to stay calm. Dan had never said anything about any feelings for her, and she had certainly never told him about her crush on him. Suddenly the moment was upon them, after a year of getting closer and closer.

"So I wanted to tell you tonight, more than anything, how I feel. Because now I know that all that crap they talk about is true."

Vicki said nothing, but her heartbeat stepped up. Dan had stopped slurring his words, he was concentrating so fiercely.

"You know that crap they say? That you never know when life can be taken or what's going to happen? That everything you have can be gone in one minute, and it will be too late? That crap?"

Vicki was pretty sure she was breathing but she wouldn't swear to it.

"Well, it's true. You can't take anyone for granted. You have to tell people how you feel about them when they're alive, because tomorrow's not guaranteed to anyone." Dan leaned over and placed his hand on hers.

Oh my God.

"Well, what I realized is that I can't imagine my life if you weren't in it."

Vicki officially stopped breathing.

"You're my best friend in the world."

Vicki's mouth went dry. She waited a minute. She wasn't sure what she'd heard, then she wasn't sure whether Dan was finished. But he wasn't saying anything more. Maybe he wasn't finished anyway? He couldn't have been, because he hadn't said what she needed to hear, which was:

I love you.

"You look weird." Dan cocked his head. "You think it's strange to have a best friend who's a girl?"

"Not at all," Vicki answered flatly. She slid her hand out from under his and got up for more wine. She would have to start drinking heavily, if they were going to keep being Friends Without Benefits.

Later, before she eased her aching body into bed, Vicki called her parents and left a message on both of their cell phones, because she knew it was the first thing they checked each morning. In the messages she told them not to worry about anything they heard on TV, online, or on the car radio into work, because she was fine.

Vicki didn't mention that she was hopelessly in love with a very married man or that, first thing in the morning, she was going to investigate a triple homicide.

SIX

THE WILLIAM GREEN FEDERAL BUILDING WAS a modern redbrick edifice that anchored Sixth and Arch streets, attached to the United States Courthouse and situated at the center of a new court complex that Vicki thought of as a Justice Mall. The Neiman Marcus of the Justice Mall would be the Constitution Center, a glitzy shrine to sell the Bill of Rights, and the Gap would be the Federal Detention Center, a generic column of gray stone, except for its horizontal window slits. The FDC almost didn't get built because nobody wanted a federal prison reminding the shoppers—er, tourists—that the City of Brotherly Love was also the City of Brotherly Robbery and Weapons Offenses. But the FDC was ultimately approved because officials agreed to construct a secret underground tunnel from the prison to the federal building, so the shoppers wouldn't know. It was through this tunnel that defendant Reheema Bristow was being escorted this morning.

Vicki waited in a plastic bucket chair in a proffer room on the secured fourth floor of the federal building. They were called proffer rooms because defendants "proffered" here, i.e., offered to tell the government incriminating information, off the record, in return for immunity or a recommendation to the judge for a downward departure on their sentence. This proffer room was unfortunately identical to the others: white boxes, uniformly windowless and airless, containing brown Formica conference tables and a few mismatched chairs.

Vicki collected her thoughts. The straw purchase case might have collapsed, but she wasn't dropping the charges until after she had questioned Bristow just one time. Nobody would be the wiser; the defense didn't know the identity of the confidential informant because Vicki wasn't required to divulge until right before trial or even before the CI took the stand, if witness intimidation was an issue. She was bending the rules a little, but Morty's death provided more than enough motivation. She'd thought of the plan last night when she couldn't sleep, replaying the awful shootings in her mind.

She crossed her legs and willed herself to stay centered; the record showed that Bristow could be provocative. Straws weren't usually held in custody, but Bristow had turned her temporary detention into an almost year-long stay by mouthing off to the magistrate judge during her hearing. Whatever Bristow brought this morning, Vicki could handle it. She brushed an imaginary hair off her black wool suit, her hair swept back into a black barrette and curling loosely at the nape of her neck. She had picked out the outfit on autopilot, then realized she was dressed in mourning. Only determination held raw grief at bay.

Suddenly, the door to the proffer room opened and the defense lawyer bustled in. "I'm Carlos Melendez," he said, and extending a hammy hand. "It's freezing cold, isn't it? They say snow this afternoon." He looked about sixty years old, his still-thick hair coiled in tight steel-gray curls, contrasting with his darkish skin and rich brown eyes. He had a cheery demeanor and a short, chubby build in a herringbone topcoat, like SpongeBob SquarePants with a law degree.

"I'm Vicki Allegretti," she said, liking Melendez immediately, despite the fact that he was technically the enemy.

"Boy, you look too young to be an AUSA." Melendez smiled.

"No, I'm twenty-eight. I'm just short."

"Ha! You're short *and* young." Melendez laughed. "Though I gotta admit, I don't know many AUSAs, I'm court appointed on this case." He wriggled out of his topcoat, releasing the scent of a strongly spicy aftershave.

"Thanks for coming on such short notice."

"Not at all, glad you called. Trial's just around the corner."

Eek. Not anymore. "Did you get my proffer letter?" This morning, Vicki had re-sent Melendez the proffer letter that the first AUSA had sent, since it had the necessary signature, namely Strauss's. The letter was a formality, setting forth the government's request for information and the ground rules for the meeting off the record. She'd had it in the Bristow file and faxed it from home.

"My secretary confirmed that we got it, thanks." Melendez opened a scratched-up leather briefcase, extracted an accordion file, and closed it again.

"Think Ms. Bristow feels chatty this morning?"

"Reheema? Honestly, no." Melendez smiled. "You'll see, Reheema's not the talkative type, but maybe she'll listen to reason. I'll be honest with you, I want her to cooperate, and I told her so." He pushed his briefcase across the dusty Formica table and eased his girth into his bucket chair. "The first AUSA had no luck with her, but he lacked your youthful enthusiasm. Maybe with you being a woman, too, that'll help. You're the same age."

"Good."

"Like I told you, I'm court-appointed, so I don't meet a lot of people like her. She's a tough nut. But she has a good heart, and I think she's innocent."

Vicki knew he'd learn soon enough that Bristow could be behind the murders of three people.

"And five years is five years. I hate to see her get set up for this."

"What do you mean? You think someone's setting her up?"

"Somebody's letting her twist, aren't they? Whoever she bought those guns for, and like you say, anything is possible." Melendez shrugged his heavy shoulders. "I don't know, she won't talk to me. Like I said, I don't usually do this kinda work, but I've never had a client who was so close-mouthed."

"Is she frightened?" Vicki was considering the possibilities. "Intimidated by someone?"

"Ha! No way. Reheema doesn't scare easy." Melendez mulled it over, looking idly at Vicki. Suddenly, his dark eyes seemed to sharpen and he focused on her face. "You know, you look a lot like that woman on TV last night. With that murder, on the news?"

"Uh, yes, that was me." Vicki told herself to act natural. It would have been only a matter of time before he recognized her. The story was all over the papers, TV, and radio this morning.

"That *was* you? An FBI agent killed and a pregnant woman?"

"He was ATF." Vicki's chest felt tight.

"Je-sus." Melendez looked shocked, his lips parting. "That must have been horrible. What the hell happened?"

"I can't really say," Vicki answered in her official voice, as a burly ATF agent in a tie and gray blazer appeared at the door to the proffer room.

"Special delivery," the agent said dryly. Usually, the federal marshals brought up the prisoners, but Vicki had asked the ATF on duty as a favor. He had to know it was related to Morty's death, but she didn't tell, to give him deniability.

"Thanks," Vicki said, and when the agent stepped aside, Vicki did a double take at the sight of the shackled prisoner.

Reheema Bristow didn't look at all the way Vicki had expected.

SEVEN

VICKI HAD BEEN EXPECTING A STREET TOUGH, but Reheema Bristow looked like a black model, albeit on steroids. She had stunning features: large almond eyes of an unusual caramel-brown, a longish nose, and a broad mouth, which was sensual, if unsmiling. She wore her dark hair back in a short, stiff ponytail and had a strong, killer body, even in the olive green jumpsuit worn by FDC prisoners. Her manner made the handcuffs seem oddly like sex toys.

Bristow was seated, cuffed and shackled, in the chair next to Melendez, and her lawyer had gone positively goofy in her presence. Suddenly Vicki understood why he'd been suckered into believing in her innocence. And also why he'd worn his cardamom aftershave.

"Reheema, how are you today?" Melendez boomed, grinning.

"I'm fine, thanks," Bristow answered, and Vicki reacted viscerally to the sound of her voice, soft, but hardly ingratiating. Streetwise, but not street. Sonorous, if it hadn't come out of the mouth of a criminal. Vicki couldn't forget that Bristow could know who killed Morty and Jackson. She could know Teeg and Jay-Boy. She could even have hired them, or maybe whoever she was buying the guns for had hired them.

"Ms. Bristow." Vicki introduced herself and explained, "I'm the new AUSA on this case. I'm replacing Jim Cavanaugh, whom you met with before. I believe that was the only proffer conference you had with my office, correct?"

Bristow nodded, and if she recognized Vicki from the TV, she didn't let it show, which proved she was one great liar. News of the triple homicide had to be all over the FDC, learned from TV or the "bowl," the way prisoners communicated after lights-out; each inmate flushed the toilet a few times to evacuate the water, enabling the plumbing to carry voices as efficiently as Nextel. The Bureau of Prisons couldn't do anything about it, short of replacing the plumbing at taxpayer expense, but nobody was funding better johns for felons.

Vicki continued, "I called you here today for a conference, and we'll start by asking you a few questions. As you know, you've been charged with two counts of a straw purchase, in violation of 18 U.S.C. Section 922." Vicki glanced at her file as she read. "The indictment charges that you purchased two Colt .45–caliber handguns and illegally resold them. As you may know, when such a multiple weapons purchase is made, Pennsylvania gun dealers are required automatically to send a report to the Bureau of Alcohol, Tobacco, Firearms, and Explosives. Would you like to see the report concerning your purchases, or the indictment against you? I have both."

"No. I told the first lawyer, Cavanaugh, I don't want to plead guilty."

"Is that because you didn't do it?"

Bristow's lovely gaze shifted sideways to Melendez. "Do I have to answer?"

"Not if you don't want to."

"No comment," Bristow answered, which gave Vicki pause. Most felons knew that "no comment" was for reporters, not government lawyers.

"Reheema, may I call you Reheema?"

"Yes."

"Reheema, you do realize that if you are convicted in this case, and you will be, you'll spend five years in federal prison, a chunk of the prime of your life?"

Bristow didn't say anything.

"I see from your file you have no priors, so you may not know that federal prison isn't as nice as the FDC, new and clean. It isn't like on TV, either."

Bristow didn't blink, which set Vicki's blood simmering. She had given this speech in three other straw cases and had never gotten this far. Unlike state jail time, federal sentencing guidelines removed the judge's discretion, so cooperating was the only thing defendants could do to help themselves. The guidelines were a huge hammer for federal law enforcement, but coming from the D.A.'s office, Vicki secretly thought they also took the sport out of the contest. They'd created a culture of snitches, and after most indictments, crooks raced to flip on their friends. Last month, Vicki even got a confession on her answering machine.

"Reheema, prison is ugly, brutal, nasty. Women beat each other up, some of them daily. Think. Five years of that."

Bristow said nothing, her expression as impassive as if she were posing for a *Vogue* cover, and Vicki guessed she had to know that Jackson had been killed and there would be no trial on the charges.

"Reheema, let's get real. You're a pretty girl, you know that. A woman as beautiful as you, it won't be nice. You'll be placed in the general population. You'll be somebody's bitch."

Bristow's perfect mouth remained closed, but Vicki kept squeezing. Bristow couldn't be completely sure the government didn't have other evidence against her. Vicki wouldn't be the first federal prosecutor to be stingy with what she disclosed before trial.

"That is, if you're lucky, it'll be one woman. It could be more. You could be the pass-around pack. You want that?"

Bristow didn't answer, and next to her, Melendez shifted his weight in his chair. Vicki was threatening Bristow, which wasn't permissible, but Melendez wanted to save his client.

"I'm not trying to scare you, I'm trying to tell you what you risk by going to trial. You bought two guns for somebody and resold them. All I want from you is the name of the person you sold them to."

Bristow didn't answer, and Vicki felt her cheeks hot with renewed anger.

"Reheema, if you're frightened, I understand. These are dangerous people, scary people. I can get you into the witness protection program. You lived in an apartment in West Philly, right?"

Bristow didn't answer, and Vicki checked her temper.

"Come on, you can answer that! It's on the indict-ment. Who did you live with?"

"Lived alone."

"No boyfriend or anything?"

"No."

If she couldn't get a date, I have no chance. "So you don't have the apartment anymore, do you?"

"No."

"Even better. I'll get you relocated to a new place, maybe even a house. I'll make sure you're okay, I swear it." Vicki meant every word, if it led to Morty's killer. "You don't have to be afraid of anybody or any-thing. Even if they're dealing drugs, even weight."

Bristow looked down, breaking eye contact, and Vicki felt her heart quicken.

"Reheema, if you give me the name, I'll tell the judge you're a cooperator. I'll give him the best possi-ble recommendation for your sentence. I'll get you in ad seg, too, out of the general population. It's a com-pletely different proposition."

Bristow kept her head down, and Vicki leaned across the table.

"Just give me a name. These guys are filth, they don't deserve your loyalty. Give me the name and you'll get back to your life. You had two jobs, you can work them. Meet a nice guy, I wish you better luck than me. You're only twenty-nine, as young as I am. Your life is in front of you, if you just say the word."

"No," Bristow answered, looking up. Her gaze was steady, two flawless brown orbs focused on Vicki, which only made her crazier. She tried another tack. Maybe if Bristow knew Vicki had her number, she'd talk.

"Reheema, who is Jamal Browning?"

Melendez's ears pricked up at the unfamiliar name and he wrote it on a legal pad, but Bristow merely looked down again and began examining her finger-nails.

"Have you ever been at 3635 Aspinall Street? It's in West Philly." Vicki had looked it up on MapQuest this morning.

Bristow continued with her cuticle, and Vicki felt her frustration rising.

"Do you know a young man, a black male aged about fourteen, about five nine, who wears his hair in cornrows and is nicknamed Teeg?"

"Objection." Melendez raised a hand, though no for-mal objections were necessary, nor did they have any legal impact at a proffer conference, which this wasn't anyway. This was a mugging.

"I'm just asking her a question. She can decline to answer." Vicki's temper sharpened her tone but she didn't bother dialing it back. She turned to Bristow. "Who's Teeg?"

Bristow didn't answer.

"How about Jay-Boy, a young black male? Goatee? Older than fourteen, maybe sixteen." Vicki couldn't give further details of his description. He was the one who had killed Morty. Her head pounded, and her chest felt tight enough to burst.

Bristow didn't answer, and Vicki was growing more furious by the minute.

"How do you know Shayla Jackson?"

Reheema's expression betrayed no recognition.

Melendez looked up from his pad, his forehead wrin-kling. "Jackson. Isn't that the name of the pregnant lady who got killed last night? I remember because it's my neighbor's name."

"I'm just asking her, does she know Jackson?"

Melendez set his Bic pen down beside his pad. "What's the difference if she knows her?" he asked, suspicious.

"I'm curious. She didn't recognize me from TV, like you did."

"So?"

Uh. "I like to be recognized. It makes me feel good about myself."

Bristow cracked a sly smile, which made Vicki want to wring her neck. The woman was getting away with murder.

"Reheema, I know you know Shayla Jackson. She was my CI in this case. You know what that means, don't you? My confidential informant." Vicki leaned across the table, almost spitting. "She was going to dime on you and you know she was murdered last night with my partner. Teeg and Jay-Boy were the shooters, but they work for someone, and I want to know who. And how you're involved."

"Vicki, what are you doing?" Melendez rose slowly, but Vicki was too far gone.

"You had Jackson killed to prevent her from testifying! You killed her and her baby! And Morty!" Suddenly, Vicki's rage boiled over. She reached across the table and grabbed Bristow's upper arm.

"No, wait!" Melendez shouted, horrified. "Stop!"

"Yo, bitch!" Reheema bellowed, but Vicki exploded.

"Why'd you do it, Reheema! Why? To save five lousy years?" Vicki couldn't stop herself and she didn't want to. She yanked so hard that she dragged the handcuffed Bristow onto the table. "They killed an ATF agent last night! My partner! My *friend*! And you know it!"

"HELP!" Melendez yelled at the top of his lungs.

The door to the proffer room flew open, and the ATF agent burst in, drawing his gun from his shoulder holster, ready to protect a prosecutor from a prisoner.

And, startled, discovered that it was the other way around.

EIGHT

"GET YOURSELF A LAWYER, KID." BALE bustled into his office, where Vicki had been told to wait for him.

"You have to be kidding."

"Not today. Strauss got a call from Melendez, Bristow's defense lawyer." Bale slid off his camel-hair coat, hung it carefully on a wooden hanger, and placed it on the wooden rack behind him, then sat down in his tall chair, shooting his cuffs by habit. "He's suing you—and the office—for official misconduct, assault, and battery."

"Assault and battery, on *Reheema*? She has six inches on me!"

"Melendez says she sustained a soft-tissue injury."

"But all her tissue is hard!"

"You twisted her arm, didn't you?"

"I couldn't! She was wearing handcuffs!"

"Not your best argument." Bale glared from behind his walnut desk, its surface marked by a clean leather blotter, stacks of correspondence, and a computer with the office's American flag screensaver, flickering madly. "You're missing the point. You shouldn't have put a finger on her, not a finger."

"I know. I'm sorry. But still—"

"No buts. You're a federal prosecutor. You behaved like a street brawler."

Vicki reddened. She was in the wrong, which sucked.

"And Melendez is filing suit on her behalf and on his own."

"What?"

"He doesn't have soft tissue, either?" Bale arched an eyebrow.

"I swear, I didn't touch *him*!"

"Says you pushed him. Your word against his."

"What about the ATF agent, at the door? He could tell you what happened."

"Oh, should we ask him? He wasn't even supposed to be there! Marshals bring prisoners up, not ATF. How'd you swing that?"

Vicki slumped in the chair. The ATF agent couldn't speak for her anyway. He had had to pull the three of them apart, like a group hug gone horribly wrong.

"I didn't think so. Either way, it's a lawsuit that could result in liability for you personally. Meeting with a defendant is within the scope of your official duties, but trying to kill one is not."

"You're not backing me?"

"Of course not." Bale's brown eyes went hard, like chocolate cooling. "You had no business setting up a proffer meeting, or a meeting of any kind, when you knew you had no case. There's just no excuse for it. What were you thinking?"

Gulp. "It was my last chance. I was gonna let her go after that."

"You shoulda dropped those charges first thing this morning. What did you use for a proffer letter?"

"The old one in the file."

"So Strauss's signature is on it? Strauss will love that, that's great." Bale pursed his lips under his mustache. "He talked with PR and they're press-releasing it. The media knows you were at the scene last night, and the press release sets forth your very sincere apology and explains that you were upset over the murder of an ATF case agent you knew very well. I dropped the charges against Bristow and she'll be released from the FDC by tonight."

No. "She knows those shooters, Chief."

"Melendez told me she denied all of it, and he believed her."

"Gimme a break. He's a man, and she's hot." Vicki felt her bile rising. "Chief, obviously, there's a connection between Bristow and the CI. The CI volunteered to testify against her, apparently out of the blue. I told you, there's a memo in the file."

"That's what you're pinning this theory on, a memo in the file? That's why you attacked a defendant and her lawyer?"

Not her lawyer, but never mind. "My CI gets shot a few days before she's going to testify and she's my whole case. It can't be a coincidence. There has to be a link."

"Melendez says you were out of control. He said that you have a big mouth for such a small woman, which I can vouch for."

"Thanks."

"Don't be a smartass. You need representation. Understand?"

"Understood." No lawyer would take this case without a five-thousand-dollar retainer, half of Vicki's savings. Her father would represent her for free, but then she'd have to tell him the truth, which was unprecedented.

"The locals are all over us now. We need good relations with the Roundhouse. I don't have to tell you that, do I? Don't make me sorry I convinced Strauss not to can your ass."

"I'm not fired?" Vicki felt her throat catch with gratitude.

"Suspended without pay, for a week." Bale rubbed his smooth forehead irritably. Rumor had it he was getting Botox injections, but Vicki would never again spread that around.

"Thanks, Chief."

"The only reason he gave it to me was that you won last month in Edwards. I went to bat for you because I know why you did it. You reacted emotionally. You were close with Morty."

Morty. Vicki looked away. A pale sun ray filtered through the windows of the corner office, landing on the electroplated plaques, etched crystal bowls, and hunk-of-acrylic awards. Black office manuals and rule books filled the shelves lining the wall.

"Hey, look at me," Bale said, and Vicki did. "I'm responsible for you now. One step out of line, and I don't go to bat for you again. You're still new here. Watch your step. We're not fast and loose, like the D.A.'s office. You got it?"

"Yes, Chief."

"Good." Bale's voice returned almost to normal.

"Melendez also told Strauss you asked Bristow about some names. Jay or something. Teeg. You gave those names to the Philly detectives last night, didn't you?"

"Of course." Vicki had. She wasn't even lying.

"And to ATF, too?"

"Yes."

"So you're not completely crazy."

"No, not completely."

"It's Friday. Morty's memorial service will be on Monday. You will attend, then take the week off without pay. If anyone from Homicide calls you to look at a photo array, you'll go, but that's it. Be back at your desk on Monday and start redeeming yourself."

"What about my cases? I have a suppression hearing in Welton on Tuesday."

"I'll reassign it, and Malloy will watch your desk while you're away. Now get outta my sight." Bale's phone rang but he let the secretary get it. "Don't stop at your office, just go home and stay home. No talking to the press, and no more shenanigans."

"Okay, Chief. Thanks again."

Vicki left the office and closed the door behind her. She walked down the hall to her office, and when she turned the corner, the secretaries were standing up at their desks and behind them AUSAs were coming out of their offices.

And all of them were clapping.

Vicki said thanks to everyone, taking only her coat from her office. She didn't need anything else from it anyway. She had the Bristow file in her briefcase.

And she knew just where she was going.

NINE

VICKI HURRIED THROUGH THE CROWDED
parking lot and checked her watch on the run: 12:45.
She wrapped her old down coat closer and reached the
concrete entrance to the medical examiners', just as an
older African-American woman was leaving. Her gray
head was bowed in grief and she carried a wad of
Kleenex in her hand. Vicki felt a pang of sympathy and
realized that she wasn't too late after all. Shayla Jackson's mother had been due here to identify the body at
noon, and the grieving woman had to be she.

Mrs. Jackson walked with another older black
woman supporting her elbow, though the woman was
struggling with two large purses, a canvas bag
stuffed with red yarn, a folded newspaper, and a
plastic-covered library book. Vicki felt vaguely like
a vulture as she swooped down on the forlorn pair,
reaching them just as one of the leather purses fell to
the parking lot, pebbled with city grit and rock salt.

Vicki scooped up the handbag before both women toppled over.

"Got it," Vicki called out, restoring the bag to the friend.

"Thank you, thank you so much." Mrs. Jackson looked at her with gratitude and managed a sweet smile, though tears pooled in her reddened eyes, behind wire-rimmed glasses. Up close, she looked about eighty years old, with sparse hair the hue of sterling silver and deep fissures for crow's-feet and laugh lines on dry, ashy skin.

"Yes, thank you," the other woman chimed in. "It's hard to carry all these things. I should have thrown away my newspaper, but I didn't get a chance to read it yet."

"I understand." Vicki held on to Mrs. Jackson, who leaned lightly on her arm. The woman couldn't have weighed one hundred and ten, including her coat. "Are you okay, ma'am?"

"Yes, I guess. I'm so tired. I had to . . . I just had to . . ."

Her friend supplied: "Her daughter was murdered."

Vicki couldn't hide the ball another minute. She introduced herself and asked, "Aren't you Ms. Jackson, Shayla Jackson's mother?"

"Why, yes." Her wet brown eyes fluttered in surprise. "Well, not exactly, I'm her auntie." She pronounced it *awn-tee*.

"Well, it's nice to meet you."

"I'm her Auntie Tillie. Mrs. Tillie Bott. Mr. Bott passed away in 1989. Shayla used to call me Auntie Tillie but now she calls me Tillie, or Mama Tillie." Ms. Bott seemed disoriented, understandable under the circumstances. "Shayla was the neighbor lady's girl, but the neighbor run off. I raised her as my own, after my children were grown."

"That was kind of you," Vicki said, touched, but Mrs. Bott shook her head, wobbly.

"Not at t'all. That child gave me more than I ever gave her. She was just so sweet—"

The friend interjected, "How did you know who Tillie was?"

"I'm an assistant U.S. Attorney. I was going to meet with Shayla last night when she was killed." Vicki noticed Mrs. Bott's hooded eyes widen and she softened her voice. "Shayla told me that she had important information for me on a case, so my partner and I went over to her house. It was my partner who was killed with her."

"You mean that policeman?" the friend interjected, again.

"Yes. He was an ATF agent." Someday Vicki would figure out why she kept correcting everybody about Morty. "I was coming here to talk with Mrs. Bott about Shayla, but I hate to bother you now. Maybe we could talk another time."

"We don't live here," the friend answered. "We're country people. We live in Florida. We're going home now. We're going to the bus. We took an airplane here, but we're taking a bus back. The airplane is too expensive."

"You're leaving now?"

"On the three o'clock bus."

"Then we have some time to talk."

"No, we don't."

Vicki wondered when library patrons got so tough. "Wait a minute, did Mrs. Bott talk to the police yet?"

"What police?"

"The Philadelphia police."

"No."

"Didn't they call you to talk about Shayla?" Vicki addressed Mrs. Bott, but she was dabbing her eyes with the soggy Kleenex ball, then resettling her glasses on the bridge of her nose.

"No, they didn't call her," the friend answered. "Now, excuse us, we have to go. We're going home and we're going to take Shayla home to rest, home with us. She'll rest better, home where she grew up."

Mrs. Bott looked so broken, and the cold air dried the tearstains on her lined cheeks, making whitish streaks in the cold. As much as Vicki's heart went out to her, she couldn't let them go.

"I have an idea," Vicki said gently. "Maybe we could go somewhere warm and talk over a cup of coffee. Before you two leave."

"No, she's too upset," the friend answered, drawing Mrs. Bott closer to her side. Vicki kept her grip on poor Mrs. Bott's other arm. If it became a tug-of-war, the library fan was going down. Vicki was younger, stronger, and a federal prosecutor, which should count for something as against the reserve list.

"I'm sorry to have to intrude." Vicki leaned over and spoke directly to Mrs. Bott. "And I'm sure the police are going to call you, but I want to find whoever killed Shayla and my friend. I'm hoping that what you know about Shayla could help me."

"Did you tell that to the police?" the friend broke in, and Vicki bit her tongue.

"Yes, but I have questions of my own."

"That's not your job," the friend shot back, and

Vicki was considering decking her when Mrs. Bott cleared her throat, lowered her Kleenex, and said:

"I wouldn't mind talkin', if it would help Shayla."

A noisy convenience store wasn't what Vicki had in mind for a quiet chat, but the one on the corner of Thirty-eighth and Spruce, down the street from the medical examiner, would do in a pinch. An instrumental version of "Love Will Keep Us Together," the *ca-chunk* of cash registers, and the endless *beep-beep* of touch-screen ordering machines filled the air. The place teemed with overgrown frat boys, exhausted med students, and university staff, but Vicki managed to find a free table in the far corner, at which she seated Mrs. Bott and her attack friend, who turned out to be named Mrs. Greenwood.

Sun streamed through the floor-to-ceiling glass window, warming the three of them, and by the time they'd started on their 184-ounce cups of brewed coffee and Southwestern wraps with suspiciously colorful ingredients, the small talk was over, Mrs. Bott had almost recovered, and Mrs. Greenwood had turned as nice as a librarian.

"When was the last time you saw Shayla, Mrs. Bott?" Vicki asked, getting to the subject at hand.

"I hadn't seen my baby girl in so long. She hardly ever came home anymore."

"How long?"

"Maybe two years now. Two Christmases ago."

"So you hadn't seen her in a while. Did you talk on the phone?"

"Surely, she'd call me, to keep up. Every other week or so."

Mrs. Greenwood nodded with approval.

"Did you know she was pregnant?" Vicki asked.

"I did. At first she didn't tell me, but then she did. She was afraid I'd get mad at her." The creased corners of Mrs. Bott's mouth turned down. She looked so lost in her heavy coat, and her hair, smoothed back in a frizzy bun, glinted dully in the harsh light. "Lord, a baby. The doctor today, he said it was gonna be a girl. Now, if she had a girl, Shayla wanted to call her Shay, after herself. Shay was her nickname. Shay."

Vicki nodded. So much pain. Who was responsible for it?

"Shay," Mrs. Bott repeated.

Mrs. Greenwood nodded again, behind her coffee. "I always liked that name," she said softly.

Vicki sipped cold coffee and let the moment pass. "When did she tell you she was pregnant?"

Mrs. Bott thought a minute. "About a month ago, she did. I was mighty surprised. I didn't know she was seein' anybody serious."

Mrs. Greenwood laughed softly. "You were so surprised, Tillie. You called me right away. You couldn't believe it, I couldn't, either. I was washin' dishes and I dropped the cookie sheet. Almost made a dent! My best one, with the air cushion." She looked over at Mrs. Bott. "You know the one, with the cushion? The air cushion down in between the layers?"

"I do, yes." Mrs. Bott nodded. "That is a good cookie sheet."

Vicki paused. "Did Shayla tell you who the baby's father was?"

"No. Jus' that they was having trouble and she might move out."

The boxes. "She was getting ready to move where?"

"I don't know, exactly. Said she wanted to find a new place and change her life."

Vicki made a mental note. "What did she mean by that?"

"I don't know. I figgered she'd tell me, in time. I was just happy to have a grandbaby comin'."

"Did she mention a Jamal Browning?"

"No, no. She didn't tell me that."

Vicki didn't get it. "I think he was her boyfriend."

"Don't know him."

"I think he may have been the father of her baby. I believe that he paid her bills, like electric and phone."

"Hmmm. I don't know that. I don't know that name."

Vicki sighed inwardly. "Who do you think was the baby's father?"

"I don't know. I didn't ask. I figgered that was her business, not mine."

"Did she date anyone that you know of?"

"Like I say, not serious. She always went out, she liked to dance. Shay was a good dancer. She liked music." Mrs. Bott paused, thinking. "A while ago, there was someone, his name was Dwayne."

Yay! "Dwayne what?"

"I don't know. Or maybe Don. Or Wayne." Mrs. Bott waved a gnarled hand. "That was years ago."

"When she visited, did she ever bring anybody? Any friends or boyfriends?"

"No. She always came alone."

Vicki was getting nowhere. "What did she do for a living?"

"She used to type. She typed. On a computer. Key-punch, they used to call it," Mrs. Bott answered vaguely.

"Did she work for a company, if you know?"

"No, different places. For a temporary, like."

"I see."

"But she never asked me for money, not once," Ms. Bott added.

"So she was independent."

"Yes, very. Stubborn."

"Did she ever mention anyone named Reheema Bristow?"

"No."

"Are you sure?"

Mrs. Bott thought a minute. "I don't know that name. I would recall that name. Reheema. That's an unusual name."

"Yes, it is," Mrs. Greenwood added, leaving Vicki frustrated.

"Who were her girlfriends, did you know?"

"Not really."

"Didn't she have a best friend? Every girl has a best friend." Then Vicki blinked. *Except me.* "I mean most girls."

"She said some names. Mar, that was one."

"Mar? Did she have a last name?"

"I don't know it. I would say Mar was her best friend, I think. Mostly she talked about Mar."

"Is Mar in Philly? Do you have her address or phone number?"

"No, I just know Shay used to call her, on the cell phone. When she was home ta visit she'd always be calling Mar. Mar this. Mar that."

Vicki made a note. Maybe there was no connection between Jackson and Bristow. But then again, it was clear that Shayla Jackson wasn't telling her aunt much about her life in Philly, or maybe Vicki was projecting. Either way, time to get down to business:

"Mrs. Bott, I have a feeling that someone close to Shay, maybe her boyfriend, sold drugs. Do you know anything about that?"

Mrs. Bott fell silent. "I don't know about that," she answered after a minute. "She didn't do anything like that, growing up. She was a good girl. She drank a little, at parties in school, but nothing like that."

"Not Shay." Mrs. Greenwood clucked a dry tongue, shaking her head.

"Do you know about any friends of hers who did drugs or sold them? Or guns? I don't think she did anything wrong, but she knew some bad people. What you know about this could help find her killers."

"I didn't know anything about that, I wish I did." Mrs. Bott looked into her paper coffee cup, then sighed. "Shay could get talked into things. She trusted people. She trusted everybody."

"So maybe she trusted the wrong people?"

"Maybe."

"Maybe that's why she wanted to change her life?"

"Maybe. Yes." Mrs. Bott nodded.

But she didn't get the chance.

"I know she was lookin' forward to that baby. She always did want children."

Vicki suppressed the image of Jackson, slain in her bedroom. "Did you ever hear the nicknames Jay and Teeg?"

"No, I surely didn't."

"I think they were involved with drugs, too."

"I don't know anything about that."

"There seemed to be a lot of money in her life. She had nice jewelry, for example."

"Shay did like nice things," Mrs. Bott answered. "When she was little, she always had to have matching bows. And braids. And dresses."

Mrs. Greenwood added. "Mmm-mh. Those little white socks, with the lace on top. The ruffle. All around."

"I made those."

"I know you did, Tillie." Mrs. Greenwood's speech fell into a soft cadence that matched Mrs. Bott's, a re-assuring call and response between old friends. "I know you did."

"And shiny black shoes."

"Oh, how she loved those black shoes."

"She was such a pretty child, a pretty little girl."

"She was."

"She surely was." Mrs. Bott smiled happily with Mrs. Greenwood, the two of them forgetting for a minute how it would all turn out, and Vicki let them be, left them to slip into a reverie of what might have been, what could have been, thinking of pretty babies in ruf-fled socks with shiny patent shoes. Vicki wished for one minute that she could replace the scenes from the med-ical examiner with those frilly, happy, pastel images. Women like these shouldn't have to see sights like that. Vicki felt terrible she'd brought up the drug thing and raised questions about Jackson's memory.

"I am so sorry for your loss," Vicki said, and Mrs. Bott seemed resigned, and overwhelmingly sad.

"Thank you very much. You know, I told her, if she comes to the city, things happen. Things like this."

And it made Vicki sad, too, that she couldn't deny it. Even in her hometown.

In time, she packed Mrs. Bott and Mrs. Greenwood into a Yellow cab bound for the bus station. She offered to buy them an airplane ticket, but they wouldn't hear of it, and she had to promise if she ever went to north Florida she'd stop in for pecan cookies. She stayed on the corner in the cold, waving to them as the cab drove off, already formulating her next step.

She hadn't learned enough about Shay Jackson, and there was someone else who might know more. Cars and SEPTA buses rumbled down the cobblestone patches of Spruce Street, spewing chalky exhaust into the frigid air, and Vicki looked for another cab. She wouldn't be doing police work, exactly. It was more like an errand.

She wasn't suspended from errands, was she?

TEN

THE SUN BURNED COLD IN THE COLD CLEAR sky, but Vicki stayed warm by keeping up, stride for stride, with Jim Cavanaugh. Cavanaugh was tall, thin, and superbly tailored in a gray wool coat he'd undoubtedly bought with his signing bonus. Former AUSAs earned $150,000 to start when they joined the big Philly law firms, so they upgraded their wardrobes, bought a car with excessive horsepower, and demoted the Jetta to "station car." Vicki experienced paycheck envy. Working for Justice paid one-third of that amount, which proved there was no justice.

"I need to ask you about one of your old cases," she said, hurrying alongside Cavanaugh down the busy sidewalk. His tie flew to the side, catching a bracing breeze as they strode down the street. He'd been too busy to meet with her in his office, but she'd insisted, so he'd agreed to let her walk him to his deposition. "The defendant's named Reheema Bristow, indicted for a straw purchase. You had the case just before you left our office."

"A straw case?" Cavanaugh wore hip rimless glasses, and his dark bangs flipped up as he barreled along. Businessmen in topcoats, workers in down jackets, and well-dressed women streamed past them on the sidewalk, laughing and talking, going back to work after lunch. "I picked up a straw case? I thought I was cooler than that."

"Two guns purchased, a CI named Shayla Jackson?"

"No clue."

"You spoke with Jackson on the phone?"

"Don't remember that."

"You must have met her at the grand jury."

"Name doesn't ring a bell. What did she look like?"

Vicki flashed on the scene of Jackson strafed with gunfire, then shifted to the photos on the mirror. "A pretty girl, black, nice smile."

"That's everybody."

Great. "Think about it. The case had a knockout for a defendant. Reheema Bristow. Tall, black, lovely face, killer body. Looks like a model."

"Oh, yeah." Cavanaugh smiled, and breath puffed from his mouth. "Now I remember the case. Who could forget Reheema? She was slammin'. Re-hee-ma."

"Yes, Reheema. You held a proffer conference with her, your memo in the file says so. I have it, if it helps."

"Let's see," Cavanaugh said, and Vicki juggled her handbag to slip the memo out of her briefcase and hold it in front of him while they walked. A kid plugged into a white iPod looked over as Cavanaugh glanced at the memo. "Yes, okay, I remember."

"It says her lawyer, Melendez, was there and also your case agent, Partino."

"Yeah, they were."

"You remember Melendez? Court-appointed, short, a little blocky?"

"Oh, yeah. Nice guy."

Unless he's suing you. "And Partino. Where's he, these days? Why didn't he stay with ATF?"

"He was a reservist and got called up. Still in Iraq, I think."

"So I can't talk to him."

"No."

Vicki refused to be discouraged. "Last night, my case agent was killed when he and I went out to see Jackson. Jackson was murdered, too, and she was pregnant."

"The CI, I read that online," Cavanaugh said, and to his credit, he winced. "I didn't realize it was that case until now. Reheema. So what do you want from me?"

"I'm trying to find out what happened."

"Don't they have police for that?"

Best not to dwell. "Okay, let's talk about Shayla Jackson."

"The CI? What about her?"

"First off, her grand jury transcript wasn't in the file, and the slip shows you ordered it. You know where it went?"

"Guilty. I admit it, I wasn't into filing. Maybe it got misfiled. I *love* having somebody to do my filing." Cavanaugh grinned. "I have my own secretary now. Well, the guy I share her with is always out of town. It rocks."

"Jackson called you and volunteered to testify, your memo said."

"Right."

"So she called you out of the blue? It's weird."

"But not unheard of."

"I know, but usually there's a reason." Vicki didn't get it. The girlfriend of a drug dealer, calling the U.S. Attorney's Office to snitch? It didn't make sense but she couldn't tell Cavanaugh about the cocaine. "Do you know why she did that?"

"No."

Vicki checked the date of the memo, flapping as they walked. Eight months ago. Shayla would have just found out she was pregnant, if she knew that early. "Did she mention that she was pregnant at the time?"

"No."

"Did she look pregnant then? She wouldn't have been far along."

"I don't know if she was pregnant. She mighta been a little heavy, but that's typical. Gold jewelry, tipped fingernails. You know. Ghetto fabulous."

Vicki got over her jealousy of his salary and began disliking him on the merits. "Okay, so Jackson came in and testified before the grand jury that Reheema resold the guns?"

"Yes."

"How did Jackson know that Reheema had resold the guns?"

"As I remember, the defendant told her she resold them."

Vicki's ears pricked up. "Bristow admitted it to her?"

"Yep."

"So they knew each other?"

"I think that's what she said. They were best friends."

Vicki didn't get it. She'd asked Reheema this morning if she knew Jackson, and it didn't seem like the name had even registered. And that was consistent with what Mrs. Bott had said, too. "Who told you that?"

"What?" Cavanaugh was distracted, exchanging waves with a man he knew.

"Who said that they were best friends?"

"The CI."

"Jackson?"

"Yes."

"Did Jackson ever call Reheema Mar, or a name like Mar?" Vicki flashed on Mrs. Bott. Actually, she was having separation anxiety.

"How the hell do you get Mar from Reheema?" Cavanaugh screwed up his nose.

"Did she?"

"I don't know. Christ."

"Did Jackson mention a Mar?"

"No."

Vicki felt confounded. "You sure Jackson said Bristow was her friend?"

"Best friend, she said."

"How did they become best friends? Don't say you don't know."

"I don't."

They barreled down the street, and Vicki shook her head. "It couldn't be from the neighborhood. Jackson lived in the near Northeast, and from the file, Reheema's apartment was in West Philly."

"If you say so."

"Did Jackson have a job?"

"No idea."

"And it couldn't be from work, even though Reheema worked two jobs." Vicki was remembering from Reheema's case file and she suspected that Jackson's temp job was history, no matter what Mrs. Bott had thought. Jackson was more likely the well-kept girlfriend of a coke dealer, not a woman who worked. But for some reason, when she got pregnant, she had dimed on Bristow and decided to change her life. "Did Jackson ever mention a Jamal Browning?"

"No."

"Do you know if Jackson had a boyfriend?"

"What is this, high school?" Cavanaugh laughed.

"Do you know the names Jay-Boy or Teeg?"

"They dogs or people?"

Vicki didn't fake a smile. "Okay, take me back to the proffer conference. At the conference, did Reheema want a deal?"

Cavanaugh held up the memo and double-checked it on the fly. "It says she didn't, so she didn't."

"Did you squeeze her?"

"I wish." Cavanaugh laughed. "Re-*hee*-ma."

"Jim, this matters."

"I'm sure I did. I used to have a good rap."

"It's odd that she didn't want a deal, isn't it? I mean, no priors, so she could get off with almost no time, if she gave up whoever she resold the gun to."

"True."

"So why didn't she want to deal?"

"I don't know."

"Didn't you wonder why?"

"Frankly, my dear, I didn't give a damn." They stopped at the red light on Seventeenth Street, where Cavanaugh faced her, shrugging in his heavy coat. "You're new, aren't you?"

"Yeah."

"You'll see what I mean. I was halfway out the door by then and I was burnt out. It gets to you. All of it."

Vicki didn't have to ask what "it" was. She'd seen "it" at the D.A.'s office, but it hadn't gotten to her. Oddly, she'd only wanted more of "it." Maybe she'd feel differently if her personal life didn't suck. Or if she owned a station car.

"I only went to the proffer because Melendez pushed for it. I was there if Reheema wanted to talk, but she didn't want to talk. She made a stink at the detention hearing, yelling that she was innocent, and got herself a permanent detention." Cavanaugh shrugged again. "These people, they make their choice, they live with the consequences. I don't try to figure out why they do what they do."

They. "You think she was too scared to name names?"

"I don't know."

"She didn't seem scared to me."

"Whatever."

"You don't remember anything other than what you told me, or what's in the memo?"

"Not really. When I started this job, I had a brain dump, I swear. I don't remember much from before." The traffic light changed, and they crossed the street. Cavanaugh picked up the pace, and Vicki hurried along, roasting in her down jacket. A woman going past seemed to recognize her and started whispering to her friends, but Cavanaugh remained oblivious. "I've been at my new firm for a year, and I tell you, it's a totally different world. This meeting I'm on my way to? It's multidistrict product liability litigation, with 137 corporate defendants. It's a city, a country! At issue is a defective disposable syringe, specifically the plunger on the syringe—"

"Excuse me, but was there any corroboration of Jackson's story?"

"It was a circumstantial case, so what else is new? The gun dealer reported that she bought them, and the best friend said she admitted reselling them," Cavanaugh said, defensively, and Vicki recognized his tone. She often had it in hers. No crime was easily proved, *Law & Order* aside.

"Who'd she sell the guns to?"

"Reheema didn't say."

"You mean Jackson *said* she didn't say." The government's case was so thin, Vicki was almost doubting it herself. "Did they ever find the guns?"

"No."

"They turn up in a robbery or shooting?"

"No."

"So the only proof in the case really was Jackson's word."

"Yes." Cavanaugh came to an abrupt halt before a massive office tower of dark glass mirrors, and people streamed into the building next to smokers taking one last drag. "Put it in context. It doesn't sound like much now, but when the indictment was filed, it did. Handgun crime went through the roof last year, I remember that much, and Strauss started Project Clean Sweep to get handguns off the street. The office was cracking down on straws, big time. We got the list of multiple purchasers from ATF, and we went after 'em. We caught Reheema and a lot of little fish in the net."

"So we had our story and we were going with it."

"Exactly," Cavanaugh answered, with a final smile. "Now I gotta get to work."

"Thanks," Vicki called after him, but he had already turned and was flowing with the others into the mirrored tower.

She stood still, momentarily stumped. Maybe she'd been going about this the wrong way.

But if she was going to try a new tack, she didn't have much time.

ELEVEN

VICKI CHECKED HER WATCH: 3:15. NOT BAD. The sky was still a frozen blue, so she turned up the heat in the car and steered her old white Cabrio out of the business district in clogged traffic. She'd gone home to get her car and cell phone, and, with a sick feeling inside, wiped it clean and plugged it into the recharger in the dashboard. Almost immediately the phone began chiming, signaling she had messages.

Vicki reduced her speed, picked up the phone, and tried to ignore the darker line of dried blood around the keypads while she thumbed through the menu to see who had called. Dan. The three messages were as predicted, and she pressed the button to call back, bound to the recharger like an umbilical cord.

Dan answered after one ring. "Woman! Holy God, what are you up to? You off your Ritalin?"

Vicki laughed.

"I heard you tried to kill a defendant! I say, who's

got a problem with that? We all clean the streets our own way. Judge not, lest ye be judged!"

"I didn't try to kill her." After last night, Vicki would never again use that word so lightly. "I just wanted a little information, is all."

"So you tried to kill her for it?"

"Not true!"

"Bale's walking around the office with steam coming out of his ears. It's not a good look for him."

"I can imagine."

"You're definitely right about that Botox. He's completely pissed off and he still isn't frowning."

Vicki felt a guilty twinge and switched lanes.

Dan said, "Isn't that a perfect vision of hell? Having all that anger and not being able to express it?"

"Sounds like work."

"Or marriage."

Vicki let it go and passed Thirtieth Street. "At least he didn't fire me."

"Congratulations. Your career is really going places."

"Thanks for your support."

"So what happened? Tell Daddy," Dan said, and Vicki filled him in completely. "Quite a story. So where are you now?"

"In the car, going to learn a little more about Reheema. She should get out of jail free in a few hours, and I wanna see what I can see before then."

"You think it's a good idea? Coke? Guns? You? One of these things is not like the other."

Vicki smiled. "The most dangerous thing I'm doing is talking on the cell and driving."

"Why do you want to know more about Reheema?"

"I'm curious, is all."

"Curiosity killed the Cabrio."

"Puns are beneath you, Dan."

"You overestimate me."

"That's a given."

"No, I mean it." Dan's voice turned serious, and Vicki could imagine exactly how he'd look when his handsome features darkened. Basically, he'd look even handsomer. "You're doing this for Morty."

"No, really?" Vicki accelerated when she saw open road.

"The cops are on it."

"Oh yeah? I just met with the CI's mom, who didn't even get a call from them. God knows when they'll get in gear, and I'm not stopping them, anyway. I'm learning about my own case. If anything, I should have known it before." Vicki swallowed hard, checking traffic in the rearview. A gypsy cab was riding on her bumper. "If I'd taken the time to get that transcript, I would have known the stuff I found out today."

"You were on trial. Don't blame yourself."

"I'm at fault."

"No, you're not."

"Enough." Vicki braked at the light at Thirty-eighth Street. She was going back out to West Philly again. Penn students crossed the street in scruffy jackets, mingling with university employees wearing plastic ID badges on lanyards. A white police cruiser pulled next to her, and the cop gave Vicki a nasty sideways look, disapproving either of her cell phone or her penchant for police work. "I should go."

"Call me as soon as you get home."

"I will."

"The minute you get home."

"Yes, dear," Vicki said, as if she were kidding. She pressed end, flipped the phone closed, and tossed it onto the seat beside her. When the light turned green, she accelerated. She was almost there, even if her thoughts were elsewhere.

With Dan.

TWELVE

"*YOU'RE* A LAWYER?" THE MANAGER ASKED
skeptically, which dispelled Vicki's concern that he'd
recognize her from the TV news. His name was Mike
Something and he was maybe thirty-five, his face dotted with old acne scars. He wore a ratty blue sweater
with jeans, and his short, dark hair was gelled and
spiky, so it stuck up like an unfortunate crown. His
eyes were narrow and blue, his nose straight, and his
teeth stained with nicotine. Vicki stood in the door to
his tiny, windowless back office, and he took way too
long to eye her up and down.

"Yes, I'm a lawyer," Vicki answered.

"You don't look like a lawyer. You're so little."

"I'm a little lawyer."

Mike smiled crookedly. "You watch *The Practice*? I
used to watch *The Practice*. I don't know why they took
it off." They were in the back office at Bennye's, a
raggedy sandwich shop in West Philly. The paneled

walls were covered with an old Miller High Life ad, a taped-up 2001 calendar from a local heating oil company, and an obscene Lil' Kim poster, which was redundant. The office reeked of leftover cooking grease, and Vicki couldn't fight the sensation that even the air was sticky. Mike sat behind a small desk cluttered with old newspapers. "I liked the blond chick on *The Practice*, you know which one?"

"Yeah, I liked her, too." Vicki didn't have all day. "Talk to me about Reheema Bristow. She waitressed here, right?" There had been a note in the file.

"You're here about Reheema?" Mike brightened, sitting straighter in his black vinyl chair. "Whyn't you say so? How the hell is she?"

"Fine." *Only because they stopped me from strangling her.*

"I went to visit her a couple times, inside. Tell her I said hi, will you?"

"Oh, I'm not her—" Then Vicki caught herself. Mike thought she was Reheema's lawyer. *Well, what's the harm?* "Sure, I will. I'll tell her you said hi."

"Thanks. My best to her mom, too. How's she doin'?"

"Her mom? Fine." *I hope.* "Now, you're a friend of Reheema's, right?" Vicki was taking her cues from Mike's demeanor, like a cable TV psychic. "She mentioned you to me. She said you'd be glad to talk to me, if it helped her out."

"I am. Anything she needs, you just ask."

"What I need most is information. Background info, for her case." Vicki thought a minute. "I don't remember her mentioning anyone but you from here. Didn't she have any other friends at work? People who know her well? I could use them for character witnesses at her trial."

"Not really. There's only the one waitress, the joint is so small. I prolly was the closest one to her, being the boss. I'd be a great character witness."

"Great, we'll get to that in a minute." Vicki made a fake note in her Filofax. "By the way, did she have any boyfriends, that you know of? We don't get time to talk girl stuff."

"A boyfriend? Reheema? No way. She worked this job in the day and the housecleaning at night, at Presby, the hospital. She didn't have the time. She was like a church girl, anyway, you know."

Church girl? Vicki blinked, nonplussed. "I know, that's what's so unfair, with the charges against her. The government indicted her for buying two guns and selling them to someone else."

"The government can kiss my sainted ass." Mike snorted. "She would never do that. Reheema was the kind of girl, you know, she took care of people. Her mother, all the customers. Reheema wasn't ghetto, like some of them."

Vicki let it go. "Let me ask you something. Why did she work here and at the hospital, if she was a college grad? If you don't mind my asking."

"Not at all, I know this ain't the Ritz. I think she used to work for the city, like a case worker or somethin', but she got laid off. I knew she'd leave when something better came along." Mike was shaking his head. "Then they picked her up. Whatever they said she did, she didn't do it."

"How do you know that? I mean, how can I prove it?"

"She never done nothin' wrong, I'll come in and testify, I'll tell 'em. Reheema, she was the best." Mike pursed his lips, and Vicki read his look. He'd had a crush on her.

"What would you say about her, in detail, if I called you to testify?"

"I'd say she worked the day shift when I started here, opened up each morning, and kept the place always clean as a whistle when I come in. And she took real good care of all the customers. The customers loved her, too. They still ask about her. She worked every day, seven days a week, always on time, super-reliable. The only time she missed work was when her mom was sick. That's four days in two years."

"What was her mom sick with?"

"Cancer. Her mom's big in the church, too." Mike cocked his spiky head. "Don't you know, about her having cancer?"

Oops. "Right, she did mention that, but she didn't go into detail. Reheema keeps the personal stuff to herself."

"She is quiet, a sweet girl. Very sweet. She's a beautiful person, inside and out." Mike got lost in thought, and Vicki could guess where he was going, but didn't want to follow. "The guys who came in, they'd all hit on her."

"Of course."

"But she'd put them off real nice, not to hurt their feelings. And if they got a little too handy, or came in drunk, she could take any of 'em." Mike straightened in his chair. "You get her offa these charges, tell her she can have her old job back anytime. My business went through the roof when she worked here. Nobody comes here for the food."

"Great, thanks. Did she ever talk to you about a girl-friend named Shayla Jackson?"

"No."

"They were best friends," Vicki said, increasingly puzzled.

"Never heard the name."

Damn. Were Jackson and Bristow friends or not? Somebody was lying or didn't know the truth. "How about Jamal Browning?"

"No."

"Jay-Boy or Teeg?"

"No. She never talked about nobody except her mom. She was a loner."

"Then how do you think she got mixed up in all this? Any idea? I mean, she just got indicted out of the blue?"

"I wonder about that, sometimes. She sure don't de-serve what happened to her. I think it's a conspiracy." Mike sucked his teeth. "The way I figure, somebody set her up. I told her so in my last Christmas card, she mention that?"

"Your Christmas card? Yes, she did mention that. She said it was very thoughtful of you."

"I send her mom a card, too. Every year."

Vicki blinked. He hardly looked like the kind of guy to keep a Christmas card list, much less one that in-cluded sick mothers. He must have had a major crush on Reheema. *Worse than mine on Dan.* Vicki hadn't realized how completely pathetic she was until she started investigating.

"She mention that, too? The card to her mom?" Mike's eyebrows lifted in a hopeful way. "I ask because I slipped a few bucks in there, you know, like a Christmas present."

Vicki got an idea. "She never mentioned the card to her mom, which does seem odd. You sure you sent it to the right address? You know, if you send cash to the wrong address, it'll never get to her."

"Hmmm, you're right," Mike said, leaning forward and reaching across the desk to a grimy old-fashioned Rolodex. He flipped through the wheel of plain white cards written in ballpoint, then stopped at one, and Vicki went over to snoop as he read. "Here we go. Arissa Bristow. Her address is 6847 Lincoln. It's in West Philly."

"Sounds right." Vicki made a mental note. "I'll check it with Reheema."

"Appreciate it."

"One more thing," Vicki said, deep in thought. None of this was making any sense. Reheema wasn't earning much at this crummy deli, so she'd have an obvious need to supplement her income by reselling guns. But the whole picture was out of whack. Reheema fit the profile of a typical straw, but it was hard to believe that a church girl or a social worker would conspire to have an informant killed. "Did anybody else come here, asking you about Reheema?"

"No."

"No detectives?"

"No."

"Cops?"

"No."

"How about the feds? FBI?"

"No."

"Another lawyer? A guy named Melendez, or somebody who works for him?"

"No."

"Well, thanks," Vicki said, mystified. What had Melendez intended to do to defend Reheema anyway? "I appreciate your help, and so will Reheema."

"Sure thing." Mike rose, a bit of gallantry. "You know, I don't believe Reheema would even know how to shoot a gun."

And for a minute, Vicki didn't either, though she had proof positive that Reheema had bought two and sold them.

Clearly, she wasn't finished with her errands yet.

THIRTEEN

VICKI HAD NEVER BEEN IN THIS NEIGHBOR-
hood, but something about it had a familiarity she
couldn't place. She was still in West Philly, bundled up
in the superbly heated Cabrio. She had no idea why
VW had stopped making these cars, but they shouldn't
have. First the Cabrio goes, then *The Practice*.

She had driven about twenty blocks west and a zillion dollars away from the campus of the University of
Penn or even Bennye's Sandwich Shop, to this rundown neighborhood. Two-story row houses lined the
streets, characteristic of Philly, but they were crumbling and scarred with graffiti. Their wooden front
porches sagged, the paint blistered and peeling, and
some houses had windows boarded up with plywood.
Vicki took a right at the corner for the third time, having no idea where she was exactly because the street
sign had been taken down. Then she took a right and
another left, passing a vacant lot strewn with concrete

rubble, beer cans, and other debris, and she finally found Lincoln Street.

She cruised to read the house numbers, crudely painted directly on the brick, fading but still readable. 6837, 6839. At least she was on the odd-numbered side of the street. She had been in bad neighborhoods before at the D.A.'s office, going to question witnesses with and without police escort. She had learned the best way to deal was to be yourself. A very white girl driving a very white Cabrio, conspicuous as all hell in an African-American neighborhood that had seen better days.

Vicki crossed Washington Street, then Jefferson Street; she detected the pattern, now that she was a big-time gumshoe. The cross streets were presidents' names, but still, they sounded vaguely familiar. In the next second, she remembered. She realized where she had heard about this neighborhood. *At home.* This was her father's old neighborhood, Devil's Corner. She'd never been here, but the name had always intrigued her. There were hundreds of neighborhoods in Philly, all of them named, but few had any relation to reason.

Vicki looked at the houses with new eyes. Her father never liked to talk about his childhood here. The neighborhood had been Italian and Jewish then, the starting place for upwardly mobile immigrant families who puddle-jumped to the City Line area and, if they were lucky, to the Main Line, the classiest of all neighborhood names.

She remembered that the brick house on the corner of Washington Street had belonged to her father's family. She circled the block, passed the cross street, and found the house, pausing as people do at funerals. It seemed somehow appropriate. Her father's old house on the corner, a squat two stories, stood obviously vacant and hollowed out, a crumbling brick shell, its windows nailed shut with cheap tin. She experienced a pang of sadness at its disrepair, unaccountably, because she had never been inside. She doubted if her father would shed a tear, either; he never talked fondly of his home or this neighborhood, spoke only of it as having "changed," which was his code for "black people moved in." But Vicki wasn't seeing changed; she was seeing leveled.

There was nobody on the street. She checked her watch: 4:26. Granted, it was cold outside and would soon be dark, but kids should be home from school, playing outside. Adults should be going in and out of their houses, too, whether mothers at home or people out of work. But no one was in sight on these blocks. The streets were oddly deserted. Vicki spotted house number 6847. She slipped into a parking space, cut the ignition, and grabbed her bag and got out of the car. She walked to the house, zipping her coat and finger-combing her hair to meet a church lady. She had been such a hit with Misses Bott and Greenwood, this should be a piece of cake.

Vicki walked to the house and climbed up the concrete steps, which needed to be repaved. The red paint on the front door had alligatored, and a tiny window on the door's top panel had been duct-taped in place. Vicki was guessing that Reheema's mother, Arissa Bristow, didn't have much money. Maybe she gave it all to the church. Or it went for medical bills.

Vicki knocked several times and waited patiently on the sunny front stoop; the door had three locks, including two dead bolts, so she knew it would take time to open. Still, she wasn't hearing anything. She waited a minute, then knocked again and called out, "Hello? Mrs. Bristow?"

Suddenly, without being unlocked, the front door opened and behind it stood a tall but frail African-American woman. Like her daughter, she wasn't what Vicki had expected at all.

"Yeah?" the older woman said, slurring her words, almost stuporous. She stood in a flowered housedress that hung on her frame, oblivious to the cold air sweeping in from the door. Her hair, gone gray-white, was sprayed stiff and uncombed from her head. Spittle oozed from the corner of her mouth, and her lips were parched and blistered.

"Mrs. Bristow?" Vicki asked, in surprise.

The woman's brown eyes registered no response. They had sunk in their sockets; deep folds creased the corners of her eyes and mouth, and she was almost emaciated, her skin stretched so tight that her face was more skull than flesh. Her body swayed slightly, her bony hand evidently hanging on to the doorknob to remain upright, her stick legs in half nylons almost giving out on her. Vicki didn't know if she was seeing the ravages of cancer, drugs, or both. If the woman was Mrs. Bristow, she should have been about fifty-five years old, but she looked twenty years older, and Vicki wondered if this was the right house.

"Are you Arissa Bristow?"

"Yeah, you got anythin' for me?" the woman mumbled. Her pupils were a pinpoint and seemed to focus on Vicki without seeing her. "I need to hit, I need to hit. You got anythin' for me, you got anythin'?"

Drugs. "I wanted to talk to you, about Reheema."

"Reheema? Reheema?" Mrs. Bristow sounded as if she'd never heard the name.

"Yes, your daughter, Reheema. May I come in?"

Mrs. Bristow opened the door and walked ahead, leaving the front door hanging open, then she shuffled out of the room, as if Vicki hadn't been there at all.

"Mrs. Bristow?" Vicki called to the receding form, but there was no answer.

A cold draft blew in, so she shut the door behind her and took a quick look around the small living room. The lack of curtains and a southern exposure guaranteed the room would be incongruously sunny, its neglect brightly illuminated. Sun shone on a tattered brown couch, next to a blue beach chair with ripped plastic lattice. Dirt, cigarette wrappers, and old newspapers littered the dark red rug, and the air was thick with filth and stale cigarette smoke. There was no TV, stereo, or radio, and it was almost as cold in here as it was outside. Against the wall, the old-fashioned white radiator had cracked, spilling blackish water onto the floor. The heat must have been turned off, so the pipes had burst. Vicki went into the next room, where she gasped.

Mrs. Bristow lay on a dirty, bare mattress, her eyes closed and her mouth hanging open.

Please don't be dead. Vicki hurried to Mrs. Bristow's side, searching her still face, and grabbed her wrist. She was feeling for a pulse when the older woman snored deeply. Vicki started, then relaxed.

"Mrs. Bristow?" she asked softly, jostling her, but the woman didn't stir. How could Vicki interview her now?

Damn! She scanned the room, stumped for a moment. The floor was strewn with empty Gallo and

Thunderbird bottles, and the end table next to the mattress overflowed with crack paraphernalia: an orange glass pipe, another plain pipe, and matches. Empty glassine envelopes of nickel bags, one-inch square, came in pink and purple plastic.

Vicki picked up one of the bags and caught the sweetish whiff of crack; she had prosecuted drug cases in state court and had sniffed more than her share. Her gaze went automatically to Mrs. Bristow's hands, resting palms up. Burns on her fingerpads, where she'd held a hot glass pipe, confirmed the obvious. Vicki was looking at a long-standing crack habit; she didn't know if Mrs. Bristow ever had cancer or if she had beaten it, or if those were lies that Reheema had told her boss.

Vicki had questions, but no answers. She checked her watch: 4:45. Reheema would be released from the FDC soon and she might come here to see her mother. Vicki left the sleeping Mrs. Bristow and went into the next room. Fifteen minutes later, she had snooped around the first floor, having learned nothing probative. Empty liquor bottles lay everywhere, some broken. The refrigerator held only fast food and take-out debris; the cabinets were empty except for canned peas, a few loose Newport cigarettes, an open box of Frosted Flakes, and, inexplicably, Libby's pumpkin pie mix. The grimy kitchen was overrun with cockroaches too bold to run even from a federal prosecutor.

Vicki checked on Mrs. Bristow, determined she was sleeping deeply, then went upstairs to snoop some more. At the top of the stairs was a small bathroom, and she peeked inside. The stench of human feces almost overpowered her, though the toilet lid was closed. The floor was wet with filth and urine that it was luckily too dark to see. Old rust streaked the sink, and water had frozen in a colossal teardrop at the faucet. A white plastic trash can overflowed with trash and toilet paper. She shuddered, left the bathroom, and went down the hall to the nearest bedroom, in the back of the house.

It was darker here, and cold, but the bedroom was empty, unused. The radiator had cracked in two, draining black water, and the bed and mattress were gone, as was the box spring and the metal rack to hold it; only a darker square remained on the floorboards to tell where a bed had been. A battered end table sat in one corner, and there was no lamp or dresser. Vicki left the room and went back down the hall. If the row house was typical, there'd be another bedroom in the front, facing the street.

She opened the door onto another bedroom, also disemboweled, with everything of value sold off. A lighter square in the floorboards sat against the interior wall, where a double bed used to be, facing the sunny windows. The rug was gone, the empty closet hung open, and a lone battered chair sat in front of a bare corner. She figured a desk used to be there because a cork bulletin board clung to the wall, colorful and cluttered with items, the one cheery sign of human habitation.

She crossed the room and found the bulletin board covered with high school paraphernalia. REHEEMA BRISTOW, read a certificate for the National Honor Society, with a tiny metal pin sunk into the corkboard. A large W made of maroon felt was next to it, with ribbons in red, white, and blue. One ribbon read PENN-SYLVANIA TRACK CLASSIC in gold letters, and next to the ribbons, a handwritten list, in a girlish high school scrawl, that was titled Personal Record: *100 meter run 2:15.71, one mile 5:02.* And underneath had been written: *GOALS, 800 meter run 2:11, 1 mile 4:55.*

She didn't get it. Reheema had been a good student and a track star in high school. When had she gone so wrong? How had she ended up in the FDC? Vicki stared at a photo of Reheema in a black track singlet, in a formal group photo with her teammates. Their singlets read Willowbrook Lady Tigers, and Vicki felt a start of recognition. Willowbrook High was her father's alma mater! He never talked about his high school days, except to say that he was in the chess club, but she knew he'd graduated from Willowbrook.

Her gaze fell to another snapshot of Reheema, lovely and smiling in the middle of her track pals, and they all stood in front of an old Ford Econoline van with a homemade sign painted on a bedsheet: PENN RELAYS OR BUST. In the driver's seat of the van sat a tall woman with a mature version of Reheema's camera-ready features and an equally dazzling smile. The driver had to be Mrs. Bristow, before she'd become a ghost of herself.

The image turned Vicki's emotions on their head. She'd thought she knew about crack addiction, but she had learned it from cases she'd tried, in a legal context. She had never seen it up close, viewed as part of a family. And in this case, it wasn't the daughter who was the user, it was the mother. And Vicki had always thought of criminal defendants as simply "the defendant"; she had never personalized a felon. But here it was, staring her in the face. She was prosecuting a girl who graduated from high school only a year ahead of her, and in National Honor Society, as she had been. A girl who worked a job and was "super-reliable," as she was. A track star who had borne up, even excelled, under odds that Vicki never had to deal with, like a mother who had disintegrated into powder. And what if Mrs. Bristow had gotten worse after Justice had put her daughter away for the straw purchase?

What was going on? Was what she was doing right or wrong? Was Reheema guilty or not? Could Vicki help Mrs. Bristow at all? She turned, puzzling, from the bulletin board and left the bedroom. She got halfway down the stairs, and the sight in the first-floor bedroom told her that she didn't have the right answers.

In fact, she didn't even have the right questions.

FOURTEEN

ARISSA BRISTOW WAS GONE. THE MATTRESS in the makeshift bedroom lay empty. And Vicki's purse lay on the floor, its contents strewn onto the filthy rug.

Damn! How could she have been so stupid? She hurried to her purse and kneeled on the rug. Her mascara, eyeliner, a lipstick, her thick black Filofax, her BlackBerry, and, happily, her car keys, had been dumped in a pile. Of course, her wallet was gone and so was her cell phone.

Vicki sat back on her haunches, angry at herself. She had set her purse down when she thought Mrs. Bristow had stopped breathing and had forgotten about it when she went to the kitchen. She couldn't be sure, but she thought she had fifty bucks in her wallet, a black nylon Kate Spade, which cost a hundred bucks. Luckily, she didn't carry her checkbook, but she did have three zillion credit cards; Visa, Amex, Ann Taylor, Gap, Lord & Taylor, Nordstrom. Her ATM card and her driver's license were gone; and worse, so were her DOJ creds, in their little black bifold.

Vicki couldn't believe it. Losing her Justice ID was an even bigger deal than losing her license. A guy at work had lost his and had to get authorization from Bale and reapply to Washington for a replacement. She couldn't even get into the office building without it these days.

"Argh!" Vicki considered calling 911, but she had no cell. And Mrs. Bristow had no telephone. She threw her stuff back in her purse, scrambled to her feet, and sprinted for the door after Mrs. Bristow. *Okay, so I haven't worked out in a few days. I can still catch a crack addict.*

She ran through the door, her coat flying open, and hurried down the steps onto the sidewalk. It was darkening now and so cold; the sky was a frozen blue. The rising moon was full, casting a cool whiteness. She looked right, then left, down Lincoln Street. The sidewalk was still deserted. The row houses stood silent, not giving up their secrets. Mrs. Bristow wasn't in sight. It hadn't been that long. Where had the woman gone? She couldn't drive; she could barely stand. Was she in a neighbor's house?

Vicki sprinted next door and peered in a cracked window, but there was no light inside and the house seemed still. She went to the next house and knocked. No lights were on inside, and nobody answered. She ran to the Cabrio, pulled the keys from her purse, chirped the car unlocked, and hopped in. She'd find the woman faster in the car. She switched on the ignition and zoomed out of the space, going the right way on the one-way street, then taking a right onto Washington

Street, another right onto Harrison, then a third right onto Van Buren.

No Mrs. Bristow. Vicki turned on the heat, and it blew a cold stream into her face. She drove around, looking. The next few minutes were a blur of American presidents until she looked to the right. Behind Lincoln was a narrow street that ran parallel to it, almost an alley. The crooked green sign read CATER STREET, but the light at the corner was out. In the moonlight, Vicki could barely see shadows moving on the street, at the far end.

There. Shuffling toward the shadows was Arissa Bristow, easily recognizable because she wore only her housedress. The poor woman had no coat on and moved through the cold night with surprising speed. Vicki pulled over to the curb, cut the ignition and put her hand on the door handle, about to get out and run after her. Then she stopped herself.

How would it look? An AUSA running down the street, physically tackling the aged, crack-addicted mother of someone she was prosecuting? Not a great idea. Vicki weighed her options. She wanted her wallet and her phone back, but she wasn't supposed to be here anyway. Also, she felt a little scared at the prospect of running down a dark street in this neighborhood. *I'm not from the suburbs for nothing.*

Then she had a better, or at least a safer, idea. Mrs. Bristow had wanted to smoke, and now, thanks to her new lawyer, she had fifty bucks in cash. There was only one place she would go—to buy more crack. It might be interesting to see where she bought it. Vicki stayed in the driver's seat and watched Mrs. Bristow travel purposefully up the street, her dress flapping like a flag. Decrepit row houses lined the street; some with lights on, some without. There seemed to be activity five houses down, at what appeared to be at a vacant lot, its entrance partially obscured by bare city trees. Mrs. Bristow approached the trees and turned right, disappearing into the darkness of the vacant lot.

Vicki's breath steamed up her windows and she rubbed out a circle on the passenger side. She kept her eyes trained on the trees. A large figure came out of the lot, with another shorter figure. The car got colder, the heat dissipating quickly through the thin convertible skin. Maybe there was a good reason VW stopped making Cabrios. She checked her watch: 6:15. She waited . . . 6:40. She wondered when Reheema would get released from the FDC. Would she come to see her mother? Vicki tucked her cold hands into her jacket pockets. She developed an ache in her neck from looking to the right so much.

The sky darkened to blue-black ink but still no Mrs. Bristow. A few people, maybe five or six, went into the lot behind the tree and came out again. The only activity on the block was at the vacant lot. It had to be drug sales, but where was Mrs. Bristow? What if the woman had been hurt or had a seizure of some kind? Or what if Mrs. Bristow had just smoked up and fallen asleep in the lot? She couldn't survive outside in the night, not at this temperature.

Vicki was putting two and two together, developing a working theory. Maybe Reheema hadn't resold the guns, but had given them to her mother, who had sold or traded them for crack. Guns were valuable currency to drug dealers, the engine powering the straw trade.

The theory was consistent with what had happened at Vicki's proffer conference and even jibed with Cavanaugh's proffer conference. It was possible that Reheema wasn't giving up the name because she wasn't about to flip on her own mother.

BOOM! Suddenly a loud bang came from the window on the driver's side. Vicki jumped in fright and looked over. A fist pounded on her driver's-side window. The Cabrio rocked with the impact. A man in a black hood loomed inches from her face.

"Get outta here, bitch!" he yelled, but Vicki was already twisting on the ignition and hitting the gas.

She sped down the street, cranking the Cabrio engine as fast as it could go, and she didn't stop speeding until her heartbeat returned to normal. At some point she came to a red light, unsure if she was in Atlantic City or maybe Maine, but she didn't care. She was away from scary guys in hoods. But she had left Mrs. Bristow behind, and that worried her.

She drove a few blocks until she spotted an Exxon station, then dug around in the car seat and retrieved a red scrunchy, a chipped grape Chiclet, and what she had wanted in the first place. She popped the Chiclet, got out of the car, and headed for the phone booth. Frigid air hit her like a blast; she hadn't realized what a cocoon the Cabrio had been. She opened the booth's squeaky collapsible door, which had left its runners long ago, fed the pay phone, and dialed her own cell phone. It was picked up after two rings.

"Yo," said a man's voice, and Vicki was pissed. Mrs. Bristow had already unloaded the phone?

"That's my cell phone, pal! Who are you?" she shouted, but the man hung up. She pressed redial and when he picked up, she shouted again, "Where's Arissa—"

He hung up again, and Vicki let it go. She took a deep breath outside the phone booth and exhaled deeply, taking mental inventory and watching her breath cloud around her like a chain smoker. She should call the cops, but that would reveal she'd been with Mrs. Bristow. Odds were that Bale wouldn't find out, but why risk it? Also, what could the cops do? Wallets got stolen all the time. Poor Kate Spade.

The air felt cold, the lights of Center City twinkled far away. Vicki was in West Philly, halfway out to suburbs like the Main Line. She had no wallet, no cell, no money, and no credit cards. She'd have to cancel them ASAP. She felt exhausted, hungry, and dumb. She could use a little comfort. She had gas in the car because she never let the tank get too low, on the advice of women's magazines. She moved her sleeve aside to check the time: 7:30.

She could be there in no time.

PART TWO

The names of the streets are mostly to be taken from the things that grow in the country, as Vine Street, Mulberry Street, Chestnut Street, and the like.

> —WILLIAM PENN,
> Instructions to His Commissioners, 1681

Q: What type of crack or what quality of crack did you see on Brooklyn Street? Was it good, was it bad?

A: What type of crack?

Q: Was it good quality or poor quality?

A: Oh yeah, the best work in the city.

Q: The best work in the city? What does "best work" mean?

A: The best crack in the city.

Q: Is that just that the amount you sold was good in terms of volume, or was it the actual quality?

A: Quality.

> —DAVID WEST,
> *United States v. Williams,*
> United States District Court,
> Eastern District of Pennsylvania,
> Criminal Docket No. 02–172, February 23, 2004,
> Notes of Testimony at 736–737

FIFTEEN

"HONEY, I'M HOME!" VICKI CALLED OUT, unlocking the front door, which opened to the shrill barking of a dog and the warning beep of a burglar alarm, set in case a psycho killer dropped in for Glenlivet, neat. She went to the keypad to disable the alarm before it went off, while her parents' Welsh corgi sprinted into the entrance hall and attacked her shoe.

"Ruby, no!" Vicki said over the beeping, shaking her toe to get the dog off. She punched her mother's birthday into the white keypad, but the alarm went off, erupting into earsplitting sound. She shook her foot but the corgi hung on, a nasty blur of tan and white. Her startled parents rushed in from the kitchen.

"Mom! Dad! Did you change the alarm code?" Vicki yelled over the din.

"Yes, it's my birthday now!" her father shouted, wincing. Vicki was trying to remember her father's birthday but it was too noisy to think. Her father hurried past her to the keypad and punched in the new code, mercifully silencing the alarm, if not the corgi.

"Ruby, no!" her mother said, but the dog growled and shook her head, with Vicki's toe still in her teeth. "Ruby, no!"

"Why does she do this?" Vicki couldn't help but laugh, finally freeing her pump. She had no idea what had possessed her parents to buy this dog. Every time she came home, the dog attacked her toe, heels, and ankles. Either the animal had no long-term memory or her name was Ruby, no! "Mom, doesn't she know me yet?"

"She's a herding dog."

"So?"

"Ruby, no! Ruby, no!" Her mother bent over in her white silk blouse and full navy skirt, tugging the determined dog by her red leather collar.

"Why does she bite me? I'm family."

"That's why she's herding you."

"She's insane," Vicki said, reaching down to pet the puppy, who only scampered away, barking and play-bowing on her short legs. She had eyes like brown marbles, legs like stumps, and a body like a Tater Tot. She kept nipping, trying to bite Vicki's toe. Adorable, for an attack dwarf.

"Why didn't you call first, Victoria?" her father asked. He was still dressed from work in suit pants and a starched white shirt, but his Brioni tie was loose, which qualified for him as casual dress. His straight, dark hair, growing sparse on top, matched dark eyebrows that capped small brown eyes. His nose curved like a hawk and his lips were thin, with a small scar on the top lip that appeared when he frowned, as now. "We didn't know you were coming."

"I have only the four lamb chops, honey," her mother added, with plain regret. Her greenish eyes softened in spite of the surgically enhanced lift at their corners, and her hair, chin-length, curved gently under her chin and shone like jet in the light of the entrance hall's chandelier. "We're on the South Beach Diet, so we have to watch. I would have bought more if you'd called ahead."

"Sorry, I didn't get a chance." Vicki wouldn't tell them she'd been stalking crack addicts. She had long ago stopped telling her parents anything. In fact, she was hoping she'd get to eat a full dinner before her father brought up what happened last night. "I was close by and figured I'd stop in. If there's no dinner, that's okay."

"Nonsense, you can have one of my chops," her mother offered, putting a silk-swathed arm around Vicki and giving her a brief hug. "Come in, we were just about to sit down." She smelled like Chanel and felt just as elegant, but it freed the dog to bite Vicki's foot.

"Mom, your dog hates me," she said as they walked into the dining room, which had an oval walnut table as its polished center, surrounded by Chippendale chairs and red wallpaper blooming with etched Chinese poppies. Against the far wall sat a mahogany sideboard, and the rug was a silk Oriental, a red-and-white pattern that complemented the Mandarin-hued borders of her parents' china, now set with cooling food in two place settings.

"Ruby just wants you to stay with the group."

"She bites!"

"Herds," her mother corrected, and they fell into step, with the dog herding Vicki's heel.

"Why doesn't she just lick my face like a normal dog?" Vicki remembered the neurotic poodle from her childhood, which looked like a saint next to this one. "Peppy never did that."

"Ruby has different instincts. She bites you only so you'll do what she wants."

"The control freak of dogs."

"Oh, hush." Her mother released Vicki with a smile and turned to the swinging door to the kitchen, in the back of the house. Ruby let go of Vicki's heel and scooted after her. "Sit down while I get you a plate. I'll be right back."

"Can I help?"

"No, thanks. Keep your father company," she called back airily, her navy silk skirt billowing gracefully behind her, her waist still svelte. Vicki became aware that her father was watching her mother with similar admiration. They stood in the large dining room, saying nothing, and she wondered if there would ever come a time when she felt completely comfortable alone with her father, without her mother to fill in the silences. There was only one subject that she and her father ever agreed on:

"Mom looks great, doesn't she?" Vicki asked, but it wasn't a question.

"Absolutely. She goes to Curves now."

"There's a Curves here? Where?"

"On Lancaster Avenue, near the tile place. And Eadeh, the rug place."

"I see those Curves commercials all the time." Vicki was putting herself to sleep with her own conversation. She was filling up the air with words until her mother got back and rescued them from each other. What was taking her so long?

"Eadeh has very nice rugs. Very nice Oriental rugs."

"I heard that."

"She loves Curves. She goes three times a week. Here. Let's sit. Dinner's getting cold." Her father pulled out his chair at the head of the table and sat down behind his plate, which held two medium-rare chops of New Zealand lamb, three florets of barely steamed broccoli, and a portion-controlled tossed salad, sparingly dressed with vinaigrette. Vicki sat down, and he gestured at his plate. "Your mother put us on South Beach, and she's right. We eat twenty grams of carbs a day, no more. It's much healthier than Atkins."

"I'm sure," Vicki said, but she hungrily wished she belonged to one of those Italian families in the Olive Garden commercials, who ate piles of spaghetti with hearty red tomato sauce. Her parents wouldn't be caught dead in an Olive Garden and now they were the only Italians in the world who didn't eat pasta.

"Our cholesterol was too high, and so was our blood sugar."

"Really."

"Now our levels are a lot better."

"Good." Vicki hid her smile. Her parents spent every minute together; driving to the office, working across the hallway from each other, then driving home in the same car. They had met at Villanova Law School, married upon graduation, and gone into practice together. Their marriage was all the more solid for their togetherness, although now that they were sharing the same blood sugar, Vicki suspected that they were physically fusing and soon would become conjoined twins.

"We use only Splenda now. It's a sugar substitute."

"Splenda. It sounds so cheery."

"Make fun, but I lost five pounds the first two weeks."

Vicki blinked. "I wasn't making fun, Dad. That's great, that you lost five pounds."

"No, it isn't. The book says you should lose seven. I listened to it in the car, on CD. Your mother lost seven."

"Five isn't much less than seven. It's only two." *Math genius.*

"Fewer."

"Huh?"

"You said less. You meant fewer."

"Oh. Sorry." *English genius, too.* "In any event, two fewer pounds doesn't matter."

"It does to me."

"Oh." Vicki sighed inwardly. It was almost impossible to agree with her father, even when you were faking it. He was a man who never took yes for an answer. She suddenly regretted coming home. She should have gone to Olive Garden.

"Sugar is poison," her father added. He unfolded his napkin and set it on his lap, then rested his arms on the side of the table. The strains of *The Marriage of Figaro* lilted from a CD player in the kitchen, followed by her mother, humming along. Her father tapped his index finger in time, though he would never sing, as much as he loved opera. He seemed preoccupied, and Vicki knew he had to be thinking about Morty and Jackson's murders.

"Dad, about last night—"

"Let's wait until your mother comes in. I know she wants to hear, too."

"Okay."

"This way you won't have to repeat it."

"Or repeat it all over again." Vicki smiled at her own joke, because somebody had to. Her father was listening to the opera wafting from the kitchen, tapping his finger. She changed subjects. "Dad, guess where I was tonight?"

"Where?"

"Washington Street."

"Washington Street?" Her father's eyes flew open. "In Devil's Corner?"

"Yes, I even saw your old house."

"Really." His eyebrows lifted higher, just as her mother returned with an empty plate, which she set in front of Vicki and filled quickly with one of her own lamb chops and two broccoli spears. Between them, it wasn't enough food for a corgi, and Vicki felt a wave of guilt.

"Mom, that's all right. I'm not that hungry."

"I won't hear of it. I had a huge lunch." Her mother smiled and went around the table to her seat. The barber of Seville was bragging in the background. The dog returned to gnawing on Vicki's shoe.

"I was saying that I was on Washington Street today, Mom. I saw Dad's old house."

"Really?" Her mother tossed her shiny helmet of dark hair. "How did it look?"

"How do you think it looked?" her father interjected. "We can't all be from Hilltown." Hilltown was her mother's old neighborhood, which was nicer, some ten blocks east of her father's. Her mother let it pass, but Vicki was puzzled by his grumpy reaction.

"Did I say something wrong?"

"Of course not, Victoria." Her mother's green eyes

lit up. "You know your father doesn't like to be reminded of his humble beginnings."

"It's not that, Lily," her father said, turning to her mother. Vicki couldn't see his face from that angle, but she knew what it would look like. "It's a horrible neighborhood now. A ruin."

You don't know the half of it.

"Washington Street, my block, it's a slum now." Her father sipped water from a glass frosty with ice.

"Did you know the alley behind it, Cater Street?"

"Of course. How do you know Cater?"

"I get around," Vicki said, to make him smile, which it didn't. "I was driving through Van Buren and Lincoln Street."

"All the best places. Hope you kept the windows rolled up." Her father stabbed a spear of broccoli, and her mother avoided anyone's eye.

"Dad, was there a vacant lot on Cater when you were growing up?"

"I don't remember."

"Do you have any old pictures of Washington Street or the house? Maybe in Grandma's stuff?" Vicki's grandmother had died ten years ago, and her grandfather well before that. As soon as her father had had the means, he had them both moved into a gated retirement community in Chester County.

"No. I don't even know where your grandmother's things are."

"In the attic?"

"No. I didn't save those things, did I, Lily?"

"You saved nothing," her mother answered.

"Too bad." Vicki thought a minute. "You went to Willowbrook High School, right?"

Her father set down his fork. "Why the questions?"

"I was just asking."

"Victoria, it wasn't high school like you went to high school. Like Episcopal or another private school with nice green fields. Lacrosse, Parents' Day. It wasn't pleasant. We were poor. You can't imagine how poor."

As poor as the people who live there now?

"My father worked day and night, three jobs, to make ends meet. I don't think I ever saw him sit down in a chair, not once."

"You've been crabby all day, Victor," her mother said softly.

"No, I haven't."

"You have, too." Her mother faced Vicki. "We lost a house client this morning. Remember Carlon Industries, the dry cleaners?"

"Sure. Jerry Solomon, right?" Vicki's parents did so much business entertaining that she had grown up around their clients and their wives, like Olive Garden families had uncles and aunts. Michael, Sam, and Carol clustered around the Allegrettis' dinner table. They counted as family, evidently until they fired you.

"Yes. Yes. Good for you."

"It wasn't Jerry, it was the son," her father said, but her mother waved him off.

"Please, it was Jerry. He's hiding behind his own son, the coward." Her mother turned to Vicki. "Anyway, Jerry had eleven locations. As you know, we've done all his closings for years, and he let us go today. It was a blow for us."

"We'll do fine without him," her father said, gruff. "The son was a slow pay anyway. Receivables of six months' standing. It's enough, already." He turned to

Vicki, miffed but trying to hold it in. "That's not what I want to talk about, anyway. Your mother and I want to know what happened last night. If I've been crabby today, that's why."

"That's not completely why, Victor," her mother corrected, but her father ignored her.

"We pieced together what we could from the newspapers. Why don't you fill us in? Our only child is on the news, involved with violence, a multiple homicide, a shooting, and we hear nothing but a phone message."

"I told you we should have stayed up for the news," her mother interjected. "Were you on the eleven o'clock news?"

"I was. A case agent I've been working with was killed last night." Vicki gulped chilled water, hoping it would get past the sudden lump in her throat. The barber was singing happily in the kitchen, an ironic soundtrack to Morty's shooting, flashing through her head. "His name was Bob Morton."

"I saw it in the newspaper account, and online. I thought I knew that name."

"We won that case together, Edwards? Morty was his name."

"Yes, I remember now. He was killed, and a pregnant woman, a black, was shot in a house." Her father's dark eyes grew hard as onyx. "It said you were inside the house at the time of the shooting. Were you?"

"No, I wasn't inside when it happened." Vicki reflected that maybe she hadn't learned to lie in law school. Maybe she had learned it at this color-coordinated table. "I was outside at the time and I'm fine."

"The newspaper said you were inside." Her mother set down her fork, waiting.

"The newspaper got it wrong. They want to sell papers."

"But you were there at the house last night, weren't you?"

"It's part of the job." Vicki checked her temper, and her father tugged the napkin from his lap and set it down on the table. She knew he wouldn't be eating another bite tonight. He could lose those extra two pounds in no time. The corgi, on the other hand, was making a meal of her shoe.

"You're in the wrong job, Victoria." Her father shook his head. "Two people killed. If this experience doesn't change your thinking, I can't imagine what will."

Morty.

"I don't know why you don't just come to work for us. This is getting ridiculous. My God, what does it take to wake you up?"

Here we go.

"If you like criminal law so much, you can practice criminal law with us. We have only the four associates now, with Rachel going on maternity leave. You can do white collar defense. We get those matters all the time, referrals from the big firms."

"That's criminal defense, not prosecution."

"Don't be so picky!"

"I'm not being picky!"

Her mother raised a hand, her mascaraed eyes widening in alarm. "Wait, Victoria. Am I to understand that you were at a home when two people were shot to death?"

"I told you, Lily!" her father exploded, turning on her mother.

"Dad, please don't yell," Vicki said, but he wasn't listening.

"Of course she was, Lily! That's what she's saying! That's what she does! She's in the gun and violent crime unit, or whatever they call it! It puts her directly in harm's way!"

"You could have been *killed*?" her mother asked, shaken.

Vicki felt stunned at her mother's pain, which appeared as unexpectedly as a tornado in the middle of Broad Street. She must have been tense the whole day, her anxiety an undercurrent to the quotidian tasks of answering e-mail, taking phone calls, and attending closings. They had probably fought about it on the way home.

"Victoria, I simply don't understand you anymore." Her mother's light eyes glistened. "How can you do that? How can you? It's as if you intentionally want to hurt us."

"Mom, that's crazy, it's not intentional—"

"I beg to differ," her father interrupted. His skin flushed so brightly she hoped he'd taken his Pravachol. Seville seemed far away, but the dog wasn't. "At this point, isn't it intentional? To persist when you know how we feel?"

"Dad, it's not about you."

"No, it's about you. Because you, for some reason, want to hurt us, when we have given you everything. You even make much less than you could earn with us and you've no equity! You're not even building toward anything!" Her father stiffened, struggling to keep a civil tongue. "You know, if we owned a family farm, you would take it on, no questions asked. But we own a family law firm, and you refuse. You feel *justified* in refusing. And to add insult to injury, it's not that you don't want to practice law, which perhaps I could understand. No, it's that you don't want to practice our kind of law. That's like saying, I'll grow alfalfa for my family, but not corn!"

"It's different from—"

"No, it isn't! You're a lawyer, Victoria, and you know about foreseeable consequences. If you can foresee the consequences, you are charged with intending them, are you not?"

"Yes, but—"

"So it's foreseeable that our firm, without anyone to leave it to, will simply be"—her father was so angry, he was at a loss for words, which was as angry as he ever got—"*defunct*. The Allegretti firm will simply cease to exist. And you know this and you persist nonetheless, so you are charged with intending that consequence. And why? Because it's not your kind of law!"

"Dad, can we seriously be having this argument again?" Vicki asked, finally getting angry. "I should have a choice, don't you think?"

"Not when you have an obligation! To us, to me and your mother! And not when it can get you killed! If a choice is what you want, then you have it! And if you want to live like a pauper, then do!" Her father rose and gestured to her mother. "Look! Look at what you're doing to her!"

Vicki looked. Her mother's glossy head bent slightly over her plate and her lips, their gloss finally worn off, pursed in pain. She was trying not to cry.

"Mom, I'm sorry, don't cry," Vicki said, feeling a tug, not for the first time. Morty was dead, and now her mother was upset. It had all gone to hell in a handbasket. She didn't want to quit. She didn't think they were right. But she was so very tired. Suddenly the phone in the kitchen started ringing.

"I'll get that." Her father rose and went into the other room, leaving them in miserable silence. Vicki knew that her mother was listening to the phone, to hear if it was a client; like most self-employed people, they worked around the clock. The two women sat in suspended animation until her father returned, his bearing erect, his features emotionless.

"The phone's for you, Victoria," he said.

"Me?" She rose stiffly, with a dog attached to her toe, which was when it struck Vicki that maybe her parents were herding her, in their own way. Biting her to keep her close. She knew that they loved her, and she loved them, too, despite their best efforts to the contrary.

"Be right back," she said, wondering who was on the phone.

SIXTEEN

"VICK, WHY IS A BLACK GUY ANSWERING your cell? Are you cheating on me?"

Dan. "I can't talk now."

"What up? You said you'd call, and when you didn't, I called your cell. What happened?"

"It's a long story." Vicki could hear stone silence from the dining room. At least her mother wasn't crying.

"I e-mailed you, too. Didn't you check your Black-Berry?"

"I didn't have a chance."

"Why does he have your phone? He doesn't even know who you are. Did you get into trouble?"

"We'll talk about it later."

"That means yes. Are you okay?"

"Fine."

"You don't sound fine. You sound upset."

I am upset. "I'm fine."

"Are you staying overnight at your parents'?"

"Are you insane?"

Dan laughed. "When will you be home?"

"An hour."

"Want me to come over? Mariella's on call."

"No thanks."

"Then call me, no matter how late. I want to talk to you. I don't like the way you sound. You're worrying me lately, with Morty and all."

"Okay," Vicki said, touched. The man could read her like a book. "Gotta go."

"No matter how late, call me."

"Okay."

"Swear?"

"Swear."

"Okay, good-bye, sweetie."

She hung up, warm inside. Dan was truly worried about her. And he didn't bite.

Vicki got back to her house around ten o'clock, where she ignored her bills, mail, e-mail, and phone messages, and tiredly headed straight for the phone in her bedroom, shedding her coat on the way upstairs, dropping her purse, and kicking off her wounded shoe. She couldn't wait to call Dan and tell him what had happened on Cater Street. He could help her sort it out. He'd been an AUSA so long, he'd have good ideas. Should they bust Mrs. Bristow's dealer? Should they get her into rehab? And Vicki wanted to work on some theories with him, about Shayla Jackson and Bristow.

She flicked on the lamplight beside her bed, slid out of her suit jacket and blouse, then slithered out of pantyhose and her skirt, feeling better once she was home. She loved her bedroom. She had painted the walls a bright cobalt blue last year, by herself, and she had a big TV/DVD player on a white metal stand affixed to the wall. Her dresser, next to the closet, was a pine four-drawer she'd bought secondhand, and the room was neat, clean, and comfy. She undressed, slipped into an old Harvard T-shirt, and tucked herself under her puffy white comforter while she called Dan.

"Hello?" a woman answered, confusing Vicki for a second. Of course, it was Mariella. She recognized the slight British inflection. Then Vicki heard masculine laughter in the background. *Dan.*

"Mariella, oh, hi. It's Vicki."

"Vicki, hey, you caught us at a bad time. A very bad time." There was more laughter, and Vicki realized that Mariella and Dan were in bed together. Dan was laughing, then Mariella started laughing. "No! No! Daniel, no tickling! Daniel!"

Vicki felt a wave of shame, then didn't know why. What was she ashamed of? That she was dying to talk to a married man? *Yes, for starters.* That he was at this moment making love to his wife? *Yes, that too.* That she would have traded beds in a minute? *A trifecta!*

"Daniel! Don't tickle!"

"Mariella, sorry, I should go," Vicki said, but Dan's deep voice came on the line, breathless.

"Vick, talk to you in the morning! Duty calls!"

She was about to say good-bye, but Dan had already hung up.

It left Vicki in her blue bedroom, alone except for the silence. She sat still for a minute, propped up by her pillows, trying to process what had just happened. Mariella must have taken a break and come home; she did that sometimes, at weird hours. Dan would have been delighted to see his wife, as he was for every drop of time she threw his way, as an afterthought or no.

He adores her, you idiot. Right now they're making love, five blocks away. GIVE IT UP, LOSER! YOU NEED A VIDEO?

Vicki stopped feeling sorry for herself, at least temporarily, and picked up the phone. There was work to do. She had made a mental list of all her credit cards and spent the next half hour getting each toll-free number from 1-800 information, then canceling the cards. She ordered a new ATM card, rush delivery, and she'd still have to get a new driver's license and DOJ creds. She sighed and lay back in the pillows, to devise a good lie to explain how they'd been lost. She closed her eyes against the lamplight. Her mind wandered and her thoughts flowed where they would. She was still for another minute, then she reached over and picked up the phone, dialed a number, and waited.

One ring, two rings, three rings, four. After five rings, the answering machine switched on and said:

"You have reached Grandmaster Bob Morton, and, yes, I *am* even better-looking than I sound. Please leave a message for me and The Commodores." The tape segued instantly into Morty's trademark song, "Brick House."

Vicki felt a wrenching deep within her chest. She listened to the song, then hung up, and dialed again. She did that four more times, and by the fifth time, she felt better just holding the receiver, listening to

Morty, feeling connected to him, somehow. Tonight she didn't know what to do about his murder, but tomorrow she would. She had to. She couldn't help feeling she was on to something, and she couldn't leave it to the cops, ATF, or anyone else. Morty was her partner. Vicki hung on to the phone long after the song had finished, and when the tears came, she let them slide down her cheeks until she fell soundly asleep.

Ring! Ring! It was the telephone that woke Vicki up, her face stuffed in her pillow. She cracked a scratchy eye at her alarm clock. The red digital numbers read 8:15. She had slept in.

Ring! Ring! She pushed herself up from the bed and reached for the phone.

"Vick." Dan, his voice unusually grave. "You near a TV?"

"Uh, yes."

"Turn it on. Right now."

"Why? I'm asleep."

"Just do it."

Vicki reached for the remote on the nightstand and flicked on the TV, set to channel ten. Grisly images flickered across the screen: yellow crime scene tape, uniformed cops standing around a row house, a black van, and a low metal gurney on wheels, bearing a black body bag. In the next scene, a pretty blond reporter said:

"Arissa Bristow was found dead this morning of multiple stab wounds. The body was discovered in Mrs. Bristow's West Philadelphia home, and police have no suspects at the present time." Then the screen changed to a commercial for I Can't Believe It's Not Butter.

My God. The news stunned Vicki. She felt suddenly chilled in the bedroom and yanked the comforter from the bed, wrapping it around her naked form.

"Isn't Bristow your straw's last name?" Dan asked. "Think she's a relation?"

"It's her mother." Vicki muted the commercials, numb.

"Her mother killed, the night after Morty? Think it's a coincidence?"

Vicki couldn't answer. Her head was spinning, tangling her thoughts. Dan didn't know what had happened last night. She hadn't had the chance to tell him. She didn't know where to begin.

"Vick? You okay?"

"I met her, I was there," Vicki started to say, but she couldn't finish. *I should have stayed with Mrs. Bristow. I should have made sure she got home safe.* Her knees went weak, and she felt herself sinking down onto the bed in the comforter.

"Vick, what's going on?"

"I wish I knew."

"I'm coming over. I'll be there in fifteen minutes."

"You don't have to," Vicki said, but she was interrupted by the ringing of her doorbell downstairs, followed by a loud pounding on her front door. The sound frightened her, unaccountably. "There's someone at the door. I have to go."

"Vick?"

"Hold on." Vicki shed the comforter and looked around the room for something to put on. She felt more naked than she was. Something felt very wrong. Suddenly, events were getting ahead of her, out of control. The knocking pounded louder on the door. She had to get dressed. She had to go. "Dan?" she heard herself say.

"I'll be right over, baby," he answered, understanding instantly.

SEVENTEEN

FIVE MINUTES LATER, A SCENE WAS TAKING place that Vicki couldn't have imagined if she'd tried. Two Philly homicide detectives sat across from her on her couch, and against the front wall stood Chief Bale. He had shifted into official mode, unsmiling under his groomed mustache, his dark eyes a mixture of distance and disapproval. He wore his Saturday best, jeans and a black turtleneck under his camel-hair topcoat, but his manner was anything but casual. The cops sat on one side of the coffee table, Vicki sat on the other, and between them on the coffee table, in a clear plastic evidence bag, was her black Kate Spade wallet.

She'd felt almost physically sick when they'd set it down like a trump card. Next to it lay two smaller evidence bags, one that contained her green-and-white plastic library card and the other a curled-up white paper card, her membership to the Philadelphia Museum of Art. Evidently, crack addicts wouldn't be seeing the new Manet exhibit. And if Vicki screwed up now, neither would she. She didn't know if Chief Bale was here as friend or foe, but you didn't have to be a former ADA to realize that the detectives were here to question her in connection with Mrs. Bristow's murder. The wallet made her a lead, if not a suspect.

"Your wallet was found on the body," the black detective said. His name was Albert Melvin, and he was young and attractive; clear brown eyes, a generous mouth, and a brawny build in a black leather jacket that seemed to retain the winter cold. He'd shaved his head completely, a macho look that struck Vicki as incongruous with his warm, if official, smile. She was guessing he'd taken the test only recently, because she didn't know him and he wasn't as dressed up as your standard Philly homicide detective. Detective Melvin gestured at his evidence array on the coffee table. "This is your wallet, isn't it?"

"Yes, of course."

"No money was in it. No credit cards, no driver's license. Just the membership card and the library card."

"I'm not surprised."

"How did Ms. Bristow get your wallet? Do you know?"

"Yes, she took it from me, last night. My wallet and my cell phone." Vicki told herself to stay calm. She could ask for a lawyer, but it would signal that she had something to hide, and Bale would fire her again, after he fired her for going to see Mrs. Bristow in the first place. She could represent herself; she knew how the Philly detectives put their cases together and she could anticipate the questions they'd ask. "I'd like to explain what happened, if I may."

"Please do," Detective Melvin answered, with his official smile. Next to him on the couch, the other detective made a note in his steno pad, his dark head bent so his pinkish bald spot showed. He wore glasses and a navy suit, with a skinny striped tie.

"First, I'm an AUSA and I had nothing to do with Arissa Bristow's murder." Vicki met Detective Melvin's eye to show him she wasn't guilty, which turned out to be harder than she'd expected. She didn't kill Mrs. Bristow, but she did feel guilty about the murder, and even she could hear it taint her tone. "I did meet Mrs. Bristow last night and may well have been the last person to see her alive, depending on what the coroner told you about time of death." Vicki waited a minute, but they weren't volunteering any information. "Let me start at the beginning, which is when I left Chief Bale's office yesterday, before noon."

Suddenly there was a loud knock on the front door, and everyone turned.

Dan. "I'll get it." Vicki practically jumped to her feet and ran to the door, opening it onto a blast of frosty air that wasn't completely weather-related. Dan was acting casual despite the fact that he was standing on the front step with two uniformed cops. Of course, they'd want to search.

"Look what the cat dragged in," Dan said, with an ironic smile. Vicki's neighbors across the street, Mrs. Holloway and the three kids, were at their window, gawking at the two squad cars that sat double-parked in front of her house.

"Come in, everybody," Vicki said, as if she were the perfect hostess. The three men trundled into the house, and she closed the door after them, getting her bear-

ings as the cops introduced themselves. She shook
their hands, still in cold black gloves. "I'd make coffee
for you, officers, but I'm busy being interrogated."

The cops laughed, and Dan quickly masked his surprise at Bale's presence. "Hey, Chief," he said.

Bale merely grunted in response.

Detective Melvin smiled again. "Ms. Allegretti, do
you mind if the officers look around?"

Dan's eyes widened. "They're really gonna *search*
your house? For God's sake, why?"

"Go right ahead, officers." Vicki had no choice but
to authorize a consent search. She signed the form
when they produced it, with Bale watching her every
move, leaning back against the wall again, his arms
crossed. She turned to Detective Melvin. "They're
welcome to look anywhere. The clothes I was wearing
last night are in the upstairs bedroom. It's a black suit,
and it's probably on the floor. You'll find hair and
fibers from Mrs. Bristow's house on my clothes, and
vice versa. I can explain all of that."

"Thanks." Detective Melvin nodded in a way that
directed the officers out of the room, and Vicki eased
onto the couch while the detectives resettled themselves on the other side of the coffee table. A bewildered Dan Malloy remained standing for a moment in
his jeans and his black down jacket, then he walked
around the coffee table and sat down next to Vicki,
who hoped her gratitude didn't show.

"Well, here's what I did yesterday, from noon on-
ward," she began, while the other detective started to
take notes. She proceeded to tell them everything, including her call to Dan, but not her call to Morty's answering machine because she was already feeling

exposed enough. In the background, the clinking of her pots and pans told her cops were searching her kitchen. Vicki took a deep, final breath. "That's the truth, and the whole truth."

"I see." Detective Melvin looked up from his steno notebook, which he'd pulled out of his back pocket in mid-lecture. His expression seemed relieved and his frown had vanished. They weren't charging her today, anyway. "I do have a few questions. Was there—"

"Wait a minute," Dan interrupted, leaning forward on his knees. "You guys can't really think that Vicki is a suspect in this murder, or, for that matter, in any-body's murder. I mean, this is ridiculous!"

"We have to investigate our leads, sir."

"Get real, detective. The wallet's not a lead." Dan snorted. He'd been a federal prosecutor for so long, he thought the locals were dummies, and it showed. "Who kills someone and leaves their wallet behind with a library card?"

"We didn't say it wasn't strange, sir."

"You know a lot of killers belong to the art museum? Obviously, that crack addict stole Vicki's wallet. I mean, what are you thinking? Vicki's a criminal? She's law enforcement. An AUSA, for God's sake!"

"Dan, let them ask the questions they need to." Vicki worried he was going too far. Behind her, the clinking from the kitchen had stopped and was replaced by the heavy tread of the officers' thick-soled shoes as they climbed the stairs to her second floor.

"But they're stupid questions!" Dan exploded, and Bale waved him into silence, at the same time that Vicki leapt in.

"Please, detective, you were saying."

Detective Melvin resettled. "Ms. Allegretti, how much money was in your wallet?"

"About fifty dollars. Also, my credit cards, a driver's license, and an ATM card. And my Justice creds," Vicki added, as if they were an afterthought, but Bale rolled his eyes. *Now they would both have to think of a lie.*

"Did you report it stolen to the police?"

"No, I didn't think it would matter. I chalked it up to bad luck."

Detective Melvin made a note. "I assume you won't mind us contacting the people you mentioned, including your parents."

Oh, great. "Of course not. Feel free." Vicki recited their addresses and phone numbers, which the detectives wrote down in unison. She would have to call her parents and explain why cops would be calling them, which bothered her almost as much as the officers searching her bedroom. She experienced the completely paranoid fear that they'd plant something incriminating in her house. Then again, she also believed that blow dryers jumped spontaneously into bathtubs.

"Now, you said you visited Arissa Bristow to investigate the murder of the ATF case agent. Did you believe that Reheema or her mother was responsible for this murder?"

"Honestly, I didn't know. That's what I was trying to follow up on." Vicki paused. If they were thinking about possible motives for her to kill Mrs. Bristow, it was a stretch. Did she kill Reheema's mother to get back at Reheema for having the CI killed? Too much. And how would the teenagers have known she and Morty would be at the house? Or was their theory more tenuous, like that Vicki killed Mrs. Bristow as revenge for Reheema having her partner killed? No, motive didn't exist. "But after what I learned, I'm not sure that Reheema was involved in any conspiracy to kill my CI or Morty."

Bale glowered, shifting his weight uneasily from one loafer to another. He didn't want her thinking about stuff like this, much less talking about it, but she couldn't stop now. And she was still curious: "Detective Melvin, the news report said that Mrs. Bristow was found in her home, stabbed to death. What was the estimated time of death?"

"Around seven-thirty last night."

The sentence struck Vicki like a body blow. *I should have gone after her. I shouldn't have been scared off by that man in the hood.*

"Ms. Allegretti?" the detective asked, and Dan put a comforting hand on her arm.

"Vick. You okay?"

Vicki found her voice. "She was killed right after I left."

"Of course, as you probably know, these things are never exact. It's always give or take a half an hour."

"I know." Vicki was trying to piece things together. *While I was eating lamb chops, Mrs. Bristow was being killed.* "My cell was already gone by that time."

"How do you know?"

"Because I called it from a gas station and a man answered. Maybe he had something to do with her murder." Vicki felt a rush of adrenaline. Had she talked on the phone to Mrs. Bristow's murderer? "Think about it. Mrs. Bristow had the wallet and cell, and she'd trade the phone and money for crack. Then she'd go somewhere—probably home—to smoke. The man could have followed her home, taken the drugs and killed her. Or maybe she bought the drugs and the man followed her home and killed her for them, then took the cell. Either way, we need to find that man."

"We?" Detective Melvin arched an eyebrow, and Bale raised his chin. "Who's we?"

"You're right. Not we." *I meant me.* "I meant you."

"Good. Now, what did the man on the phone sound like?"

"A black male. Gravelly voice."

Next to her, Dan was nodding with vigor. "Exactly. He did sound gravelly. I called her cell, too. A man answered and he didn't identify himself when I asked him. He's the one you want to go after, not Vicki."

"What time did you call, sir?" Detective Melvin made a note.

"Around nine o'clock, I guess." Dan ran a finger-rake through his unruly red hair, as he always did in court. "You heard what Vicki said as well as I did. Bristow was a crack addict, wandering the streets in a lousy neighborhood with fifty bucks in cash. Vicki is right. The likeliest scenario is that Bristow was followed to her house and killed for the drugs."

"That's certainly possible, sir."

"It's a helluva lot more likely than an AUSA knifing her to death!" Dan raised his voice, but Vicki cut him off.

"Dan, really, it's okay."

"You should be on Lincoln Street right now, or Cater," Dan continued, heedless. "Wherever it was, right now, you should be canvassing the neighbors! Checking out who went in and out of Bristow's house last night!"

"For your information, we canvassed already, sir." Detective Melvin raised his large hand, with a Bic pen stuck between his thick fingers. "So settle down. We have to ask your girlfriend a couple of questions."

"I'm not his girlfriend," Vicki said for the record.

Dan shot back, "Who are you kidding? You're searching her house!"

Bale stepped forward, easing off the wall. "Malloy, enough!" he said firmly. "Let the detectives complete their investigation. You and I know Vicki didn't kill anybody, but they have to do their jobs."

Vicki sighed with relief. So Bale was on her side. It emboldened her, or maybe she just liked her promotion to Dan's girlfriend. "Detective Melvin, who found Mrs. Bristow's body?"

"Her daughter, Reheema."

Vicki felt a sympathetic pang. She couldn't imagine how horrific that would be, finding your mother knifed to death. "Where was the body in the house, exactly?"

"A bedroom on the first floor."

"When was she found? I don't know when Reheema was released from the FDC."

"Let's see." Detective Melvin flipped back in his notebook, then ran a thumb down the page. "You met with the daughter yesterday in the morning, right?"

"Right." Vicki had almost forgotten, it seemed so long ago. A loud thump came from her bedroom, which everybody pretended not to hear.

"The daughter wasn't released until after midnight last night."

"Why so late?"

"There were paperwork issues, I understand. She

went straight to her mother's house and found her body. We caught the case at about one in the morning."

How awful. "The report said Mrs. Bristow was stabbed to death. I assume you didn't recover the knife."

"Not yet. It wasn't pretty. The victim was stabbed nine times."

My God. Vicki's stomach did a backflip. "That sounds like rage, as if it were personal, or maybe drug induced."

Dan added, "Like a crack addict."

"Was she found with any crack?" Vicki asked. "Had she used or what?"

"We field-tested the pipe next to the bed, which was positive. Toxicology tests on the body aren't finished yet."

"She'll be positive." Vicki thought a minute. "Where was my wallet?"

"Still on the victim's person, in a pocket in her dress. It was minus whatever credit cards and money you had."

"Reheema found the body and called the cops?"

"Right."

"Who found the wallet, you or Reheema?"

"The daughter."

"So Reheema knows that it was my wallet. She must have been surprised by that."

Detective Melvin nodded. "She was extremely angry. She demanded we question you, and I told her we were coming right here."

"She can't think I killed her mother."

"I can't speak for her, Ms. Allegretti." Detective

Melvin made a note. "Now, about this man who answered your cell phone. What's your phone number?"

Vicki gave it to him, and he wrote it down. But she couldn't stop thinking about Reheema. Did she think Vicki murdered her mother?

"And what type of phone was it?"

"A Samsung, the newer model. It has one of those special covers, it's silver and has blue daisies with little green centers on the front."

"Now *that* should be a crime." Detective Melvin smiled, but Vicki couldn't.

"How will you run that down, detective? Look for the phone? Tap the line? You have enough for a warrant."

"Leave that to us. I'd ask you not to terminate the service, to help our efforts."

"Of course."

Detective Melvin flipped his notebook closed. "I understand that you have a personal interest in this case, but you have to leave matters to us. My partner and I have the highest clearance rate on the Homicide Division. We know what we're doing."

"I respect the Philly police, I was an assistant district attorney." Vicki decided to press her luck. "Though I did wonder why you hadn't called Mrs. Bott, to talk to her about Shayla Jackson."

"We did call, but there was no answer and she didn't have an answering machine. Then we understood she was going to ID the body at three yesterday, not noon. It was a simple misunderstanding." Detective Melvin didn't look happy about it, either. "A little knowledge is a dangerous thing, Ms. Allegretti. Everybody thinks he's a detective. You could have been hurt last night, if not killed."

Standing behind Detective Melvin, Chief Bale wasn't saying anything. He didn't have to.

"But what about the drug activity on Cater? Is anybody going to do anything about it?"

"Ms. Allegretti." Detective Melvin frowned all the way to his shaved scalp. "As you well know, we have a Narcotics Division. That's their job. I'll make a point of notifying them of your observations of drug activity on Cater, and I'll also notify the captain in charge of that district. I'm sure they'll step up the patrols. If there is drug activity, they'll deal with it. You can't. In fact, Chief Bale has informed us that you're on a one-week suspension."

"It is indefinite now," Bale interjected, with a deep scowl. "That's without pay."

No! "Chief—"

"Don't even, Allegretti." Bale warned her off with a raised index finger.

"Fine, Chief."

"I don't need your permission," Bale shot back, and in the next minute, his attention was redirected to the stairs. The two uniformed cops were coming downstairs, carrying the brown paper bags they used to collect evidence.

"You found my suit?" Vicki asked, though the thought of her clothes in an evidence bag was tough to take.

"Yes, thanks. Took the shoes, too." The cops looked calm, so she assumed they hadn't found a murder weapon. She didn't want to think what her bedroom looked like.

"You didn't toss the place too bad, I hope."

"We improved it," one of the cops said, with a smile. "Give us a chance to make a mess here, too, will ya?"

"No problem," Vicki answered, and everybody rose and stood as the cops split up and began to turn over cushions in the couch. In the meantime, Detective Melvin slid his notebook into his back pocket, as did the other detective.

"Looks like we're done here, for now," he said. "Thanks for your cooperation. You know the drill. Don't leave the jurisdiction."

"You have to be kidding," Dan interjected, but Vicki touched his arm.

"Understood, gentlemen."

Bale was leaving, too, shifting his topcoat higher onto his shoulders and heading for the door. "I have a meeting to go to. Call you later, Vick." He glanced at Dan. "Malloy, put her under lock and key until further notice."

"Yeah, right," Dan said, but he didn't smile. He was watching the uniformed cops search Vicki's books, sliding them out and looking behind each one. She went to the door and opened it to let Bale and the detectives out, but a wet chill blew into the room. It had started snowing lightly, and large, flat flakes floated from the gray sky. The Holloway kids reappeared at their front window, ogling the uniformed cops.

"Thanks for coming," Vicki said, shutting the door, and she and Dan stood uncomfortably aside as the cops searched her living room.

"Almost finished, officers?" Dan asked, though they clearly weren't, and Vicki felt touched by his loyalty. He stood by her side, staring the cops down until they had finished destroying her living room, when she ushered them out the door. It was snowing with flakes too wet to stick, but the Holloway kids were out in heavy coats and mismatched mittens, pinwheeling in the snowflakes and sticking out their tongues stiff as spatulas. Their mother, Jenny, was laughing with them, taking pictures with a disposable camera. The Holloways stopped when the cops filed out of Vicki's front door and climbed into their respective squad cars, banged the doors closed, and started the cruisers' powerful engines, spewing exhaust into the chill air. Vicki waved a don't-worry-it's-just-business, and in the next minute, the kids resumed their spinning, with their mother snapping happily away.

Vicki watched them for a minute, then closed the door.

Hatching a scheme to get rid of her boyfriend.

EIGHTEEN

SNOW FELL STEADILY, MUFFLING THE WORLD
with nature's own insulation and filling Vicki's small
kitchen with soft, natural light. It would have been
cozy if Dan weren't somebody else's husband and she
didn't have murder on her mind. She had to think of a
way to kick him out without making him suspicious.
"You sure you don't have to get home?" she asked.

"Nah, I want to help you clean up."

"I'll clean later. I have some errands to do."

"I do, too. Let's clean up and do them together." Dan
scooped coffee grains into the paper filter with a brown
plastic measuring spoon. "First, we need coffee."

Argh.

"It's so ridiculous, them questioning you. I just can't
get over it."

"Let it go. They're just doing their jobs."

"Clowns. Jokers. Keystone Kops." Dan put the coffee back in the cabinet, then extracted the glass pitcher

from the coffeemaker and filled it up with tap water. He had taken off his coat and was wearing his jeans with a blue crewneck sweater and no shirt underneath, which forced Vicki to imagine him naked. Finally she understood why men found bralessness sexy.

"They're not so bad," she said idly, but Dan turned, incredulous.

"A library card? Exhibit A?"

Vicki couldn't laugh. She still felt bad that Mrs. Bristow was dead, so horribly murdered.

"What's the matter?"

"I feel crappy, is all."

"Why?" Dan poured water into the top of the coffeemaker, put the empty pot in the machine, and switched the black knob to brew.

"Because I was so naïve. Not only to go to Mrs. Bristow's house, but to leave my wallet." Vicki couldn't stop shaking her head. "If I hadn't been so dumb, she would be alive today. I'm screwing up so much lately and it's *killing* people. Jesus."

"How do you figure that?"

"I gave her the money that bought her the rock that got her killed." Vicki bit her lip. "It's the urban version of the house that Jack built."

Dan snorted. "Gimme a break. You didn't give her the money, she stole it. You didn't buy her drugs, she did. She got herself killed, and you had nothing to do with it."

"I don't know about that." Vicki wished she could agree, but she didn't. Why was everything going so wrong? First Morty and Jackson, now Mrs. Bristow. She rubbed her eyes, feeling sick inside.

"Stop blaming yourself. You're not to blame. By the

way, sorry I blew you off last night." Dan turned away and went into the cabinet to retrieve their two go-to mugs, Harvard and Elvis. He set them on the tile counter with a harder-than-usual *clink,* suddenly preoccupied. The coffee gurgled away, filling the kitchen with the aroma of brewing coffee.

"No problem. I'm sorry I called. I thought Mariella was at work."

"She stopped home."

"That's what I figured." Vicki hated talking about Mariella. Snow drifted onto her windowsill in wispy cartoon scallops, but it didn't lift her spirits the way it usually did. Looking up from the coffee mugs, Dan noticed it, too.

"When did it start snowing?"

"Not long ago."

"I didn't realize." Dan kept looking out the window, the reflected light illuminating his handsome features. His blue eyes drooped with morning fatigue, and reddish stubble dotted his chin. He frowned. "Snow is funny. You never know when it starts. It just sneaks up on you and there it is. Before you know it, you're in a snowstorm."

"I guess."

"This is pretty terrible, what's happening here." Dan turned from the window, still frowning, but Vicki wasn't sure what he meant.

"That Mrs. Bristow was killed?"

"No. You, on indefinite suspension."

Vicki blinked. "At least I'm not fired."

Dan didn't say anything. The coffeepot gurgled, and he bent over to make sure it was dripping, without meeting her eye.

"Well, I'm not, am I? If I were fired, Bale would have said I was."

"With the detectives there?"

"Sure, that would make it more fun."

"Good point." Dan laughed. "You're right. Bale likes you. I think you're his favorite."

Vicki smiled, mystified. "I thought you were."

"No. Strauss likes me, Bale likes you."

"But Strauss is Daddy and Bale is Mommy, so you win."

"It's not a contest," Dan shot back, and Vicki put up her hands.

"Whoa, don't shoot."

"Sorry, it's not you. I didn't sleep well, last night. We had a fight."

"Who?"

"Mariella and me."

Suddenly Dan had Vicki's full attention, especially being braless and all. But she knew she had to act as if she didn't want to hear everything or she'd never get to hear anything. She reached for the coffeepot, interrupting its brewing cycle, and poured coffee into his Elvis mug. She said lightly, "Forget it. Don't worry. This, too, shall pass."

"Not this one." Dan accepted his mug and took a thoughtful sip. "This was a big, big fight."

"It'll pass," Vicki said, though the Malloy/Suarez family never had big fights. In fact, they rarely fought at all. They didn't see each other enough to fight.

"I'm not so sure."

"Sure you are." Vicki poured coffee into her Harvard mug. The day she'd been admitted, her parents had bought three hundred of them. She tried to think of a new subject, which wasn't hard. "How about that guy who answered my cell phone?"

"You'd think the cops would wake up when they heard that. Instead they're in your face. Jerks."

"They'll get to it, in time." Vicki waited and sipped. The coffee tasted good and hot. Snowflakes blew outside. The kitchen fell silent.

"You wouldn't believe what the fight was about," Dan said, after a minute.

"It doesn't matter. The fight's never about the fight, anyway." Vicki knew this from her parents, two major love affairs, and Dr. Phil.

"Mariella thinks we spend too much time together."

"Who?"

"You and me."

"You and me, spend too much time together?" Vicki felt accused and convicted, both at once. His words had broken through some veneer. The fight was about *them*?

"She accused me of having an affair with you."

"*What?*"

"You heard me."

Vicki flushed. "But we're not!"

"Of course we're not, but I can't convince her of that. It's not even the first time we've fought about it."

My God. "It isn't?"

"You look surprised."

"I am! I had no idea. Why didn't you tell me?"

"Why would I? I didn't want to, it's between me and her. And I know it's not true, so I don't sweat it." Dan shrugged. "But I can never make her believe me, and lately, it's all coming to a head. It started when I caught her checking my BlackBerry, for e-mail from you."

"Really?" Vicki felt instantly guilty. "Well, we do e-mail."

"We're allowed to."

"And we do spend a lot of time together. A whole lot."

"But we're just friends."

Right. "Maybe we should cool it a little."

"I don't see why."

"So she won't be upset, or suspect you." Vicki felt a wave of shame for secretly wanting him. He belonged to Mariella, and it was obvious now what should have been obvious all along. "Look, our friendship is undermining your marriage."

"No, it isn't."

"Dan, it is."

Dan frowned. "But she's wrong to be upset!"

"That doesn't matter. Her feelings are her feelings. She's your wife."

"And you're my best friend."

"So, friends take breaks. Maybe we shouldn't have lunch together, every damn day. In fact, I'm sick of you." Vicki faked a smile. *You and your bralessness.*

"No." Dan set his mug down, and coffee sloshed around the side. "She's not around anyway, and we're just keeping each other company. She should trust me."

"Maybe she does, but she still doesn't like it." Vicki had to admit that Mariella wasn't being unreasonable. "You two were in bed together when I called. She doesn't like it; no woman would."

"I told you to call, and so what? Things are going crazy lately, with Morty being killed and now Bristow's mother. She acts like that's not happening. My

God, it's like I have this whole life she doesn't know about!"

"You have to be sensitive to her," Vicki said, managing not to choke on the words.

"Plus, she doesn't know what it's like to work in our office, to try to move up there." Dan raised his voice, his tone sharpening. "She doesn't know what it's like to be on trial, day after day. Write motions at night. Meet with witnesses around a court schedule."

Nobody knows what that's like, except another AUSA, Vicki thought, but would never say it, because it was way too true. People at work shared things that outsiders would never understand.

"She doesn't know what it was like to lose Morty. I worked with him for two years, had three cases with him. You saw him every day for a year, on Edwards. You knew him, and now he's dead!" Dan's voice broke, in pain. For Morty. For her. For himself. Vicki felt like hugging him but knew she couldn't. It confused her. She wanted him, but not this way, and she didn't want to cause trouble for him.

"Dan, calm down. Mariella just wants more of your time."

"I want more of hers!"

Ouch. "Right. So you both want the same thing, and this will blow over." Vicki set down her mug. "She's at home now, right?"

"Yes."

"You left her to come over here?"

"Yes."

"Smooth move, Malloy."

"I wanted to help you! You're in the middle of a mess! You needed me!"

Vicki's cheeks got hot. A day ago, she would have loved hearing that. Now, it was a problem. "You helped me, and I appreciate it. But you should go home."

"I'm not supposed to be home, anyway. I'm supposed to go buy salt for the sidewalk, then pick up the dry cleaning."

"Then go home and ask her to go with you. Or take her to brunch."

"She'll say she's too tired. She's been on call for three days."

"Then she'll like that you asked." Vicki waved good-bye. "Go. See ya."

"But what about Bale? He said he'd call you. And your house is a mess, from the cops."

"I'll handle it. Sayonara." Vicki put her hands on Dan's strong shoulders, which felt painfully good, then turned him around and pushed him out of the kitchen, grabbing his coat on the way and handing it to him. "Here. Put a bra on and go home to your wife, who loves you."

"Huh?"

But Vicki had already opened the door. She didn't bother to explain and she ignored the hard knot in the middle of her chest. Doing the right thing was no fun at all. Her only consolation was that she was getting rid of any interference.

So she could get busy.

NINETEEN

THE SNOW WAS STICKING, COMING DOWN heavily with more predicted, but Vicki wasn't worried about the weather. The Cabrio was great in snow, the windshield wipers thumped energetically away, and she had bigger things on her mind. Devil's Corner lay under a thin blanket of fresh snow, two inches so far, according to AccuWeather. Through the window she could see that Mrs. Bristow's block was as deserted as it had been yesterday, except that the fresh snow covered the trash, debris, and filth she knew lay underneath. No children played out in front of the houses; no tongues caught snowflakes. There wasn't a snowman in sight.

Vicki found a parking space down from Mrs. Bristow's house and got out of the Cabrio, setting a loafer into wet slush. A chill wind hit her like a blast, jolting her to a realization. No official vehicles were parked out front; no crime scene techs or police cruisers with their engines idling. She hadn't seen a cop in front of

Mrs. Bristow's house, guarding the crime scene and logging personnel in and out. In fact, there wasn't any yellow crime scene tape or police sawhorses. She checked her watch. Noon. Only hours after Mrs. Bristow had been found knifed to death, the scene was already closed.

She hurried toward the house, head down against the driving snow, her thoughts churning. She couldn't help but remark on the contrast between this murder scene and Morty's. There'd been tons of uniforms there, not to mention detectives, crime scene techs, FBI, ATF, and DOJ personnel. Admittedly, Morty was a federal agent and the scene had been a triple homicide, but Vicki didn't think that completely accounted for what she was seeing. She reached the step, hesitating before going in. She didn't relish what she had to do, but she knew she had to do it.

She knocked on the closed door once, then again. There was no answer. Snow blew sideways into her ears and hair; she had gone out without a hat, she'd been in such a rush. Wind bit her nose; it was twenty-five degrees. She had no gloves on, either, and pounded the door once more, hard. It creaked open.

Vicki blinked. The door hung ajar. She didn't want to simply barge in. "Hello?" she called out. "Hello, anybody home?"

There was no answer.

She felt a shiver all the way to her toes, and it wasn't the cold. A woman had been killed here, and the last time she had walked through an open door, Morty had been killed. Too much violence, too much death; all these row homes, awash in blood. Not even the snow could cover it up and hide it, not forever.

"Anybody home?" she called out, louder, knocking again on the open door. A chill wind blew harder, carrying her voice off with the snowflakes and opening wide the front door.

Crap. Now Vicki was standing in an open doorway, watching snow blow into the dark living room. She conceded the obvious and stepped inside, shutting the door. She blinked away the snow blindness, waited until her eyes adjusted to the interior light, then turned around.

The living room looked completely different from yesterday. It was much darker because newspapers had been taped up against the windows like temporary curtains, and only indirect light streamed in. The beach chair lay folded on the brown couch, which had been moved into the center of the room and was loaded with black Hefty trash bags, their yellow drawstrings pulled tight. The dark red rug had been rolled up and also placed on the couch, resting on the two armrests, and every bit of trash in the room had been picked up. The floorboards looked swept and had even been washed clean; wet spots dried here and there, and a lineup of empty water jugs sat against the wall, next to a metal dustpan and new corn broom. The air smelled a little more normal, but it was still as cold inside as out.

"Hello?" Vicki said. The house was still. She braced herself and went into the bedroom where Mrs. Bristow had been killed. The dirty mattress had been lifted up and was standing on end, with the bloodstained side evidently against the wall. Still, it emitted an awful stench; rotting, human blood.

Vicki turned away. The end table had been pushed against the mattress, she guessed to hold it upright, and this room had been cleaned, too, all the debris and crack paraphernalia swept into trash bags and piled in the center of the bedroom. She went into the kitchen, expecting more of the same, and she was right. The cabinets hung open and empty; all the food and cigarettes had been taken out and, presumably, disposed of in the trash bags in the center of the room. The floorboards had been swept and mopped; a large white Rubbermaid bucket sat in the corner and a lemony Pine-Sol odor filled the room. A cockroach skittered across the counter, but Vicki sensed he'd be history soon.

"WHO'S IN THERE?" someone shouted, all of a sudden, and Vicki startled, whirling around.

She froze at the sight of Reheema Bristow, aiming a small, lethal Beretta at her. The black woman's mouth set in a grim line, and she stood tall and four-square, her feet planted wide apart, as if she were ready to fire.

"I'm within my rights to shoot you dead, Allegretti." Reheema's dark eyes glittered under a navy-blue watch cap. Snowflakes dotted the cap and her broad shoulders in a navy-blue pea coat.

Stay calm. "That's the third gun pointed at me in two days, and it's getting old. Why don't you put it away before I arrest you for ag assault and weapons offenses?"

"You're trespassing."

"Then I'll go. I came to tell you I'm sorry about your mother." Vicki's chest tightened. She was pretty sure Reheema wouldn't shoot her, but pretty sure had too much wiggle room when it came to small-caliber weapons.

"Why was your wallet on her?" Reheema shot back, her tone icy as winter.

"Put the gun away and I'll answer you. I don't like being threatened."

"I don't like being put in jail. I *said*, why'd I find your wallet in my mother's pocket?"

"Okay, she took it out of my purse. I came to see her and when I went out of the room—"

"How'd you know she lived here? The phone book?"

D'oh. "That would have been too easy. I found out from your old boss at Bennye's."

"Why'd you come here?"

"To learn about you."

"What did you wanna know?"

"If you had anything to do with my partner's murder. If you had Shayla Jackson killed so she wouldn't testify against you, or if someone did that on your behalf. If you resold the guns, and to whom, which I'm still wondering since the one in your hand isn't one you were indicted for. And that's just for starters. Now, put the gun away."

"Ha." Reheema let out a short burst of laughter, like semiautomatic fire, then unlocked the trigger, lowered the weapon, and shoved it inside her coat pocket like a pack of gum.

"Thanks."

"Don't mention it. Now we're even." Reheema snorted. "You attacked me at the conference."

"Oh, that. Shall I go?" Now that the threat was over, Vicki had lost her sense of humor. It seemed as if it should be the other way around, but she was too angry to puzzle it out now. "I'm finished with the condolences. You blew the mood."

"Not yet." Reheema yanked the cap off her head and

shook her hair out. It had been mashed flat under the cap but she didn't seem to care; she was still strikingly beautiful, for a stone bitch. Her cheekbones curved almost delicately, and her mouth was soft and full, however nasty her expression. "Why do you think I was involved with what happened to your partner and Jackson?"

"Because you're the one who benefited from Jackson's murder. The timing's too coincidental, and Jackson dimed on you. She told my office that you two were best friends. She testified before the grand jury to that effect and she was ready to go to trial to convict you."

"I told you, I don't know the girl. She lied."

"She was under oath."

"Oooh. Nobody lies under oath." Reheema grinned crookedly, and Vicki reddened.

"You sure you don't know her?"

"Never met the girl."

"Jackson also said she knew who you sold the guns to. She was my confidential informant in the case."

"That's a lie, too. I didn't sell the guns to anybody."

"What did you do with them?"

"None of your business."

"It would help if you told me."

"Tough."

I should have strangled you when I had the chance. "If it's true that you didn't know her, then it would mean that Jackson, a complete stranger to you, framed you for a straw purchase charge. At risk of perjury, by the way. Why would she do that to you? How would she even get your name?"

"I don't know and I don't care." Reheema's gaze

didn't waver. "I care about getting this house cleaned up. You're leaving."

"Not so fast. What did you do with the guns?"

"I *said*, it's none a your business."

"How about I tell you? You gave them to your mother, who sold them or traded them for drugs. Or you sold them yourself and gave her the money or the drugs."

"I would never give my mother drugs."

"But you bought the guns for her, didn't you? One for you and one for her? Then somehow she traded them both. That's why you wouldn't take the deal I offered you. You wouldn't give her up."

Reheema blinked, and Vicki knew she had scored.

"Just tell me. If you tell me, I'll go."

"You'll go anyway."

"No, I won't. I can be a real pain in the ass."

"I know," Reheema answered, unsmiling. "Fine. Whatever. She said she wanted a gun for protection. I left mine here when I moved to my apartment, and she took it."

"She sold them for drugs?"

"She'd sell me for drugs. She sold everything I owned." Reheema's tone was beyond bitter; it was utterly without affect, but Vicki still felt strange speaking ill of a woman who had been murdered in this very room.

"I know where your mother bought drugs last night."

"You proud of yourself?"

Well, yeah, Vicki thought, though the question may have been rhetorical.

"You think I don't know that?" Reheema arched an

eyebrow. "You think I didn't find that out five minutes after I found her?"

"It's on Cater Street."

"I know, the vacant lot. They opened a store there."

A store? "Did you go there?"

"That's none a your business."

"I was there, last night. I followed your mom, after she took my wallet."

"You?" Reheema laughed, less like gunfire this time. "A white girl?"

"In a white car." Vicki smiled. *Yay! We're bonding!*

"Why?"

"First I wanted to get my wallet back, then I wanted to see where she bought her drugs."

"Why?"

"Curiosity." Vicki felt tougher by the minute, just talking to someone so tough. In fact, she was sure she'd never experience another emotion again. "You wanted to know, too. You went over there, to see who killed your mother."

"Wrong. I know who killed my mother. My mother killed my mother. Whatever junkie finished her off did her a favor."

Vicki couldn't speak for a minute, the thought was so cruel.

"Time for you to go, lawyer. I got a U-Haul out front and I got to get to the dump before this snow gets too deep."

"Just one thing. Do you really not know Jamal Browning?"

"Don't know him," Reheema answered, her response quick, direct, and believable.

"I think he was Shayla Jackson's boyfriend."

"Whatever."

"How about Jay-Boy and Teeg?"

"I told you, no."

"They're drug dealers, or work for one." Vicki didn't tell her about the fish-scale coke. It wasn't prudent to reveal police business to a gun-toting ex-con.

"Time to go." Reheema gestured to the door, but Vicki stayed put.

"Jay-Boy and Teeg were the shooters. They killed my partner and Shayla Jackson, who was pregnant. I saw them."

"Life in the city. Now, get out."

"Your mother, she was very beautiful, when she was younger," Vicki heard herself say, then wondered why. If she was trying to make some connection, it was futile. Reheema's face remained impassive, and she had already started picking up Hefty bags, two in each hand, and lugging them to the door, which she opened with difficulty.

"Leave."

Vicki swallowed hard and walked to the door, then stopped in the threshold. "I'm gonna bust whoever sold those drugs to your mother."

"You go, girlfriend." Reheema dropped the bags and began to clap, and her ironic applause followed Vicki as she walked out the door.

And into the snowstorm.

TWENTY

SNOW FELL HARD, AND VICKI HURRIED TO her car, her head bent against the icy flakes that bit her cheeks. She reached the Cabrio, got inside, but didn't pull out of the space right away. Snow dusted her plastic back window, but she could see in her outside mirror that Reheema was carrying Hefty bags out of the house and tossing them into the bed of an orange-and-white pickup, double-parked out front.

She turned on the ignition and watched Reheema work, pretending she was letting the engine warm up. Clearly the woman was determined; a Lady Tiger, indeed. Carrying concealed and aiming without blinking. Cleaning the house the same morning her mother was killed. Being practical, levelheaded, and emotionless about all of it, even her mother's addiction. You didn't need to be Dr. Phil to guess that Reheema might have been the parent growing up, taking care of her mother. Even buying her a gun for protection. Had Reheema been fooled, or did she know? Was she telling Vicki the truth? Either way, Reheema had taken the rap, spending almost a year at the FDC. And she would have been convicted if Jackson hadn't been killed.

Jackson. Morty. Who was Jackson to Reheema? How were they connected, if at all? Was it possible that Jackson knew Reheema but not vice versa? How?

Vicki yanked down the emergency brake and eased out of the spot. There was no one on the street, playing or driving. Not a living soul except Reheema, coming out of the house with another load of bags, a tall, dark figure with dark bags against the white snow, receding in the rearview mirror.

Vicki reached the corner and turned, noticing things about the houses that she hadn't before, now that it was daytime and the street felt more familiar. Here and there, lights glowed inside the houses, and in one of the windows flickered an electric candle, ringed by a plastic holly wreath left over from Christmas. There was still life in Devil's Corner; still families making their way, and people like Reheema, moving in and trying to set up house.

Vicki cruised ahead, the car interior warming, and approached Cater. The corner at the mouth of the alley was empty. No scary guys in dark hoods. She drove forward slowly and eased to a stop, looking to the right as she had last night. She parked and scanned the street, which looked different in the daylight. There were no cars parked on it, so she could conceivably drive down it, and it was lined with houses, many of which had lights on and trash at the curb collecting snow, their black bags like misshapen body bags. But even in the terrible weather, she could see people milling at the far end of the street. They seemed to be going inside the vacant lot.

The store. Vicki reached into her purse for her Filofax and pen, then started taking notes. Whether it was the bad weather or the fact that the cops had been at the Bristow house, the watchers hadn't come out yet. She shivered in the cold car, but she didn't quit because she'd never get another chance.

In time the foot traffic fell into a pattern; customers walking into the vacant lot, then leaving five to ten minutes later. A few cars came down the opposite cross street, driving toward Vicki, the windshield wipers pounding to keep the snow off. They stopped at the vacant lot to let somebody out and back in again after the buy; the transaction was never made curbside. Only a car or two drove past her and up Cater, because the vacant lot was closer to that end, and she noted their license plates.

She documented everything in her pocket-size Filofax. Every hour or so, the same man, a short man in a black leather coat and black leather baseball cap, would leave the vacant lot, walk down the street away from the Cabrio, then return in about twenty-five minutes to half an hour. Alternating with him, but making the same trip on roughly the same schedule, was a taller man in an Eagles jacket and black knit cap. Vicki theorized that they were the go-betweens, going back and forth to a crackhouse that supplied the store.

On the third trip by the man in the Eagles coat, Vicki set aside her notes and started the Cabrio engine. She cruised forward in the driving snow, finally turning on the heat and switching the defrost to MAX to keep the windshield clear. She took a right at the corner and sped to the end of the street, her windshield wipers pumping to keep up with the snowfall. She stopped at the traffic light, striking a blow for lawful behavior everywhere, and turned right.

By the time she was on the cross street, the man in the Eagles coat had reached the top of Cater Street on foot. Vicki slowed the Cabrio to a crawl and double-parked by a salt-covered Taurus to watch him. Eagles Coat had his back to her, the emblematic bird flying high, its talons splayed. The street was quiet; there was little traffic. Nobody was out in the snow; on the drive over, she'd heard reports of a big storm.

Eagles Coat got into a battered blue Neon parked at the middle of the line-up of cars. Vicki waited while he started the Neon, and when he pulled out of his space, she let a black Ford truck get between them for cover, then took off after him. They cruised to the top of the street together, his speed quicker than hers. She stepped on it, tailgating the black truck. Her heartbeat picked up as the Neon took a left onto Cleveland Street and headed west.

The black truck went straight, leaving her exposed, but a pile of fresh snow covered the Neon's back window, and the driver made no attempt to defrost it. The Neon had to be ten years old, with a large dent buckling the back fender. Vicki had heard that drug dealers kept the nice cars for driving around in and used crummy cars for "work," because they were less conspicuous. The felonious version of a station car.

The Neon sped forward heedless of the weather conditions, with icy snow streaming sideways across the street. Pellets hit the window, making *tinck tinck* noises, and the windshield wipers worked frantically.

Vicki drove as fast as she could, letting the occasional car get ahead of her to minimize her chance of being spotted, since snow on the back window of the Neon was sliding off.

They threaded their way out of Devil's Corner, and Vicki could see through her steamy window that the neighborhood was worsening. They took a right and a left, and the Neon turned quickly onto a street, then parked. She drove past it because she couldn't stop fast enough and she wanted to avoid being spotted. She went around the block to the street into which the Neon had driven and glanced at the street sign. It was crooked, but its bright green was readable in the snowstorm:

ASPINALL STREET.

Whoa. Vicki flashed on the envelopes on Shayla's dresser, in the row house. They were being forwarded to her boyfriend, Jamal Browning. He lived on Aspinall Street.

Vicki's heart thumped harder. She leaned forward over the steering wheel but the Neon was parked too far away to see much. She waited. Trying to stay calm. Wishing she had a cell phone. Who would she call? The cops. Dan. Somebody. Anybody.

She assumed that Eagles Coat was going to Jamal Browning's house on Aspinall Street, because it seemed unlikely that there were two drug dealers on Aspinall Street. That meant that Jamal could have been supplying the drugs to the new store on Cater, where Mrs. Bristow had bought her drugs. Could that be the connection? Had Reheema given her mother the guns, then her mother sold or traded them on Cater Street for crack, which was in turn supplied by Jamal Browning?

Did that mean the guns had ended up with Browning? And what was Reheema's connection?

Vicki got so excited, she almost missed Eagles Coat leaving a house in the middle of the block, then making his way down the snowy sidewalk. He got into the Neon and took off, presumably back to Cater. Vicki hit the gas, steered the Cabrio onto Aspinall, and drove down the street, not daring to pause at the house. It was a rundown brick row house with a yellow plastic awning bowing with disrepair and snow.

Number 3635. Jamal Browning's house.

"Yes!" Vicki shouted so loud her voice reverberated in the tiny Cabrio. But now what did she do?

She wasn't about to knock on Browning's door, but she knew how to accomplish the same end.

TWENTY-ONE

AN HOUR LATER, VICKI REACHED THE ROUND-house, Philadelphia's police administration building. It looked almost pretty in the snow, only because the whiteness hid the cracked windowsills and stained concrete of its aging facade. The building was composed of two joined circles, hence its nickname, and its design had been positively space-age in the 1970s. She parked in the press space in the lot, as she used to as an ADA, switched off the ignition, and got out of the Cabrio. The cold tightened her chest, and she pulled her down coat tighter around her. It was almost six and the sky was dark. The parking lot was only partly full, which was deceptive; the Roundhouse wasn't closed for business on the weekend, but only got busier. She'd been here more times than she could count, and hurried to the entrance, kicking snow onto her ankles, and went inside the revolving door.

Ten minutes after that, Vicki found Detective

Melvin in the ratty squad room of the Homicide Division. The blue paint on the walls had dulled to grime, and large institutional desks dotted the room, defying any normal path of travel. Water-stained curtains hung from uneven valances along the far wall, which curved with the south side of the building. The air smelled of cigarettes, though smoking wasn't allowed. On TV, *Cold Case* showed America a sanitized replica of the squad room every week. Nobody would believe how crummy it really was, which was the problem with the truth.

"Have a nice chat with my parents?" Vicki asked, sitting down in the old metal chair next to Detective Melvin's desk.

"Not yet. Is that why you're here?"

"No," Vicki answered, and told him the whole story in detail. By the time she was finished, Detective Melvin was looking at her like her father did, which wasn't good.

"Wait a minute," he said, holding up a hand. "In the beginning, you said you went to see Reheema, to explain to her why her mother had your wallet. You felt you owed her that."

"I did."

"So why were you taking notes on drug trafficking on Cater?" The detective gestured to Vicki's Filofax pages, spread out on the cluttered desk.

"I know what I saw, and so do you." Vicki leaned forward. "The opening of a crack store on Cater, supplied by a dealer on Aspinall. And Browning is connected to Shayla Jackson because of the bills in her house. It's a silver platter."

"It's good, but it doesn't prove anything yet."

"I make out an affidavit of what I saw, to get you probable cause for search of the house and for arrest of the two street dealers and whoever's at that crack house. Business is booming and will only grow. We can end this thing right now."

"We?"

"Yes, we. This could lead to whoever killed Shayla and Morty, and maybe even Mrs. Bristow. It's a good lead."

"I agree, it's a good lead, I didn't say it wasn't a good lead."

"Not to mention that the drug business will take down the street, then the neighborhood."

"I've heard that happens, yes." Detective Melvin was already gathering up Vicki's notes, his muscles flexing in the gray pullover he must have been wearing under his leather jacket this morning. Hard to believe that was the same day; Vicki was already feeling like they were old friends, though she could have been delusional.

"Did you see Browning yet? Did you question him?"

"Not yet, but we will."

"What's the holdup?"

"We have procedures, Ms. Allegretti."

"Please, call me Vicki when you lie to me."

"I'm not." Detective Melvin pursed his lips.

"What procedures, then? The homicide procedures I remember are running down leads. Browning is a clear lead in Jackson's and Morty's murder, and they may all be connected."

"This is a complicated situation, and I'm not at liberty to discuss the particulars of the investigation," Detective Melvin answered firmly, and Vicki eased back into her chair. Being pushy was getting her nowhere fast, and she could see Melvin wasn't happy about the situation, either.

"Does that mean we can't talk about wiretaps? Are you going for a wiretap on my cell? You could get one, based on these facts."

"We understand that and we're investigating it."

"I know ATF would get a Title III tap."

"We'll investigate our way, not yours or ATF's."

"Which would be what?" Vicki knew she was on thin ice, and Detective Melvin's eyes went hard.

"Look, I don't have to keep you apprised. If I call your boss and tell him what you've been up to, he'll fire your ass."

Gulp. "But if you could just tell me what you've been doing, maybe I can help."

"I don't need your help, thank you. I thought I made that clear this morning." Detective Melvin stacked her notes into a little Filofax tower, like silver-dollar pancakes. "I'll talk to my sergeant about what you learned today, about Browning on Aspinall and the Neon. And I'll turn your notes over to the Narcotics Strike Force."

"The Narcotics Strike Force? But what if the Cater Street store is connected to the murder of my partner?"

"We handle that part, they handle the other. They've had other complaints from the neighbors. They know about the situation, but they're taxed. They'll give this attention if it comes from Homicide."

"Will they coordinate with the feds?"

"I'm sure they will, but there are jurisdictional issues."

"Who has jurisdiction, state or federal?"

"I'm not at liberty to discuss that with you," Detective Melvin answered, but Vicki couldn't let her hard work fall between the cracks.

"I say you have jurisdiction over the whole case. It's a murder, at bottom, whether a federal agent or not, and I think it has to stay with you, not the Narcotics Strike Force." Vicki was thinking out loud, issue-spotting in criminal procedure. She knew that Homicide could run-and-gun in a way the feds never could. Making a federal case wasn't just an expression.

"Thanks for the vote of confidence." Detective Melvin's forehead relaxed, and his voice softened. They both knew that jurisdiction was a question of legal power, so it always became a legal power play, and this situation would only make it worse. "But at this point, we think it's a local offense, so it's ours. Doesn't mean we don't have to coordinate."

"With whom?"

"A task force."

"Oh no." Task force was police code for a committee. Vicki could only guess the pressure he was under. "But somebody has to be running the store, right now. Time matters in a murder investigation."

Melvin managed a smile. "I've heard that, too."

"What's the precedent in cases like this?"

"There isn't any."

"There has to be," Vicki said in disbelief. "Morty couldn't have been the first federal agent killed in the line of duty."

"Actually, in Philly, he is. Except for one case that doesn't help us much. An FBI agent, Chuck Reed, was killed making an undercover buy in the nineties, remember? In a car at Penn's Landing?"

"No." Vicki was at Harvard Law in the nineties, but

she never dropped the H-bomb unless she had to. "Remind me."

"It was a buy-bust that went wrong, in that yuppie cocaine ring. The dealer was coked up and panicked. He shot Reed, who shot back. They were both killed." Detective Melvin winced with the regret that cops show at another's passing. Grief was the one thing that crossed jurisdictional lines.

"So there was no need for an investigation to find Reed's killer."

"Right, there's no precedent on this one."

"But it is a state law matter, and civilians were killed, too—Jackson, her baby, and Mrs. Bristow, if her murder is related." Then even Vicki thought better of it. "Still, everybody at ATF loved Morty. They'll want to take care of their own."

"Right, of course. So would we." They fell silent on their respective sides of the desk. Vicki felt the tug of conflict, and Detective Melvin sighed, a resigned sound that came from deep within his broad chest. "We already scheduled a meeting about your partner's murder with top brass at your office, and with ATF, DEA, and FBI."

"Why would FBI have jurisdiction? Because they take it?"

"I didn't say that."

"No, I did." Vicki considered the situation. The FBI was the grabbiest federal agency in existence, after the IRS. "When is the task force meeting?"

"They were talking about Tuesday, but realistically, it'll be Wednesday. They need a day after the memorial service of your partner."

Morty's funeral. Vicki felt a tightness. She'd been so

wrapped up in catching his killer, she hadn't thought about his burial. "When is the memorial service scheduled for?"

"I got a memo. The wake is tomorrow night, the memorial on Monday."

Vicki checked her emotions. "Wednesday is when you all meet? That's forever, in a murder investigation."

"This has to be done right," Detective Melvin said, but even he didn't sound like he believed it, and Vicki was shaking her head.

"Procedures?"

"In a word."

"So we have a tangle over whether it's state or federal, then we have a tangle over which federal it is, ATF, FBI, or DEA."

Detective Melvin looked almost as miserable as Vicki. "I'm not even invited to the meeting, only my captain and the feds."

"All that law getting in the way of justice."

Detective Melvin smiled crookedly, but Vicki was already rising to her feet.

"Got a Xerox machine?"

"Sure, why?"

"Time's a-wastin'."

Vicki reached over and picked up her notes.

TWENTY-TWO

IT WAS ALMOST SEVEN BY THE TIME VICKI made her way through the snowstorm to the United States Custom House. A frigid wind gusted from the Delaware River, snow flurries flew around the building, and the American flag at its top flapped madly. Custom House, only ten minutes by Cabrio from the Roundhouse, was a stolid gray edifice that anchored the corner of Second & Chestnut Streets and housed a number of federal agencies: the passport office, the FDA, GSA, and ATF. The building looked positively bureaucratic in contrast with the funky restaurants, art galleries, and bistros dotting Olde City, and only a single couple was out in this bitter night, walking cuddled together against the storm. Vicki hurried past them, up the cleared granite steps, and into Custom House.

At this hour, the building was closed to the public, and the lobby was empty except for two weekend security guards at the metal detector. She barely knew the unfriendly one sitting at a standard-issue wooden desk, reading the movie listings in the *Daily News*, but the other, her pal Samuel, looked up from peeling his fingernails. He blanched when he recognized Vicki, and she knew why.

"Yo, Samuel." Vicki was about to produce her ID when she remembered it was gone. "I don't have my ID with me, okay?"

"No sweat, Vicki." Samuel waved her around the metal detector. She'd been here almost every day last year, while she and Morty interviewed witnesses and laid out their case at the ATF offices.

"Appreciate it. Anybody up there still?"

"Oh yeah, plenty, even the brass."

"Great."

"Sorry about Agent Morton," Samuel said when Vicki had almost passed. It came out as an after-thought, though she knew it wasn't; he must've been getting up his nerve to say something, which touched her all the more.

"Thanks." Vicki checked her emotions before they got out of control. She was already feeling shaky, being in this lobby. The last time she had been here was with Morty. They had gone out to pick up hoagies and fought over who ordered the sweet peppers.

I swear I did, he had said.

Nah, you always get hot.

I'm evolving.

Vicki crossed to the small, circular lobby, which was vintage Art Deco. She knew its history, thanks to Morty, who had loved this building; Custom House had been built in the 1930s as a WPA project, and he had always claimed it was to keep South Philly stonemasons busy, because the lobby was fashioned completely of carved marble. A rosy-bronze marble covered the curving walls of the entrance rotunda, and remarkable royal-blue marble pillars, etched with long lines that lengthened their two-story stature, stood in a ring that anchored the domed ceiling. Gold-leaf florets twinkled in the dome against a celestial blue background, giving the entire lobby a heavenly, ethereal feel.

Morty.

Vicki hurried past and went upstairs, the clatter of her footsteps muffled by residual snow. She hit the second floor as she always used to, noting again the oddly painted mauve doorjambs, and pressed a code into the keypad by the unmarked purple door. It was an entrance used only by ATF agents, who bypassed the glass-walled reception area, and Morty had told her the code. She opened the door and had almost succeeded in setting her thoughts about him aside when he was suddenly staring her in the face.

MEMORIAL SERVICE FOR BOB MORTON, read the typed headline, and an almost life-size photo of him hung on the wall, grinning in a tie he wore only for picture day. It was a photocopied announcement of the details of his wake and funeral. Vicki had almost forgotten how handsome he was; she swallowed hard and took a right turn down the hall into an off-white warren of offices, most of which were empty with the lights off, but some of which were not. The Philadelphia office of ATF contained one hundred agents in its several floors, and she could only imagine how busy these halls had been the past few days, buzzing with agents talking about Morty, comparing notes, and consoling one another. Given what had happened, she had guessed that people would be working this weekend; in fact, because the agents spent so much time in court, many routinely worked nights and weekends, catching up on paperwork, interviewing witnesses, and generally giving the lie to the cliché about "government work."

Going down the hall, Vicki waved briefly at the agents who looked up from their desks, nodding to acknowledge her; she hadn't gotten to know them with only a year on the job, much of it spent with Morty. She traveled down the purple-patterned carpet, feeling out of place without him. A sharp solvent smell filled the air in the next hall, and she passed a small room containing a trio of men in long white coats, cleaning rifles on a table. She finally reached the threshold of the large corner office, knocked on another purple doorjamb, and braced herself to meet the boss.

"Mr. Saxon?" Vicki began, then shut up, because he was talking on the telephone and taking notes. He saw her but didn't wave her in, and she wasn't surprised since she wasn't sure he knew who she was. In the meantime, she tried not to listen to any top-secret conversation.

"Eggs, milk, low-fat, no fruit in Phase I," Saxon said into the phone, and Vicki smiled. The whole world was on South Beach. The phone conversation sounded like an instant replay of Vicki's dinner with her parents, before they'd bitched her out. Maybe that was their problem. Not enough carbohydrates.

"Brown or white eggs, does it matter?"

Vicki eyed his office, the largest she'd seen here. The three windows were dark behind closed window shades, and the wall behind his desk bore the requisite framed movie poster from *The Untouchables* with Kevin Costner. ATF jocks loved *The Untouchables*, Hollywood's version of the beginnings of their agency, and they uniformly revered the real-life Elliott Ness. Every year, Morty had gone to the Elliot Ness party they held in Baltimore and returned with a killer hangover.

"Ricotta? Maggio? That has to be low-fat, too? Gimme a break here, Kath."

An American flag stood to the right of the desk, in the far corner, and a coat rack stood on the near corner, holding a baseball cap, winter coat, and navy-blue bulletproof vest that read ATF in characteristically bold yellow letters. The desk was large and simple, of light wood, and immaculately clean except for a plastic party-favor statue of Jesus Christ, still in the box, which sat next to a nameplate that read JOHN SAXON, SPECIAL AGENT IN CHARGE.

"Pistachios, almonds, not roasted, unsalted."

Saxon made a note with a Bic pen, his oversize hand curling around the paper; he looked like an overgrown schoolboy except for the fact that his gray-blond hair showed a large bald patch. Saxon himself was king-size, easily six four, with broad muscular shoulders in a white cotton polo shirt too thin for winter. His nose and cheekbones were large and pronounced; his eyes an overworked and bloodshot blue, and even his complexion looked ruddy, with a touch of rosacea. Still, he was handsome in a middle-aged alpha-wolf way, and Vicki liked him because he hung up the phone by saying, "Love you, too."

Saxon looked up at Vicki, who introduced herself as

she walked in and extended a hand, which he shook, half rising. "Allegretti, how do I know your name?"

"I'm the AUSA who worked with Morty. We got the conviction in Edwards, and we were on Bristow."

"Of course. Morty." Saxon frowned and pursed his lips, which were thin and chapped, as he eased back into his high-backed chair. "Jesus, God. Poor Morty. Siddown, kid." He waved at one of two padded brown leather chairs in front of his desk. "You were with him, right?"

"Yes." Vicki flashed on the scene of Morty at the doorway, blood bubbling at his lips, then forced it away.

"I read your statement. You did a good job, lots of details. It must have been tough." Saxon eyed her, appraising her. "Well, you know, we're all so sorry. Sorry for all of us. Sorry for Morty. He was a great agent. A thorough, professional agent. He would investigate a case no matter how long it took." Saxon ran a massive palm over his forehead, which only messed up hair that was baby-thin in front. "He was such a good guy, even his ex-wife called to say she's sorry." Saxon smiled, and so did Vicki.

"Morty always said he was married to the job."

"He was. ATF was his family, all the family he had. The office is in a state over it."

"I can imagine." Vicki felt a twinge at having cut ATF out of her jurisdictional analysis. She felt oddly as if she had betrayed Morty's memory.

"So what can I do for you?" Saxon checked his watch, a gold-toned Seiko. "You heard She Who Must Be Obeyed. It's late and I gotta go."

"I wanted to talk to you about the investigation of Morty's murder."

"Right now? On a Saturday night?" Saxon raised blond, furry eyebrows. "Pretty girl like you, you must have somewhere you have to be."

Actually, no. "I've been upset over Morty, so I've been doing some digging on my own."

Saxon's eyes narrowed. "You're an AUSA, right?"

"Yes, and I was an ADA before that. I've been an acronym for a long time." Vicki was trying to lighten his sudden bad mood, but it wasn't working.

"What do you mean, digging on your own?"

"Just asking some questions and—"

"You have no business doing that." Saxon frowned. "We sent your description of the doers to every ATF office in the country. That's where you end and we take over. We'll find those scumbags."

"Does that mean ATF will be in charge of the investigation?"

"Why do you want to know?" Saxon's features flattened to a bureaucratic mask, and Vicki shrugged.

"Because I care. About Morty."

"ATF cares about Morty, too." Saxon laughed without mirth, his manner growing unfriendlier by the minute, and Vicki sighed. What had she said wrong? Or did this guy just need more carbs?

"I didn't say you didn't. It's just that I found out some things today that are related to his murder."

"What things?"

"That's what I came to tell you." It wasn't the way Vicki had expected this conversation to go, but at least he wasn't pointing a gun at her. She began the story in chronological order. "I guess you heard about the murder this morning of Arissa Bristow."

"Bristow?" Saxon frowned. "How do I know that name?"

"It was on the TV news."

"What's that have to do with Morty?"

"Arissa Bristow was the mother of my defendant in the straw purchase case, the one that Morty and I went to see the CI about. The CI was named Shayla Jackson."

"Jackson, I remember. But Bristow? When was she killed?"

"This morning, it was on TV," Vicki repeated. "Didn't Chief Bale call you, or someone from Philly Homicide?"

"No. What happened?" Saxon leaned across his desk, and Vicki filled him in about Mrs. Bristow, Reheema, and Cater Street, and finally Aspinall Street and Jamal Browning. She gave him a copy of her notes from her purse, which she took him through in detail. His eyes widened as she spoke, and he took notes on the same legal pad as his shopping list. When she was finished, he leaned back in his chair and set down his pen, deep in thought.

"I think Mrs. Bristow's murder is related to Morty's, and the drug traffic to all of it." Vicki was thinking out loud again. "A loose end is that guy who has my cell phone. He has to know something. I figure this is more than enough for a Title III tap on the cell, don't you?"

"This concerns me," Saxon said, but he wasn't speaking directly to Vicki anymore. His gaze strayed to the windows, but the blinds were drawn. Still he kept looking in that direction, maybe by habit. He seemed to have forgotten that she was even there. "I'm not happy I wasn't told about this situation."

"I'm not, either." Vicki sensed this would be the falling-through-the-cracks part. The jurisdictional turf war. These agencies would have to talk to one another if they wanted to catch Morty's killers. "Who has jurisdiction in the investigation, as you see it? I know ATF will want to follow up because of Morty, but as a legal matter, I think Philly Homicide should—"

"I'm not going to discuss that with you."

Vicki blinked. "I thought we were discussing it."

"No, we weren't. Relations between ATF and other federal agencies on a specific case isn't appropriate for us to discuss."

Vicki felt slapped down. He didn't mind discussing the case when she was the one giving information. "I guess that will be decided at the meeting on Wednesday."

Saxon lifted an eyebrow. "How do you know about that meeting?"

"I've kept it completely confidential, of course."

"That's not the point. How do you know?"

Vicki paused. She didn't want to rat on Detective Melvin. The plastic Jesus doll stared at her. Behind Jesus was John Saxon. For a minute she didn't know what to say.

"Allegretti," Saxon said sternly, "you're way out of line, what you've been doing. Going to Bristow's house, surveilling Cater Street, following a suspect to Aspinall. You're not a professional, and this is dangerous work. You shouldn't be taking any part of an investigation on yourself."

"I didn't intend to, I was just following up when I went to see Reheema."

"You shouldn't have done that, either. It's better left to law enforcement."

Vicki was getting a little sick of hearing that. "I am law enforcement."

"You're a lawyer."

"I'm an AUSA and it's my partner who got killed."

"A loose cannon is what you are," Saxon said, as if it were an official pronouncement, and Vicki finally got mad.

"You know, if I hadn't made any progress, you'd have a point." Suddenly, the emotion, pain, and exhaustion she had been suppressing for two days caught up with her, and Vicki rose to her feet. "But I don't need this. All I know is that Morty's dead, and I'm the one driving around after the bad guys. So excuse me if I don't knuckle under."

"You're way outta line, kid." Saxon rose behind his desk and pointed a thick finger at her. "Does Bale know what you've been up to?"

But Vicki was too angry to answer. She turned her back on him and headed for the door.

"Don't you walk out on me, Allegretti! Answer my question! Does your boss know what you've been doing?"

"Tell you what." Vicki turned on her heel at the threshold. "You go food shopping, and I'll let you know when I get my next lead, okay?"

And she walked out before he could shoot.

When Vicki got home, she took an even greater risk than surveilling a drug dealer or questioning the masculinity of an ATF chief—she called her parents. She wanted to explain about Detective Melvin's call. She pressed in the number and took a fifty-fifty chance that the parent she actually liked would answer. After two rings, her mother picked up. *Yes!*

"Mom? Did Detective Melvin call you yet, from Homicide?"

"Goodness, yes, we just hung up," her mother said, alarmed. "What *is* going on? Are you okay, dear?"

"I'm fine."

"Thank God! Did you actually need an alibi?"

"No, not really."

"Your father's at the gym. I'm beside myself. Are you sure you're okay?"

"I'm fine. My wallet was stolen last night by a crack addict, who was killed last night."

"But you were here last night, and you didn't tell us anything about this."

And I'm still not. "We kind of had a fight, remember?" Vicki felt a tug. "I'm sorry I upset you, Mom."

"I'm sorry, too, dear." Her mother's tone softened.

"And for the record, I don't live like a pauper."

Her mother sighed. "You know your father."

"Uh, yeah."

"Maybe I won't mention to him that the detective called."

"Thanks." Vicki felt touched. "I have to go now, Mom. Don't worry too much."

"Just be careful."

"I will. Bye. Love you."

"Love you, too. Good-bye."

Vicki hung up, ignoring the knot in her chest. She thought about calling Dan but she didn't want to cause more trouble for him. She felt a little disconnected from the world. Without Morty. Without Dan. And after Saxon called Bale, without a career.

Vicki considered it. The smart thing to do was call Bale and preempt Saxon, but she'd get fired for sure. She turned it over in her mind, but her brain kept skidding on the ice. She was too tired to think. She needed to eat something and she needed a good night's sleep.

And only after that would she know what to do next.

TWENTY-THREE

VICKI WOKE UP IN THE MORNING TO A DIS-tinctive sound of winter: the *sc-c-c-crape*, *sc-c-c-crape*, *sc-c-c-crape* of a neighbor shoveling his sidewalk. She groaned and checked her bedside clock. 10:49. Late. She felt a wave of guilt. She'd have to get up and shovel her sidewalk so she didn't get sued. Growing up with both parents as lawyers, Vicki had been indoctrinated to shovel before the dreaded underlayer of ice wreaked havoc with the American system of civil liability.

She turned over and stuck her head under the pillow. She hated to shovel snow and put it off as long as possible, a rebel with a Back-Saver shovel. She consoled herself in her own childishness. It was nice and dark beneath her pillow, and her bed felt soft, comfy, and warm. The radiator hissed in a reassuring way, whispering *stay asleep, stay asleep, stay asleep*, but it couldn't drown out *sc-c-c-crape, sc-c-c-crape, sc-c-c-crape*, and neither noise stood a chance against

YOU'LL GET SUED, YOU'LL GET SUED, YOU'LL GET SUED.

Vicki turned over and squeezed her eyes shut, but it was inevitable. Nothing could silence her lawyer's conscience, and no pillow could block the realization that today was Morty's wake. It was still hard to believe he was dead. She flung off the pillow, rolled out of bed, and tried not to have another thought that would make her sad while she went to the bathroom, pulled on old sweatpants and a crimson hoodie sweatshirt, then trundled downstairs in the chilly house, put on her winter coat, boots, mittens, and stupid Smurfy hat. Then she went to the basement to retrieve her shovel, trundled back upstairs with it, went to the front door, and opened it into a blast of cold air.

The snow had stopped; the sky was clear and blue. The Holloway kids had already been out playing, evidenced by a snowman with a tiny head like Beetlejuice and M&M eyes dripping blue tears. Her street had been plowed, snowing the parked cars in until the next decade, and almost all the sidewalks had been shoveled, including her own.

Huh? In the middle of her perfectly shoveled walk, leaning on a snow shovel in his down coat and a Phillies cap, stood a grinning Dan Malloy.

"Nice hat, babe," he said.

Vicki clapped with delight, though her mittens made a *muh muh muh* sound that had no payoff. "What did you do, Dan?"

"That'll teach you to think about moving. All the neighbors in Center City are mean."

"This is so nice of you!"

"Will work for coffee."

"Done!" Vicki waved him inside. Ten minutes later, they had shed their boots, coats, hats, and mittens and left them by the door in a jumbled pile of his-and-her things, the sight of which made Vicki unaccountably content. She padded barefoot on the cool pine floor into the kitchen, going ahead of Dan. "That was really great of you. I hate to shovel."

"I know that."

"You do? How?"

"Because you told me once."

"I did?"

"Yes." Dan smiled and sat down in his customary chair at the kitchen table, while she reached in the cabinet for the coffee grounds, a role reversal for them. He looked typically unshaven, and his reddish bangs sprayed over his blue eyes, making even hat head look good. Luckily, today he was wearing a bra, in the form of a ratty white turtleneck under the same blue crewneck sweater.

"So you just decided to come over and shovel my walk?"

"Yeah. Mariella had to go in, so I have the day free."

The M-word. Vicki, in denial, had almost forgotten. Dan's snowboots might be parked next to hers, but his bedroom slippers were next to Mariella's. Meantime, he had on her favorite jeans, which were soaked from snow at the lower legs. If they were in a movie, Vicki would ask Dan to take his pants off so she could throw them in the dryer, and they'd end up in each other's arms. Unfortunately, they were in Philadelphia, where things like that never happened and people sat around in wet pants.

"Catch me up, Vick. What's going on? I haven't seen

you since they tried to arrest you. You gotta get a new cell phone."

"I will." Vicki poured tap water in the back of the coffeemaker and turned the button to On. "You want breakfast?"

"You have food in the house?"

"There's eggs." Vicki knew because she'd had some for dinner last night, and Dan was already on his bare feet, heading to the refrigerator.

"Scrambled, okay?"

"Fine."

"My specialty." Dan took out the eggs and a stick of butter, and Vicki drew way-too-pathetic pleasure from the fact that they were cooking side by side in her kitchen. Dan set the eggs and butter on the counter and went into the base cabinet for the fry pan. "So I know you've been up to no good, because Bale called me this morning, asking where you were."

"He did?" Vicki turned, surprised. Funny the things husbands don't tell you. Other women's husbands, that is. "What did he say?"

"That he's been calling here and there's been no answer. Said he was trying to find you."

"When did he call?"

"Last night and this morning."

Saxon must have called Bale. "Oh no, I must have slept through it. I conked out as soon as I hit the pillow."

"I called late last night and this morning, too."

"I guess I was really sleeping. I didn't even hear the Holloway kids making the snowman."

"You didn't check your messages?"

"No, I was too tired when I got in." And truth to tell,

she hadn't wanted to know if Dan had called. Since his fight with Mariella, she didn't feel as if she should call him back. Vicki tabled that for now. "What did Bale say? Is he mad? I'm pushing it, I know."

"He didn't say. You'd better call him, but not until after you tell me what happened yesterday."

Vicki was getting tired of giving everybody reports, but Dan was a great sounding board and he was on her side. The coffee started to drip, and its wet aroma filled the air. The kitchen was bright, quiet, and still; if the snow had been insulation yesterday, it was a cocoon today. Vicki retrieved their Elvis and Harvard mugs, interrupted the coffee in mid-stream, and poured them both a cup.

"Thanks." Dan melted butter in a Calphalon pan, as Vicki leaned against the counter and began the account of what had happened. By the time she was finished, they were sitting before plates of leftover eggs and Vicki was on her third cup of coffee, which was weak because she had interrupted the brewing process.

"I hate when I do that," she said.

"What?"

"Mess up the coffee, so the first cup is too strong and the ones after it suck. I'm my own pet peeve."

"You're too impatient." Dan set down his fork.

"Is that possible? Can you be just impatient enough?"

"*You* can't." Dan smiled. "That's part of the reason you're getting yourself in trouble with the brass."

"Let the lecture begin."

"No lecture here. You know what you're doing is nuts."

"Insulting Saxon?"

"Yes, and stalking drug dealers." Dan's mouth made a grave line.

"I don't want to talk about that. I want you to help me figure out the connection between Jamal Browning and the Bristows, if there is one."

Dan cocked his head. "Well, lay the facts down and organize them, as if they were evidence. Build your case, only undisputed facts first. Then we'll go from there."

"First, Browning supplies crack to Cater." Vicki counted off on an index finger. "Two, Browning was the boyfriend of my CI."

Dan shook his head. "That's not undisputed. The mother never heard of him."

"But it's likely, and the mother never heard of anybody."

"Not good enough." Dan spoke in his official jury-closing voice. "Second undisputed fact is that Mrs. Bristow was killed right after she bought drugs at Cater."

Vicki resumed finger counting. "And, three and four, the things I'd bet money on are that Jamal Browning was the boyfriend of Shayla Jackson, and that Mrs. Bristow gave the guns that Reheema had given her to the Cater Street dealers, in return for crack." Vicki considered it, then decided she was right. Funny how that always worked. "It's just too coincidental that the CI turns up dead in a houseful of fish-scale coke, and she happens to be the girlfriend of the dealer who sells to Cater Street."

"It's a baby drug business, from the sound of it, and that's a small world in Philly, believe it or not. Coincidences abound."

"Possibly. And we know that Reheema didn't know Jackson or Browning."

"Wrong. You don't know that at all."

"I do know it. I believe Reheema."

"Why?" Dan asked in disbelief.

"Because she convinced me, and so did that stuff I saw about her on her bulletin board. And the fact that she didn't know Jackson was corroborated by her boss."

"Jackson testified they were best friends."

"People lie under oath," Vicki said, because Reheema had taught her such things.

"And as between Jackson and Reheema, you believe Reheema, a known felon? Just because she ran track?"

"It's just a feeling I have about her. Reheema's different. And she's not a felon, because she wasn't convicted." Vicki sounded idiotic even to herself, and Dan's mouth dropped open.

"She pulled a gun on you, Vick!"

"She thought I was trespassing."

"So? If you thought somebody was trespassing, would you pull a gun on them? Would you even have a gun to pull? Or would you run out and call the cops?"

Vicki gathered it was rhetorical.

"Of course not. But just as it's second nature to you to call the cops, it's second nature to Reheema not to. Her experience of the cops is completely different from yours. For you, the cops are saviors. For her, they're enemies. You're the enemy." Dan nodded. "This is where Episcopal Academy comes in."

"What's that supposed to mean?"

"Vick, you're a rookie in this subculture, for want of a better word. You come to it with new eyes, and it's kind of exciting."

"It wasn't exciting, what happened to Morty."

"That's not what I meant and you know it." Dan flushed red, and Vicki regretted her words.

"Sorry."

"What I meant was the whole gangsta thing. The jewelry, the coke, the nicknames."

"I'm not new to it. I saw it at the D.A.'s office."

"Not this. Not with stakes this high. If these boys get caught, they go away for life. The boys who play that, they're a different breed. They're what the NBA is to high school ball. They like the big money—tens of millions of dollars—and they kill for it."

"I know all that," Vicki said irritably, but Dan leaned forward, intent.

"No, you don't. You bring this Main Line thing to it. You believe Reheema when she tells you, 'No, I didn't resell the guns, I gave them to my mommy.' 'No, I don't know Jackson.' You believe her because you tell the truth and you project that onto her. You believe her because you were raised in a world where people told the truth."

Obviously, he'd never eaten dinner at the Allegrettis'.

"No offense, but you're completely naïve. You can't believe her. You can't believe any of them. They lie to you all the time. Lying is a way of life for them, especially lying to you, an AUSA."

Vicki didn't like this new side of Dan. "You sound racist. Everything's 'them' and 'they.'"

"It's got nothing to do with race. I know these people, the mentality."

"What people?"

"People like my father."

It took Vicki aback. He never talked about his father. "How do you mean?"

"A liar, a cheat. A bad boy who grew up not knowing how to make a dime, so he learned how to steal it. Scam for it. Smile for it. The guy could charm the pants off you and you'd never know they were gone until you looked down." Dan shook his head. "How can I make you understand? My dad grew up in a poor neighborhood, just like your dad did. Some kids become straight arrows, like your dad. Go to school, make A's, graduate. Others shuck and jive and look for the angles. The quick buck. They want to be a big shot. My dad's as white as Irish lace, but he's gangsta to the core."

Vicki felt moved by his vehemence but she couldn't see it pertaining to Reheema. "I hear you, and I appreciate what you're saying. But keep an open mind. There's a person in there, even in the baddest gangsta. Even your dad."

"Not in my dad." Dan smiled, without mirth, and Vicki got back on track.

"Let's assume Reheema is telling the truth. Look at the facts. There's something we're missing. Maybe Reheema doesn't know Shayla Jackson, but Shayla Jackson knows her."

"How is that possible?"

"You can know someone who doesn't know you." Vicki was thinking aloud, a bad thing to do in front of a boss but a good thing to do in front of scrambled eggs. "You see them around, and someone tells you who they are. You know them but they don't know you."

"Okay, right. So?"

"So assume that Shayla and Jamal are boyfriend and girlfriend, and Shayla visits him at Cater Street."

Dan arched an eyebrow. "How do you know Jamal

goes to Cater Street? At his level, odds are he doesn't go to Cater Street ever, and the runner in the Eagles coat delivers the crack to the store."

"Okay, well, let's say once he does. Once, in the beginning, like when he's scouting locations or doing whatever drug dealers do before they open a store."

"Usually, they hang the sign—Grand Opening."

"Right, the sign and the lights." Vicki was too preoccupied to smile. "Or he drives by and he sees Reheema at Cater Street and she's with her mother."

"Not Saint Reheema. People don't buy crack with their mothers unless they use, too."

"Okay, let's say that Jamal drives by the neighborhood with one of his underlings and he sees Reheema in front of her mom's house, and he says to his pal, 'Who's that girl?'" Vicki could imagine the scene. "And the friend says, 'That's Reheema Bristow, and her mom buys from us.' And Shayla's in the car at the time." Vicki considered it and decided that she was right, yet again. "It's possible, isn't it?"

"It's not likely."

"But it's possible."

"Yes."

Yay! "Then maybe it happened." Vicki felt excited, but Dan looked dubious.

"So why would Shayla Jackson frame someone she saw on the street, a total stranger, on a straw charge?"

"I can think of one reason, but you won't guess it because you never met Reheema."

"Why?"

"She's gorgeous. She's stunning. She's like Beyonce, only cranky."

"You mean the gun."

"Exactly."

Dan laughed. "So?"

"If my boyfriend were showing an interest in her, or even asking who she was, I'd be worried." Vicki felt thunderstruck; it made so much sense. Maybe she had actually deserved to get into Harvard. Or maybe she just knew a lot about jealousy. "If I were in love with someone, but he had his eye on someone else or started to stray from me, I'd hate her. I'd want her gone."

"You're vicious." Dan was oblivious, even for a man.

"A straw charge is perfect, and Shayla would guess correctly that Reheema wouldn't dime on her own mother."

Dan was listening now, cocking his head.

"If Jamal started showing an interest in Reheema"— Vicki flashed on the bills on Shayla's dresser—"that would threaten Shayla's support."

"Not bad, but Reheema told you she didn't know Jamal. Is she a liar?"

"No, let's say she didn't know him, but he knew her, like with Shayla. He doesn't approach her, or even hit on her. Maybe he jokes about it or asks his friend about Reheema and Shayla finds out."

"That would be a very jealous woman."

"They exist." *Look across the table, pal.* "And we know that Shayla and Jamal did break up, because she was forwarding bills to him. If she were still seeing him, she'd just give them to him." Vicki felt excited. It was coming together, or at least part of it. "Shayla would know about the guns, because if Mrs. Bristow traded them for crack, they might find their way to Jamal. Or at least he'd know about them. If Shayla knew the guns had been bought by Reheema, she'd know enough to set her up for a straw charge. All it takes is a call."

"Not bad." Dan reached for his mug, which was empty.

"More coffee? I'm getting some." Vicki started to get up but Dan waved her down.

"Don't, you're caffeinated enough."

Vicki smiled. "So what do you think? Am I a genius or not?"

"You're a genius." Dan was nodding. "I think it's all very interesting."

"The question is, what do I do about it?"

"Nothing," Dan answered firmly.

"What? Why? I have to call Bale, I should tell him."

"Tell him later. If you call him now and start talking like this, he'll fire you for good. He didn't sound happy last night, and Saxon will have called him already." Dan relaxed back in his chair. "Lower the temperature of the situation. Let it sit for today. It's Morty's memorial, you know about that?"

"Sure."

"That will suck."

"Yes."

"Mariella might be able to go, if she can get somebody to take her place."

I could take her place. "That would be nice."

"So I say, let it be. Let Saxon forget your conversation and let Bale cool down."

"But they should follow up."

"They will. If you figured it out, they can figure it out. They really are professionals, Vick. Tell them next week and let them take it from there." Dan's tone turned almost plaintive. "Get real, girl. You did great, but Jamal Browning is a killer. A bona fide killer. You're out of your league."

Vicki knew it was true. She didn't have the stuff to go after Jamal Browning. She couldn't prove if he was behind Shayla's murder or if someone else was. And she didn't know if he or his underlings had anything to do with Mrs. Bristow's murder. She knew only that she had the information that would support the wiretaps and surveillance that would lead to the truth.

"Okay, I call Bale now and I'll play it by ear." Vicki rose to go to the phone, newly nervous. She couldn't afford to lose this job, but she wouldn't tell Dan her money worries. No one wanted to hear rich girls plead poverty. God bless the child. Vicki lifted the phone receiver. "I'll apologize for what I said to Saxon, then if Bale sounds like he's in a good mood, I'll tell him the theory. If he fires me, I'll shut up."

"Sounds like a plan. Should I stay or should I go?"

Is holding my hand an option? Vicki thought, but what she said was: "Stay." She picked up the phone and pressed in Bale's cell. It rang a few times, then his voicemail picked up, so she left a message, and managed to avoid begging for her job.

But she hung up with a bad feeling she couldn't quite explain.

PART THREE

The soil is good, the air serene and sweet from the cedar, pine and sassafras, with wild myrtle of great fragrance.

   —WILLIAM PENN,
   in an early description of "Penn's Woods,"
   the emerging colony of Pennsylvania and its
   capital, Philadelphia

Q: All right. Now, at the time, were you all selling drugs?

A: Well, at the time "G" had various corners that he was supplying, but there was those corners and I was selling drugs down the street from my grandmom's house at the projects, 55th and Vine.

Q: And when you say Gio had various corners, do you remember what the corners were that Gio had at the time?

A: Well, back then, a corner called 56th and Catherine was one of the major corners and he was serving the guys on Ithan Street quantity, small quantities of drugs back then.

Q: What does "serving" mean in the trade?

A: It means when the guys buying stuff off you. Like you go to the store you buy something.

Q: Uh-huh.

A: They just call it serving. It's slang like.

Q: So if you were "serving" somebody that meant you were selling them drugs?

A: Yes.

—JAMAL MORRIS,
United States v. Williams,
United States District Court,
Eastern District of Pennsylvania,
Criminal Docket No. 02–172, February 19, 2004,
Notes of Testimony at 255

TWENTY-FOUR

VICKI HAD NEVER BEEN TO THE WAKE OF AN officer killed in the line of duty and hadn't realized that it would be a state occasion. At least a thousand mourners packed Prior's Funeral Home in the Philly suburb of Fort Washington, filling it to capacity. The reception line flowed out of its largest viewing room, spilled into the hallway, and continued outside the funeral home, where massive loudspeakers had been set up. Top brass from ATF in Washington, masses of ATF, FBI, and DEA agents, politicians, U.S. Attorneys, several federal judges, squadrons of uniformed police, support staff, and more than a few reporters made up the massive throng, which was somber and businesslike in mood.

Vicki had arrived early, and even so, stood in line, just outside the viewing room in the entrance hall. She had heard that only family was invited to the funeral tomorrow morning, and now she understood why. She couldn't see the front of the viewing room for the crowd, and multicolored roses, carnations, calla lilies, and gladioli filled every available spot. A large ATF plaque covered with a crepe sash hung on the front wall. The scent of the bouquets thickened the air, commingling with mint aftershaves, heavy perfumes, and cigarette smoke every time the front door opened.

Vicki counted herself lucky to be inside the funeral home at all, and the distance from the hallway to the main room gave her time to deal with the situation. For her, this wasn't an official function, and she knew that Morty would be lying in a casket at the front of the room. The thought left her with a numbness throughout her body. She felt stiff in the navy wool suit, with a white silk blouse, which she wore under her down coat. She bowed her head to marshal her strength, hearing snippets of the conversations buzzing around her.

"We don't need Lawn Doctor, honey," the woman in front of her was saying in a wifely tone, to a gray-haired man who was obviously her husband. "I don't like those little green balls all over the lawn."

"They keep out the crabgrass and the dandelions."

"But I like the dandelions."

The husband chuckled. "I do, too. Have we met?"

Vicki screened them out in favor of the couple behind her, also talking quietly.

The man was saying, "The best was when he comes up with, 'I make good choices, Daddy!' At seven years old, can you believe that?"

The woman answered, "Dave, how many times you gonna tell that story?"

"As many times as I can," the husband retorted, and they both laughed.

Vicki looked up, wondering where Dan and Mariella were. Somewhere in the thick line of married people, standing two-by-two, like animals loading onto Noah's ark. She scanned the crowd but didn't see him. Or Bale, Strauss, or any of them. They'd be at the front, where there was movement, then the unmistakable sound of someone tapping into a microphone.

"Sound check, sound check," boomed a man's voice, and the room quieted. "Thank you, people. Excuse me, may I have everyone's attention?"

Saxon. Vicki recognized that sonorous bass. She considered running for her life but angled for a better view, standing on tiptoe and coming between the married couple in front of her. Where were Dan and Dr. Bitchy?

"Thanks to all of you for coming today." Saxon towered at the head of the room, a big blond bear in dark suit and tie. "I thank you on my own behalf and on behalf of the ATF family, who gathers on this tragic occasion to honor one of our finest agents, Special Agent Robert Morton."

Vicki swallowed hard. Women sniffled, their heads bowed, and men in suits studied their wingtips. Everyone stopped talking. The only sound was the scratchy undertone of the microphone and the echo of Saxon's voice amplified outside, slightly delayed.

"I'd like to introduce the director of the Bureau of Alcohol, Tobacco, Firearms, and Explosives, here from Washington to attend in Morty's honor. Director Louis W. Bonningtone."

Saxon moved aside for the director, a distinguished man whose short stature prevented Vicki from seeing him, given the heads in front of her. She tried to listen to his speech, which was generic, formal, and laden with government-speak, leaving her with the impression that the director had never met Morty in his life. Saxon retook the floor, and then Vicki could see the speaker again.

"Thank you, Director," Saxon began, shifting his weight. "I won't talk long, though I wanted to reiterate how vital Morty was to the agency, how valuable his skills and his tenacity were, over seventeen years. Morty ran the Boston Marathon in his younger days, and I always thought of him as a marathoner, mentally and physically. And he was a handsome devil, even if he was too skinny for my wife's taste."

There was laughter, and even Vicki smiled.

"Morty never met a case that didn't completely absorb him. If others were style, he was substance. He was the best of us, and we won't rest as a family until we bring to justice those responsible for his murder."

At this, there was clapping, and Vicki wished she could believe it, and almost did.

"Let me take a brief minute to introduce to you His Honor, the mayor of Philadelphia, then Ben Strauss, the U.S. Attorney for the Eastern District of Pennsylvania, and finally, Anthony Cardinal Bevilacqua, of the Archdiocese of Philadelphia, who will pray with us. Mr. Mayor, sir?" Saxon gestured grandly to his left and the mayor stepped in front of the microphone, and a ripple of curiosity went through the crowd, acknowledging his celebrity.

Vicki only half-listened to the mayor's speech, an adequate lecture by a man who had never met Morty, either, and looked around the room for Dan. He would have arrived early, because he always arrived everywhere early, so he'd be in this room somewhere. When the crowd shifted at the front, Vicki spotted Chief Bale with his chic wife. Bale squared his shoulders, because Strauss was taking the microphone.

"Welcome, everyone. I'm Ben Strauss, the U.S. Attorney for our district, but I consider myself honorary ATF today. But don't let me anywhere near a weapon. It wouldn't be the first time a lawyer shot himself in the foot."

People laughed softly, even agents who couldn't abide Strauss. All was forgiven today, and death had a way of persuading people to set aside their differences. Everybody, that is, except Vicki.

"Frankly, I didn't know Morty that well, at least not as well as my AUSAs knew him. For that reason, I'd like to introduce one of them who knew Morty exceptionally well, Dan Malloy, who will say a few words on Morty's behalf."

Whoa. Vicki's ears pricked up. Dan hadn't mentioned it at breakfast. Maybe it came up after? In the next minute, he emerged from the crowd at the front and stood tall before the microphone. His hair had been combed back, wet as a little boy's, but his suit was sharply tailored and Italian. He looked like a candidate for something, and even though Vicki was miffed that he hadn't mentioned it to her, she would have switched parties to vote for him.

"Welcome, everyone." Dan managed a smile, but it was shaky. "Morty worked closely with so many of us AUSAs that sometimes I thought he was a prosecutor. He knew more criminal law than most lawyers, and he had more street smarts than most crooks."

People laughed, nodding, and Vicki bit her lip. It was true. *Tell it, Dan.*

"I loved Morty. He was everything a federal law enforcement agent should be, and everything a man should be. Morty always said he would lay down his life for his job, and he died the way he lived—in the service of all of us." Dan paused, swallowing visibly, and Vicki wondered for a minute if he'd lose control. "I knew Morty very well and saw firsthand all the hard work he did—work that, frankly, I got the credit for. Morty made me look good, and that's the way ATF, FBI, and DEA agents are—they make us prosecutors look good, and we get the glory while they labor, literally, undercover."

Around the room, ATF and FBI agents nodded, and conferred briefly.

"Morty, I'm speaking for each and every AUSA in the Philadelphia office when I say: we love you and we miss you already. I'll never play 'Brick House' without thinking of you. Thank you."

People sniffled, and ATF agents hung their heads. Even if they didn't know Dan, his words had identified him as a real insider. Only someone who knew Morty would know he loved "Brick House." Dan had comforted all of them, even Vicki. Cardinal Bevilacqua himself then took the microphone, saying a brief prayer, and everyone bowed his head. When Vicki raised hers, her gaze found Dan, standing between Strauss and Mariella. Mariella had her arm around him and her head close to him; his broad shoulder shook slightly and his head hung. Vicki felt a stab of sympathy for him. She wished she could comfort him, but Dr. Bitchy was on the spot. Bitterness edged Vicki's thoughts, and she willed herself to banish it. Wives and husbands belonged together at times like this.

I have to get over him.

The reception line started to move so people filtered past the casket, and Vicki's throat felt tight as she reached the front of the line. She spent the next hour in a fugue state of heart-wrenching images. Bent gray heads in line. A flag holder on a stand next to the coffin, the red, white, and blue a neatly folded, thick triangle. An open casket, and Morty. His face still in death: his cold hand tacky to Vicki's touch, from whatever makeup they'd put on his skin. Photos of Morty at the Elliot Ness party were placed in his coffin with paper notes and a Commodores CD. And gallows humor; propped on an easel, an enlargement of a silly photo of Morty in a T-shirt that read, I HAVE A RESCUE FANTASY.

Vicki blinked back her tears and shifted over, shaking hands with the few family members who stood beside the casket, Morty's cousins or something, then Strauss, a priest, and finally, Bale. She was way too emotional to be talking to Bale about Aspinall Street, and he hardly met her eye anyway. She escaped the room and was in the entrance room on the way out when someone touched her arm.

"Vicki?" It was a man's voice, and she turned. A tall, dark-haired man about her age stood there, looking attractive in a dark, pinstriped suit. "I'm Jim Delaney, I don't know if you remember me. I came to the D.A.'s office right when you were leaving. I'm in the Insurance Fraud Unit."

"Right." Vicki remembered him only vaguely. "We met at that party."

"Ken Stein's barbecue, in Merion."

"Right."

"I'm sorry about what happened to Agent Morton."

Delaney looked at her with obvious sympathy. His eyes were a watercolor blue. "I read in the newspaper that you two worked together."

"Thanks." Behind Vicki, the front door opened and a cold gust blew in. People shuffled ahead in the reception line, the women drawing their coats tighter around them.

"Are you leaving? I'll walk you out."

"Sure." Vicki turned, zipped her coat on the fly, and went outside, descending the granite steps. Her hair blew in her face, and she almost tripped at the bottom, where Delaney put a steadying hand on her elbow.

"You all right?"

"Yes, thanks." The cold air stung tears drying in her eyes.

"How about I walk you to your car?"

"I'm parked in the far lot." Vicki pointed, and they took off.

"Are you going to be okay, after this?"

"Sure." Vicki nodded.

"It must have been awful, to be there when he was killed. That's traumatic."

"It was," Vicki said, though she hadn't thought of it that way until now.

"You know, people at the D.A.'s office still talk about you. You were a great prosecutor, quick on your feet. I saw you in court once, I don't know if you know that. I was at Dechert at the time. You were trying the Locke case."

"Locke." Vicki flipped through a mental file cabinet. "Home invasion. Wait, I lost that one."

"Yes." Delaney laughed, and so did Vicki. "But you made me want to try cases. Criminal cases."

"I did?"

"I made my decision that day," Delaney answered warmly, which was when Vicki realized what was going on. His hand hadn't left her elbow, and since he didn't have a wedding band, she wasn't pushing it away.

"Really? Little old me? Tell me more about how great I lost."

Delaney laughed again. His dark, curly hair blew in the wind, and he had a nice laugh, too. "Listen, I know this isn't the best time, but the way I see it, I owe you dinner."

Wow. "You do. A really nice dinner."

"So, if you don't have any plans right now and want some company, how about I take you out? You shouldn't be alone, and I can offer you an excellent shoulder to cry—"

"VICK!" came a sudden shout from behind them, and Vicki turned.

Dan. Running toward her. Concern creased his forehead, and she wondered if something was wrong. He was winded when he reached her, his chest heaving and his breath puffing white in the chill.

Dan nodded to Delaney. "'Scuse me, can I borrow this girl? It's important."

"Sure." Delaney released Vicki's arm and stepped back.

"It might take us a while, friend," Dan said brusquely, and Delaney nodded.

"Vicki, maybe I should give you a call, another time?" Delaney asked, and before she could process it, he had edged away.

"Yes. Do."

"You in the book?"

"Yes," Vicki said, and Delaney said good-bye, then walked away as she turned to Dan, concerned. "What's the matter?"

Dan cracked a wry grin. "Sorry to interrupt. Who was that?"

"Mr. Right."

Dan laughed. "Since when?"

"Okay, Mr. Right Now. Which would have worked for me."

"You can't be serious. What a geek."

"He's not a geek, he's an ADA."

"Not in Major Crimes, he's not. I can tell."

"He's in Insurance Fraud."

Dan fake-snored, closing his eyes and dropping his head to the side.

"Very funny."

"Shhh, I'm asleep."

Vicki looked over Dan's shoulder. Delaney was long gone. The reception line shifted forward in the cold. "Where's Dr. Mariella?"

Dan fake-woke up. "In the ladies' room."

Hmmm. "So what's the matter? Is something going on?"

"Yes, I need to talk to you."

"I'm parked this way," Vicki said, and they walked together into the wind. Dan took her arm, but she missed the way Delaney had held her. Also, he was single.

"Listen, I fixed everything between you and Bale," Dan said, under his breath, and Vicki looked at him in surprise.

"What do you mean?"

"I told him what we talked about this morning, all

about your theory, and he said it sounded like you made a real connection. He said he's going to talk to Saxon about it, smooth some feathers, and ask ATF to get the surveillance squad on Jamal Browning."

"You're kidding!" Vicki felt off balance. As happy as she was that they'd go forward on Browning, she wished she had been a part of the discussion. "When are they going to start surveillance? I know they have a big meeting, but it's not until Wednesday."

"Bale didn't say."

"I wish I could be there. They should do it right away. They don't need a warrant or anything, it's plain view."

"And guess what?" Dan strode on. "ATF is already running down a lead on your cell phone."

"What's the lead? The guy with the gravelly voice?"

"I don't think Bale knows. It's ATF. They got tech experts in Philly and D.C. on it, Bale says."

"D.C.? Then it will never happen."

"Don't be so negative."

"All they have to do is go to Cater Street and ask around. My cell phone has blue daisies on it, for God's sake." Vicki shook her head. It felt colder out, but it could have been her imagination. "No self-respecting drug dealer will carry that around for long."

"Bale thinks they'll ask the judge for a tap."

"With what? Don't they need my affidavit for probable cause? Or my notes?"

"Evidently not," Dan answered, then waved at a phalanx of uniformed Philadelphia police, attending a black Cadillac hearse. Morty's hearse. Vicki looked away.

"Well, what else do they have on Browning? The bills at Shayla's house? That's not enough."

"I didn't ask, and he wasn't telling. I got the idea it was confidential."

"When are they going for the tap? They can't do anything until this meeting, unless they moved it up. Did they move the meeting up?"

"I didn't cross-examine him, Vick. I was just happy to hear you're still gainfully employed." Dan picked up his pace. "He got your phone message."

"Think I could be at that meeting?"

"Honestly, no. But he's not even that mad that you were harassing drug dealers. Great result, huh?"

"Great. Thanks."

"You're happy, right?"

"It's Morty's wake, how happy can I be?"

Dan stopped in his tracks, frowning beside a powdery mound of plowed snow. "You know what I meant."

"Yes, and I appreciate what you did." Vicki felt confused, her thoughts a grief-stricken jumble. "I wish I had talked to Bale, though. I want to be the one to indict on this case."

"You're too junior, Vick, and you couldn't try it anyway. You're a fact witness. You were there."

"I could still be on the indictment. I want to work that case. I want to be the one—"

"Stop." Dan put up a hand. "You're getting ahead of yourself. It doesn't matter who's on the indictment, does it? The only thing that matters is that they get the conviction."

Vicki shook her head. The only thing she agreed with was that they couldn't discuss this now, or here, beside Morty's hearse.

"You know I'm right."

"For now, maybe."

"Good." Dan smiled, cocking his head. His hair blew sideways in the cold, drying stiff from the mousse. "Then isn't it time for the magic word?"

"Huh?"

"'Thank you.'"

"You're shameless, Malloy." Vicki rolled her eyes. "*Please* is the magic word, anyway."

"Wrong. You didn't read the statute. It's in the definitions section, right up front." Dan folded his arms. "You gonna say it or not?"

"Okay, thanks."

"You're very welcome."

Vicki tried to buck up, and started liking Dan again. Or loving him, as the case may be. "I'm just sad, is all."

"I know. Me, too." They started walking again.

"They're not moving fast enough. I mean, did you see it in there? All that brass? Morty almost gets lost in the process."

"No, he doesn't. They care."

"But they need to get moving! Washington? It's a murder case, not a Senate hearing. So will they keep us posted?"

"Bale said he'd give you a call when the suits leave."

"Good, I need a paycheck." Vicki shook her head. "Am I off suspension yet, did Bale say?"

"No."

"Argh!"

They reached the Cabrio, and Dan put a hand on her shoulder. "Take it easy, sweetie."

"I have no choice." Vicki dug in her purse for her car keys. "So what about my cases?"

"I got your back. Chin up." Dan gentled her chin upward with a cold hand. "By the way, what did you think of my speech, in there?"

"It was great."

"Thanks. It wasn't easy." Dan appraised her, his eyes ice-blue in the bright sun, the pupils telescoped to pinpoints. "You gonna be okay, Vick?"

"Yes. You?"

"I've had better days." Dan checked his watch, then frowned. "I gotta go."

Vicki unlocked the Cabrio door. "Give her my best," she said, but when she turned back, Dan had already taken off.

Leaving Vicki alone with her questions.

And her impatience.

TWENTY-FIVE

BY NOON ON MONDAY, VICKI HAD DONE everything possible to get her life back to normal. She had cleaned her house, paying special attention to the rooms that the cops had upended, then went out to buy a new cell phone and get groceries. When she came home, she organized her closet, worked out on the elliptical, and finally pasted her hair with a conditioning "masque" that made it greasier than ever. She ran for the telephone every time it rang because she thought it would be Dan or Jim Delaney, which it wasn't.

She sat now at the kitchen table, ignoring half of a turkey sandwich, sucking down another cup of coffee, and paging idly through the newspaper. It was all murder all the time, and she closed the page. It had stopped snowing, leaving a foot on the ground, so she and the Holloway kids had a snow day. Only one of them was happy about it. It wasn't easy to sit around and leave important matters to federal agencies, especially the investigation of Morty's murder. Vicki was in mourning, with a side order of cabin fever. She hadn't spoken to another human being in a whole day, and she couldn't remember the last time she'd convicted anybody.

Her new cell phone lay beside her, and she gave in, picked it up, and flipped it open. She called Dan at the office, but he was in court, so she left her new cell number. Then she thought about it. She didn't have to be so passive with the very single Mr. Delaney. She called the D.A.'s office, but he was out, so she left a message with a receptionist who was too new to know her. Who else could she call?

She looked out the bright kitchen window. Bare tree branches swayed in the bitter wind. She had two good girlfriends from law school, both married, but one had had a baby and left the world, and the other, Susan Schwartz, was in-house counsel at Cigna. Vicki called Susan but she was on vacation. As a last resort, she called her parents, but they were in a meeting, so she left her new cell number with the receptionist. Then she was fresh out of people to not reach, so she ate the turkey sandwich and stared at the discarded newspaper, reading beneath the fold. Which was when she saw it.

And ran upstairs to get dressed.

Vicki entered the room and sank unnoticed into an empty chair in the last row. The wake was completely different from Morty's, as the crime scene had been completely different from Morty's. The funeral home was in the city, not the suburbs. The viewing room wasn't large and well-decorated, but small and shabby, with a dark navy-blue rug that had been worn almost threadbare at the door, where Vicki lingered. Lemon-scented Glade, not flowers, perfumed the air, and only two bouquets of red roses flanked the plain casket, which was mercifully closed, of course. And instead of being crowded, only a handful of people were in attendance, leaving rows of empty brown folded chairs. Vicki counted six mourners, including Reheema.

The mourners faced the front of the room, and there was no representative of the funeral home in sight. Reheema sat alone in the front row, her head bowed, her dark hair smoothed into a tiny, stiff ponytail. She wore a black dress and black flats. In the row behind Reheema sat five women, all older African-American women, dressed in heavy coats and small velvet hats. They looked like the church ladies that Vicki had expected Mrs. Bristow to be, or perhaps used to be.

Vicki felt a twinge of guilt. She didn't know if she should be here. She didn't know if she had a right. She'd come because she'd felt she had to pay her final respects to a woman whose murder she might have caused. It was the least she could do; it was the beginning of setting it right, which she hoped would end with convicting the killer. She would stay for Mrs. Bristow.

But her gaze remained on Reheema. It was only thirty feet to the front of the room, and Vicki could see Reheema's shoulders shaking just the slightest bit. Was she crying for the mother she had spoken so cruelly of?

Of course.

So Vicki wasn't the only one who had mixed feelings about her parents. She flashed on the scene at Morty's funeral, when Dan had gotten upset and Mariella had comforted him. If Reheema was crying, no one was consoling her. The church ladies were talking among themselves, off to the side. Reheema sat alone in her grief.

Like me.

Vicki squirmed in the hard chair. She felt an unrealistic urge to go sit with Reheema, though she knew it was out of the question. Reheema would have her thrown out. Or shot on sight. Instead, Vicki stayed put, bowed her head, and said a prayer. But when she looked up, Reheema was walking down the aisle on the side of the room, tears streaking her cheeks. Her wet eyes flared a bloodshot red when she spotted Vicki.

"I'm leaving," Vicki said preemptively, rising to bolt, and Reheema grabbed her upper arm, propelling her toward the exit door.

"You're damn right you are. What are you doing here?"

"I wanted to pay my respects to your mother."

"Get out of my life." Reheema pulled her to the front door and yanked it open with her free hand. Brutal cold slapped them both in the face, and Reheema's eyes narrowed against the chill. "Go. You got no business here."

"If it's any comfort, I made progress on her killer."

"I don't need comfort from you." Reheema shoved her through the open door, where Vicki turned, suddenly resentful.

"You know, you could show a little interest."

"I'm not interested."

"In your mother? The one you're crying over?" The words came out more harshly than Vicki intended, but she might never get another chance. She softened her tone. "I'm sorry, it's just that I'm so close, I could get to the bottom of this, if you helped me."

"Helped you?" Reheema's lips parted in disbelief and she forgot her tears. "Why would I help you?"

"It's not about me and you. It's about your mother and my partner. I think their murders are connected. I found out it was Jamal Browning who supplied the store on Cater Street. He was Shayla Jackson's boyfriend."

"Gimme a break."

"And even though you don't know these players, I think you might have something to do with it."

"Me? I was in the FDC, thanks to you."

"I didn't buy her the guns. You did."

"You tellin' me I killed my own mother?" Reheema blinked, angering, and Vicki shook her head.

"No, but you're the only link I know of between these events and people. You. You could help me. If we work together, Reheema, we can figure it out." The words came pouring out before Vicki realized what she was proposing. This time she was thinking out loud before her enemy, which was even dumber than doing it before your boss. "I can't do it alone anymore. I stick out like a white thumb in your neighborhood. But you wouldn't."

"You're so full of it!" Reheema tried to close the door, but Vicki stuck her navy pump in it.

"I'm asking you to think about it."

"Think about what?" Reheema closed the door on Vicki's foot, where Ruby the Insane Corgi had chewed. It might be time to retire her shoe, if not her toes.

"Think about helping me find her killer. She was a beautiful woman once, and she loved you. She raised you. Somebody got you to school."

"I walked."

"I saw the picture of her, with the Penn Relays van."

Reheema pushed harder on the door. From inside the funeral home, an older man in a dark suit was rushing to assist her, followed by a clutch of church ladies.

"The woman who drove you in that van is the woman you're crying for." Time was running out, so Vicki made her final pitch. "Show her the respect she deserves. Bury her, then call me." She edged away from the door, then hurried into the cold night, her pumps clattering on the sidewalk.

When Vicki got home, she checked her messages. Dan had called back on the home phone, telling her not to bother calling back, which she knew was code for Mariella's-home-now-so-don't-call. He hadn't called on her new cell though he'd had the number, which meant that he wanted credit for returning her call, but didn't actually want to talk to her.

Definitely have to get over him.

Vicki pressed the button for the next message but there wasn't any. She checked the message machine for a call from Delaney; no messages, just a big, red, digital zero. She hoped the moment hadn't passed. She skipped dinner, discouraged, and climbed the stairs, undressed, and went to bed, where she barely slept. She didn't know what had come over her at the funeral home, shouting at someone who had just lost her mother, and she doubted that Reheema would call.

Which was why she was surprised when the phone rang.

TWENTY-SIX

THE NEXT MORNING, VICKI DROVE STREETS still being plowed and salted, in traffic lighter than usual because of the snowstorm, which was more than big enough for Philadelphians to credibly ditch work. She drove past closed stores, restaurants, and offices, and made her way back to West Philly, where fresh snow blanketed the trash cans, fire hydrants, and sagging porch roofs, reflecting the bright sunlight. She blinked against the glare.

Vicki hit the gas, barely able to move in a jacket, white cotton turtleneck, fisherman's sweater, and flannel-lined jeans. She had dressed for the weather this time, and whatever might come. So much was unknown about what had happened and what was going to happen that she couldn't help feeling nervous. She hadn't taken risks like this before in her career, much less her life, but she wasn't going to do anything crazy. Just a little legwork that the cops couldn't do, or weren't doing fast enough.

She turned onto Lincoln and had barely cruised toward the curb in front of the house when Reheema, on the sidewalk, flagged her to a stop and opened the car door.

"You didn't have to wait outside," Vicki said, surprised. "It's cold."

Reheema didn't reply, but climbed into the car, letting in a chilling burst of air. She slammed the door behind her and folded herself into the passenger seat, her legs so long that her knees ended up at chest level. "Gotta get a new car."

"Your seat adjusts. The lever's on the side near the door."

"That's not the problem." Reheema reached down and slid the seat back anyway, stretching her legs out. She had on her navy pea coat with her black knit watch cap pulled down so low it grazed her naturally long eyelashes, drawing attention to dark, lovely brown eyes, if only by accident. It would have been a fetching look, if Reheema had been smiling instead of frowning. "This car won't work."

"What do you mean?" Vicki was about to start the engine, but she held off. "This car works great."

"Not for what you're talkin' about. It won't do. Uh-uh."

"You mean, for our plan?" Vicki got finally up to speed. Reheema was a woman of so few words, it was like playing connect-the-dots.

"For *your* plan. I'm just along for the ride."

"Not really."

"Yes, *really*."

"You said on the phone you'd cooperate."

"*Cooperate* means snitch," Reheema shot back, and Vicki bit her tongue. She had suspected their relationship wasn't going to be roses, but she had to make it work if they were going to do the job.

"That's not what I meant."

"That's what you said."

"Okay, poor choice of words. Sue me."

"I am."

Oops. Vicki had almost forgotten. The lawsuit that Melendez had told Bale about. "You're still going through with that?"

"Sure."

"Even though you said you'd help me? That you'd work with me?"

"I *am* workin' with you. You oughta see me when I'm not."

"I have," Vicki said, her tone harsher than prudent for someone Trying to Make Friends.

"When?"

"The Beretta, remember? The lethal weapon part? The aimed-at-me part?" Vicki managed a smile, which she thought was big of her, but Reheema's eyes flared in ready anger.

"*What*? *You* started it, at the conference. That's why Melendez is gonna file. You pulled me across the desk! I was in handcuffs, I couldn't even defend myself!"

Okay, besides that. "At least I was unarmed."

"Unarmed? No United States Attorney is *unarmed.*" Reheema scoffed. "A U.S. Attorney is armed with guns you can't see."

Assistant U.S. Attorney. Common mistake.

"You have guns that put people away. Guns that put me away!"

"Hold on. You did buy two very real guns, ones you can see."

"And you couldn't prove I resold them, so I shoulda been free." Reheema pointed in her black wool gloves. "You had me brought up to a conference when you *knew* that."

Okay. Vicki gritted her teeth and bit an imaginary bullet. "I'm sorry." She paused, waiting, but there was no response. "You sorry, too?"

"For *what*?"

"For pointing a gun at my favorite heart."

"No."

"Reheema, we're trying to clear the air here."

"My air is *clear*."

"I said I was sorry. You can say you're sorry."

"Why?"

"That's how it works."

"Go to hell."

Or not. "Fine." Vicki gave up, faced front, and squeezed the steering wheel. It was hard to look tough in J. Crew red mittens, but she was trying.

Reheema cleared her throat and faced front, too. "We need a new car. This car is too conspicuous. You said so yourself."

"I was joking."

"You were right. For once." Reheema smiled in spite of herself, which Vicki took as an apology. She looked over.

"Why is it conspicuous? Because it's white?"

"Where you from?"

"Philly."

"You were *not* raised in Philly, girl."

"Well, specifically, I grew up in Devon, but I consider it—"

Reheema's eyes narrowed. "That where they have that horse show?"

"Yes, the Devon Horse Show."

"You ride horses?"

"When I was little, I had lessons." Vicki was tired of being defensive. Especially on her salary. "What's this have to do with my car?"

"It's suburban."

"What's suburban about a Cabrio?"

Reheema snorted. "Convertible's suburban, automatically. You keep this car in the hood, the homes slit the rag top. Take the CD changer, air bag, all gone. Wouldn't last an hour."

Oh.

"And that little red H on the back window? That doesn't help, either, Harvard."

"It's crimson, not red." *But never mind.* "Black people go to Harvard, too, you know."

"But not to Avalon."

"What?"

"Your bumper sticker—'Avalon, Cooler by a Mile'? Black folks don't go to Avalon, New Jersey."

Which could be why my parents bought a house there.

"White girl and a black girl in a car's conspicuous enough."

"It happens."

"Not in Devil's Corner. The car's got to go. They might recognize it. If that lookout sees you again, he'll remember the car." Reheema shook her head, and Vicki suspected she was enjoying this way too much.

"I don't want to sell my car. I love my car."

"Then don't. You got the dough, buy us a new one." Reheema looked out the window. "Now let's go."

A half an hour later, Vicki found them an open dealership, parked beside a pointy mound of freshly plowed snow, and cut the ignition. The peeling sign over the lot entrance read PHILLY PRE-OWNED AUTOS—USED TO EXCELLENCE! SALE OR RENT! Red and white plastic pennants flapped from a sagging string, and fake-gold tinsel glittered in the noonday sun, its ends frayed from twisting in the elements. Old Jeeps, Tauruses, Toyotas, and an ancient Pinto sat in the lot, in obsolete shades of avocado, diluted lemon, and bright blue.

Vicki looked at the dealership with satisfaction. "This is perfect."

Reheema curled her upper lip. "I said, a *new* car. This is the brokest-ass car lot I ever saw."

"We're supposed to be inconspicuous."

"We can be inconspicuous in a new car. And we can look good doin' it."

"Come on." Vicki slid her keys from the ignition and grabbed her purse, but Reheema stayed put.

"I thought we were *cooperating*."

"I'm paying, you're cooperating."

"Oh no, you didn't just say that."

Vicki got out of the car, yanked on her mittens, and walked onto the plowed lot, making a beeline for a grimy white Camaro with a dented front end. She skimmed the sign: AS IS, 1984 CHEVY CAMARO, 60,374 MILES, BUY FOR $1250, RENT FOR $50/WEEK. MPFI FUEL-INJECTED, TRANS REBUILT 10,000 MILES AGO. "Sounds good, and the price is right. We'll rent."

Reheema came up behind her, hands shoved deep

into the pocket of her pea coat. "What is it with you and white cars?"

"I'm suburban, with a little H."

"Crimson, not red."

"Correct. Details matter."

"Hold on, check this." Reheema went one car over, to a sports car that had been repainted cobalt-blue, with metallic shimmer. "That's what I'm talkin' about!" She read the sign aloud. "'1986 Nissan 300ZX, 110,000 miles, Z-bra included.'"

"How much?"

"Three grand to buy, a hundred a week to rent."

"That's some bra. No."

"But it's in great condition."

"Too much money."

"I would look damn good in this thing." Reheema couldn't stop gazing at the sports car. "You're single, right?"

"Yes." *But he's not.*

"Got a boyfriend?"

"Not a prayer."

"Not for long." Reheema spread her arms wide. "In this."

"No," Vicki said, with regret. She shifted over to the next car, a black sedan with a dented fender and a black rubber strip peeling from its side door. She skimmed the sticker out loud. "'1995 Pontiac Sunbird, four cylinders, 120,000 miles, $1,500 to buy, $75 a week to rent.' Not bad."

Reheema walked over. "I'm not feelin' it. S'boring."

"Exactly." Vicki peeked inside. "Only one problem. It's a gearshift. I don't drive a stick."

"Can't you learn, Harvard?"

"You know how to drive a stick?"

"Sure, I went to a real college. Temple."

Vicki was distracted by a short white man in a gray coat, coming out of a one-room building in the middle of the lot, presumably the office. A Fotomat sign was a painted ghost under the building's grimy white. Vicki said under her breath, "Let me do the talking."

"No, I'll do the talking."

"But I know how to negotiate."

"So do I."

"*I'm* the lawyer."

"You couldn't get me to plead out."

Ouch.

"And you can't even drive a damn stick."

"Okay, fine. Go get 'em, girlfriend."

Reheema's eyes shifted under her cap. "Black people stopped saying girlfriend a long time ago. We talk just like you white folks now, since you done give us the vote."

"Gimme a break," Vicki said, just as the little salesman came chugging up, his breath puffing in the cold air like a toy locomotive.

"Welcome, ladies!" he sang out. His bald head looked cold and the tip of his nose had already turned red. His blue eyes were bright behind thick glasses and he clapped his gloved hands together, as if to generate excitement. Or heat. "How are you two lovely ladies doing today?"

"Fine," they answered in unison, with equal enthusiasm, which is to say, none.

"Great day to buy a car! You girls have my undivided attention! No waiting, right? Ha ha!"

Reheema stepped forward. "I want me a cheap car

that don' look like crap. And don't be rippin' me off. You messin' with the wrong girl."

Huh? Vicki did a double-take at the appearance of Street Reheema, especially after the lecture she'd just received.

"Certainly, certainly." The salesman edged away from Reheema and looked at Vicki. "And, miss, you are?"

"Her life partner."

Reheema burst into startled laughter, and Vicki smiled to herself.

Half an hour later, Reheema was driving the Sunbird off the lot with Vicki in the passenger seat, because they didn't have time for her stick lesson after dropping the Cabrio back at home and going to the bank, where she had withdrawn the cash to rent the car. They had jointly negotiated ten bucks off the price, and the dealer had agreed to "detail" the car, that is, hose it down and spray the interior with Garden in a Can. The Sunbird was a washed-out light blue inside, and its floor was covered with aftermarket shag rugs, somebody's idea of pimp-my-ride. Armor All greased the blue vinyl bucket seats, and there was no cute little H on the rear window, in crimson or even in red.

By noon, the two women were rolling, and one of them was missing her Cabrio very much.

TWENTY-SEVEN

VICKI AND REHEEMA STAKED OUT CATER
Street, parking the Sunbird behind a tall snowbank
made by a city plow when the cross street had been
cleared. The tall, triangulated mound hid them from
view of the lookout, smoking a cigarette halfway down
the block. And both women were in extraordinarily
professional disguise; Reheema's knit cap covered her
hair and Exxon-station sunglasses hid her eyes, and
Vicki wore Dan's Phillies cap and Chanel sunglasses,
to fashionably conceal her forbidden whiteness. Even
so, she was pretty sure that they looked like two
women, one white and one black, driving while blind.

Cars couldn't drive for the snow on Cater, which
hadn't been cleared yet because the street was too narrow to fit the conventional wide plows, and only a few
row houses had their walks shoveled, but it didn't deter
steady foot traffic to the vacant lot. The pace was as
brisk as the other day, and addicts braved the elements,

showing unusual hardiness. Vicki wondered if watching them bothered Reheema, so soon after her mother's murder.

"You okay?" she asked, looking over at that perfect, if impassive, profile.

"Fine." Reheema nodded, her sunglasses reflecting the snow. The woman of few words had become the woman of no words. Vicki had been previously unaware that you could be a woman and say so very little. It seemed biologically impossible.

"Is this weird for you, since what happened to your mother? Is it upsetting?"

"I look upset?" Reheema didn't move, just kept gazing out the windshield, and then Vicki gave up and looked, too. A bundled-up couple, a man and a woman, walked in the snow to the vacant lot, arm in arm, like a crack date.

"You recognize them?"

"No."

Vicki had hoped otherwise. This was Phase One of the Master Plan. They'd been here an hour, and Reheema hadn't recognized either of the lookouts or any of the customers. "But they're your neighbors."

"I don't know the neighbors."

Vicki didn't get it. "You lived here, right?"

"Moved here senior year high school, and not since then."

"Where were you before you moved here?"

"Somewhere else."

That clears things up. "And your mother stayed here. When did she start using, if I can ask?"

"I was in college."

"Is that why you didn't come back?"

"Yes."

Now the conversational ball was really rolling. "It must have been hard."

Reheema didn't say anything.

"What did you major in?"

"Business."

"Did you like it?"

"No."

Try another tack. "You know, my dad lived right on your street. He had the corner house on Washington. He went to Willowbrook, too."

"Where'd you go to high school?"

"Episcopal."

"Private school."

"Guilty," Vicki said, and she was. They both watched as a young man in long dreads and a brown coat walked down the street, kicking snow as he shuffled along, heading for the hole. "How about him? Do you know him?"

"You know, he does look familiar."

"Goody!"

"Did you just say *goody*?" Reheema peered at Vicki over the top of her sunglasses. "Never. Again."

Excited, Vicki handed Reheema a pair of binoculars she'd brought from home. She'd packed her backpack full of equipment they might need for the Master Plan, including guacamole Doritos. Episcopal Academy taught its grads to plan well for their stakeouts.

Reheema turned and raised the binoculars to her eyes. "Yo, that's Cal!" she said, dangerously animated.

"Cal what?"

"Cal Moore. Was in my math class. I think he dropped out, and now he's a crackhead." Reheema lowered the binoculars. "Always was a loser."

"It's sad."

"No, it isn't."

Vicki let it go and noted Cal Moore's name in the Filofax. So far his was the only name. Phase One wasn't working out so hot, but then again, it took only one name for a lead. She dug inside the backpack again, grabbed the silvery Cybershot camera, pressed the button so the lens was on telephoto, and snapped a digital close-up of Cal Moore.

"Why're you doin' that?"

"In case we need it."

"Why would we need it?"

Good question. "I don't know yet. But this is what the ATF would do on a stakeout, and so I'm doing it, too." Vicki knew the basics from Morty, but she was trying not to think about him today. "If it turns out we need an ID on Moore, we have a picture." They both watched as Moore trudged through the snow to the vacant lot, then went inside, past the bare trees. Vicki couldn't help but wonder. "What do they have in there anyway? Like a shack or something?"

"You mean, what's in the hole? Just the man, standing there, behind some trash cans and an old wood wall from one of the houses."

"A wall in the middle of the lot?"

"Toward the back. Looks like the house got torn down and the old wall, like maybe the backyard, got left. It makes a screen, so you can't see what's goin' on from the street."

Vicki tried to visualize it. "So this guy just stands outside, in the hole?"

"Yeah."

"I guess the overhead's low."

"'Cause there's nothin' overhead," Reheema said, and they both laughed.

More bonding! Bonding like crazy! Then Vicki sobered up. "They won't do business outside forever, will they?"

"No, not for long. They're just gettin' a hold. Established. They'll move into one a the houses soon."

"When do you think?"

"Soon as they find one." Reheema snorted. "Hell, I'll sell 'em mine."

Vicki assumed she was kidding. "And that will be the end."

Reheema didn't say anything.

Vicki set the camera down and skimmed the Filofax notes she'd made today, in her lap. She had counted foot traffic again, and business was better than yesterday; sixty customers in the past hour, even in the bad weather. At sixty bags an hour, for a dime bag, which was conservative, the dealer made six hundred dollars an hour. Vicki looked up from her notes. "Wonder when the go-betweens will show up, the black leather coat or the Eagles coat. They're late."

"Maybe he stocked up because of the snow."

"Funny that they started an outside business in winter."

"Lotta competition in the city right now. Everybody wants to open a new store." Reheema's tone was so certain, Vicki had to wonder.

"How do you know that?"

"Just got outta jail. The FDC's fulla crack dealers. All the talk is turf, who's stealing customers from who. Who's expanding, who's not."

Vicki considered it. "Maybe we can put the word out

in the FDC. See what anybody knows about Jay and Teeg, or Browning's operation in general."

"Did that already."

"You did? When?"

"Soon as it went down with my mother."

Vicki felt a twinge. "Did you learn anything?"

"No. Everybody's afraid to talk about it. Hey, Cal's back." Reheema raised the binoculars, and Vicki raised the camera to watch the young man walk out of the hole, hands thrust in pockets and head down, his dreads coiled into a thick rope that came to a point like an alligator tail.

"What's with the hair? This would be a black culture question."

Reheema snorted. "Don't ask me, I hate it. Cal had his that way since high school. Hasn't been washed in five years."

At almost the same moment, a shiny maroon Navigator turned onto Cater from the opposite direction and powered toward the vacant lot, spraying fans of fresh snow in its wake, like a speedboat. "Lookout," Vicki said, taking a photo, and Reheema whistled behind the binoculars.

"Nice ride!"

"Four-wheel drive."

"We got Daddy's car today!"

Vicki snapped another close-up as the Navigator stopped in front of the hole and the driver's door opened. In the next instant, the short man in the black leather coat and cap stepped out into the snow. Vicki took his close-up when he turned. She had never been so happy to see a criminal before. "Bingo!"

"Goody!" Reheema said.

Vicki let it go and took another photo. "Do you know him?"

"No."

"Damn."

"More like it," Reheema said. Vicki looked through the telephoto lens to see him better. Mr. Black Leather had large, round eyes, a short nose, a tiny little mustache, and photographed rather well. He hustled inside the vacant lot, raising his knees high to avoid getting his feet wet, kicking snow as he went. The Navigator idled in the street, sending a chalky plume of exhaust into the air. Vicki eyed it through the camera but, because of the snow's glare on the windshield, couldn't tell if somebody was in the passenger seat. Only a drug dealer could leave a car like that unlocked and running in this neighborhood.

"He might come past us on the way out. Get down." Vicki lowered the camera and slunk down in her seat, and Reheema laughed.

"Sit up. You're embarrassing yourself."

Vicki edged up in the slippery seat and watched the scene again through the camera. Moore was at the top of the block and turned right. "Wonder where he lives. Do you know, from high school?"

"We didn't travel in the same circles."

"He wasn't in National Honor Society, huh?"

Reheema shot her a look. They fell silent in the next minute, and Vicki raised the camera again when Mr. Black Leather reappeared, hustled out of the lot, and to the Navigator, knocking snow off his shoes before he climbed inside. The Navigator backed out the way it had come, and Vicki raised the camera to see if she could shoot his plate number. When the Navigator turned at the top of the street, she tried to catch a glimpse, but it was too far away.

"Rats!" Vicki said, and Reheema's only response was to start the engine of the Sunbird, which struggled to life.

Half an hour later, the women sat parked in a space on Aspinall Street down from Jamal Browning's house, and they were on their second girl stakeout. Unlike Cater, there was no activity on Aspinall; it was a static scene of a snow-covered city street. No one had answered the row house door when Mr. Black Leather went inside, and there were no comings or goings for Reheema not to identify people. Vicki had taken all the pictures she needed and none of them mattered. In short, she was beginning to doubt the viability of Phase II.

"Cheeto?" Vicki offered, discouraged, pointing the fragrant end of the bag to Reheema. "It's lunch. And dinner."

Reheema didn't say anything.

"You're not *feelin'* the Cheetos?"

Reheema didn't smile.

"You didn't want the Doritos either. You off carbs, too?"

"No, just food that glows in the dark."

"Seems unduly restrictive." Vicki brushed orange dust off the front of her parka. She had consumed one 64-ounce Wawa coffee, and six hundred thousand calories. The Sunbird reeked of Cigar-Smoke-in-a-Can and her Master Plan sucked. Vicki scanned the cars parked in front of the house, but they were covered with snow mounded like sugar frosting. "Wonder which car is Browning's. They use the crappy ones for work, right? So which is the crappiest?"

"Ours."

Vicki eyed Browning's row house, her frustration intensifying. "This isn't going well, none of it. You know, I feel like your neighborhood is right on the brink of something. Like it could go either way, up or down, depending on what happens on Cater. You know what I mean?"

Reheema didn't say anything.

"The crack dealers get established in the hole, making addicts, then they buy a house and sell crack in it, making more crack addicts, and there goes a perfectly fine neighborhood, with law-abiding people and Christmas wreaths. And if that happens all over the city, pretty soon the city is lost. And city after city, it happens all over."

Reheema still didn't reply.

"That's why I want to shut them down, get them behind bars. Not only because of Morty and your mother, but because we can actually save your neighborhood."

"It's not my neighborhood," Reheema said, finally. "You keep saying Devil's Corner is my neighborhood, and it's not. I told you, I'm only living there until I sell."

"It's my dad's old neighborhood."

"Oh, I get it. *That's* why you care." Reheema snorted. "You're doing it for your daddy. To get Daddy's approval."

"No. He hated it there."

Reheema faced Vicki, her sunglasses masking her eyes. "Then why do you care?"

"Why don't you?" Vicki asked, glad for some reason that she was wearing sunglasses, too. Suddenly, something caught her attention at Browning's house.

The front door was opening. She grabbed the camera and snapped a photo as a man emerged. But it wasn't Mr. Black Leather, it was Eagles Coat. "Here's the other go-between. So they take turns. Alternate, like last time."

"So there's two on a shift," Reheema said, from behind the binoculars. "And two shifts a day, maybe three. I don't see anybody at the door."

"Me, neither." Vicki took a photo anyway, then lowered the camera and watched Eagles Coat walk to the Navigator, get in, pull out of the space, and take off. This time she got a clear shot of the license plate and lowered the camera. She knew cops who could run the plate for her, and maybe Dan would have an idea. Then she realized she'd gone the whole day without thinking about him; she'd even left her phone turned off. She was in Married Man Rehab.

Reheema twisted on the ignition, but Vicki raised a palm.

"Don't follow him. We know where he's going. Probably back to Cater, if the pattern is the same, right?"

"Probably."

"So he's just the runner, he brings the crack back and forth." Vicki was thinking out loud, which was okay to do in front of someone who barely liked you, and vice versa. "He's not the one we really want."

"What do you mean?"

"This is Jamal Browning's house, where he brings the stuff and bags it for sale. Odds are he doesn't live here, right? You tell me, you're the bad-guy expert." Vicki thought back to what she knew about the crack trade. "I mean, I know that most drug dealers have a separate car for business. Do they have more than one address, too?"

"Yeah. Browning won't live here. This is where he does his business."

"That's what I thought." Vicki flashed on the unopened bills of Jackson's. "And where would he keep his supply? Here?"

"Probably."

"Not at his house."

"Not usually. The idea is to keep that clean."

"And he'd keep some at a stash house, like his girlfriend's. Shayla Jackson." Vicki couldn't put the memory of the murdered Jackson out of her mind. Or Morty. "I want to get to Browning, not his delivery boy. I want to understand this whole organization, then I can bring it down."

"You serious?" Reheema slid off her sunglasses, her gaze dead even. "This could be big, an operation this size, this much money, two guys on each shift, three shifts. Plus two lookouts on three shifts, and the dealer, three of them twenty-four/seven?" She rattled it off like the business student she used to be. "Probably got three cooks and coupla baggers. And an army of young 'uns like the ones you ran into, Jay and Teeg. Helpers. Runners. Gofers. That's a lotta personnel, and this might not be Browning's only operation."

Okay, I knew that. "Then that's all on the Master Plan."

"Browning might even be a connect."

"Meaning the one who deals weight?" Vicki asked, but it wasn't a question. The answer was the bricks in Jackson's house. "He might be. If he is, he's going down."

"Why? He's not the one who killed your partner. You know who killed your partner, those kids did."

"That's right, but they were just kids. Pawns." Vicki thought a minute. "It's all of a piece. I'm gonna find and indict those kids, but that won't go far enough. This month it's Morty, but next month it'll be another agent, or a cop, or an AUSA. This has to stop."

Reheema smiled crookedly. "What got into you?"

"It's time to change things, to get things right. I'm tired of the way things are. And I'm tired of eating Cheetos and crushing on the wrong guy." Vicki sensed there was a connection, but she had no idea what it was. She pointed at Browning's house. "Either Browning's in that house and he's got to come out. Or he's coming here. Or he's not in there at all and he won't be coming anytime soon."

"Somebody's in there."

"So let's see who comes out, and see if he looks like Browning, the guy in the photo on Shayla Jackson's dresser. If it's him, wherever he goes, we follow him." Vicki liked it the more she thought about it. "We don't take any unnecessary chances. We just take a little ride and a few pictures. No big deal."

"We got the car for it." Reheema laughed, her features relaxing into a beautiful smile, for the first time since they'd met.

"So, you wanna?"

"Why not?" Reheema settled back into the driver's seat, facing the house.

"Goody." Vicki did the same, newly content in the passenger seat, and after a minute, Reheema asked:

"So, who's the wrong guy?"

TWENTY-EIGHT

"GO!" VICKI COULDN'T HELP SHOUTING. IT was almost midnight and there was finally activity at Browning's house. The front door opened, barely visible in the streetlight, and two men emerged, mere shadow figures.

"Not yet. I'll start the engine after they're in their car. Then they won't hear it."

"Of course. Right. Good thinking. That's what I meant, too."

"Calm down, girl." Reheema laughed softly

"I can't." Vicki fumbled to find the camera, shivering with cold and excitement, as the two men walked down the steps in front of the row house. It was impossible to tell if either of them was Browning. "Damn!"

"Don't take a picture."

"I won't use the flash." Vicki disabled the flash and used the telephoto to see the men more clearly. It was absurd in the dark, but she took three photos anyway.

They were both about average height and wore thick dark coats and dark knit caps, pulled low over their foreheads. "What is it with the knit caps?"

"Another black culture question? It's cold out."

"Damn it to hell! I can't see their faces." Vicki still couldn't tell if either was Browning and she gave up trying, for now. The two men walked close together, and she could tell they were talking because little clouds puffed from their mouths. It had to be twenty degrees outside and ten in the Sunbird. Circulation to her extremities had stopped four thousand Doritos ago. Reheema turned on the ignition as the two men walked to a snow-covered car, three down from the row house. The two men straight-armed snow off the car, clearing the hood and roof in one swoop.

"They'll never get it out. Look at the wheels." Reheema pointed at the car, and Vicki took pictures as the one man cleared a cake of snow from the back window with his arm and shook the powder off, and the other pounded the car door to break ice on the lock and get the key inside. She laughed behind her camera.

"It's not easy being a drug dealer."

"Maybe we should help 'em out." Reheema smiled.

"The car's a white Neon, same one as the other day." The women watched with amusement as the men struggled for fifteen minutes, then went back inside the house and came back out with a Back-Saver snow shovel, a blanket, and two cans of beer. "Drug dealers care about their backs, too."

"Nobody wants back trouble."

"So the maroon Navigator is Browning's good car."

"Yeah. He lends the go-between the four-wheel drive to get down Cater."

"He has to take the chance, because of the snow. When it clears up, he won't. He can't risk the car being spotted."

Vicki raised the camera and took a picture of one of the dealers shoving a blanket under the car tires and digging them out, while the other slid into the driver's seat and hit the gas. "Tell you which one I think is Browning, if it is Browning."

"The driver."

"Right." Vicki laughed. "I still can't tell if it's Browning for sure."

"So let's follow him anyway. We got nothin' better to do." Reheema sat up, and after ten more minutes of struggling, the dealers had freed the Neon. She leaned forward in her seat and rested her hand on the ignition key. "Okay, good to go."

"Finally!" Vicki said, and when the Neon took off, Reheema started the engine and so did they, following from a safe distance and at lawful speed. There was enough traffic to provide the Sunbird great cover, especially since it was dark and nondescript, and Vicki was able to take as many pictures of the Neon's license plate as she wanted, though one would have sufficed. She felt her adrenaline ebb away. "Not quite the high-speed chase I imagined."

"These guys don't want to get picked up for anything. This'll be the safest ride you ever took. Sit back and relax."

So Vicki did, but when she looked over, Reheema's mouth was tense.

"Home, sweet home," Vicki said, when the Sunbird pulled up at the end of the block. They had been driving for an hour and had ended up in one of the middle-class residential neighborhoods in the city, Overbrook Hills. The brick row houses here were semidetached, sitting together in pairs, like happy couples. Each double house had a front yard, bisected by a cyclone fence and dotted with children's bikes and plastic play-houses, padlocked to the fences.

"We don't know if this is home or his supplier's," Reheema said.

"It doesn't look like a drug supplier's house."

"Tells you nothin'."

"It's the end of the day. Browning has to get tired sometime, doesn't he? I'm gonna say this isn't his sup-plier's, it's his house."

"How you know he hasn't been sleepin' all day? When do you think he makes his pickups, in broad day-light?" Reheema's mouth formed a grim line, and her eyes glittered in the dark interior. "If they both get out of the car, it's the supplier."

Vicki nodded. Reheema was right. They were mak-ing assumptions, but reasonable ones. They both leaned forward as the Neon's doors opened and the two men got out. Vicki took pictures of the driver, al-beit too dark and too far away, as he hurried from the car and toward the row house. The streetlights were brighter here, but the man's features remained impos-sible to discern, so she still didn't know if he was Browning. The passenger went around to the driver's side of the car, got inside, and drove off. Vicki lowered the camera. "So if it's Browning, it's his house."

"How you know the one got dropped off is Brown-ing? You didn't recognize him. We got two players."

Vicki sighed. She was getting tired, and ATF legwork was harder than she'd thought. "Our theory was that the driver was Browning, or the boss, and this confirms it. I say, the boss gets dropped off."

"I agree, but we need to cover all bases." Reheema started the ignition.

"We're leaving? I wanted to get another picture."

"Get it another time. We know where he lives."

Vicki took a final picture as the Sunbird took off and snagged a close-up of the back of Browning's knit cap, where a shiny silver shield caught the light. She recognized it in the telephoto. "He wears a Raiders cap."

"Everybody likes football," Reheema said, and hit the gas.

Half an hour later they were in a lesser neighborhood closer to the city, with attached brick row houses in various stages of disrepair. The Sunbird followed as the Neon drove around, evidently hunting for a parking space. Huge piles of plowed snow sat at the corners of the block and cut down on the number of available spaces.

Vicki said, "The only thing more boring than watching a drug dealer dig a car out is watching him find a parking space."

"A day in the life."

"I'll have the same problem when I go home," Vicki said.

"No, you won't. You can't drive this crate, remember?"

"Oh. Sorry."

"No sweat. I'll drop you off. I'm a night owl." Reheema turned the car to the right, lingering almost a full block behind the Neon, and Vicki realized that one of them would be going home to a very cold house tonight.

"Reheema, you don't have heat in your house, do you?"

"I got a coupla blankets."

"You want to come over my house, to sleep? I have a pull-out couch."

"Like a pajama party?"

Vicki smiled. "We don't have to do our nails or anything."

Reheema was silent a minute. "Nah."

"You sure?"

"Wait. Here he goes." Reheema slowed the Sunbird to a stop as the Neon finally found a space, when another car pulled out.

"It's almost two. Doesn't anybody sleep in this neighborhood?"

Reheema didn't answer, and Vicki sensed she had withdrawn again. It was the invitation that did it, somehow. They watched as the second man got out of the car, hustled to one of the houses, and went inside.

"So that's where Number Two lives," Vicki said.

"Right."

"Can we find it again? I'm not even sure where we are."

"I can." Reheema started the engine. "Let's get you home, sleepyhead."

"Thanks." Vicki felt a twinge. "You sure you don't wanna—"

"No. Thanks." Reheema kept her eyes straight ahead and they drove in silence to the expressway, which was the last thing Vicki remembered before they pulled up in front of her house and Reheema was jostling her shoulder, waking her up, saying, "You're home."

"Oh. Sorry." Vicki straightened in the car seat stiffly,

stretching and vaguely bewildered. "How did you know where I live?"

"Got it from information, on your cell. I don't have my own yet." Reheema handed Vicki her own phone. "Soon as I turned it on, though, it started ringing and it's been ringing off and on all night."

"I slept through it?" Vicki held the phone and reached down for her backpack, and Reheema laughed.

"You woulda slept through anything."

"Sorry." Vicki felt off balance. The Sunbird clock read 3:30. Her street was quiet, still, and frigid. She grabbed her purse, and her phone beeped, signaling she had voicemail. A tiny electric envelope appeared on the screen. "There's a text message, too."

"That'd be the wrong guy."

"I know," Vicki said, with a tired smile. She reached for the door handle.

"Take my advice and leave him be." Reheema nodded. "No married man should be callin' any woman other than his *wife* this time of night."

"I started getting over him, today." Vicki meant it. "Nothing's ever going to happen with him. It's time to let him go, for good."

"Right."

Still. "He's a friend, maybe he's worried about me. I don't usually keep the phone off all day."

"Don't be stupid. That man's a *dog*."

Yikes. "Thanks for everything," Vicki said, and got out of the car.

"Be back at eight in the morning."

"Okay," Vicki called back softly, so as not to wake the neighbors, and trundled up the front walk, dripping backpacks, purses, and cameras. She'd check the messages when she got inside, not in front of Reheema, who was waiting out front with the Sunbird idling. Surprising. Vicki let herself in and waved from the front door, and the Sunbird took off.

Once inside, Vicki dropped her stuff on the floor, hit the light switch, and checked her text message, which was from Dan.

NEED TO C U TONITE. CALL MY CELL

"No," Vicki said aloud. "Fool me once, fool me twice." She wasn't about to call him again and catch him in bed with Mariella, and she doubted he'd meant her to call him this late anyway. She double-bolted the front door, turned off the living room light, and went upstairs with the cell phone, but the bedroom phone started ringing almost the moment she hit the landing, a jarring sound in the still house. She went down the hall and picked it up on the third ring. It was Dan.

"You home? Where were you?" Dan sounded stricken, not angry. "I was worried out of my mind! Or were you with that guy?"

"What guy?"

"The guy from the wake."

Delaney. "Of course not."

"Then can I come over?"

"*Now?* It's after three!"

"Vick, please. I wanna come over." Dan's words came out in a rush. "See you in five."

TWENTY-NINE

IT WAS A REVERSE OF THEIR USUAL SITUA-
tion, with Dan sitting at her kitchen table, unusually
calm for the situation, and Vicki pouring them both a
half glass of cold Chardonnay, left over from the other
night. His eyes looked a washed-out blue, with anxious
circles underneath, and his mouth formed a slash of
resignation. He wore khaki pants and a blue-plaid flannel shirt, put on so hastily it was buttoned wrong.

"Drink up." Vicki brought Dan's glass to the table,
set it down in front of him, and took her customary seat
opposite. "Now, begin at the beginning."

"Mariella's been having an affair with another doc, a
big-time plastic surgeon, an older guy, in Cherry Hill."
Dan's voice remained even, and he took a drink of
wine. "She's divorcing me to marry him. She's been
cheating on me for three years. We've only been married four."

Vicki sipped her wine, for something to do. She was

shocked and sympathetic, hurt and confused, all at the same time. "How did you find this out?"

"I'll tell it in chronological order, to make it easy. This morning, she served the papers on me at work. Can you believe that? Right at work?" Dan shook his head. "I'm in a meeting with Bale, and they get me out and say Louie's in reception for me. You know, Louie the process server?"

"The process server we use?"

"Mariella, or her lawyer, musta hired the same outfit. What a coincidence, I know." Dan shook his head in amazement. "So here's Louie, serving papers on *me*. I open them up and they're my own divorce papers! So, obviously, I think it's *a joke*. One of Bale's pranks, you follow?"

"Oh, God." Vicki's mouth fell open.

"Wait, this is when it gets good. So I go back to the meeting, I tell Bale, you dumbass, I wasn't born yesterday, to fall for this one. He tells me it's no joke and he's lookin' at me like 'you poor slob.'" Dan kept shaking his head. "And I mean, he's not kidding, and it's *no joke*."

"Oh no." Vicki cringed, humiliated for Dan. No wonder he'd been calling her all afternoon. His world had exploded today. Her heart went out to him.

"After I get the papers, I call Mariella on her cell, and she doesn't answer. I go to the hospital because she told me she's on call, but it turns out that my bride hasn't been on call for two days." Dan paused, significantly. "Then I go home to see if she's there, and the house is cleaned out! Cleaned *out!*"

"*What?*"

"The whole house is empty." Dan's eyes widened, and he smiled, incredulous. "Everything is gone, every stick of furniture, everything but my clothes. The old lady next door told me Mariella had the moving van there an hour after I left for work. She even took Zoe."

"The cat?" Vicki couldn't believe it. "You love that cat!"

"I know, and she doesn't even like the cat! She didn't even take her meds."

"Whose meds?" Vicki was confused.

"Zoe's. She needs atenolol for a heart murmur, but Mariella didn't take the medicine with her. She doesn't even know the cat needs medicine, half a tab, every morning." Dan shook his head. "I must sound so friggin' *stupid*. God, I mean, it's a cat, suck it up!"

"You don't sound stupid."

"Or gay. So *gay*." Dan raked fingers through his hair, already out of place.

"No, you don't. Then what happened? How did you find out?"

"Okay, so, at home, taped to the living room mirror, is a note that says call her at this number I never heard of, in the 609 area code. I do. She answers the phone and tells me that it's over, the marriage is over." Dan waved at the papers on the table. "That I better sign the property agreement. That she's in love with this other doc, who's *Brazilian*. He's forty-five or something. He's leaving his wife and two kids, and she's leaving me."

Vicki winced.

"Oh yeah, and then she says, 'Have your lawyer call my lawyer. Good-bye.'"

Vick felt stunned. She couldn't imagine it.

"That's when I realized, *that's* why she accused me of cheating on her!" Dan's eyes flashed with sudden anger. "You know, that fight the other day, the big one I told you about?"

"Yes."

"*That's* why she accused me, to hide the fact that *she's* been cheating, all along. To throw me off. The best defense is a good offense." Dan smiled ruefully. "How cold *is* she?"

"Wow." *I always knew that.*

"So I spent all this past year, since you and I have known each other and done *nothing wrong*, being so careful about her feelings, when, the whole time, she was cheating on *me*! And accusing *me* of cheating! Ha!" Dan smiled. "Diabolical, isn't she? She's an evil genius!"

Vicki couldn't smile. "On the other hand, maybe she really thought it, since she was doing it. People do project themselves onto others, the way liars always think people are lying."

"No, it was a scam and it worked." Dan curled his upper lip, where reddish stubble sprouted. "I never suspected her of having an affair. I thought she was working hard, to become a surgeon. I knew what that job took, and I figured she's paying her dues, like you are. A woman in a man's world. I just got suckered."

Aw. "That's awful!"

"I tell you, what's awful is being lied to, all that time. I don't like thinking that all those calls she got, emergency calls, weren't really from work. That, I don't like. I was stupid. Blind."

"No, you trusted her." Vicki remembered one of those emergency calls herself. They were in a restaurant and Mariella took a cell phone call, then left the dinner. "You can't question somebody when she leaves to save a life."

"Exactly." Dan exhaled and leaned back in his chair,

his manner surprisingly accepting. "So, my marriage is over, but it's weird, I'm not even that upset. I don't even feel sad, not about the marriage ending. I didn't even cry."

Vicki eyed him with doubt, and Dan read her mind.

"Really, Vick, believe me, I know it's okay to cry. I know I'm supposed to cry. But I don't feel like crying."

"Are you in denial?"

"No, I'm in reality."

"But you loved her, didn't you?" *Say no.*

"I don't think I did, really. It wasn't a very good marriage." Dan shrugged. "Funny. After she told me, I went to the gym, but there was no game that late, so I took foul shots until they closed. Then I went home to my completely empty house and took a good, long shower. I think I *sweated* that woman out." Dan smiled. "And I dried myself off with toilet paper, because she took all the towels."

Vicki laughed. "Did that *work*?"

"Yes, if you like white balls stuck in your leg hair."

"That's *so* hot."

Dan smiled. "Bale said there's like starter marriages, practice marriages. He thinks that's what this was."

"Bale's been married three times."

"He's still practicing," Dan shot back, and they both laughed. Then he grew serious. "So that's that. She can have the stupid furniture. I'll sign the agreement, which gives her half our money, and it will be over and done with."

Vicki frowned, sipping her wine. "But didn't you earn most of it? I mean, what does she make, as an intern?"

"What's the difference?" Dan paused, as if waiting for an answer, but Vicki didn't have one. "She can have it. I don't want to fight, I want to move on. We'll sell the house and split the proceeds."

"Don't you want to talk to a lawyer first?"

"No, I am a lawyer. But I want Zoe back. A man needs his kitty cat." Dan got up with his full glass and took it to the sink, and Vicki rose.

"You don't like the wine?"

"It's fine, I've had enough. I'm going to be a good boy and wash my glass."

"Let me." Vicki came up behind him. "You shouldn't have to do dishes on a night like this."

"Why not? I always do." Dan flipped on the hot water and regulated it with care. "I always stand at this sink, just like this, with you hovering at my right shoulder, yakking away while I wash dishes."

Vicki smiled. "I wash, sometimes."

"Sometimes you do, but mostly, it's me. Cooking. Making coffee. I *am* completely gay."

Vicki laughed. "You're just a good friend."

"I'm your *best* friend, am I not?"

"Actually, you are." Vicki smiled, feeling a rush of warmth. It was the wine, partly. And partly not.

Dan turned from the sink, his blue eyes frank and direct. "And you are mine."

Vicki nodded, and a silence fell between them.

Dan turned off the water, set the wineglass upside down in the sink, and then looked at her again. "And *that*, my dear, is why I'm not going to fight over the china. Because Mariella was right about one thing."

"What?"

"I *was* in love with somebody else, all along."

Gulp. "Really?"

"Really. I share everything with this woman.

Chicken dinners and jury closings and funny e-mails on the BlackBerry. And the amazing thing is, I feel like she's with me all the time, even when she isn't. Wherever she is, and wherever I am, I am connected, profoundly *connected*, to her."

Vicki's heart thumped. All of a sudden her organs were very noisy.

"I never had an affair with her, but to be honest, I wanted to." Dan's voice softened. "I never touched her that way, but I imagined her touch. I've never seen her without clothes on, but I know exactly what her body looks like, naked. And I've made love to her so many times, in my head, that I can't count them all."

Vick felt strangely like she was going to cry. *I sure hope this girl is me.*

"I told you, and I realized that night, when I thought that I might lose you, that you are my best friend. Remember that night?"

Vicki nodded. There were tears in her eyes. She had wanted to hear what he was going to say for so long, it somehow hurt to hear it now, as if its sweetness were too much.

"Well, you are my best friend. And so, I love you." Then Dan leaned over slowly and kissed her, gently, and she kissed him back, just as gently, until she sensed his hips shift closer to hers and felt his tongue flicker just inside her mouth. In the next instant, his arms closed strong around her, and Vicki breathed in the hard soap scent on his scratchy cheek.

But then something made her heart pull back. "Is this a good idea?" she asked, worried, and Dan smiled softly, holding her in his arms.

"Do you love me?"

"Yes," Vicki answered, because she did, and she had, for so long.

"Then it's a *very* good idea." Dan grinned.

"But is this a rebound?"

"No, my rebounding sucks. This is love."

Vicki smiled. "And it's really happening?"

"If you ever shut up, it is."

Vicki laughed, and Dan laughed, too, and the laughter ended with a happy kiss, and then another, and next a deeper one, which was joyful in a different way, more serious. And the serious kissing didn't stop when the touching began, or when his flannel shirt came off and then her heavy fisherman's sweater and her white turtleneck and next her old Harvard T-shirt and eventually her pink-waffle thermal undershirt, which was when Dan started laughing, mystified.

"Vick, *what* were you dressed for?"

Oops. "Sledding, with the kids across the street."

Dan kissed her again, then his mouth made a path down her neck to her chest, and he reached around and unfastened her bra, slipping the silky straps from her shoulders, taking her fullness into his mouth. Warmth surged through her, leaving her weak, and Vicki arched her back involuntarily, giving herself to him, loving the feel of his mouth on her skin and his hands everywhere on her body, and in the next minute, she heard herself whisper.

"Let's go upstairs."

Vicki awoke to knocking on the front door and cracked an eye at the alarm clock. The red numbers glowed 8:15. She blinked against the noise until her brain started to function.

It's Reheema. I am so busted.

She moved aside the covers quietly enough not to wake Dan, climbed out of bed, and hurried for the bathroom. She had no time for a shower, and she grabbed her pink bathrobe and wrapped herself in it on the run. Dan remained fast asleep on the far side of the bed, his head buried sideways in the pillow, his strawberry hair a lovely rumple.

Dan Malloy is in my bed. Yippee!

Vicki ran downstairs and flung open her front door into the frosty air and an unusually cheerful Reheema Bristow. Reheema's eyes were darkly bright and her smile broad, and she wore her customary knit cap, pea coat, jeans, and Timberlands. In her hand was a tall pink-and-orange Dunkin' Donuts coffee covered with a plastic lid.

"Yo, girl." Reheema offered the coffee. "You look like you need this."

"Jeez, thanks," Vicki said, in a low tone, so Dan didn't wake up. She accepted the coffee and pulled her robe around her, feeling guilty. "I'm really sorry, I'm running a little late."

"S'all right." Reheema stepped inside the living room, looking around. "Nice place."

"Thanks," Vicki said softly.

"Why are you whispering?"

"I'm not whispering," Vicki whispered.

"You are, too," Reheema said, then her eyes narrowed to disapproving slits. "Oh no, you didn't."

"I'll explain later. Follow me." Vicki signaled her out of the room, past the dining room and into the kitchen, then she set the coffee down and started digging for her stakeout outfit among the clothes heaped on the floor.

"In the kitchen?" Reheema's tone sounded admiring, if surprised. "You did it in the *kitchen?* Damn!"

"Turn away, I'm embarrassed," Vicki said, and when Reheema turned away, she dropped the bathrobe and yanked on her jeans and panties.

"*Embarrassed?* You weren't *embarrassed* last night, when you were doin' it on the damn *floor.*" Street Reheema had returned and she was having a good laugh. "You weren't *embarrassed,* you were *bare-assed.*"

"Very funny." Vicki slid into her bra, thermal underwear, T-shirt, turtleneck, fisherman's sweater, and then two pairs of white thermal socks, one of which was suspiciously large.

"You *had* the *man* in the *kitchen?*"

"Wait here, please." Vicki ran past Reheema in stocking feet, out of the dining room, and up the stairs. She didn't want Dan to know what she was up to today. She'd rather get busted by Reheema than him. She reached the bedroom, slid on the hardwood floor in her soft socks, and hurried around to the far side of the bed, where Dan was just waking up, muzzy and rubbing an eye with a balled fist.

"Vick?"

"Baby." Vicki leaned over and gave him a quick kiss on the cheek, deliciously stubbled. "Stay asleep. The house is yours. The door locks when you leave. Take care of yourself today. I have to go."

"What? Where?" Dan lifted his head and opened his eyes, in pale blue confusion. His breath was just as bad as hers, which was the only lucky thing that had happened so far this morning.

"I'll call you later. Go back to sleep. I love you." Vicki kissed him again, then straightened up, hurried out of the room, and ran down the stairs, where a gloating Reheema waited at the front door, holding the coffee and red snow boots.

"In the *kitchen*?" Reheema whispered, grinning, and Vicki ignored her while she grabbed the boots and stuck her feet inside, then snagged her purse and backpack on the fly, and opened the front door.

From upstairs, Dan called out, "I love you, too!"

Vicki hustled them both outside and closed the door before Reheema could say, out loud:

"Oh no, it's not like *that*!"

THIRTY

GRAY AND WHITE SNOW CLOUDS COVERED
the sky, and Vicki and Reheema circled the block on
which they thought Jamal Browning lived, in Overbrook Hills, scoping it out before settling into a parking space. In the daylight, his home was a well-kept, if
modest, semidetached row house, and its front yard,
bounded by a costly wrought-iron fence, contained a
snow-covered Little Tikes slide, a Razor scooter, and a
black BMX bike with training wheels.

"I don't see a padlock on that BMX bike," Vicki
said, snapping a picture through the telephoto.

"Ain't nobody takin' *that* child's toys." Reheema
pulled the Sunbird into a parking space down the street
from the house, next to a curbside pile of dirty snow
and in front of a side yard, so that no house was directly in front. The street was more residential than
Cater and Aspinall; the girls couldn't sit here forever,

undetected. Reheema cut the Sunbird's ignition. "This one's the best we can do."

"Maybe we drive around in a little while, keep moving." Vicki looked around. Schoolkids with Spider-Man lunch pails and backpacks were gathering on the far street corner with their watchful mothers, evidently waiting for a school bus. Vicki couldn't help but smile at the scene. "Aren't those kids so cute?"

Reheema sipped McDonald's coffee, where they'd stopped for bathroom and breakfast.

"They're so small, aren't they? I can't believe we were ever that little, but we were."

Reheema looked over. "You gonna be like this all damn day?"

"Like what?"

"You know, all happy and white."

Vicki laughed. "What?"

"You gotta get over this."

"Why? I can't help it." Vicki flashed on an instant replay from last night, erotic enough to keep her dreamy for hours. She'd had one hour's sleep and three orgasms, a superb ratio. "I love the man."

"Too soon for that."

"Are you kidding? It's been a year. One *year* of foreplay." Vicki had told Reheema about Mariella and Dan, which, for some reason, hadn't completely allayed her concerns. But Vicki was too happy, or too tired, to hear any objection. "He's a great guy. He's just great."

"Hard to get excited about a U.S. Attorney."

Assistant. "Not that hard."

"So." Reheema paused, with a sly smile. "*How* hard?"

"Hard enough, and that's all I'll say about that."

They both laughed and returned their attention to the house.

"I don't think he'll be comin' out anytime soon," Reheema said. "Drug dealers don't start the day early, but I didn't wanna miss him.".

"Sure. Makes sense." But Vicki was thinking about love, especially as applied to Reheema. "I was surprised that you weren't seeing anybody."

"Nobody special."

"Why not? I mean, you're beautiful, you're smart, and your body is phenomenal."

"Calm down."

Vicki smiled. "You look like a model, even in that dumb hat."

"Means a lot, coming from a girl who wears fireman boots."

They laughed again. They were more relaxed together today, if only a fraction. "So?" Vicki asked, after a minute.

"What?"

"Give."

"There used to be a man, now there isn't." Reheema looked over, her emotions opaque behind her sunglasses, though she was smiling. "And that's all I'll say about that."

Vicki turned as a school bus appeared and rolled to a stop at the corner, belching sooty smoke. The doors slapped open, and the kids piled on willy-nilly, collecting last-minute kisses and hugs. The bus pulled away from the waving mothers, and Vicki noticed the front door opening at the house. "Check it, Ree."

Reheema raised the binoculars to her sunglasses. "My mother used to call me Ree."

Oops. Vicki took a photo as a pretty young black woman left the house, tugging along an adorable little boy, who looked about four. That they were mother and son was undeniable; they had the same tall, thin build, same large, almost black eyes, and same short hair, cut natural. They even wore matching red Sixers jackets, the sight of which chased Vicki's love flashback away, replacing it with an awful memory of the night Morty had been killed. She took another picture, glad that the camera covered her face.

"Now we get to see which car is theirs." Reheema raised the binoculars. "I say the Lexus. What do you say?"

Morty. Vicki had lost her appetite for their guess-the-car game. She watched as the young mother stopped to light a cigarette, a purple mat tucked under her arm, then greeted the other mothers now scattering from the corner. Then she said good-bye and walked with the child to a gold Explorer, chirped the door unlocked, and they got inside.

"Losin' my touch." Reheema clucked. "Hell no, what's that under her arm? The purple roll? Tell me that's not a yoga mat!"

"It is." Vicki took a photo of the license plate as the gold Explorer pulled out of the space. "I don't think we should follow her. I think she's taking the kid to pre-school and I don't wanna miss our man."

"She's got herself a yoga mat? A *yoga mat*? She gonna smoke that cigarette in the damn yoga class?"

Vicki lowered the camera, and Reheema peered at her over the top of her sunglasses.

"You okay, Tinker Bell?"

No. "Are we getting closer to whoever killed my partner?"

"We're doing what we can do."

"Tell me we can get them."

"I can't do that. I can only tell you that we'll try."

Vicki blinked. "Fair enough."

Two hours later, a white Neon finally pulled around the corner, coming toward them, and both women saw it at the same instant.

"Driver's here!" Reheema said, sitting suddenly upright, and Vicki grabbed the camera, aimed it at the Neon's windshield, and shot quickly. It reflected the cloudy sky, but maybe they could get something off it on the computer. The women watched, tense, and a minute or two later, the front door to the house opened and a tall man emerged, with a black Adidas bag.

"It's him!" Vicki almost shouted, recognizing Browning's face through the telephoto. It was the same man as in the photo! "Reheema, do you recognize him?"

"No, never saw the man before."

"Rats!" Vicki fired five great shots of Browning's face, in close-up, as he hustled to the Neon, his Adidas bag swinging, then opened the passenger-side door and jumped inside.

"Get down!" Reheema said quickly, and they both ducked so their heads didn't show as the Neon drove past.

"Thought you said that was dumb," Vicki said, excited, and Reheema popped up and switched on the ignition.

"It's dumb when you do it, not when I do it." Reheema maneuvered the Sunbird quickly out of the space.

"Go!" Vicki said, needlessly, because they were already driving down the block, taking a right at the corner. "We gotta stay with him. We can't lose him."

"We won't lose him," Reheema said, bearing down. "I never lost a man I wanted to keep."

Later, after having followed the white Neon through noontime rush hour into the city, past buses and cop cars and snow plows and salt trucks, then finally out to South Philly, Vicki and Reheema sat parked at the drug dealer's first stop. A Toys "R" Us.

"I can't believe this!' Vicki said, edging up in her seat. Five minutes ago, Browning and his pal had left the Neon, grabbed one of the shopping carts, and wheeled it into the store. "What kind of drug dealer goes *shopping*? At Toys 'R' Us?"

"Prices are good." Reheema laughed. "Maybe he needs a board game."

"He's supposed to be a *drug dealer*!" Vicki fairly shouted, then caught herself before she cursed. She had been raised better than to use profanity. But not better than to have three orgasms. Her frustration boiled over. "Could this man's day be *more* boring?"

Reheema was laughing. "I don't know, the wife's at yoga class and he's at Toys 'R' Us, doin' the shoppin'. You ask me, that boy needs a marriage counselor. He's whipped."

"This would be funny if it weren't such a waste of time." Vicki sat watching the entrance. The Toys "R" Us anchored the huge strip mall, which drew customers from everywhere in the city. The parking lot, two city blocks long, was crowded with cars and minivans looking for spaces. Women and kids walked this way and that with strollers and shopping carts. Vicki sighed. "How will we ever learn something about Browning? His supplier, or even his connection to you?"

Reheema stopped laughing. "What do you think is the connection to me?"

"If you don't recognize Browning, I don't know. Unless he knows you and you don't know him."

"Only one way to find out." Reheema slipped off her sunglasses. "I'm goin' shoppin'."

"What do you mean?" Vicki felt panicky. This wasn't in the Master Plan or the New Master Plan. "What are you gonna do?"

"Walk by the man, see if he knows me, see if he says anything to me." Reheema opened the door, and a cold blast of air blew inside the car. "You're not the only one gettin' impatient here."

"I don't know." Vicki couldn't process it fast enough. "He might be dangerous."

"In a toy store?" Reheema climbed out of the driver's seat and shut the door.

"Wait, be careful," Vicki called after her, opening her passenger-side window, but Reheema was already striding away from the Sunbird, making a beeline for the Toys "R" Us entrance. She made a tall, dark silhouette with the knit cap, pea coat, and jeans, and in the clunky Timberlands looked almost like a man from the back, but for the sexy swing of her walk. She waded through the moms and kids, grabbed a shopping cart, and wheeled it inside the store. Vicki reached for the camera, to watch her better through the telephoto lens.

Rring! Rring! Vicki jumped at the sound. Her cell phone. She reached quickly into her backpack, resting on the Sunbird's blue shag, and pulled out the cell. The electronic display read DAN. Good and bad. She had to get it or he'd be suspicious. Also, she was crazy about him. She juggled the camera to flip the phone open.

"Dan, I'm crazy about you but I can't talk now."

"What are you wearing?"

"No time for that. I have to go."

"Listen, last night was—"

"The best night of my life, but I have to go." Vicki kept watching through the camera, in close-up.

"Hold on, I have a question. Did you take your clothes off the kitchen floor and wear them again?"

Uh. "No, I took them to the dry cleaners." Shoppers with their kids in hand moved in and out of the glass entrance doors of the Toys "R" Us. No Reheema.

"You dry-clean your jeans?"

"Sometimes, and I have to go."

"Where *are* you?"

"Shopping."

"Where?"

"Neiman Marcus."

"In the suburbs?" Dan *hmmm*ed. "But your car is still in the garage."

"A friend picked me up."

"I don't believe you, my sweet. What are you really up to?"

Busted. "Okay, it's a surprise. A surprise for you. Now tell me you're okay so I can hang up."

"I'm better than okay. I'm getting divorced."

"Already?" Vicki watched the store entrance through the camera. An old man in a walker went in, but no sign of Reheema.

"I signed the papers and messengered them to her lawyer, and she's agreed to give me Zoe. She's having *his maid* drop the cat off. Also, that meeting is today, at five, with the FBI and ATF, about Morty's investigation."

The meeting. Vicki had forgotten, with all that was going on. "I wish I could be there."

"I'll tell you what happens. I may get to go."

"Really?" Vicki eyed the Toys "R" Us entrance, distracted. Two little boys were having a tug-of-war with a new scooter. "Then you have to tell me everything."

"Of course. Be home after, okay?"

It had a nice ring. "Light a fire under 'em." Vicki figured it sounded like what she would say if she were at Neiman Marcus. "I have to go. Call you later. Bye."

She flipped the phone closed, set it down, and focused her attention on the store entrance, through the telephoto. Her heart was thumping again, but she didn't know if it was true love or true anxiety. If Browning knew Reheema, would he hurt her? Vicki put a hand on the door handle, tempted to go after her, but stopped herself. Vicki's picture had been all over the news, and she could be recognized, even in the sunglasses and Phillies hat. And Browning wouldn't hurt Reheema in a public place, would he? Still, if Reheema wasn't out of the store in five more minutes, Vicki was going in.

She kept her attention on the entrance, taking a few photos of the scene. A salesclerk in a blue apron collected shopping carts from the lot. A white work van slowed near the entrance, waiting for a parking space. A man and his wife, huddled together against the cold, entered the store with two kids, followed by a woman with three kids, holding hands in a daisy chain. And in the next minute, through the telephoto, Vicki recognized Reheema, mostly because of her distinctive walk.

"Yay!" Vicki yelled in the car, and then she couldn't

believe her eyes: Reheema was leaving the store with Browning!

What? Vicki kept her eye plastered to the camera and took a series of photos, in amazement. As they walked, Reheema was putting on her cap against the cold, smiling, and Browning was smiling, too, carrying a plastic bag of red-and-white Huggies. The two of them were talking like old friends, and on Browning's other side walked his driver, also carrying a bag of Huggies.

Reheema was not only safe, she had scored! Vicki didn't understand it, but shot another picture. Did Browning know Reheema or had she struck up a conversation with him inside the store? How did they get to be friends so fast? What the hell was going on? This wasn't in any Plan at all.

Suddenly Vicki heard an earsplitting *pop pop pop* from the store entrance. She blinked, uncomprehending. She knew that sound. It was unmistakable.

Gunfire.

THIRTY-ONE

"REHEEMA! RUN!" VICKI SCREAMED. SHE
dropped the camera, flung open the car door, and ran
for Reheema.

Pop pop pop! Reheema took off as if from a starter
pistol, sprinting in the heavy Timberlands, pounding
toward the Sunbird. Mothers screamed in terror, scoop-
ing crying toddlers into their arms. A little boy turned
toward the gunshots, covering his ears. Two little girls
fled in panic, their ponytails flying.

Pop pop pop came more gunfire, like a war zone.
Browning crumpled to his knees, his face hitting the
asphalt. A little boy near him was shot, trying to run
away. Browning's driver was cut down, dropping the
Huggies. A toddler fell beside her mother, the child's
pink snowsuit splashed hideously with red.

Pop pop pop! The salesclerk ran for his life but was
cut down. A mother was strafed and tripped, dropping
an infant. The white work van that had been idling

near the store entrance flew out of the parking lot, its tires squealing. Vicki couldn't read its license plate on the run.

"REHEEMA!" she screamed.

"Back to the car!" Reheema grabbed Vicki by the arm and together they ran back to the Sunbird and jumped inside. Police sirens blared nearby. In this busy part of town, help was already on the way.

"You okay?" Almost breathless, Vicki slammed the car door closed, grabbed her cell phone, and dialed 911. Men and women ran from the store to the victims, and one salesclerk came running out, shouting into a cell phone.

"I'm alive!" Reheema floored the gas pedal.

And they were outta there.

The Sunbird came finally to a stop at the first Irish pub off the expressway. By that time, the two women were finally breathing normally, wet-eyed and shaken as they sat side by side at the far end of a crappy wooden bar. The shellac on its wooden surface peeled like clear nail polish, and its stacks of cocktail napkins smelled strangely of Lysol. The place was empty except for two drunk guys who sat near the bartender at the other end of the bar. The TV overhead was on mute, but Britney Spears sang "Toxic" loud enough to make it almost a song.

Vicki stared stunned at the shot glass in front of her, which was full of amber fluid. "I never drink hard stuff."

Reheema sat slumped before her glass. "I don't drink."

"Then who ordered the shots?"

"You, or maybe me," Reheema answered, then picked up her glass. "Let's do it to it."

Vicki picked up her glass. "One, two, three." They downed their shots together, swallowed in unison, and set the shot glasses down at the exact same moment, with a restaurant-grade *clunk*. Vicki said, still stunned, "It didn't help, did it?"

"No. Nothing can." Reheema shook her head. "I have never seen anything like that in my life. And I've seen some terrible things."

Vicki nodded, her throat burning. "That was carnage. I mean, they shot everywhere. They didn't care who they hit. Little kids. Babies." She tried not to cry. She was too stunned to cry. She wanted to understand. "But they got who they were after. Browning."

"Looks that way."

"We should have stayed to help."

"They had it under control. The cops were on the way."

"So tell me what happened."

"You *saw* what happened." Reheema wiped her eyes, but Vicki needed to know the details.

"Tell me what happened inside the store, and we'll see if we can piece this thing together. I'm two minutes from going to the cops."

"Another round!" Reheema called to the bartender, who arrived after a minute, poured them both a shot, and wisely withdrew. She sighed, shaking her head. "Oh man. This is bad, real bad."

"Try to focus and tell me."

"Well, I walked by Browning twice, in the store. I had my hat and sunglasses off and made sure he saw my face. He looked me over both times, like I was a stranger. I don't think he knew me."

"You're sure?"

Reheema downed her second shot. "Yeah. He was in the diaper aisle, and he and the driver were joking. It sounded like he forgot which diapers he was supposed to buy, and I walked down the aisle. I was pretending I was buying some baby oil, and he asked me what size diapers do six-month-olds get." Reheema started rolling her empty shot glass on its end. "I knew that was crap, because it says it on the package."

"I wonder what baby he's buying for? The kid we saw was about four." Vicki tried to reason, despite the gunshots reverberating in her ears. "If there was a baby in that house, his wife, or whatever, wouldn't have left it alone to go to yoga."

"The man is a playa, a gangsta." Reheema's tone was weary. "He got kids everywhere."

"Okay. Right."

"He asked me about my kids." Reheema kept playing with her glass. "I said I didn't have any, I wanted the baby oil for my skin."

"Good save."

"Then he asked me my name and I said Marcia, and I asked him his and he said Jamal, and he said did I live around here, and I said no, I was in from D.C. for the day, visitin' my sister."

"You're a better liar than I am."

"My mother's daughter."

Ouch. Vicki felt a twinge of sympathy, and regret. "Look, maybe we should wait a little to talk about this. We're both upset, and you almost got—"

"I'm fine."

"You could have been killed."

"I wasn't." Reheema stop playing with her glass. "So, anyway, he and I, we kep' talking and the driver got the diapers, then Jamal said could he walk me out and I started to get worried, and I said I was gonna take the bus, and when we got outside he asked me what was my number and I was about to give him a fake one when the shooting started."

"That's it?"

"That's all."

Vicki eyed her second shot, untouched. "So what have we learned? One, Browning doesn't know you. Two, somebody wanted Browning dead and he got his wish. And three, the new bad guy drives a white van."

"Wait, look." Reheema pointed above the bar at the TV, and on the screen was a blue BREAKING NEWS banner.

"Can you turn that up?" Vicki called to the bartender, who reached up and increased the volume loud enough to overcome Britney. The TV screen switched to a scene of the parking lot, above a red caption that read TOYS "R" US MASSACRE. A pretty reporter came on in a red suit and stiff haircut, saying into a bubble microphone:

"Seven people were shot and killed, and fifteen more wounded, five critically, in what appeared to be a drive-by shooting this afternoon at about twelve-thirty, in front of the Toys 'R' Us store on Regon Avenue. The injured have been taken to area hospitals—"

Vicki could barely watch, sickened. *Seven dead. Browning. His driver. The salesclerk. The mother. The baby, the toddler, other children, who else?*

The reporter continued, "Police are on the lookout for a white Dodge van, 2003, which had a small American flag decal in the back left window, and was being driven without license plates. We realize there may be many such vans in the Delaware Valley area, but viewers who see a 2003 white Dodge van, with a flag in the rear window, are encouraged to call the police tip line or *Action News* at . . ."

Vicki's shoulders sagged. *Morty. Jackson. The baby.*

The TV screen switched to the next story, a warehouse fire, in the Northeast, and both women turned away. Reheema sighed. "So where were we?"

Vicki straightened up. "Now it's possible that Jay-Boy and Teeg, the kids who shot my partner and Jackson, don't work for Jamal Browning at all. I had thought they did and that the attack was against Shayla Jackson, because of you or your trial, and because Jackson and Browning were evidently breaking up." Vicki forced her brain to reason, despite the shock and the whisky. "But after this, and because Browning didn't know you, I think the real target was Browning, and he's being attacked by a rival gang."

Reheema nodded. "You mean, the teenage kids who shot your partner worked for the white van guy or his boss?"

"Yes."

"But why would they shoot the guy's girlfriend? 'Cause she was pregnant, to hurt him?" Reheema frowned, puzzled. "That man, Browning, he got enough kids already."

The fish-scale coke. Vicki made a judgment call and filled Reheema in, then concluded, "So the rival gang, if that's what they are, struck at Browning to steal his coke stash. They only killed Jackson because she was there, in the way."

"So it wasn't personal. Okay, I'm with you. Lotta business at stake." Reheema thought a minute. "Still doesn't say why your snitch set me up."

"No, it doesn't. That's an open question." Vicki made a mental note. "It must be a turf war."

"And we walked into the middle."

"Wonder if it's over Cater Street."

"There's a thousand Cater Streets in this city."

Vicki nodded. "At least we know it's directed at Browning."

"Oh, it's *directed*, all right." Reheema laughed, but it was hollow.

"The problem is that now we don't have anybody to follow back up the chain."

"Unless the white van supplies from the same place."

"Right."

"How likely is that?"

Reheema's eyes glittered under her cap. "Likely. It's the little guys that fight it out, block by block, brick by brick. The supplier doesn't care who moves his product."

"So we gotta find the white van."

"Us and *Action News*. And, oh yeah, the cops. A white work van with an American flag? No license plate? No sweat."

"Hold on, I have an idea," Vicki said, her thoughts racing ahead. "Let's go."

Vicki sat in front of her desktop computer at home, wolfing down a Big Mac while Reheema ate a McDonald's shaker of salad over her shoulder, watching the screen.

"Okay, they're loaded," Vicki said, snapping in the photo card and clicking to slide show, and they both sat back and watched. The pictures, downloaded from her digital camera, started last night in the dark and played out like a short film with a miserably unhappy ending. A shot appeared of Browning and his driver digging the car out, almost pitch black, then bright shots of Browning's wife and son coming out of the house, getting in the car, and the photos continued all the way to the Toys "R" Us, with Reheema going in and out, then finally appearing with Browning, slipping on her cap and smiling at him.

Vicki clicked and pointed. "There, in the right corner. The front bumper of the white van."

"Got it."

"I thought it was waiting for a space. What an idiot."

"Keep going."

Vicki double-clicked and the slide show restarted, each picture dissolving into the next, in that corny way the software dictated, horribly inappropriate in context. The scene changed to a laughing Browning and Reheema, in close-up, cutting out the white van, and then the last shot caught the salesclerk going down, before Vicki had dropped the camera in horror.

"Sweet Jesus," Reheema said, and Vicki put down her sandwich, her stomach upset.

"Somebody has to stop these guys. This is just lawlessness. They're turning the city into the wild, wild West. No order, no justice. Only money and murder." It gave Vicki a second wind. She clicked through the slide show, searching. She had taken so many pictures, one had to have the driver of the white van. The van had been pointing out of the lot, ready to make a quick getaway, and the driver's side had been facing Vicki, full on. She'd been only half a lot away. She had to have him on film. She moved the mouse to the right corner of the photo, then clicked. The front end of the white van peeked onto the corner of the frame.

"Yes!" they both said.

"Gotcha, you animal." Vicki eyed a perfect shot of the driver's window, but it was small and dark.

"Can you make it bigger?"

"Watch and be amazed." Vicki moved the mouse to the toolbar and clicked away. Ten clicks later, her large Gateway monitor had a pixelated photo of the driver, dim but visible.

"All right, girl!"

"Thank you, thank you." Vicki scrutinized her hand-iwork. The photo was dim and too grainy to be perfect, but the features of the driver were clearly visible, and he was young and white.

"Ha!" Reheema snorted. "Ice, ice, baby."

"How does a white boy take over the trade on Cater, street level?"

"He doesn't show his face, that's how. He's the man who talks to the man. He has his boys do his dirty work." Reheema set down her salad.

The driver looked about twenty-five, his face young and unlined, with large, light eyes, maybe blue or hazel. His hair was shaved into a fade of a light hair, its color impossible to ascertain in this light. Next to him in the seat sat a shadow. Vicki couldn't make out the features of his accomplice.

"Now what do we do?"

"First thing, we get the photo to the cops. Philly, ATF, FBI, the whole alphabet."

"Show our hand?"

"No, not if we don't have to. I still need my job. And I have another lead I want to follow up." Vicki paused. "If I e-mail this, they'll know where it came from."

"Then what?"

"We do it the old-fashioned way." Vicki checked her watch. Three o'clock. Then she remembered. "They're having a meeting today at five with all the brass, about Morty's investigation."

"Goody."

"Just so they get *started*," Vicki said, and they both smiled. She hit Print. "Maybe this actual photo of the *murderer* will help?"

"Least we can do." Reheema laughed. "So what's the old-fashioned way? Drop it off and run like hell?"

"Bingo." But Vicki was thinking about that meeting, and what would happen when Dan came home.

THIRTY-TWO

IT WAS COLD AND DARK BY THE TIME VICKI and Reheema had finished their mail run, delivering enlargements of the white van driver to receptionists at the U.S. Attorney's Office, the FBI, ATF, Philly Homicide, and the four major news stations. They completed the task in disguise, having Reheema drop off where Vicki would be recognized and vice versa. Vicki had considered taking the next step in the Former Master Plan, but she was exhausted and wanted to find out from Dan how the big meeting had gone. And the shooting had taken a toll on Reheema, who seemed exhausted and had reverted to being remote. After a side trip for some groceries for each of them, they pulled up in front of Vicki's house.

"You sure you don't want to come in?" Vicki asked. "I'm feeling very domestic. I could make you a quick dinner."

"How would you explain me to your boyfriend?"

"Oh, right. I forgot." Vicki wasn't used to coming home to anything but bills.

"I'm wiped out, anyway. I'm gonna go home and make myself a nice chef salad."

"Didn't you have that for lunch?"

"If it comes in a glass, it ain't a salad."

Vicki had noticed Reheema shopping with a sharp eye on prices at the Acme. "Can I ask what you're doing for money?"

"Using the same green as you."

"You can't have much, after being in the FDC so long." Vicki was choosing her words carefully, especially because she was responsible for putting Reheema there. "And you have to pay bills, get the utilities on. You need infrastructure, right?"

"I'm okay for a while. After we're done, I'm gonna get a job."

"Not at Bennye's."

"God, no."

"Can I lend you some money?"

"No, I'm fine." Reheema stiffened, and Vicki regretted it instantly.

"Okay, just let me know. See you tomorrow morning, later, like nine, after Dan goes to work?"

"Fine."

"I'll let you know anything I find out."

"Good." Reheema faced front, nodding.

"Bye." Vicki got out of the Sunbird, retrieved her groceries from the backseat, and closed the door with a final slam, feeling oddly as if she had lost something.

A friend.

Or her innocence.

*   *   *

Vicki opened her front door to a grinning Dan Malloy, standing on her front step in the frigid night, dripping calico cat, the animal's black-and-orange legs draped over his arm. "Well!"

"Zoe, we're home!"

Vicki laughed. "Come in, it's cold. How'd you get her here?"

"Cab. She loved it. She has caviar tastes." Dan stepped inside, then leaned over the cat and kissed Vicki, his mouth an intriguing mix of cold and warm. She kissed him back, then again, and then another time, before they parted.

"Wow." Vicki closed the front door.

"I agree."

"I could get used to this."

"You'll have to, until I get new furniture." Dan looked her over with a smile. "You know, as good as you look right now, you'd look better in bed."

"Thank you." Vicki had showered, which made her feel almost human again in fresh jeans, a pink cashmere sweater, and no sunglasses. "Come into the kitchen and see your surprise."

"I'm getting a surprise?"

"Of course." *Only because I'm so smooth.*

"Look around, Zoe." Dan set down his briefcase and cat, and followed Vicki into the dining room. "Does the surprise involve you naked?"

"No."

"In a nurse's outfit?"

"No."

"A nun's habit?"

"That's so wrong, Malloy." Vicki reached the kitchen, and in the middle of the floor sat a pink plas-

tic litter box, filled with gourmet litter and its own little scoop, resting casually against the side of the tray.
"Romantic, huh?"

"Terrific! Thank you!" Dan grinned, pulling her to
him and holding her close, and she could feel the cold
air clinging to the scratchy wool of his topcoat. "I
didn't know they sold litter boxes at Neiman Marcus."

Oops. "Uh, no, they don't. I didn't get the litter box
there. I got it from the Acme, where I got groceries for
dinner."

"Oh, nice." Dan released her to slide out of his topcoat and put it on the back of the kitchen chair. "What
am I making?"

"Hey, I'm making it. We're having filet mignon,
with onions and baked potatoes. It'll be ready in a
minute. I'm Martha Stewart, preincarceration."

"Funny, I don't smell anything."

D'oh! Vicki crossed to the oven and turned it on.
"Okay, so we won't be eating in a minute."

Dan smiled. "Doesn't matter. What'd you get at
Neiman Marcus?"

Eek. "Nothing. So what happened at the big meeting? Did you go?"

"Yes." Dan's expression changed, suddenly troubled.
"Did you see the news, Vick? The shooting at Toys 'R'
Us? Seven people killed, three of them kids, and they
say a fourth might not make it. It's disgusting."

"Horrible."

"They should hang that guy. And one was Jamal
Browning, shot dead."

No, really? "I heard that on TV. Jackson's
boyfriend. Incredible."

"Don't worry, they're gonna get the guy. They already ID'ed him."

"How?"

"You're not gonna believe this. At the end of the business day, somebody sent us a photo of the shooter." Dan reached excitedly inside his jacket pocket and pulled out the photo she'd taken. "Look."

Vicki looked at the photo as if she'd never seen it before, which wasn't easy. "Somebody sent this to us?" *And was she wearing Exxon sunglasses or Chanel?*

"Dropped it off at the office. FBI, ATF, everybody got a copy, like manna from heaven. The FBI thinks somebody from the neighborhood took it and they're too afraid of retaliation to come forward."

The FBI are geniuses. "Probably."

"I'd be afraid, too. What kind of man guns down kids in a Toys 'R' Us? They coulda hit Browning anywhere, if that's who they were after. It's true scum who does something like that."

Vicki nodded.

"Anyway, it's damn lucky they took the photo, though. The cops had no flash on the shooter. The Toys 'R' Us surveillance cameras were pointing at the wrong side of the truck, and the eyewitnesses were so freaked out, their descriptions were all over the place. Philly police couldn't even get a composite they had faith in. Then this came in."

Damn, I'm good. "So who is he and what are they doing about it?"

"His name's Bill Toner. He has a record of bush-league crack dealing and ag assault, in Kensington. Philly put an APB out on him, with his last known address." Dan eyed the photo. "Dude's ugly as sin. A cold, cold killer."

"So Toner killed Browning?" Vicki fake-mulled it over. "Do they know why?"

"Not yet." Dan shook his head. "Or at least they're not saying so in an open meeting, with Strauss there."

"Strauss was there? Was Bale?"

"Yep."

"The triumvirate." Vicki would have felt left out if she hadn't been doing something more important. *Like their jobs.*

"I missed you today." Dan smiled, set the photo on the table, and reached for her, drawing her close. He didn't feel so cold anymore, his chest warm and strong, and Vicki pressed herself against him, his loosened tie silky on her cheek. She felt guilty deceiving him, but if he knew what she'd been doing, he'd try to stop her. She accepted his embrace, and the real, solid comfort it afforded, after the awful afternoon.

"It looked horrible, on TV. These poor people, getting shot."

"I know, I saw it, too. These are real bad guys. Dangerous guys." Dan's voice softened, and Vicki felt the reverberation within his chest as he spoke. "Problem is, you shoulda seen this meeting. The Toys 'R' Us shooting threw a major wrench into the works. The mayor's on the phone, the city's in an uproar. Then the chamber of commerce starts screaming. Everybody's running around like a chicken and you could see it happen. It was like a tide shifting. I watched Morty go to the back burner."

"Why?" Vicki asked, stricken. "Browning's murder is related to Morty's. These things are of a piece, they have to be."

"Doesn't matter now." Dan frowned in disappointment, too. "Now it's about innocent people being killed while they shop, you can see that. Strauss has to shift priorities to the safety of shopping in the city, to babies and kids getting shot up on the evening news. You can't blame the man."

"But the CI was Browning's girlfriend and she got killed when his coke was stolen. Maybe somebody from the Toner crew, if not Toner himself, is trying to take over Browning's operation."

Dan nodded. "I'm not saying they won't follow up on that, but jurisdiction is still a live issue, unfortunately, and Toys 'R' Us is an emergency. The situation is acute, and we're in triage. The murder of an ATF agent and a druggy girlfriend in a stash house will not get the same attention as kids shot up when they're at a Toys 'R' Us. They're already pulling uniforms off the street."

No! "But Morty's life matters and so does hers. And what about her baby?" Vicki felt like the case was slipping away. "If you fix one, you fix the other, don't you see? They can't let Morty go!"

"Wait, there was one thing, hold on, I'll get it." Dan left the kitchen and returned with his briefcase, set it on the chair, and slid some papers out. "Look." He put the papers down on the kitchen table, next to the place setting.

Vicki came over. The papers were charts of first names and numbers in computer printing. The names ran down the left side of the chart, the numbers, ten digits, ran down the middle, and then after that was a second column of numbers. After a minute, she recognized the ten-digit numbers in the middle as phone numbers because they all began with 215, the area code for Philly. Vicki asked, "A list of phone calls?"

"Yes. It's called a Call Frequency Chart. It's fascinating. ATF developed the software program that generates it, for HIDTAs."

"HIDTAs?"

"High Intensity Drug Trafficking Areas. It's a task force within the agency, and ATF assigned the investigation of Morty's murder to them. They specialize in drug operations with an especially high level of violence."

Gulp. "And what does HIDTA do, exactly?"

"Investigate, tap, surveille, you know, get the info for search and arrest warrants, in the most dangerous cases." Dan returned to studying the charts. "HIDTA has developed its own program for investigations of cell phones. You see, dealers have to communicate with each other all the time, and they use Nextel phones or cell phones. It's very mechanical, the drug business."

Vicki had thought the same thing, when she and Reheema were following the dealers the past two days. It was almost primitive.

"HIDTA starts with a normal cell phone, one that's seized, let's say, during a search. They call that the 'known phone.' They analyze the data in it, like the directory, and figure out the phone numbers associated with each person called. You follow?"

"Yes."

"Then they subpoena the records for the known phone, over a long period of time, and they load all the information about the calls into the computer. The program they wrote generates a Call Frequency Chart. That is, it makes a record of how often the owner of the known phone calls certain numbers." Dan ran a finger-nail across the first line of the list. "This first page is a sample, and you can see the first name on this list is Lik, which they tell me is the nickname for Malik."

"Okay."

"Lik's number is this one, and the chart shows that the owner of this phone called Lik's number the most frequently of all other calls, in a month's time. The column on the far right is the number of times the owner of the phone called Lik in a month, which is 354. You can look down the chart at the first three people the owner called the most. Lik, Tay, and Two. See? He called them 354, 322, and 310 times, respectively."

Vicki did.

"Now, they tell me that drug dealers change cell phones all the time. They use 'burnout phones' or 'drop phones,' they call them. Let's say the owner of the phone, the bad guy, drops this phone. He throws it away to avoid the cops."

"Okay."

"The problem used to be that when the bad guy dis-carded a phone, all the investigation of his activity and calls were gone, and HIDTA would have to start over again. No more." Dan went to the next sheet of num-bers. "Now they can figure out which cell phone he picks up next, using this software."

"How?"

"Because, as a logical matter, he tends to call the same set of people he called before, at the same fre-quency. See this second chart? This new caller called Lik's number ten times that day. HIDTA does the same thing for the other people called, Tay and Two, and they do it over a long period of time, to enhance the reliability of their conclusion. The odds are that it's the same person making those calls, regardless of which phone he uses. Correct?"

"Correct."

"So then we can reason backward, and say that therefore, the bad guy is now using *this* cell phone. We can figure out that that's his new cell number and pick up activity on the new phone, losing no time on the investigation. In other words, the fact that they change phones doesn't defeat us."

"Great."

"Now this software has other applications for investigations. For example, what they told us at the meeting is that *your* cell phone, with the blue daisies"—Dan smiled—"is currently being used by a known mid-level drug dealer. His name is Ray James."

"What?" Vicki was astonished. "How do they know *that*?"

"Here's his chart, but it's only for a few days, so it's not rock-solid by any means." Dan set two charts side by side. "But see? They had Ray James's known phone from a previous arrest, and they did a Call Frequency Chart for him on the known phone. Then, because they knew your cell number, they began a Call Frequency Chart for your phone after it was stolen."

"So they tapped my cell phone?"

"No, they don't have to tap the phone to get this. They just can get a pen register, a record of calls made by the phone, as opposed to actually listening in to the call."

"Okay."

"So now they load your Call Frequency Report into the computer and ask it for a match, and it comes up with Ray James. In other words, Mr. James, who used to use *this* known phone"—Dan pointed to the chart on the left—"is now using *your* phone, because his old Call Frequency Chart matches the one for your phone, on the right."

"My God." Vicki's eyes widened. "So they know Ray James killed Reheema's mother!"

"Not yet."

"But they go and pick him up and question him about the murder, don't they?" Vicki was so tempted to call Reheema, but she couldn't. "Either he killed her or he knows who did!"

"Slow down. They don't do that yet. Why are you getting so excited?"

"But it was only days ago! It's most likely him! Ray James could be the guy with the gravelly voice, that we both talked to!"

"Vick." Dan smiled and held up a warning hand. "Settle down. You know better than that."

"I do?"

"Yes, you do. Think about it, calmly. All it means is that Ray James has the *phone* from somebody who might know that. Or that Ray James found the phone in a Dumpster or on the street. Or that he bought it from somebody who bought it from somebody else who found it on the street after the killer threw it there." Dan cocked his head, his blue eyes tired. "All we really know for sure is that Ray James has your cell phone."

"We can still ask the man, can't we?"

"Not consistent with that pesky Constitution, we can't. ATF can't, and they won't." Dan laughed. "This is way too soon to be sure, and they don't show their hand until they have the goods. You should know that they would need to show a judge at least a few months of calls to establish probable cause." Dan smiled. "So your phone is hard at work for the common good."

"So what will they do about Ray James?"

"Try to learn more about him, build their case, record his calls. Do it right."

"He has a record?"

"Ag assault, firearms, possession and distribution, the works. His record's in my briefcase; they gave us all copies. They'll follow up, it's just a question of time. You know how they investigate. Morty was the most methodical agent I knew."

Morty. Vicki tried to simmer down. "Ray James doesn't bring us any closer to Morty's killer."

"Not really, no."

"And he's on the back burner."

"For the time being. Then the heat will die down, but they won't forget about him. I won't let them." Dan began to gather his charts. "But we have been told to deal with Toys 'R' Us, top priority. I put a press release together for Strauss. There's a conference at eleven tomorrow. Everybody's gonna be there, from the mayor on down." Dan put the charts into his briefcase. "Plus, I forgot, they do have the one other guy, a loose end. This guy who was with Browning. They said they'll track him down when they get the chance."

"What guy? The guy who got shot, that one? I thought he was killed."

"No, not that one, another one. Tall guy, walked out of the store with Browning. The FBI thinks he mighta helped set him up for the kill. They're lookin' for him everywhere."

Huh? "I didn't see him on TV."

"He's there, walking with Browning. They picked him up on the surveillance cameras at Toys 'R' Us. He had some kinda cap on and they only got his back."

Oh no.

"Tall guy, black, that's it. He ran when the shooting started."

Reheema.

"And they're looking for a car that was waiting for him. They got a shot of it on the surveillance camera. He was working with another guy and he ran to him and the car when the shooting started."

That would be me. "Could they ID the other guy?"

"No. Short white guy. The FBI thinks this new gang is multiracial. Gives you hope, doesn't it?"

Eeek. "Did they get the make of car?"

"I think so, but no plate either." Dan slipped the charts into his briefcase, then straightened up with a smile. "No more work for today."

The FBI was looking for Reheema and her, crossdressing.

"Do you know how nice it is to come home to you?" Dan reached for Vicki and pulled her into his arms, kissing her softly. "You made me very happy today, on what could have been the worst day of my life."

Aw. "Really?"

"Yes, I'm basically homeless, but you made me feel at home. I love you for that. And I cannot stop thinking about last night, which was epic." Dan looked over at the clock on the oven. "I figure we have half an hour before dinner. That's enough for a nap."

"But I'm not tired." *And I have to go rent another car.*

"What a coincidence." Dan kissed her softly. "Can I interest you?"

"You already have," Vicki answered, kissing him back, and she let him take her hand and lead them both out of the kitchen. She would force herself to have great sex with him, so he wouldn't be suspicious, and her orgasms would only lend realism to her ruse.

But she took one last look backward, filled with lust. For his briefcase.

PART FOUR

Right is right, even if everyone is against it, and wrong is wrong, even if everyone is for it.

—WILLIAM PENN

Everybody, if you in the drug business, your object is to reach the top and do business with the connect. Nobody who's in the business stay at the bottom; not unless you's a fool. If you do something, you do it your fullest. So your object was to be like the Monopoly game. You start at Go and you want to go around and pass the board. So, that's what your object would be. To reach the top.

—JAMAL MORRIS,
United States v. Williams,
United States District Court,
Eastern District of Pennsylvania,
Criminal Docket No. 02–172, February 20, 2004,
Notes of Testimony at 429

THIRTY-THREE

FIRST THING THE NEXT MORNING, VICKI AND
Reheema picked out another new-to-you car, a nondescript beige Intrepid, vintage 2000, automatic trans-
mission, 78,000 miles, which rented for a hundred a
week. They parked the Sunbird in a garage, at thirty
bucks a day, because they couldn't take the risk of
turning it in, even though Vicki was worrying about
her skyrocketing stakeout costs.

They parked the Intrepid down the street from the
diner closest to their new favorite car dealership and
settled into a table for breakfast. Only a few tradesmen
were in the restaurant, which had wood-paneled walls,
harsh fluorescent lights, and red Formica tables that
were permanently greasy. They chose the restaurant
for the TV, not the decor or the food, and they weren't
wrong. The big-screen Panasonic was mounted on a
plywood stand high in the corner, and the scrambled
eggs arrived in a blue plastic basket.

Vicki sipped her coffee as Reheema read Bill Toner's police record. On TV, *Live at 10* was running a special feature on the Toys "R" Us shooting, and the newspaper headlines this morning had been all about the bloodbath. The city had reacted emotionally, and Vicki knew the pain would only intensify as funerals for the children began. Morty's murder paled in newsworthiness and official attention.

Reheema looked up. Her eyes were bright and alert, her hair hidden by a new Eagles hat, and she wore a plain gray sweatshirt under her pea coat. If it bothered her to know the name of the man who had almost shot her to death, it didn't show. "You got these papers from your boyfriend?"

"Yes."

Reheema frowned. "You told him what we're doin'?"

Not exactly. "No, I went in his briefcase while he was asleep. I scanned the documents and printed them."

"Damn, girl!" Reheema's eyes lit up with admiration.

"Hey, I'm not proud of it." Vicki couldn't have taken the papers or Dan would have known. She'd also copied the HIDTA charts and record of Ray James, but she hadn't told Reheema about him yet. She wasn't sure when, how, or even if, she would. How do you tell someone that you may/may not have the name and address of her mother's murderer?

Oblivious, Reheema was still smiling. "You stay outta the kitchen last night, you ho?"

Vicki winced. "Stop. I love the man."

"Slow down, girl. He left his wife two days ago."

"She left him."

"All the more, and he's not divorced yet."

"That's only the legal part."

"You're a lawyer."

"I hear you. Enough." Vicki checked the TV, where the T-Mobile commercial was over and a BREAKING NEWS banner was coming on. She edged forward in her seat. "Heads up. It's the press conference."

"Ooh, wow."

Vicki watched as the TV screen showed Strauss behind a podium, with the American flag on his right, standing next to a phalanx of suits that ended in Dan. Her heart leaped up. "That's Dan, on the end!"

Reheema turned to the TV. "He's *white*?"

Vicki laughed. "He's strawberry blond. Hot, huh?"

"He's all right." Reheema smiled.

Vicki looked again at the TV. Bale wasn't on-screen. Odd.

Strauss was saying, "No one needs to remind anybody of the appalling scenes that took place yesterday at Toys 'R' Us. Men, women, and children were murdered, and the cowards who killed them must be stopped so we can live our lives, shop with our children, and enjoy the great opportunity this country offers us all."

"What's that man running for?" Reheema asked, pushing her eggs away, half eaten.

"To accomplish that, my office is pleased to announce an initiative entitled Project Clean Shopping, whereby the highest priority will be given to the prosecution of shootings, assaults, and other crimes that take place in the shopping areas, strip malls, or indoor malls of the city of Philadelphia."

Vicki thought of Morty. *Mr. Clean.*

"You have already heard at the mayor's press conference, earlier this morning, that the Philadelphia police will double the number of patrol officers to our city's shopping areas and strip malls. Law enforcement will work together to protect the safety of our citizens and the economy of this thriving city. So please, go about your business. Mourn these victims, honor them by enjoying yourselves and by living your lives. Don't permit a few thugs—or your fears—to keep you from shopping for your family and yourselves."

"S'all about the money," Reheema said, sipping her coffee.

"I'll take questions in a minute, but I'd like to introduce you to Dan Malloy, one of the best prosecutors in my office, who will be heading up Project Clean Shopping. The press release we distributed today lists Dan as the contact point, so you now have his phone and e-mail. Please, folks, feel free to ask Dan all the hard questions. Leave the easy ones for me."

Wow! "Wow!" Vicki couldn't hide her surprise. Dan hadn't mentioned it last night. She felt confused and proud, both at once.

"Dan the man," Reheema said, smiling, and Vicki felt the proud part surge to the fore.

"Good for him. He deserves it."

"Wonder if they know he does it in the *kitchen*."

"Behave." Vicki watched the rest of the press conference, in which Strauss answered softballs with a politician's expertise. When it was over, she scooped up a forkful of eggs. "We'd better get going, we have our work cut out for us, playing catch-up. Dan says ATF assigned a special group to this case, because of the level of violence, and after yesterday, we have to be careful. Let's just see what goes on and try to stay away from the guns, huh?"

"Including mine?"

Vicki set down her fork and eased back into the booth seat. "*On* you?"

"Yeah."

"Where is it?" Vicki eyed Reheema's pea coat. "I'm not wearing my X-ray specs."

"My coat pocket."

"You got bullets, too?"

"They go inside the gun, Harvard. No fun without."

Their eyes met over the leftovers. Vicki said, "Well, I won't tell you you're wrong, and you wouldn't listen anyway."

"True."

"Where did you get it, by the way?"

"Around."

"What's that mean?"

"In the neighborhood."

"Wait. When you wanted guns before, you bought them in a gun shop."

"Went to jail in between. Learned a lot." Reheema smiled, tight, and picked up her fork. "Finish your breakfast."

But Vicki had lost her appetite. *Guns. HIDTA. Bill Toner.* Maybe they were in over their heads. For the first time, she felt afraid, and ironically, it was because they were armed now, too.

"By the way, can I take you up on your offer last night, about the money?"

Good. "How much do you need? I got some cash."

"To get started, three hundred, if you can manage."

"I think I have it on me. I took out extra for the new car." Vicki reached for her wallet, counted out the bills, then stopped. "But I want collateral. The gun."

"What?"

"Give me the gun and I'll give you the money. I need collateral."

Reheema cocked her head, her lovely eyes narrowing. "You just don't want me to have a gun."

"No, really?" Vicki made a *duh* face, but Reheema didn't laugh.

"It won't help either of us if you have it. You don't know how to use it. You're good with a computer, but a gun is something else."

"You're no better than I am."

"Am, too."

Vicki clucked. "Have you ever shot a gun?"

"Yeah."

Oh. "At somebody?"

"Of course. How else you gonna hit 'em?"

Maybe National Honor Society only goes so far. "Still."

"Fine." Reheema shoved her hand into her pea coat and took out a gun as easily as car keys. It was a revolver with a silver barrel and a black handle, and she set it on the red table with a *clunk.*

"What are you doing?" Vicki snatched up the gun and put it on her lap before anybody saw it, not that there was anybody around to see. And even on her lap, the gun felt unsafe, as if it might spontaneously combust. Vicki had never been this close to a loaded weapon that wasn't pointed at her.

"Now gimme the money." Reheema stood up, hand outstretched, and Vicki handed her the cash. She folded it into a wad and stuffed it into her jeans pocket. "And don't think I can't take that gun from you, anytime I want it."

"Be that way." Vicki slid the gun into her purse, then stood up and tried to recover her dignity. It seemed oddly beside the point, now that she was carrying concealed.

Vicki and Reheema circled Lincoln Street a few times in the Intrepid, getting a bead on the new Cater Street operation since Browning's death. There were unfamiliar lookouts at both ends of Cater, but the same steady stream of customers flocked to the hole. The smaller snowplows must have come, because Cater had been cleared, permitting car traffic and curbside crack takeaway to recommence, busy as Outback Steakhouse.

Vicki had given up trying to figure out why having a gun made her feel less safe, and they forgot their lovers' quarrel and focused on the goings-on on Cater, once the Intrepid was parked behind their favorite snowbank.

"Same wine, different bottle," Reheema said, and Vicki nodded. Bright light flooded the car's crappy black interior, reflecting off the leftover snow. They actually needed the sunglasses, if not the dumb hats.

"Wonder if it's a whole new crew."

"Crew?" Reheema looked over the top of her sunglasses. "Where'd you learn that?"

"MTV."

"Proud a you." They both laughed, and Reheema asked, "So what's the plan, we wait for the go-between?"

"Right. I still wanna go up the chain, especially now that we're on to something. I think it's Toner's crew that hit Jackson's house that night and killed her and Morty. Now we have to find the equivalent of Brown-

ing, but in Toner's crew, then go on up to the connect."
Vicki started digging in her backpack for her camera.
"I assume this organization works the same way."

"Gotta sell the crack, then gotta get more, and somebody got to bring it to you."

"Right." *Mechanical.* "So we watch and wait. We are *the* stakeout professionals."

"'Xactly, lil' home."

Two hours later, they had moved the Intrepid a few times because the lookouts in Toner's crew were more watchful, spending no time smoking or talking to the customers, which made sense because they didn't know them. It got Vicki thinking. "This is a tougher organization."

"Why?"

"They're not from the neighborhood. This is a business, to them."

"It was a business to the others, too."

"It seemed more like a party, in comparison. Not like these guys, and the go-between doesn't come as often." Vicki checked her watch. "Browning's crew would've had Mr. Black Leather here once already."

"Might mean they got more than one seller in the hole. Double the supply." Reheema eyed the customers. "Weather's better, volume increasing. They're more competitive. Survival of the fittest."

"I stopped counting customers, but I could start again."

"Don't bother, it's a lot."

"Sure is," Vicki said, taking a picture.

Half an hour later, a black van barreled around the corner from the far end of Cater and stopped in front of the house, idling exhaust. "Look alive," Reheema said.

"The company car." Vicki snapped a photo as a man got out of the driver's seat in a puffy Eagles jacket and black knit cap. "Finally, a Philly fan."

"Got a passenger, too."

Vicki took a picture even though she couldn't see a thing through the windshield because of the glare. In the next minute, the man reached back inside the van and came out with a black Nike gym bag, then turned and hustled with the bag into the hole.

"Ain't that nice? He works out." Reheema put on her seat belt, but Vicki felt too tense to joke around and put on her belt, too. In the next minute, the man hustled back to the van with the Nike bag, jumped inside, and the van took off toward them. The women ducked in unison, and as soon as it was almost out of sight, the Intrepid took off.

With a nervous Vicki riding shotgun.

THIRTY-FOUR

"LOOK, IN THE FRONT SEAT, THE PASSENGER seat." Vicki worried, three blocks later, that they'd been spotted by the go-betweens in the black van.

"So what?" Reheema maneuvered the Intrepid behind a Toyota pickup but stayed on track. They were traveling down a numbered street, and in her panic, Vicki had lost her sense of direction.

"The passenger has a ball cap on, so you can see the brim every time he turns his head."

"Okay, so?"

"He turns around a lot. I can see the brim every two minutes, practically. I think he's watching us."

"Calm down. It's only been five minutes."

Vicki tugged down her Phillies cap. "They know we're following them."

"No, they don't."

"Yes, they do! They could. These guys are smart."

Reheema stopped at the traffic light, two cars behind the van. "So what do you wanna do?"

"Let 'em go."

"Oh, come on!"

"It's daylight and this is too risky. Better to be safe than sorry."

"Don't be stupid."

"Take a left. Bail. Abort, abort, abort."

"Oh, all right." Reheema steered the Intrepid to the left and they turned onto the side street.

"We can pick them up after dark. We'll come back."

"Dumb." Reheema pulled up to the curb and found a parking space behind a PECO truck. She cut the ignition and looked over. "Why you so damn jumpy?"

"I don't know."

"You all right? You look white." Reheema smiled. "Too white."

"I'm fine," Vicki said, queasy. "My stomach feels funny. Either it's the plastic eggs or the thought that we're gonna get killed."

"You want some water? I know you put a bottle in that backpack." Reheema reached back and got the backpack.

"No! Wait!" Vicki shouted, a moment too late. Reheema already had the backpack and was pulling out Ray James's arrest record and mug shot.

"Yo, this guy's from my neighborhood. This address is near me."

"Yeah." Vicki reached for the papers but Reheema was already reading the record.

"Why do you have this? Says here he's done time for assault, with a knife."

Vicki shuddered. For a minute she didn't know what to say.

"Who is this guy?" Reheema held up the record, her eyes searching Vicki's in a way that compelled the truth. "You holdin' out on me? You get this record the same way you got Toner's?"

"Uh, yes." Vicki felt her heart pounding. She should have left the records at home, but she'd been afraid Dan would come across them. And now that Reheema knew about James, Vicki couldn't lie to her.

"What aren't you tellin' me?" Reheema asked, her voice wounded, and then she came up to speed. She tore off her sunglasses, and her dark eyes hardened with a familiar distrust. "He has something to do with my mother."

"Maybe, maybe not. They're not sure."

"Tell me!" Reheema said, but it came out like a command, dispelling the warmth between them.

"I will, but—"

"I have a right to know what happened to my mother."

"You do—"

"She's *my* mother. Tell me what you know!"

"Calm down and I will."

"Fine."

"Good. Thank you." So Vicki began, thanking God she had gotten the gun from Reheema first. She told Reheema everything, taking her through the HIDTA records, too, and by the time she was finished, she could see that Reheema was calmer, more reasonable. "So as much as you would love to get him, he may not be the killer."

"But he could be. Or he could know who is."

"No. Ray James has my phone, is all we know."

"So when do these ATF suits go talk to him?"

"ATF may not have jurisdiction and they'll have to work with Philly, because murder is a state-law crime. The Philly cops were represented at this meeting last night, and this would come under their jurisdiction—"

"Stop." Reheema held up a palm. "Bottom line."

"Your mother's murder is a matter for the Philly police. They're on it. You met Detective Melvin that morning, right? He's a good guy. He'll question James as soon as he lawfully can. Understand?"

"Understand."

"Any questions? It is kind of complicated."

"No questions." Reheema turned in the driver's seat, twisted on the ignition, and backed out of the space. She went forward too fast, almost hitting the bumper of the PECO truck.

"Reheema, where are we going?"

"Where'd you think?"

"Reheema, we can't go over there." Vicki held on tight, literally and figuratively, as the Intrepid took off down the street.

"I can."

"It could compromise their investigation."

"They ain't investigatin'."

"Yes, they are."

"No, they're not." Reheema hit the gas to pass a furniture truck. "My mother's last in line, behind your ATF friend and the little blond kids at the Toys 'R' Us. You said so yourself."

Vicki flushed. "We can do this the right way."

"I'm not gonna do anything wrong."

"You can't."

"I'm not." Reheema ran a red light, ignoring a loud HONK! "All I'm gonna do is go over and ask the man a few questions."

"But it's not our place to do that."

"It's my place."

"I have another idea."

"Me, too, but you took my gun."

Vicki was pretty sure Reheema was kidding. "Instead, why don't why we call Homicide and ask them what progress they're making? Make sure that they got the word about Ray James? Find out what they're doing about him?"

"Go ahead. Call 'em. Tell 'em I said how they doin'." Reheema barely slowed at the corner of the street, then took a right, heading for the main road.

"Okay, I will." Vicki reached in her purse, bypassed the loaded gun, and retrieved her cell phone, then dialed Philly Homicide. She knew the number from her old D.A. days. "Detective Al Melvin, please."

"He's not in," answered a gruff male voice, which Vicki knew belonged to the desk officer, a detective stuck with answering the phones this tour.

"Detective, this is Vicki Allegretti. I'm an AUSA and I'm calling about the Arissa Bristow case."

"Who?"

"Allegretti."

"No, the case."

"The victim's name is Arissa Bristow."

"Is it open?"

Reheema's eyes shifted knowingly, and Vicki hit a button to lower the volume on the cell.

"Yes, of course, it's open. Ms. Bristow was killed

last Friday night, stabbed to death in a house on Lincoln Street."

"What's your office have to do with it?"

"I'm calling as a friend of the family."

Reheema snorted. The detective asked, "Okay, how can I help you?"

"Detective Melvin was investigating the case, with a partner."

"Melvin and his partner are both over at City Hall."

Gulp. "Is there a number there where I can reach them?"

"Listen Mrs. Bristow—"

"Allegretti."

"I'll leave a message you called, that's the best I can do."

"When will they get the message?"

"Soon as they can. We're all a little busy lately, with what happened at Toys 'R' Us." Sarcasm tinged his tone. "You seen the news lately?"

Reheema's mouth flattened to an I-told-you-so line, and Vicki got mad.

"You know, I wouldn't think you guys would drop the ball just because another murder comes along. There was an ongoing investigation, and I'm here with a member of the victim's family."

"My condolences to the family, and I assure you, Detective Melvin is working the case. Is that what you wanted? What you called for?"

"No. I wanted to know what progress Detective Melvin had made, and specifically, if he has contacted a lead named Ray James yet."

"I'll let him know you asked. Thanks for calling."

"Thank you." Vicki gave him her cell number and flipped the phone closed as the Intrepid veered around a corner, racing to Lincoln Street. At this point, they were half an hour away.

"So, did they say hey?"

"We're not gonna go crazy here."

"No one's goin' crazy," Reheema said, and ran another red light.

"You keep running the lights, we're gonna pick up a cop."

"No, we won't. Didn't you see your boss on TV? The cops are at Toys 'R' Us."

"Think of it this way," Vicki said, changing tacks. "If we go there now, we'll be showing our hand, like you said. Right now, James doesn't know that HIDTA is recording his phone calls. He doesn't know they're building a case against him. If we go over and start asking questions about the phone, he's gonna ditch the phone for sure."

"You might be right."

"Good," Vicki sighed, relieved.

"You might also be wrong. Or what happens to him after might not matter."

Vicki felt her first tingle of true fear. "He's dangerous. James is a dangerous man."

Reheema smiled. "You got a gun."

"I won't use it, and neither will you."

"I'm dangerous, either way."

"Oh, that's great." Vicki started to lose her temper, which she knew wouldn't help her cause. "Reheema. I guarantee that however tough you think you are, James is a lot tougher."

"I can handle him. Record says he's five six, one

fifty. I got a couple inches on him and I've been lifting for almost a year."

Yikes. "That's not the point."

"Listen, if you're scared, don't come." Suddenly Reheema twisted the black wheel of the Intrepid to the right, yanked the car to the curb in front of Popeyes fried chicken, and pressed the brakes. The car lurched to a stop. "Get out."

"What?" Vicki asked, startled.

"Go. Leave. This is a decent neighborhood, you'll be fine. Get yourself some chicken wings and I'll come back for you."

"No." Vicki knew she should go, at the same moment she knew she'd stay.

"Get out."

Vicki sat stiff in her seat. "I don't want to."

"Why not? You'll lose your job."

"Not if you behave yourself, I won't. I'm in. You need me."

Reheema burst into merry laughter, like her old self, and the two almost became friends again.

"I'm saving you from yourself, Reheema."

"The hell you are!"

"Also you'd miss me. You'd have separation anxiety."

"No, I wouldn't."

Vicki waved a hand. "Go ahead, tough girl. Drive."

Reheema laughed again. "You're kiddin'."

"Go." Vicki turned to her, grave. "But I'm watching every single move you make. And if I have to shoot *you*, I will."

"*Damn!*" Reheema said, and hit the gas. They arrived at James's house faster than most rockets, and the Intrepid pulled up in front of a crumbling brick row house. Reheema cut the ignition, took out the key, and started to leave the car, when Vicki put a hand on her arm to stop her.

"How about this?" Vicki asked, as a last-ditch effort. "How about you let me do the talking and we don't tell him who you are?"

"How about not?" Reheema's features had fallen into lines as fixed as dark marble.

"If I question him, maybe I can convince him to come in and confess, as opposed to muscling him."

"I *want* to muscle him."

Vicki experienced another fear tingle. She'd had so many on the way over, she felt electrified. "Reheema, I'm begging you, please be smart."

"Enough talk." Reheema broke Vicki's grasp and got out of the car, slamming the door behind her.

Oh, great. Vicki jumped out of the passenger seat and ran around the other side as Reheema climbed the concrete steps to James's front door in two bounds and started pounding. James's row house stood in the middle of the block, in worse repair than the rest of the neighborhood. It had only one black shutter on the first floor, for two windows, and its front door had been painted a bright, mismatched green, as if bought used or poached from a junkyard.

"Stay calm," Vicki said, but Reheema kept knocking.

"James! Ray James!"

"Calm!" Vicki eyed the street, which was still except for Reheema's banging on the door. In one of the houses, a dog started barking.

"Ray James! Open up!"

"Maybe he's not home."

"James! Open this door!"

"We could call him on the cell, see if he's home."

"Open this door!" Reheema shouted, and before Vicki could realize what was happening, much less could stop her, Reheema had reared back and shoved the door with all her might, breaking it open at the lock. *"That's* what I'm talkin' 'bout!"

"Reheema!" Vicki shouted, terrified.

But Reheema was already pushing the door the rest of the way open and breaking into the house.

THIRTY-FIVE

"JAMES! RAY JAMES!" REHEEMA SHOUTED over a blaring TV, and Vicki hurried inside the dark row house after her. A short hall ended at an arched entrance to a living room, where the noise was coming from.

"Oh! Who're you?" a man asked, his voice fearful.

"You Ray James?" Reheema demanded.

"Yes, don' hurt me!"

"Reheema! Stop!" Vicki rounded the corner just in time to catch Reheema yelling at a man who was lying in a bed in the darkened living room. He raised his arms partway, as if she had a gun. He was youngish, black, and obviously ill, because the bed was an adjustable hospital bed with an orange-and-green Brophy's Medical Supply sticker on the footboard. Next to it sat a plastic white commode with the same sticker, and the coffee table was serving as a makeshift night table, littered with tall brown bottles of medication, a pebbled plastic pitcher, a box of blue

Kleenex, and a scalloped paper plate holding two pizza crusts.

"Reheema Bristow! Know that name? BRISTOW!" Reheema yelled, and Vicki grabbed her arm.

"Get a grip! The man is *sick*!"

"So what?" Reheema shot back, her fury abated, if only by degree, like a hurricane downgraded to a tropical storm. She turned to James.

"Gimme your cell phone!"

"Okay, okay, okay." James's eyes widened in fear and he fished a cell phone from the bedcovers, then thrust it at Reheema. "Here. You can have it. Take it."

"Ha!" Reheema grabbed the phone with its blue daisy cover and showed it to Vicki. "Yours?"

"Reheema, take it easy, look at the man," Vicki said, holding fast to Reheema's arm. Something was wrong with James. His head listed to the left, he hadn't shaved in days, and his words slurred slightly when he spoke. He wasn't drunk but seemed loopy, as if he was on medication.

"Where'd you get this phone?" Reheema demanded, brandishing it.

"My home."

"Who?"

"Wha'?"

"TELL ME WHERE YOU GOT THE PHONE!"

Vicki squeezed Reheema's arm. "Reheema, take it easy."

James's eyes flared. "Chucky! Chucky gi' it to me."

"Chucky WHO?"

"Call him Chucky Cheese. Look like the Chucky doll."

"Where's Chucky live?"

"Dunno," James answered.

"Yes you do! Where!" Reheema broke Vicki's grip with ease, stepping to the edge of the bed, so Vicki stepped neatly between them and faced the prone man.

"Mr. James," she asked, "do you know where Chucky lives? Just tell us and we'll go. We're trying to find out where he got the phone."

"I forget the street name. The street, with the bank."

"Which bank?"

"Dunno. Blue sign, 'bout ten blocks up." James pointed over his head, and Reheema shoved Vicki aside.

"The PNC that's on Jefferson Street?"

James nodded weakly.

"Okay, he lives on Jefferson. What house number on Jefferson, Ray?"

"I dunno."

"THINK!"

Vicki jumped. "Reheema, don't bully him!"

"Middle . . . of the block, red . . . door," James stammered, and Reheema exploded.

"You got this phone when you killed my mother!"

"No!" James's eyes widened, holding his hands higher. "I ain't killed *nobody*! I been inna hospital, gettin' ma damn foot cut off! Look!" He lowered a hand, pulled back the bedcovers, and revealed a bandaged stump on his left foot, sitting in a foam-blue holder. Vicki hid her surprise at the sight, and even Reheema took a step back.

"When'd you get that?"

"Saturday morning."

Vicki interjected, "So you were in the hospital Friday night?"

"Yeah. They took me in to run the tests, then they cut it off the next day, jus' like that."

Vicki planted herself in front of Reheema. "Mr. James, when did you get the phone?"

"When I ge' home, next day."

"When was that?"

James blinked dully. "What's today?"

"Thursday. When did you come home from the hospital?"

"I come home Saturday." James seemed to lose focus, his eyelids drooping to a close. "Saturday mornin'."

Vicki nodded. "So Chucky gave you the cell phone on Monday."

"Yeah, Chucky gi' it to me."

"Did Chucky tell you where he got the phone?"

"No."

Reheema couldn't take it anymore, demanding, "Where'd you get the phone, Ray?"

"I tole you. Chucky. Chucky got everythin', everythin' you need, he got it. Chucky like a store," James mumbled, his eyes still closed. "Alls I do now lay here and talk onna phone. Can't do no business, can't do nothin'. I watch the TV and talk to my homes, all day long."

Hmm. Vicki realized that would explain the HIDTA frequency reports; James was making the same calls but the substance was different, and in time the call pattern would change. ATF never would have gotten the warrant for James, on that record.

"You better be tellin' me the TRUTH!" Reheema spat out, and James waved her away like a fly.

"Le' me alone, le' me in peace. I din' kill nobody. I din' do *nothin'*."

"Thank you, Mr. James," Vicki said, then turned to Reheema. "I think we're finished here, don't you?"

"Hmph!" Reheema edged away from the bed.

Now. Vicki walked ahead of her, because she had a Secret Plan. She couldn't let this happen again. Suddenly, she bumped Reheema's side like a common pickpocket, grabbed the car keys from her hand, and ran down the hall and toward the front door with them.

"What are you doing?" Reheema shouted, caught by surprise and momentarily left behind.

Go, go, go! Vicki flew out the front door and into the cold, ran for the Intrepid and jumped inside, locking the doors.

"What the HELL YOU DOIN'?" Reheema reached the car a split second later and hit the glass window, furious.

But Vicki wasn't staying to answer. She'd twisted on the ignition, hit the gas, and driven off, with Reheema giving chase.

Yikes! Vicki hadn't counted on Reheema trying to run down a *car*, so she floored the gas pedal. The Intrepid picked up nicely, and she tore down the street and took a swift right onto the main drag, heading for the PNC Bank at Jefferson Street. She checked the rearview, and Reheema was sprinting down the block. Vicki hit the gas, caught the next two green lights, and spotted the PNC Bank. By then, Reheema had disappeared from the rearview mirror.

Yippee! Vicki turned right onto Jefferson and raced toward the house with the red door. She would get this job done without bullies, interference, or illegality. Chucky Cheese didn't sound dangerous. And if Vicki had to defend herself, she had a law degree.

It turned out that Chucky was not only harmless, he was eighty-proof, and he leaned way too close to Vicki as they sat in the front seat of the Intrepid. They had parked behind a CVS three blocks from his house, where Reheema would never find them. Chucky was about sixty-five years old, African-American, and a diminutive five foot three in a thick green parka. He had shrewd brown eyes with a mercantile glint and, as James had suggested, served as the eBay of the hood.

"Ya want information, that'll be twenty bucks," Chucky said, his breath scented with Budweiser.

"*Another* twenty?" Vicki had already spent twenty to get him in the car with her, once she had convinced him she didn't want to "party."

"Money talks, or Mr. Chucky walks." Chucky grinned, showing the gap between his front teeth that had undoubtedly given him his nickname.

"Fine." Vicki reached into her wallet yet again and handed him the twenty. "Okay, so tell me—"

"Ya need a watch, a new watch?"

"I got a watch."

"Classy girl like ye'self, ya gotta wear *Rolex*."

"I don't want a fake Rolex, Chucky."

"Ain't fake!"

"Of course it is." Vicki had already bought from him a fake Vuitton bag, a counterfeit pink-and-black Burberry scarf, and a bootleg copy of *Indiana Jones and the Temple of Doom*. The stuff sat between them on the seat like a barricade of knockoffs. She watched with dismay as Chucky started digging again in the backseat, where he'd insisted on putting his bedsheet, like Santa with his bag of copyright violations.

"Ya *need* a Rolex, Miss Vicki." Chucky plopped

back into the passenger seat, holding a fake stainless Rolex. "Ya need ta buy this."

"No, I don't."

"Ya do if you wanna know where I got that cell phone."

"Do you really know where you got it?"

"Yes, I do, swear I do." Chucky nodded, his bald head dotted with tiny gray hairs, covering a veiny brown scalp.

"I don't believe you. I'm guessing you sell a lot of cell phones."

"I do all right with the phones, this time a year."

"So tell me what my phone looked like."

"Little silver one, Samsung, blue daisies, green center in each one."

Vicki couldn't help but be impressed. She liked a fence who knew his inventory.

"Watch is thirty dollars." Chucky handed her a Rolex that gleamed like Reynolds Wrap.

"Thirty dollars for *this*? Come on!"

"'Scuse me, twenty."

"Excuse *me*! Ten!"

"Twenty."

Maybe bribes are deductible. Vicki handed over another twenty, and Chucky slipped it into his pocket.

"You won't be sorry, Miss Vicki. Lemme show you what I been savin' for you, special for you." Chucky reached for the backseat, rummaging again.

"No, I'm not buying anything else. Now tell me where you got that cell phone."

Chucky sat down and dangled a fake gold chain with a humongous Mercedes symbol. "Like it?"

"No."

"It's real big."

"True, no subtlety there."

"Eighteen karat!"

"I'm sure."

"P. Diddy got one just like it." Chucky swung the necklace back and forth like a cartoon hypnotist. "Yours for twenty bucks."

"No. Absolutely not."

"Come on! Ten bucks! You got ten bucks, girl!"

"No!" Vicki raised a firm, final hand. "Now tell me what I need to know."

Half an hour later, Vicki was steering the Intrepid back onto the main drag. She had dropped Chucky off at his house and picked up Reheema, who had been sitting on his front steps, simmering despite the frigid temperature. Reheema didn't say anything, remaining opaque behind her sunglasses and knit hat. Or maybe she was just thawing out.

"Reheema, you don't have to talk to me, if you don't want to." Vicki slipped on her sunglasses against the sunlight. "Even though I bought you all this nice stuff, including that lovely Mercedes-Benz necklace."

Reheema looked out the window.

"P. Diddy has one, you know. It's twenty-four karat."

Reheema didn't respond.

"Okay, have it your way. I found out where Chucky says he got the cell phone and I'm taking you there, right now. I'm taking you with me this time, because even you will behave yourself in these circumstances."

Reheema stayed turned away.

"I understand why you're angry, and I would be, too. Very angry and very hurt. In pain. But you were way out of line with James, and I couldn't let you do that again. It was wrong."

Reheema didn't budge.

"We're trying to find out who killed your mother and bring him to justice. Maybe it's not technically our job, but we aren't doing anything wrong or illegal." Vicki paused for a response that didn't come. "You crossed the line with James. You can't terrorize someone in the name of justice. If you do, you're worse than the worst criminals. You're shooting kids at Toys 'R' Us."

Reheema didn't speak, but by this point, Vicki was thinking out loud anyway, and for once not worrying about whether it was a good thing to do or not.

Ten silent minutes later, the Intrepid found Pergola Street and pulled up in front of the house.

THIRTY-SIX

THE KITCHEN WAS PAINTED A BRIGHT WHITE, ringed with refaced white cabinets, and smelled pleasantly of baked chocolate and watered-down Lysol. A white plastic tablecloth with scalloped edges covered the table, topped with a chipped plate of crusty brownies. Vicki and Reheema sat catty-corner in two chairs, opposite Mrs. Bethave. She wore the cheery red-and-white uniform of a waitress at Bennigan's, but her eyes sloped down at the corners with evident fatigue. Next to her sat her son, Albertus, an undersize eight-year-old engulfed by a hooded gray sweatshirt. He sat behind an open math book, a notebook page with a pointy protractor lying on it, and a half-eaten brownie on a pebbled napkin next to a glass of milk.

"I'm Vicki Allegretti, as I said at the door, and this is my friend Reheema Bristow. Thank you so much for letting us in."

"Fine," Mrs. Bethave said coldly. "I don't have a lot of time. Soon as the sitter gets here, I gotta get to work."

"Okay, I'll make this quick. We're here because I just met a man named Chucky, who lives a few blocks away on Jefferson Street. Do you know Chucky?"

"Everybody knows Chucky." Mrs. Bethave half-smiled, but Vicki was watching Albertus for a reaction. The boy had huge brown eyes and a somber milk mustache.

"Chucky said that last weekend, on Sunday afternoon, he paid your son Albertus five dollars for a cell phone that he had."

Albertus blinked, one movement of his baby-camel's eyelashes.

Vicki continued, "I need to know if that's true, and if it is, where Albertus got the cell phone, and when."

"Why do you want to know?"

"It's my cell phone and it was taken from me—"

"Albertus don't steal."

"I didn't mean that. Of course he doesn't. The phone was stolen from me by a woman who was later murdered." Vicki gestured to Reheema. "Her mother, Arissa Bristow."

Mrs. Bethave's eyes shifted to Reheema and back again.

"The cell phone was an unusual one," Vicki said. "It had a cover with blue daisies on it. It was pretty."

Albertus blinked again, his forehead creased with the guileless anxiety of a child. He was afraid he was going to get in trouble.

"I think that whoever stole my cell phone from Mrs. Bristow might have information about who killed her."

"Or mighta killed her hisself," Mrs. Bethave shot back, her tone colder.

"Yes, of course, that's possible. We're following the cell phone back in time, to see where it leads." Vicki tensed, now that their cards were on the table, and Mrs. Bethave must have sensed it, too, because she turned to Reheema.

"You wanna know who killed your mama."

"Yes, I do," Reheema said, and Mrs. Bethave turned back to Vicki.

"What about you? Why'd you care?"

Reheema answered for her, "She's my friend."

Wow.

Mrs. Bethave thought a minute, then looked down at Albertus. "Mook, you know what these ladies talkin' 'bout?"

Albertus glanced timidly up at her face, then nodded.

Yes! Vicki felt like cheering.

"Look at me, son." Mrs. Bethave cupped Albertus's chin and turned his face up to her. "Chucky gave you fi' dollars for the phone?"

Albertus nodded, his chin tight in his mother's hand.

"Where'd you get that phone? You find it somewhere?"

Albertus shook his head, no.

"Then where'd you get it?"

Albertus raised his hands and signed rapidly, his dark fingers flying, and Vicki held her breath for the translation. Chucky had told her that the little boy was deaf and that he read lips.

Albertus finished signing, and Mrs. Bethave's eyes filled with alarm. Her hand dropped from his chin and her lips parted. She jumped to her feet so abruptly, she bumped the three-ring notebook, startling all of them.

"Oh no! No, no, no!" Suddenly panicky, Mrs.

Bethave hurried around the table and almost lifted Vicki bodily from her chair. "Go now, out, you two! That's the way it is, you two got to go."

"Mrs. Bethave, please, what did he say?" Vicki rose rather than be thrown out, but Reheema stood her ground.

"I'm not goin' anywhere, lady! Whoever gave him that phone killed my mother! Who gave it to him?"

"I can't, I can't say, you have to go."

"I need to know who!"

"You wanna get my child killed?" Mrs. Bethave shouted back, standing toe-to-toe with Reheema. With a mother's ferocity, Mrs. Bethave more than matched the taller and younger woman. "I'll never tell, no matter what! That man is a killer! He kills for money and he'll kill my boy, sure as we stand!"

He kills for money? The words broke the standoff, and Vicki and Reheema exchanged looks.

"Go! Don't tell anybody you were here!" A terrified Mrs. Bethave shooed them both out of the kitchen and to the front door. "Please! Jesus!"

"Wait, no!" Reheema shouted, recovering first, but Mrs. Bethave had pulled open the door and was physically pushing them out into the cold.

"Never tell anybody you were here, never!"

Mrs. Bethave slammed the door closed and deadbolted it with a loud, final *ca-thunk*.

Vicki steered the Intrepid onto the cross street, driving from the Bethave house faster than necessary. She worried for Mrs. Bethave's safety and for Albertus, and it had been all she could do to stop Reheema from breaking down the Bethaves' front door.

"Look, we got our answer, for the present time,"

Vicki said. "We followed my phone down the line and we know where it ends. And it leads to another question. Why did she say it was someone who kills for money? What did she mean by that?"

Reheema was shaking her head. "I shoulda broken down that door."

"I had assumed it was an opportunistic crime. An addict or someone from the neighborhood." Vicki thought back to that night, to poor Arissa straggling in only her housedress down the cold street. The older woman had been easy prey for anyone, but Vicki didn't need to draw a picture for her grieving daughter. "It doesn't seem likely it was a murder for hire. Maybe that's not what she meant. You think that's what she meant?"

"You can sit here and guess all you want, but Bethave knows who killed my mother."

"And we're not going to get her killed for it, or that little boy. She's protecting her family."

"And I'm protecting mine. I *shoulda* beat it out of her."

"You don't mean that, and she wouldn't have told you anyway." Vicki looked over to double-check, but it was darkening in the car, and Reheema had her sunglasses on. "Look, it's getting late. Let's grab something to eat and go over to Cater."

"I'm not hungry."

"Then let's go over to Cater now and pick up the black van. It's dark, and I feel better."

"I feel worse." Reheema was still shaking her head. "She knows who did it, and we're drivin' away like it's nothin'."

"We'll figure it out, just give me some time." Vicki tried to think of a lawful solution but kept coming up dry. "If we tell the cops, that'll put her in danger, and she'll deny she said anything anyway. At least we know where she lives and we have the information."

"What if she leaves?"

"She won't. She has a job and a kid in school."

"What about witness protection? Don't the feds do that all the time?"

"Only for federal crimes, like racketeering. Murder is a state-law crime."

Reheema scoffed. "Lawyer talk."

"I'm sorry," Vicki said, meaning it. She had been raised with a reverence for her profession, but for the first time, she was beginning to understand what people meant by legalese.

"You talk about making sense, now something else makes sense. I couldn't figure why a killer would give up a cell phone like that. But he gives it to a kid who can't talk."

"Yeah." Vicki nodded. It was why Chucky hadn't known when or where Albertus had gotten the phone. The child hadn't been able to tell him.

"But why not throw the phone away? Why take it at all?"

"Maybe he liked Albertus, was trying to do him a favor."

"A killer with a heart of gold. Stabbed my mother to death. We should go back."

"No."

"Turn around. I want to go back."

"No."

"I'll go back without you. Ditch you like you ditched me."

"Then I won't let you out of my sight. We'll have a sleepover at your house. I'll bring the nail polish. You got popcorn?" Vicki accelerated into light traffic, which had picked up now that people were coming home from work. She switched lanes, then took a right, a left, and another right, and in time, Reheema looked over.

"Where you goin'?"

"Cater Street."

"Then turn around, Harvard," Reheema said, with a soft chuckle, and Vicki knew they were back on track.

Darkness descended as Vicki and Reheema sat in the front seat of the Intrepid, parked near the end of Cater. They'd found a new parking space across the street; they were changing things to avoid signaling the watchers, and now that they'd identified the van, didn't need to see it pull up in front of the vacant lot.

"They'll pull in from the far side, and we'll see them when they come out. This is safer." Vicki eyed the watcher at their end of the street, four houses up from the corner. He wore a long green army coat and a dark knit cap, and he tended to face the other end of the street. "It helps that the action comes from the far side. We caught a break."

"Yeah." Reheema's tone echoed in the cold, hollow interior of the car. She had grown progressively quieter since their discovery at the Bethaves' house, and Vicki's heart went out to her.

"We'll find your mother's killer."

"You're damn right, we will. Your way or mine."

Vicki let it go, her eyes retrained on the dark street. Thick clouds conspired to hide the moon. "Hope we didn't miss the run to the supplier's."

"Yeah." Reheema checked the car's dashboard clock. "It's seven already. Won't your boyfriend wonder where you are?"

"I left him a note, saying I'd be out shopping."

"He'll believe that?"

"I shop a lot." Vicki reached in her pocket for her cell. "I figured I'd call him about now and say hi."

"Go for it."

Vicki retrieved the phone and flipped it open, making a bright blue spot in the car. She was about to press in Dan's cell number when she heard a car engine and looked up.

"It's them!" Reheema said, pointing needlessly, as the black van veered around the corner, spraying snow.

Vicki closed the phone and twisted on the ignition, and they took off.

THIRTY-SEVEN

AN HOUR LATER, VICKI AND REHEEMA HAD successfully followed the black van from Devil's Corner through the city to a seamy section of Southwest Philly, on Getson Street, not ten blocks from Aspinall, where Browning lived. Dilapidated row houses lined the street, but lights shone from within some. Vicki could see that people lived here, but not as many or as middle class as the solid families of Devil's Corner. Fewer cars stood parked outside and many of the houses were dark shells, tall black rectangles that stood out like missing teeth against the lighted homes.

Vicki pulled into an empty space near the end of the street, about six houses down from the row house that Eagles Coat had gone into with his gym bag. As far as she could tell in the dark, the row house was number 8372 Getson; it was two stories of brick facade with a tumbledown front porch and snowy AstroTurf on its front steps. Lights were lit inside but curtains covered the windows. Getson Street stood silent except for the occasional car driving down it, and nobody walked dogs or set out trash; it was too cold or dangerous for anybody to be outside tonight. On one corner was a seedy bar, and at the corner opposite a lighted yellow sign read THE RITE SPOT; it hung over a mom-and-pop grocery store, with black bars covering the door and a smudgy plastic window, a bulletproof square of fluorescent light.

Vicki cut the ignition. "Maybe this is his work home, or whatever they call it."

"Yeah." Reheema looked around, sliding off her sunglasses. "This neighborhood isn't nice enough to be where he lives."

"Good, and it's only eight, he has to be still doing business tonight." Vicki double-checked the clock. "Maybe he'll even pay a visit to his connect."

"It's possible. You got the gun?"

"We won't need it."

"Probably not, it's not like they're violent or anything." Reheema smiled. "Is it still in your purse?"

"Not telling."

"Backpack?"

"No comment." Actually, Vicki had moved the gun to her left coat pocket, where it could shoot out an ovary.

"Have it your way."

"The plan is we wait and we watch. Then if we see Toner, we call the cops. Otherwise, we follow where they go and give that info to the cops."

"You sure you don't want to gimme my gun?"

"Absolutely not." Vicki eased back in the driver's seat, her adrenaline buzzing. It had been more exciting to follow the van than she wanted to admit and she became acutely aware of her body; the residual ache of the teenager's blows still hurt her sides, and she could almost recall the tenderness of last night, in bed with Dan. So much had happened in such a short time, since Morty had been killed. Vicki felt oddly as if she'd lived her entire life in one week and realized that perhaps she hadn't been living it well enough before.

"You should call your boyfriend. We don't want him calling later."

"Yeah, thanks. I'll make sure of it." Vicki retrieved her phone from her purse, covered the blue light so it didn't give them away, and pressed speed dial for Dan. His phone rang, then his voicemail picked up, and Vicki faked a light tone. "Hey, babe, I'm out shopping and ran into an old friend from law school, so I'll be home late. This new phone keeps cutting out, so if you can't get through, don't worry. See you way later or I'll call. Love you." She hit the Power button, turned off the phone, and slipped it back into her pocket. "Okay, we won't be interrupted."

"Good."

"Maybe I'll take some pictures." Vicki dug in the backpack, retrieved the camera, disabled the flash, and snapped away. She didn't know how much she could get in this low light level, but she was committed to the picture taking since it had actually paid off with Toner. Fifteen photos later, she had shot every scene she could conceivably take from the car. She set the camera down and watched the house with Reheema. No one left it or went inside. Eight o'clock became nine o'clock, and Reheema touched her arm.

"You awake?"

"Yep."

"I have to go to the bathroom. Do you?"

"Of course, we're girls. And I'm hungry." Vicki twisted around and eyeballed the grocery store and the bar. "I vote for the store. I'll bet they'll have a bathroom they'll let us use."

"If we go quick, we won't miss anything." Reheema tugged down her knit cap and got out of the car, as did Vicki, who grabbed her purse and joined her.

They crossed the street with a wary eye on 8372 and hustled together toward the grocery, like an urban version of Mutt and Jeff. Vicki felt the gun inside her coat pocket, which was when she realized that you couldn't shoot a gun in mittens anyway. They reached the store, and close up, Vicki could see it had once been a glass storefront, now boarded up with plywood panels that were littered with old keystone-shaped stickers for the Pennsylvania Lottery, a faded picture of the cartoon camel smoking a cigarette, and a sticker that read WE ACCEPT FOOD STAMPS.

Reheema opened the door. "Make this fast. Stay with me."

"You my passport?"

"No, your bodyguard."

They entered the store, and the older salesclerk looked up. He was about sixty, with deep wrinkles, small dark eyes behind crooked bifocals, and a dour down tilt to his mouth. He wore a quilted vest in army green and a black sweatshirt, and he'd been reading the sports page of the *Daily News*, spread open on a grimy white counter that was almost engulfed by stacked cartons of cigarettes on the top, and on the sides by multicolored bags of Cheetos, Doritos, Snyder's Hard

Pretzels, Rold Gold pretzels, Beef Jerky, and Fritos. The store was small, dusty, and smelled of the Newport he'd been smoking, resting in a filthy metallic ashtray with a beanbag bottom in incongruous tartan.

"Help you?" the salesclerk asked warily, eyeing them.

"We need to buy some food and use the bathroom, too."

"It's only for employees."

"Great, I need a job." Reheema slid off her knit cap like a hip-hop Joan of Arc and flashed him a beautiful smile. "When do I start?"

The salesclerk laughed, which ended in a single cough. "Oh, okay, young lady, it's in the back, past the cleaning supplies. Hurry up now, almost closin' time."

"Thanks," Reheema said, and the salesclerk waved her down the single aisle between a wall of Friskies and Tide detergent.

"Turn off the light when you're done," the salesclerk called after her, too late. "Don't nobody ever turn off the light."

"I bet," Vicki said, just to make conversation, feeling like she did at home, when her mother left her alone with her father. She pulled two crinkly bags of Lay's chips from the rack and set them on the counter. "You got any sandwiches?"

"No."

"Okay."

"If it's okay with you or not don't matter, 'cause we got no sandwiches. It's not like a 7-Eleven here, we don't got everything. It's just me here, I don't even own the place. Koreans own it."

"I see," Vicki said pleasantly, and continued buying

stuff in hopes that the salesclerk would like her and, by extension, white people in general. She stacked Doritos, Fritos, and Cheetos on the counter in a pile of saturated fats, then went into the aisle for Chips Ahoy and Pecan Sandies, stalling until Reheema finally returned and the salesclerk brightened.

"You live around here?" he asked Reheema, as Vicki traded places with her and went down the cramped aisle to the employee bathroom. It turned out that the bathroom was just as lovely as she'd expected, and she got out of there quickly, hurrying back into the store, where she froze on the spot.

Buying a carton of Winstons, pushing two twenties across the counter next to Reheema, stood the teenager who'd almost shot her the night Morty was killed. He wore his Iversons and a black jacket instead of the satin Sixers jacket, but she would never forget that face.

"Reheema, grab him!" Vicki shouted, lunging for the teenager, who reacted instantly and ran for the door, banging it open and getting away.

"Wha?" Reheema turned to Vicki, her mouth open.

"That's him! The kid from that night!" Vicki ran past the startled salesclerk and out the door with Reheema right behind her.

The teenager sprinted across Getson Street in the dark, running straight, his big sneakers two white blurs. Vicki darted after him, almost on his heels. Her heart pumped frantically, her legs churned, and her red boots skidded on icy spots, but she managed to keep up the pace. She felt the anger and pain she had been suppressing take over, powering her forward. The teenager had almost killed her. He knew who had killed Morty.

Vicki reached into her coat pocket as she ran, holding the gun so it wouldn't fly out. It felt heavy and right, even in her mitten. The teenager might have a gun, but there was no stopping her. She couldn't let him get away.

Vicki flashed on the night Morty was gunned down. The sight of the kid brought it all back. The sound of the bullets. The way Morty fell. The smell. The watery blood on his lips. Morty's last words. Rage coursed through Vicki's body. She picked up the pace.

"Move over!" Reheema shouted, passing Vicki on the right and taking off like a missile after the teenager.

Go, go, go! Astounded, Vicki kept running, her lungs about to burst. She had never seen anyone run so fast. She thought of the race times on Reheema's old bulletin board. Willowbrook Lady Tigers.

The teenager bolted across the next street, his jacket catching the wind like a dark spinnaker, and Vicki and Reheema pounded after him. The three of them barreled past abandoned cars, vacant row houses, and dumped car tires, heedless as the neighborhood worsened. Vicki kept running, and ahead of her, Reheema's trajectory was the purest of straight lines, a laser on target.

Vicki's breath came in ragged bursts, one block then the next, cold air filling her lungs and her boots slipping on the slick ice. Her legs ached, but emotion supercharged her.

The teenager veered left down the side streets, his arms pinwheeling to keep himself from falling. Reheema took the curve like a sports car, hugging it tight despite the snow and ice cold. They both disappeared around the corner, and Vicki marshaled her strength and put on the afterburners. She couldn't fall behind. She had to get this kid.

She hit the corner and saw Reheema ahead, closing in on the teenager. The gap between them shrank from six row houses to five, then to four. Reheema almost had him! Vicki sped up and prayed he didn't have a gun.

Reheema was reaching out to grab his flying coat. The teenager glanced back in fear. Vicki held her breath, hoping he didn't draw.

Reheema lunged forward, grabbing him by the coat with one long arm and tackling him to the snowy sidewalk. They went down together, sliding into the wall of a vacant row house.

Vicki's heart leaped to her throat, fearing for Reheema. Hoping she caught the kid. It was too dark to see what was happening. Reheema and the teenager appeared to be tussling in the snow, and in the next minute they both vanished inside the alley, out of sight.

"Reheema, watch out!" Vicki shouted, out of breath. "He could have a knife!" Her heart felt like it was jumping out of her coat. She tore to the mouth of the alley and was confronted by an unlikely scene.

Reheema was standing off to the side, her chest heaving and her hands on her hips, and the teenager was holding his hands up high, his dark eyes panicky and wide, his Iversons planted, and his back against a snow-covered Dumpster.

"Please, lady!" The teenager appealed to Vicki, his voice choked with panic. "I'm no cop killer! I didn't kill no cops! I didn't shoot you, remember? I'm Teeg, Teeg Brumley, you know me? I'm the one told Jay not to shoot you, that you were a cop! I saved your life! Please, don't hurt me!"

"Wait, calm down!" Vicki said, stunned. Her chest formed a knot of fury and pain. She couldn't catch her breath.

"I didn't know Jay was gonna kill nobody, I swear! I didn't know cops were gonna be there! Or the pregnant girl or the white cop!"

Morty. Vicki still couldn't catch her breath, and it wasn't from exertion. The teenager was giving her a full statement. She didn't know if she could even listen without Miranda warnings, but she couldn't *not* listen. She had to know the truth.

"Tha's all I know, I swear! I didn't shoot nobody! Jay did it all! Jay Steptoe's the cop killer, not me! He works for the boss, too! He's on Getson right now, at the meetin'!"

Vicki gasped. So Jay Steptoe was the name of the man who had murdered Morty. He was only a few blocks away, right now. For a minute, she couldn't speak, then she got her bearings. She couldn't compromise the indictment against Steptoe. "Listen, wait, Teeg, you don't have to say any of this, you have the right to remain silent—"

"We was supposed to go get the brick, is all, I swear! Me and Jay! All I know is Jamal wasn't paying the boss for the brick. He didn't pay the boss, so the boss sent us over to get the brick back!"

Vicki couldn't believe her ears. The kid was telling her why Morty had been killed, but it wasn't why she thought. It wasn't a battle between mid-level suppliers at all. It was a dispute with a creditor, and taking back the drugs was a gangsta version of a repo. "Teeg, you have the right to remain silent, and anything you say can and will be used against you in a court of law—"

"I know all that, you gotta believe me! You give me protection, I'll give you everything. The boss sent me there, it wasn't my fault! Preston Courtney sent me there!" The kid was growing hysterical, spilling his guts. "He does business with Jamal, with all of them, all over the city! He's the big boss! He supplies everybody! He's the connect!"

Vicki's eyes widened. *The connect.* "Teeg, in a court of law, we'll use these statements against you, and you have the right to have an attorney present at any questioning—"

"The boss is at Getson right now, with all them! That white guy in the van that they're lookin' for? He's there, too! They sent me out for cigarettes! I don't come back, I'm dead. You gotta protect me now!"

Vicki held up a hand. "If you can't afford an attorney, one will be appointed for you. Do you understand these rights? Teeg, do you hear me?"

"Yes, I understand! You gotta protect me! Courtney's the one who sent Jay and me! It's his fault the cop got shot, not me! I didn't do it! I didn't do nothin'!" Suddenly the teenager fell to his knees in the snow, beginning to sob. "I didn't do it! They did! I never killed nobody! Now they're gonna kill me!"

Vicki found herself taking a step back, trying to process it all. The teenager had dissolved into tears, doubled over in fear, like the child he was inside. Preston Courtney and Steptoe were responsible for Morty's death. And they were both at a meeting on Getson Street, right now.

"Vicki?" Reheema asked.

Vicki turned to the unaccustomed sound. She had never heard Reheema say her name and heard it now as if from far away. Courtney and Steptoe had killed Morty. They were only a few blocks away, within her grasp. They wouldn't be there forever. Vicki's head pounded, her heart hurt.

She put a hand into her pocket.

THIRTY-EIGHT

WITHIN FIFTEEN MINUTES OF VICKI'S PHONE call, an astounded Chief Bale swept into the alley with unmarked cars bearing armed ATF agents in navy windbreakers, and the remaining hours of the night pulsed with police activity. Teeg Brumley was arrested and taken in handcuffs to the FDC, where Strauss and Bale themselves videotaped his statement, and Vicki, Reheema, and later Dan watched from behind a two-way mirror to the interrogation room. Vicki prayed that Brumley would repeat everything he'd told her, and the teenager had a court-appointed lawyer present while he gave his statement again, elaborating on what he'd said in the alley and even admitting that Vicki had informed him of his Miranda rights. Dan gave her a hug for that, though it was otherwise strictly business. As much as Vicki needed the comfort, there was no time for romance.

Strauss and Bale brokered a deal by which Brumley

pleaded guilty to a lesser offense in return for cooperation and testimony in court against the others. Reheema gave her statement and went home, while Vicki, Dan, and a cadre of AUSAs and staff worked all night to prepare complaints and warrants against one Preston Courtney and Jay Steptoe for conspiracy to murder Special Agent Robert Morton, in addition to complaints and warrants against ten other individuals for numerous counts of crack cocaine sales and distribution, as well as various weapons offenses. It turned out that ATF had been surveilling the Getson Street house from an apartment on the street, waiting for the right moment to make a drug and firearms bust. The right moment had finally arrived.

Dan worked alone on the complaints and warrants for William Toner for the conspiracy to murder the seven men, women, and children who had been killed at the Toys "R" Us, then gave them to Vicki at five in the morning. She took the complete stack into Bale's office, set them down in front of him, and took a seat in the chair in front of his desk.

"Time to make the doughnuts, boss," Vicki said. As hard as she'd worked, she felt only energized.

"Ready, kid?" Bale turned from his computer keyboard, swiveling in his black Aeron chair, and for a moment they looked at each other over the papers. A new morning broke behind him, the sky turning a lovely pink-gray from the bottom up, gleaming off all the mirrored skyscrapers, setting them aglow. Either that, or Vicki was tired to the point of delirium.

"Good to go."

Bale smiled wearily, his skin tight from the night's effort and his eyes reddish but alert, with something like amusement. He had taken off his trademark gold cuff links and rolled up his sleeves, but with care, so that the folded cuff made a perfectly flat panel against his strong forearm. A tiny tattoo of an American flag peeked from its underside.

"You have ink?" Vicki asked, surprised, and Bale smiled.

"That's why I never wear short sleeves. Don't tell."

"I won't."

He pointed a stiff finger at her. "And don't spread any more BOTOX rumors about me, you brat."

Busted. "How'd you find out?"

"Debbie Hodill."

Vicki leaned forward. "So, is it true?"

"Of course," Bale answered, and they both laughed. "Now, to business. We have a judge to wake up, and then some bad guys." He took the stack of papers and pulled them toward him, his fingers a dark contrast against the pristine white.

"This would be the happy ending, right?"

"Not yet."

"You mean after we arrest them?"

"Shhh." Bale raised a slim finger to his mustache. "Can you be quiet, just for once? We're not finished. These are just paper, right now. They need the proper signatures, then they assume the force of law."

The force of law. Vicki liked the sound of the phrase, more powerful than a mere gun. Reheema had been right about that, but she hadn't realized it before.

"Let's see." Bale slid the first paper off the stack, with the caption that read UNITED STATES V. PRESTON COURTNEY AND JAY STEPTOE.

Vicki felt a deep satisfaction. She had written it herself. "That's the complaint and indictment for Morty's murder."

"I know, that's why they call me Chief. Now, hush." Bale took the warrant, read it completely, and finished at the signature page. The usual procedure was merely to initial the papers, but given the high-profile nature of the case, the office had decided to have them signed in full.

"Here's your pen, Chief." Vicki slid a black Mont-blanc from its immaculate crystal pen holder and handed it to him, but Bale swiveled around in the chair and slid a new piece of paper out of the computer printer behind. Vicki set the pen down, puzzled. "What's that?"

"A new page. I corrected a mistake you made. I noticed it when I read it earlier."

"A mistake on Morty's papers?" Vicki's mouth went dry as Bale signed. "I proofread them a zillion times. What was wrong?"

"This." Bale handed her the page across the desk, and Vicki looked at it. He had added a new signature line, left blank, and underneath the line, it read:

"For the United States: VICTORIA ALLEGRETTI."

"Sign, please." Bale handed the Montblanc across the desk.

Vicki felt herself tear up, then blinked it away.

"Better hurry and sign. We got some killers to catch." Bale waved the pen, and Vicki took it.

"Does this mean it's my case?"

"Absolutely." Bale nodded, with a smile. "My sign-off is pro forma. I can't think of anybody more deserving."

"Thanks, Chief," Vicki managed to say, and signed the complaint and warrant without crying all over it, which was a feat.

"I would let you handle it through indictment and trial, but we'll need you as fact witness, describing what happened and making the ID of the shooter. You know you can't do both, under the rules."

"I know." But Vicki could at least handle the initial appearance and work behind the scenes at trial. She gave the papers back to Bale. "Thanks."

"Now shut up while I sign the rest." Bale sat down and started reading, which gave Vicki time to recover her composure.

"I guess this means I keep my job?"

"Unfortunately. I can't fire you now." Bale didn't look up from his reading. "I want you at the press conference."

"Yay!" Vicki couldn't help herself. Outside the window, the sun was rising and a new day dawning, but she was pretty sure it was a coincidence.

"And at the conference, we will provide no details at all about how this case went down. You keep those details to yourself and let Strauss and ATF do all the talking." Bale kept reading. "Don't blow this, or Strauss will have my head."

"Agreed."

"But you know what I think, don't you? I told you last night." Bale looked up, pen poised and eyes narrowed the way they had at about two in the morning, when he'd lectured her over pizza about the dangers she'd caused herself and others. "Never again, you promise?"

"Promise. But I'm going to the arrest, aren't I?"

"You stay in the car, like a good pup."

"Arf!" Vicki barked, and Bale got busy reading again. She watched, then took a flyer, since he was in an admitting kind of mood. "You have to admit I did a good job, boss."

"No, I don't, because you didn't." Bale didn't look up, but kept signing. "You got good results, but your methods were terrible. Dangerous. I'm putting you on another drug case, Kalahut, pairing you with ATF agent Barbara Pizer. She'll keep you too busy to think about playing detective."

"Understood," Vicki said. She decided to shut up and start taking yes for an answer.

But she found herself thinking, unaccountably, of her father.

Vicki had never been part of a major federal drug bust, and the takedown played out with a coordination and precision that would have amazed the average taxpayer, if not combat veteran. Twenty ATF agents in full gear, deployed with assault rifles and fresh warrants, reinforced by FBI agents and Philly SWAT teams, conducted, at exactly eight-seventeen on Friday morning, surprise raids on the homes, businesses, and street corners worked by each of the fifteen defendants. Dan had gone with Strauss to watch them execute the warrant on Toner for the Toys "R" Us murders, but Vicki, protected in a heavy black Kevlar vest and ensconced in an unmarked escort van, watched as ATF knocked and announced themselves at the row house of Jay Steptoe, then burst in to execute. The agents emerged without gunfire or event only ten minutes later, with a struggling Steptoe, dressed in black sweatpants and a white T-shirt.

Vicki gasped. Steptoe was cursing and fighting the agents, his expression showing the same malevolence it had the night he'd shot Morty to death, then turned the gun on her. She peered out the tiny porthole of the van, deriving great satisfaction in seeing him dragged down the front walk, kicking and screaming, and into a waiting squad car.

"Woohooo!" Vicki turned to the right, by habit, but Reheema wasn't there. As a civilian, she hadn't been permitted to come, and Vicki had barely had a chance to say good-bye to her, and thanks, before she'd put her in the elevator.

Wouldn't have got him without you, Lady Tiger, Vicki thought as she watched the squad car drive off, with its siren blaring.

Vicki wasn't completely surprised to find the press conference as carefully staged, timed, and coordinated as the drug bust. U.S. Attorney Strauss, Chief Bale, brass from ATF, FBI, Philly police, and finally Dan and Vicki stood at the front of the room, in the glare of klieglights and at least forty-five still cameras and videocameras. Strauss took the podium precisely at 12:10, arranged to give the local networks the time to broadcast the warehouse fire du jour, then cut to the press conference.

Strauss cleared his throat. "My office today is announcing that a major victory has been won in Project Clean Shopping to keep the city of Philadelphia free of violent crime. Today, we have arrested and captured one William Toner, the individual who, as part of a drug conspiracy, is charged with the murder of two drug dealers and five other innocent citizens in front of Toys 'R' Us the other day."

Photos snapped, motor drives whirred, and there was even applause.

"In addition, as part of the same master raid, we have today arrested one Jay Steptoe for the murder of ATF Special Agent Robert Morton, whom you may recall was shot down last week in the line of duty."

There was applause at that, and Vicki looked down.

"Here are the charges, and the defendants, in summary," Strauss continued, and Vicki didn't listen to the rest, not after the part about Morty. She was thinking about what Bale had said, about the force of law, and how in the end, it had prevailed. The office would have to try the case against Steptoe and she would have to make sure they won, and something told her that she would, for Morty.

"Finally," Strauss concluded, "it is very important at this time for me to give credit for his fine investigative and supervisor efforts in connection with this matter, which, as you can imagine, was a Herculean task." Strauss paused, and the silence made Vicki look up, bringing her out of her reverie.

"I would like to publicly thank Chief Howard Bale, Section Chief, for his unwavering commitment both to justice and to the safety of our citizens in this highly dangerous and vitally crucial area of law enforcement. Chief Bale?" Grinning, Strauss extended his long arm, like a game show host, at Bale. The audience clapped, and Vicki joined them spontaneously, and Dan followed suit so she wouldn't look stupid. She would have to thank him later, in bed.

Bale took the podium and said a few words, then the ATF and FBI brass, and finally the mayor, the police commissioner, the deputy mayor, and the president of the chamber of commerce, who invited everybody to come out and shop, shop, shop in safety. The press conference finally ended, and Vicki couldn't help but wonder if Reheema had been watching TV and what she thought of the show.

Which reminded Vicki that she still had some unfinished business.

THIRTY-NINE

VICKI LAY WITH HER HEAD HAPPILY NESTLED on Dan's warm chest, at home, in the quiet dark of the bedroom she was coming to think of as theirs. She knew the thought was premature, but it was hard to think clearly after really terrific sex with a man she loved, under a white baffle comforter, with a calico cat curled into a variegated ball at the foot of the bed. Especially when you've left work early to make love. Vicki considered making hooky sex her new hobby.

The late afternoon sun, which had been outside the bedroom window when they had come home, had long gone, swept away by the frosty blue blast of a winter sky. It had to be six o'clock, or later. Vicki focused dreamily on the blue square over the half curtains, but couldn't tell if it would be cloudy again. As a little girl, she used to watch for the stars before sleep, imagining them in winter as hard as diamonds, fired by the cold of heaven.

"So that was my reward?" Dan asked, his voice soft and deep.

"Yes. I'm a fan of positive reinforcement. Lucky you."

"In that case, it'll have to do."

"Very funny." Vicki pinched Dan's side, and he squirmed.

"I'm still mad at you, though."

"Aw. Don't start all over again."

"I am. You've been rewarded, too, by my fabulous sexual prowess, but you should be punished."

"Spank me."

"I'm not kidding. Going into my briefcase? Stealing my papers? Staking out dangerous felons? Lying to me, day after day?"

"I'm sorry I lied to you."

"You even acted like you hadn't seen that photo of Toner, when you *took* it!"

Vicki winced. "I'm sorry about that, too."

"What about the other things?"

"I'm not sorry about them."

"You should be!" Dan didn't sound like he was smiling, and it was killing her postcoital stargazing.

"Look, I won't make a habit of it, but I got the guy who killed Morty and I'm proud of that. And aren't you happy we got Toner?"

"You and Reheema could have been arrested, too! She's the one who got you into this."

"No, she didn't," Vicki said, defensive. "If anything, I got her into it."

"I don't like her. The woman is hostile."

"I like her. Hostility is part of her charm."

After a minute, Dan said, "Vick?"

"What?"

"Your behavior was really inappropriate."

Vicki smiled. "You sound like the school principal."

"Maybe because I am. Or at least, I will be."

"What do you mean?"

"I'm not supposed to say."

"Tell me. What's going on?" Vicki lifted her head and looked up at Dan, and in the semidarkness, his lips were curving into a mysterious smile.

"Well, some promotions are in the wings. It's unofficial now, but they're going to announce it on Monday, to the office and the press."

"Announce what?" Vicki shifted excitedly onto her elbow, and Dan was already propping himself up on a pillow.

"I'm going to be the new chief."

"*You!* Congratulations!" Vicki's heart filled and she reached for Dan, and he hugged her back warmly.

"Isn't that amazing?"

"It's great!"

"I get a raise, too, three grand." Dan grinned. "There's a transition period. The promotion becomes effective a month from next week."

"What's happening to Bale?"

"He's gonna be the new U.S. Attorney."

"Wow! No wonder Strauss thanked him at the conference."

Dan nodded. "Strauss told me he's setting up the press."

"And Strauss is going to be what?"

"He's about to be nominated to the Third Circuit. They've been talking about it behind the scenes for months."

"You're kidding! I had heard that was what he wanted."

"Yeah, and with the bust today, he was told it's been put on the front burner and he'll be confirmed with no problem. I think he's heading for the Supremes, but I don't know."

"Well, good for him. Dan, jeez! You, *chief*?" Vicki began to process the news. "Wait, does that mean I'm sleeping with my boss?"

"Honestly, yes. If we keep this up." Dan's smile faded, and Vicki felt a note of worry.

"What do you mean, if? Of course we'll keep it up. We love each other."

"I'm not saying I want to give you up. I just got you."

"Me, too. I mean, me, neither!" Vicki was too tired to think. She hadn't slept in twenty-odd hours. Her eyelids felt suddenly leaden, but it could have been a stress reaction. "We can keep these things separate. Love and work, you need both."

"In the same place? What about the way it looks? There'll be gossip."

Vicki didn't like his tone of voice. She wished it weren't so dark so she could see his face more clearly. "They gossiped about us when you were married, too. Who cares about gossip anyway?"

"We both do. People don't know about us now, but I have discretion, as Chief, in giving out cases. Promotions, raises. It'll look like I'm favoring you."

"Well, you won't." Vicki felt her heart tug. "What, do you stop loving me when you get a promotion?"

"No, of course not," Dan answered softly. "I do love you, sweetie." He reached for Vicki and pulled her close, where she burrowed back into his chest, reclaiming him. He sighed. "Look, let it go, for now. This was an endless day, and I have no idea when was the last time you slept. Let's just get some rest."

"I can't sleep after this!"

"Yes, you can. You're beat." Dan shifted down in bed, still holding Vicki, and pulled the comforter over them both. "Just go to sleep and don't worry about a thing."

"I am worried."

"Everything's gonna be all right," Dan said, kissing her head. "Good night."

"Good night," Vicki said, but she was remembering something about relationships. Men always slept better after a fight. In fact, a good fight was like Tylenol P.M. for men. She tried to relax and kept watching the sky to see if the stars came out. But they didn't.

The next time Vicki opened her eyes was 9:17 at night. The bedroom was dark and quiet except for the hissing of the radiator and Dan's regular breathing. The cat wasn't in her spot any longer, but had left for her nightly walkabout, which included scratching noisy newspaper, crawling into noisy shopping bags, and meowing out the window, noisily, at streetlights. Vicki liked Zoe, but stepcats had their drawbacks.

She turned over and remembered what she and Dan had been talking about just before they'd fallen asleep. She turned and tried to put it out of her mind, without success. She got up, went to the bathroom, then came back to bed, sat down carefully, and watched Dan sleep the peaceful sleep of the newly promoted.

I love you, sweetie.

Vicki felt nervous, worried, hungry, and disoriented. She had been up and active for so many nights, she'd become as nocturnal as Zoe. She found herself wondering what Reheema was doing. They hadn't spoken since the morning. She looked down at Dan, arms thrown up behind his head, and knew she'd never fall back to sleep. If she went back to bed, she'd just wake him. She needed to think, and she needed a friend. So she got up, got dressed, and left her new boss a note on the pillow.

An hour later, Vicki was back in her beloved Cabrio, listening idly to KYW radio's continuous loop of coverage of what they were calling the Toys "R" Us Arrests and the Major Drug Bust. The mayor was quoted at length, then Strauss, on audiotape, and Vicki was enjoying hearing great things about truth, justice, and the American way when she remembered something she had forgotten.

She fumbled in her pocket for her cell phone, bypassing that pesky gun from the night before. She found the cell, flipped it open with a thumbnail, and pressed speed dial for her parents' home number, so it didn't look like she was playing favorites by picking one cell or the other. She had a fifty-fifty chance. The phone stopped ringing and the call connected.

"Mom?" Vicki asked, hopefully.

"Hello, honey!"

Yes! "Just wanted to say hi. I figured you guys would have seen me on the news. We arrested the man who killed my partner, the ATF agent."

"Yes! It was very exciting!" Her mother sounded genuinely happy, and in the background, Ruby the Insane Corgi barked and barked. "What a wonderful result, and you looked so nice up there. Your shoes were perfect."

"They always are." Vicki smiled. This phone call

would be easy, because the party line was completely sanitized. This time the United States Attorney was lying to Vicki's parents, though she welcomed the help.

"Hold on a sec. I'll get your father on the extension."

No! The only thing worse than her father on the phone was her father on the extension. Her mother covered the phone while she called for him, and he picked up after a traffic light changed to green.

"Victoria?" her father said. Now there was barking in stereo.

"Yes, hi. I just wanted to say hello, and tell you things are going well. I guess you saw the press conference and the news."

"Yes, I read the account online, too. Sounds very interesting, and the phones have been ringing at the office all day. Harry and Janet Knowles, you know what nice people they are, called and so did Maureen Thompson and Gail Graves."

Their client family. "That's nice."

"Also her sister, Lynne Graves Stephenson, you remember her, from Chester County. Will Donato called, too, and one other. Oh yes, Karen Abdalla-Oliver and Mama Jean Brightcliffe."

You sure that's everybody?

"And Phyllis Banks, from South Philly."

"South Philly Phil?" Vicki smiled at the memory. She missed Phyllis.

"Yes. She's very happy for you. You and your colleagues must be very pleased."

"I am." *But you will never be.*

"It sounds like a very big case, fifteen defendants, all manner of counts."

Her mother added, "Well, I hope you're getting some rest, dear. You did look a little tired, on TV."

It's the sex. "Well. I gotta go, Mom. It's late. I just wanted to check in."

"Good, get some sleep, honey," her mother said, and her father added:

"Pleasant dreams."

In time, Vicki crossed into Devil's Corner and had reached Lincoln Street, surprised to see lights, commotion, and activity. She drove down Lincoln, closer to whatever was going on; one block, then two, until she had to stop. Reheema's block had been cordoned off by police sawhorses, and a crowd of people filled the street, milling around outside, even in the frigid air. TV klieglights sliced the night sky, calcium-white beams knifing the cold cobalt-blue, and the white microwave antenna of a mobile newsvan towered almost as high as the row houses.

Vicki's mouth went dry. She flashed on the scene outside Shayla Jackson's, the night she'd been killed. Reheema's block looked like a crime scene. What could it be? She had listened to the radio on the way over, and the news had been dominated by the Toys "R" Us arrests and the drug busts. She hadn't heard anything about trouble in Devil's Corner. Maybe it had just happened and hadn't hit the media yet.

Alarmed, Vicki slammed on the brakes, yanked up the emergency, and parked the car. She jumped out and hustled toward the crowd and the TV lights, her heart lodged somewhere in her throat. She reached the crowd and heard noise, talk, and shouting coming from near Reheema's house.

"What's going on?" Vicki asked a man in a down parka, but his thick hood was up and he turned away. Then she heard rap music and what sounded like singing.

Huh? Vicki wedged her way through the crowd, which was buzzing and chattering happily away. People carried homemade signs that they pumped in time to the *thumpa-thumpa* rap. A handwritten poster on a stake read, KEEP THE DEVILS OUT OF DEVIL'S COR- NER! Another sign, Magic Marker on oak tag, said, TO HELL WITH THE HOLE!

Vicki relaxed, smiling. It wasn't a crime, it was some sort of block party. She wedged her way toward Reheema's, where she smelled hot dogs and grilling barbecue. Nelly rapped about Nellyville on a boom box, and neighbors danced, laughed, smoked, and talked on the street and sidewalk, heedless of the temperature. It was a joyous sight for a street that used to be so deserted, and in the middle of the crowd, dancing tall above the other heads, there bopped a familiar knit cap.

"Reheema!" Vicki called out, making a mitten megaphone. Reheema looked over at the sound, but couldn't see a very short AUSA among the revelers. "It's me!"

A few neighbors looked over curiously, but most clustered around a TV reporter, watching the interview and making funny faces in the background. The TV reporter was the only other white face in the crowd, and he held a bubble microphone in front of a mother cradling a bundled-up toddler on her hip. The mother said into the mike: "This is a celebration of the families who live in Devil's Corner! We're takin' back our neighborhood! We shut down the store on Cater Street and we're gonna make damn sure it don't come back!"

The TV reporter looked a little nervous, the neighbors cheered, and Vicki threaded her way to the knit cap.

"Come 'ere, girl!" Reheema shouted above the din, smiling broadly when she recognized her. "What're *you* doin' here!"

"I missed you!" Vicki shouted back, and they made their way to the fringe of the crowd, where it was quieter.

Reheema beamed. "Check it! What do you think of our party?"

"It's great! What's going on?"

"We tore down the wall on Cater, threw out the trash, and cleaned out the hole. And we got teams signed up for a neighborhood watch." Reheema waved at someone who had been calling her name. "Gonna walk around. Wear orange safety belts, like in grade school."

"For real?"

"*Believe* it! It's a party!"

"Ding, dong, the witch is dead!"

Reheema blinked. "Say what?"

"White culture thing."

Reheema smiled. "Whatever, isn't it great? I never met these people, now they're all coming out, meetin' each other. Organized. Together. And guess what, I'm block captain!"

Vicki saluted.

Reheema laughed. "I gotta give you the credit. I'm not gonna sell this house. I bought and paid for it, and my mother lived here. I *belong* here. And I started to figure, why does this Harvard girl care more about where I live than I do?"

Vicki smiled, touched.

"When they had that press conference today, all those suits, and then *you,* I said to myself, All right, let's see if we can keep it clean here, on our own. So I went door to door and they all took it up." Reheema grinned. "They were just scared, is all."

Vicki looked around, happily. "Well, they're not anymore."

Reheema eyed the crowd, too. "No, they're drunk!"

They both laughed, and if they'd been girly girls, they would have hugged. But that wasn't happening, and the stars weren't diamonds, either.

Vicki said, "I wanted you to know I appreciated your help, all last week, and with that kid. I never could have caught him. You were so brave, and you can run!"

Reheema shook it off. "I owe you, too. You gave me back my house."

"I didn't forget about your mom."

"I knew you wouldn't."

"Good." Vicki liked the sound of that. It was trust, which was even better than a hug. "Tomorrow morning, at nine?"

"Ha! You got a plan?"

"What do *you* think?"

And they slapped five. Black glove against red mitten.

FORTY

SATURDAY MORNING, VICKI AND DAN GOT UP
early, showered, dressed, and went down to the kitchen
together, making coffee more silently than usual. Vicki
worried that something was wrong. First, Dan hadn't
wanted to make love when they woke up, but she tried
not to let that bother her. Maybe he was the one man
on the planet who didn't automatically want to make
love in the morning. Second, when Dan brushed
against her elbow on his way to the coffeemaker, he
said, "Excuse me." Vicki tried not to give that much
weight, though she was losing that battle, too. Loss of
libido and good manners were sure signs that a couple
was circling the toilet.

"Are we breaking up?" Vicki asked, turned suddenly
from the sink.

"What? No. Of course not." Dan's brow furrowed,
and he looked at her like she was crazy.

"I'm not crazy."

"I didn't say you were."

Oh. "Last night you said we might break up, because of your promotion."

"No I didn't." Dan hit the Brew button. "I said I was worried about how our being a couple would affect work, and vice versa, but that doesn't mean we're breaking up."

Vicki blanched. "It sounds like it does."

"Well, I didn't mean it that way." Dan smiled. The coffee began its happy gurgling, and he came over and gave her a hug. He was wearing Vicki's favorite baggy jeans and navy crewneck, and even that didn't cheer her up. "How about we go on a date tonight? A real date, go out and celebrate?"

"Celebrate what?" Vicki whined, and enjoyed it. Nobody could whine like a suburban girl.

"Celebrate that the good guys won, and, in this case, they happen to be in love with each other."

"Okay."

"Good." Dan gave Vicki a quick kiss, which she worried was too wife-y and not girlfriend-y enough, then he patted her on the butt, which was downright quarterback-y. "Now we gotta get to work."

Go, team! "We do?" Vicki checked her watch. 7:38. She was supposed to meet Reheema at nine.

"Yeah, we do. We executed a coupla warrants yesterday, if you remember." Dan laughed softly as he opened the dishwasher, grabbed their Harvard and Elvis mugs, and set them on the counter. "We have to start preparing for the grand jury hearings. We'll need scripts for cross-examination, for witnesses, subpoenas prepared, you know this drill." Dan's cell phone started ringing in its belt holster, and he twisted it upward to read the display. "Unknown number, that's the press. I told Strauss I'd be in at nine."

Great minds. "Uh, well, I was going to meet Reheema this morning."

"Your friend from last night." Dan's face lengthened under his fresh shave. "What trouble did you two get into, anyway?"

"None, we just said hi." Vicki cheered up. "They were actually having a party in the neighborhood, and they're gonna keep the crack out. We actually helped them. That neighborhood will survive now, and Reheema's organizing it."

"Is that the truth?" Dan lifted an eyebrow, and Vicki made a decision.

"I'm not going to lie to you anymore. That's all we did. But we still don't know who killed her mother or why she was set up for the straw purchase, and I want to help her with that."

"Oh, you do."

"I was wondering what you thought, too, about something else. Can you listen without freaking out?" Vicki didn't wait for an answer. She had told him last night that she'd taken Toner's record from his briefcase, but she hadn't mentioned she'd taken the HIDTA charts of Ray James, too. Time to come clean. "I'd love to have my sounding board back."

"Go right ahead," Dan said, pouring them coffee, so Vicki accepted her mug and filled him in about her taking James's records and tracing her cell phone to Albertus. Dan wasn't smiling when she was finished. "So it's hired killers, now."

"Even I think I might be in over my head."

"But you're not gonna stop, are you?"

"Dan, Reheema ran down that kid for me, and he could have been armed, for all she knew. I owe her."

"No, you don't."

"Then it's the right thing to do." Vicki couldn't believe his stubbornness. "Even a crack addict is somebody's mother. This one was Reheema's. She deserves justice as much as Morty does, isn't that the point? Equal justice under the law?" *Chief?*

"Okay. You want my help?" Dan set his mug on the tile counter, with a ceramic *clank*. "Let's make a deal."

"What?" Vicki smelled another fake Vuitton.

"Let me handle it. I'll ask Strauss to make a phone call and get the Bristow homicide a top priority for the Philly cops. VIP treatment. They'll have time, now that the Toys 'R' Us case is cleared. I also give him a heads-up, off the record, about Bethave and her son. See if he can get a patrol car on their block, keeping an eye out."

"Great!" Vicki felt better already, and Dan was already smiling at her the way he used to. Yesterday.

"In return, you and Reheema don't investigate hired killers. This really is a matter for the cops. You've done great legwork, but it's too risky to go further. Deal?"

"Deal." Vicki nodded. "Only one loose end. I still don't know why Shayla Jackson set Reheema up for the straw purchase. None of the busts yesterday explain that at all. I don't even know how Jackson knew Reheema."

"What's the difference, Vick?" Dan asked, with a weary smile. "Reheema is fine now, and the guy who killed your CI is in custody. No harm, no foul."

Vicki almost laughed. "Except that Reheema lost almost a year of her life in jail."

"If she had told us she had given the guns to her mother, she probably wouldn't have been charged."

"But her mother would have been. It's still a loose end."

"Life is full of loose ends. You can't know everything, babe." Dan smiled. "Now. You coming to work with me?"

"Not yet. I have something to do this morning."

"Not with Reheema?"

"Yes."

Dan laughed. "What now?"

Vicki told him, but she wasn't asking permission.

And, in the end, it wasn't given.

An hour later, the morning sun was climbing the clouds in the sky and Vicki was back driving the Cabrio, supplied with fresh coffee and newspapers. She'd have to return her rental fleet, but that was low priority today. Stopped in traffic, she read the newspaper headlines. TOYS "R" US GUNMAN IN FEDERAL CUSTODY, announced a banner on the *Philadelphia Inquirer*, while the local tab went with KID KILLER KAUGHT. Both papers had a short sidebar and bio on Morty, including a photo and quotes by Strauss. Neither newspaper had a sidebar on Shayla Jackson.

Vicki glanced up but traffic was still stalled, so she went back to reading. Both papers covered the stories every which way, including sidebars on the ATF SWAT team methods, new security measures in shopping malls, use of surveillance security cameras, and the crack cocaine trade. She paged to the *Inquirer* op-ed, where an editorial entitled IGNORED AT OUR PERIL emphasized the connection between the crack cocaine trade and random violence at toy stores. Vicki counted that as progress.

The traffic freed up, and she took off, and in no time entered Devil's Corner and turned onto Lincoln Street. The sawhorses were gone, but crushed paper cups, soiled napkins, and beer cans littered the street, and they were being picked up by a small cadre of neighbors carrying black trash bags. Reheema, in her pea coat, was one of the hardy few, and she dumped her Hefty bag in a can and waved good-bye to her neighbors when she spotted the Cabrio.

Vicki pulled up at the curb, leaned over, and opened the passenger door for Reheema, who looked like a new woman. Her hair was pulled back into a sleek ponytail, gold studs made bright dots in her ears, and a light swipe of pink gloss gave her full lips a shine.

"Wow, you look great!" Vicki said.

"No more disguises, thank God." Reheema folded herself into the passenger seat, and almost immediately the Cabrio interior filled with a lavender fragrance.

"You even *smell* great. I have a girl crush."

"I showered!" Reheema smiled. "I got heat, electric, *and* water."

"Party! We so love our utilities."

"We so *do*!"

"In fact, how about I buy the Intrepid, and you can pay me back when you get a job." Vicki felt flush, now that she had her job back. "Or you can have the Sunbird. I'm your vehicle, baby."

"I'll think about it, thanks a lot." Reheema grinned. "Now, where we goin'?"

"First, let me tell you what's going on with your

mother's case." Vicki hit the gas and pulled away as she filled her in about the deal with Dan. Reheema nodded, listening with her head slightly inclined.

"So Dan the Man is gonna pull some strings?"

"He'll get the case VIP treatment, he said."

"We'll see what he comes up with, for the time being. I want to know who killed her."

"Of course," Vicki said, praying that Dan came through. "If the cops pick up this hired killer, that frees us to try to figure out why Jackson set you up."

"Wonder if they're connected."

Vicki looked over and almost ran the red light. "Think out loud."

"What?"

"Tell me what you're thinking. Maybe we can figure it out together. I do it all the time."

"I never do."

Vicki smiled. "Go ahead. Try."

Reheema paused. "Okay, well, it's just that Jackson framed me, about a year ago, and then somebody killed my mother. It's like a puzzle, and if you just look at that one piece, it kinda makes you think somebody doesn't like the Bristows."

Vicki blinked. "True. Any ideas?"

"If my dad weren't dead already, I woulda thought of him, first."

Vicki kept her own counsel. It made her family issues look like comic relief. "Any other relatives?"

"No, just her and me, long as I can remember. I had an uncle but he's gone, too."

"What about that boyfriend you mentioned?"

"Gone and married."

"I'd wonder about the FDC, but the timing's wrong, you were set up before."

"I got no enemies."

"Hard to believe," Vicki said, and they laughed, now that they were friends. Almost.

"Think they're connected?"

"Possibly." Vicki was kicking herself. She should have thought of that herself, but she had been so focused on Morty. "It doesn't change what we have to do. Let's let the cops work from that end and we'll work from ours. If we meet in the middle, we still win."

Reheema nodded. "So, what's the plan?"

"We canvass the neighborhood."

"Which means what?"

"Well, our problem is that we don't know why Jackson set you up. We have to learn more about Jackson and figure out her connection to you. So we ask her neighbors. Cops do it all the time after a murder. It's only because this time they had an eyewitness—me—it wasn't so necessary. Or if they did it, I don't know."

"What about what you thought before, that maybe Jackson was jealous of me? That Browning and her saw me and so she set me up."

"That's one of the reasons I want to find her friend Mar, who her mother told me about. Mar could tell us if Browning even knew you." Vicki remembered that missing file of grand jury testimony. "Without support, it's far-fetched."

Reheema fell quiet as the Cabrio wound its way through traffic, and so did Vicki, until a thought struck her:

"What if you're in danger now, Reheema?"

"What?"

"What if whoever was hired to kill your mom intended to kill you, too?" Vicki's fingers squeezed the steering wheel, as the possibility began to dawn on her. "I mean, you were supposed to be released from the FDC earlier that day, and the paperwork got held up. Maybe you were the real target, and your mom was just there. Or they meant to get you both." Vicki locked eyes with Reheema and they both knew it wasn't that crazy. "Whoa."

"Yeah." Reheema winced as Vicki dodged a SEPTA bus passing on her left. "But who would know I was being released? Had to be somebody at your office."

"What?"

"Think about it. If that's true, the only people who knew I was being let out of the FDC were the people in your office, whoever they are. Or the Philly cops, or the ATF guys. Did any of them know?"

Vicki scoffed. "Then that's not what happened. Forget it. That's impossible."

"Is it?" Reheema lifted an eyebrow.

"Of course it is. But it is possible that you're in danger, so it's all the more reason we have to learn more about Jackson. Her mother told me that Jackson had decided to change her life and was going to move. We know she was packing." Vicki toted it up. "I think she broke up with Browning and wasn't dating anyone."

"Okay. So?"

"None of us lives in this life alone. She had a friend. Mar." Vicki was thinking out loud, too, and it was nice to have someone else as a sounding board. Maybe that was the Almost Friend part. "Did she go to a gym? Did she go to a doctor? She was pregnant, so she'd need prenatal check-ups. Who's her doctor?"

"Okay, so we go to the houses and we ask questions."

"Right." Vicki took a left turn, and Reheema frowned.

"You're lost, aren't you?"

Vicki nodded. "Don't start with the Harvard stuff again."

"Did I say anything?"

FORTY-ONE

AN HOUR LATER, VICKI PARKED THE CABRIO, grabbed her bag and the newspaper, and they walked together in the cold sun to Jackson's house, a two-story brick semidetached. The crime scene tape was gone, though a shred of yellow strip flapped in the bitter wind. Vicki felt herself shudder at the sight. Coming back to where Morty had been killed was easier in theory than in practice. Somehow, having his killer in custody didn't ease the pain.

She and Reheema walked up the concrete front steps of the row house attached to Shayla Jackson's and knocked on the front door. The door opened, an older man answered, and Vicki stepped forward. "Sir, my name is Vicki Allegretti, and I'm trying to learn a little about your neighbor, Ms. Jackson, who was killed the other day."

"Didn't know her," the man answered, and slammed the door shut.

"Nice technique," Reheema said, and Vicki smiled as they went down the front walk and to the next house.

Vicki knocked on the door, and an older woman answered, so she introduced herself and said, "I'd like to ask you a few questions about your neighbor, Ms. Jackson, who was killed the other day. It won't take long."

The woman looked from Vicki to Reheema, behind her bifocals. "What do you wanna know?"

"May we come in?"

"No."

"Did you know Ms. Jackson?"

"Not very well, she kep' to herself."

"Did you talk to her much, even casually? Like if she had to borrow something, or you did?"

"No. I saw on the TV they caught the guys that killed her."

"They did. Were you here that night? Did you see or hear anything?"

"I was at work, I clean at night. I missed the whole thing."

I didn't. "How long did Ms. Jackson live here, if you know?"

"She moved in two years ago, maybe less. I hardly talked to her but once or twice, when the trash man didn't come, during the strike, you know."

"Did she work?"

"I don't think so. She stayed in a lot. Played her music, I use ta hear it through the wall."

Vicki made a mental note. "Do you know if she owned or rented?"

"Rent. We mostly rent on this street. From Polo Realty, in Juniata. They own all these houses."

"Did she live alone, as long as she lived here?"

"Yeh."

Vicki held up the newspaper through the plastic storm window. On the second page were photos of the people killed in the Toys "R" Us murders, with a sidebar about Browning and his driver, whose name was David Cole. Vicki pointed at Browning. "Ever see this man visit Jackson at her house?"

"That was her boyfriend."

"Why do you say that?"

"He was here a lot."

"When would that be about? From when she moved in or later?"

"When she moved in, I think. He helped her move in. I seen him."

"Was she pregnant then?"

"She was pregnant?" The woman's graying eyebrows raised. "Oh yeah, I heard that on the TV but I didn't know that, for myself."

"Okay, ever see the other two?" Vicki pointed to the pictures of Cole and Bill Toner.

"No."

"Ever see any other men visit?"

"No."

"Ever see girlfriends visit?"

"No."

"No one girlfriend in particular? You know, like girls have a best friend?"

"No."

"Ever hear her mention a girlfriend named Mar?"

"No, I hardly talked to her." The woman looked behind her. "I gotta go now. I got a cake in the oven."

"Thanks so much for your time," Vicki said, and the door closed.

Reheema said, "She was lying about the cake."

"I would, too."

Vicki and Reheema tried the next seven houses, stopping at the end of the street; two of the neighbors wouldn't answer the door, and the other five knew progressively less about Shayla Jackson. Then they went back to Jackson's and resumed at the first house on the other side, with Reheema pressing the bell. A black teenage boy answered, his eyes widening when he saw a gorgeous black woman standing on his doorstep, having stepped out of his dreams.

"I'm Reheema Bristow, is your mother at home?" she asked, and the kid nodded.

Suddenly, Vicki's cell phone started ringing in her purse, so she stepped back and pulled it from her bag.

Groaning when she read the display.

Vicki stepped off the elevator into work, surprised to find the floor crowded and abuzz with action. Reporters, and photographers spilled into the elevator bank, talking and laughing in groups, with still cameras hanging on their shoulders and steno pads stuffed in the back pocket of their jeans. ATF personnel, Philly uniformed cops, and an older AUSA stood talking to the press. She had to barrel through the throng to the reception room, and heads began turning as reporters recognized her and began to call to her.

"Just one comment, Ms. Allegretti!" "One question, Ms. Allegretti?" "Picture, Vicki, how about a picture?" "Nice bust, Allegretti!"

Vicki put her head down and called "No comment" to the reporters mobbing her. The reception desk was fully staffed behind its bulletproof glass, and both receptionists buzzed her in with matching grins and a thumbs-up. Beyond the door, AUSAs, ATF agents, secretaries, and paralegals were going back and forth in the halls, and they all congratulated Vicki on the fly. She acknowledged so many snippets of "Sweet!" "Great work!" and "Go get 'em!" that she felt like a celebrity.

AUSAs in jeans and sweaters worked in their boxy offices off the hall, but heads popped up from their desks and smiled at her when she passed, and a group of senior AUSAs stood talking near her office, their heads turning as one when she walked by. "Way to go, Vicki!" called one of the nicest, Marilyn Durham, and an AUSA next to her, Martin Frank, called out, "Allegretti, sweet!" A third, Janie Something, hollered, "'Bout time, sleepyhead!"

"Thanks!" Vicki called out and ducked into the office's formal conference room. She opened the door, and everyone who was anyone was in mid-meeting. It was a large, modern room with a panel of windows on two sides, and the noonday sun streamed cold onto Strauss, presiding at the head of the table, then Bale, Dan, and the office's public relations flack, ATF chief Saxon, a top tier of FBI and ATF agents, the commissioner of the Philadelphia police and two of his white-shirted deputies, and the deputy mayor. The room smelled pleasantly of aftershave, and they all sat with fresh coffee around the glistening table, each with a black three-ring binder bearing the gold DOJ emblem.

"Good morning, Vick!" Bale chirped up, too classy

to give her in public the grief he'd given her on the phone.

"Sorry I'm late," Vick called out, avoiding Dan's eye.

"S'all right, you deserve the extra rest!"

Strauss nodded. "Sure do, young lady! It's been a long trip since that tragic night, but it's all over now." There followed nods and smiles all around, even from Saxon.

"Vicki," Bale continued, "we just got started and we'd like to give everybody an overview, so we're all on the same page." He pointed to an empty chair at the table. "Why don't you grab a coffee and take your seat, so we can get this party started." Everybody smiled. "By the way, before I forget, at noon tomorrow you'll meet with Special Agent Barbara Pizer on Kalahut, that new case. It should take all day." Bale turned to Saxon. "Barbara's a very experienced agent, right, John?"

"One of our best," Saxon answered. He'd lost some weight, and Vicki felt happy for her new friend.

"So, Vick, you'll be multitasking for a while, working the new case and prepping for the grand jury, but you can handle it."

"Thanks," Vicki said, bypassing the coffee and taking her seat in the sun. She felt a wave of guilt that Bale had had to call her to come in. She had hated to leave Reheema to finish the canvassing alone, lending her the Cabrio and her cell phone, but Vicki could see now that she had to be at this meeting. Even though she was one of only three women in the room, and undoubtedly the youngest of all, Vicki felt for the first time as if she belonged here. She had finally become an Assistant United States Attorney. Now all she had to do was figure out how to be in two places at once.

After the meeting, she felt recharged and went to her office and worked all afternoon, preparing scripts for the grand jury in Morty's case. The first script she prepared was for herself, painstakingly setting out each question she should be asked and the answer she'd give, so she'd be able to give a smooth presentation, devoid of emotion. It didn't mean preparing it wasn't emotional, because it required her to relive that night. AUSAs and other staff bustled up and down the halls, but she managed to tune them out and focus on the task at hand.

As the afternoon wore on, she found herself thinking about Reheema. Vicki had called her cell but there was no answer, and her voicemail picked up, so she'd left a message, asking her to call back. She'd told Reheema her voicemail code so she'd be able to retrieve her messages.

When it started to get dark and Reheema still hadn't called back, she began to feel anxious. Was Reheema in danger? Why hadn't she called? Had she found out something? How long did it take to canvass Jackson's street, anyway? Twilight turned to nighttime, and Vicki worried through the pizza the office had ordered. She'd come back to her desk and called her cell again, but voicemail had picked up. By nine o'clock at night, she understood completely why her parents acted like jerks when they were worried about her.

I want a corgi.

"Snack time!" came a voice from the door. It was Dan, grinning, with a large brown bag in his hands, and the office filled instantly with a delicious aroma.

"What's in there?" Vicki asked, and he came in and kicked the door closed with the back of his Adidas.

"Room service from Joe's Peking Duck, just for my baby. That's right, I *am* a great boyfriend." Dan set the bag down and raised his arms. "Reward me, woman."

"Yay!" Vicki rose and gave him a warm hug, which he returned, then found her lips with a very good kiss. "Wow. Taking a chance in the office, aren't you?"

"Just one more." Dan kissed her again, and she felt like his girlfriend again. They broke the embrace, and he started digging in the take-out bag, hauling out the white containers with funny red dragons, one after the other. "Here we have your favorite entree, chicken curry, and cold sesame noodles for an appetizer."

"Yum. Where's yours?"

"I ate with Strauss and Bale and them, at Joe's Peking Duck."

"The big boys." Vicki felt mildly hurt. "You didn't invite me?"

"Aw, babe, it was sort of a spontaneous, late-night thing." Dan winced. "I'm sorry."

"It's okay." Vicki let it go. She didn't want to prove his point that they couldn't have a relationship at work, even if they couldn't. "I'm just worried about Reheema."

"Reheema? Fill me in, and I promise not to get mad." Dan took a seat opposite her desk and leaned back in the chair the way he always did, while Vicki fished in her desk drawer and found a pair of disposable chopsticks, then sat down with her chicken dish and dug in.

"First, did you talk to Strauss about the hired killer and the Bethaves?"

"Yes, I did, and he said he'd talk to him after the meeting today. You saw, the commissioner himself was there." Dan smiled. "Good things are gonna happen now. You'll see."

"Great. Thanks." The chicken tasted wonderful, hot and spicy, and Vicki cheered, momentarily. "Well, Reheema and I kept our side of the bargain today, but I'm worried about her."

"Why?"

"I think she could be in danger. That maybe her being framed and her mother's murder are related, and that whoever went to kill her mother was supposed to kill her, too."

"What?" Dan's eyes went a bewildered blue. "Why would anybody want Reheema dead?"

"I don't know, but then again, I don't know why they'd want her mother dead, either, and that happened." Vicki set down her chicken curry. "She wondered if it is someone at the office, since the only people who knew she was getting released from the FDC were us."

"That's crazy. You guys are going crazy." Dan rose, and Vicki bore down.

"You promised not to get mad."

"I'm not mad, I'm frustrated. You can't believe that. That someone from *here* is plotting against Reheema?" Dan shook his head. "It's like I told you, people like Reheema, they have a different view of the world, coming from a different experience. I don't have to tell you that blacks and whites view the justice system differently, do I?"

"No."

"So of course she's gonna think law enforcement is plotting against her! It's as old as O.J.!"

"Look, obviously, it's no one from here, but I am worried about her."

"You know what bothers me? That there was a roomful of top brass today—every agency in the friggin' city—all sitting around a table, working to make her life better, and she doesn't think of that!" Dan was getting red under his freckles. "Cops and ATF risk their necks every day, and she doesn't think of that! Morty got *killed* running down a CI, and she doesn't think of *that*!"

Whoa. Vicki put up a hand. "She does, and so do I. Please, Dan, sit down. If she's paranoid, she's entitled to it."

"But you should know better." Dan met her gaze evenly, and Vicki didn't flinch.

"Not when she was arrested on the say-so of somebody who said she was her best friend and didn't know her at all. I'm concerned enough to make her stay at the house tonight, so she's safe."

"Stay with *us*?"

"On the couch."

"You're overreacting!"

"I don't want her alone, and I wouldn't sleep worrying like this." Vicki checked the window, where the gray of twilight was deepening toward an inky blue. "I have no way to reach her, short of grabbing a cab and going looking."

"Don't even think about it, Vick. Bale and Strauss are still working. You have to be here."

"What if something happens to her?"

"They're already talking about you."

"What?" Vicki's mouth went dry.

"They're questioning your commitment. Even Bale, since you won't let it go."

"My *commitment*?" Vicki couldn't believe her ears. "We made the bust of the century, at least partly because I put myself out there! *Way* out there!"

"But you did things they don't want you to do. Running around, playing cop." Dan sighed. "Just because they're with the program to the media doesn't mean there aren't doubts about you around here. They're just closing ranks."

Vicki couldn't process it fast enough. So much for her fifteen minutes of fame. She felt suddenly stupid for believing the press releases. It had all gone to her head. *Is it possible to like positive reinforcement too much?*

"They think you're in too deep, because of the trauma of being there, when Morty was killed. You're too emotionally involved because of Morty, and now with Reheema."

"Who thinks that?" Vicki asked, stung.

"They all do." Dan's eyes softened, and he sat back down into his chair. "They wanted to talk to me about staffing at dinner. That's why I didn't ask you to come."

Oh no. "So what did you say?"

"I went to bat for you, of course. You're a great young prosecutor, the best in your class." Dan's mouth flattened with a sort of sadness. "But I'll tell you something, because I love you—they're watching you."

"You're making me paranoid."

"You should be. Your credibility is in question. Your reputation. To me, that's worse than being fired any day."

"But you're going to be chief. You know me."

Dan leaned over. "Vicki, listen to me. You have to stop this. This running around with Reheema. This talk. It's jeopardizing your career and it's embarrassing."

"To whom?" Vicki asked, then she realized. *To him.*

"You have to make a choice."

"Between Reheema and you?"

"No. Between Reheema and *you*."

Suddenly the phone rang on Vicki's desk, and she grabbed the receiver. "Allegretti."

"Yo, girlfriend." It was Reheema.

"Where are you? Are you okay?"

"Fine. Sorry, I had the cell phone off."

"I was so worried!" Vicki said, and in the background, Dan got up and went to the door. "Reheema, wait, hold on a minute." She covered the receiver with her hand. "Dan, wait!"

Dan turned at the door, his hand on the knob. "I'll be at a hotel tonight. You two have fun." Then he walked out and closed the door behind him.

"Vicki? Vicki?" Reheema was saying, and Vicki swallowed the tightness in her throat.

"Yeah, I'm back."

"I'm okay, but I have real bad news."

"I'm all ears," Vicki said, her gaze on the closed door.

FORTY-TWO

"WHAT'S THE BAD NEWS?" VICKI ASKED.

"Mar's dead."

"No." Vicki looked out the window, a black, moonless square that reflected her own unhappiness. There were no stars again. "How?"

"Drug overdose. Crack."

Whoa. "That's terrible. For her and for us."

"I know, right?"

"When?"

"July."

"Last summer. How'd you find out?"

"Long story short, I canvassed the street and got nowhere. Nobody knows Jackson, nobody sees her. Then I remember that lady near Jackson's house, who said their landlord was Polo Realty in Juniata, so I call their offices and go there."

"Good for you."

"I asked can I see the lease, I was Jackson's cousin

and maybe I would rent the place, to keep her memory alive."

"And he bought that?"

"He's white. He thinks black people got some weird ways."

Vicki laughed.

"He's right. Look at Michael Jackson. Man's a freak."

"Okay." Vicki laughed again. Despite the bad news, Reheema was evidently flushed with success, and one of them needed self-esteem right now.

"Well, Jackson signed the lease, but the deposit check, for the earnest money, was from a Martella Jenkins."

"Mar."

"Right, and her address was right on the check."

"Yes! Where does she live, or did she live?"

"Northeast, so I went over. By the way, that Cabrio's a nice car."

"You're not getting the Cabrio." Vicki smiled. "The Intrepid has your name all over it."

Reheema chuckled. "Anyway, her brother told me how she died. He didn't know Jackson, though. He just got back from the army. Been gone five years."

"Great work!"

"Thank you, thank you."

"Where are you now?"

"Still in the Northeast, 'bout an hour away."

"Perfect. Pick me up at the office, will you?"

"Oh, sure. Driving Miss Vicki."

"Gimme a break. Also, I think you should stay at my house tonight."

"No way," Reheema said, and hung up.

*　　*　　*

By eleven o'clock, after a short but intense car ride, they arrived at Vicki's house, but they were barely speaking. Vicki trundled downstairs with a sheet, a thermal blanket, and a feather-filled pillow, while Reheema sulked on a chair in the living room. Zoe rubbed against the leg of her jeans, her tortoiseshell tail curled into a question mark.

"Here we go," Vicki said, hitting the living room. "I'll make up the couch. It'll be nice and comfy."

"I want to sleep in my own house."

"Somebody could be trying to kill you. Namely, me." Vicki dumped the bedclothes on the coffee table.

"This is dumb."

"It is not."

"It is, too."

"I'm taking no chances."

"If somebody's gonna kill me, they could kill me here. This way, you're in trouble, too."

Eek. "Nobody can hurt you with a tiny but very potent AUSA like me on guard." Vicki looked at Zoe, who blinked, green-eyed. "Also, a cat with a heart problem."

"I want my gun."

"No." Vicki made a mental note to take the gun from her purse and put it in a drawer upstairs. She couldn't get it through the metal detectors at work; they kept confiscating it at security and giving it back to her. Evidently she wasn't the first AUSA to be carrying, but it was a huge pain in the butt and was making her nervous, besides.

Reheema got up, grabbed a white sheet, and helped Vicki tuck it around the couch cushions, a task they finished jointly, albeit in silence.

"You still pouting?"

"Yes."

"Sorry." Vicki smiled and sat down on the couch, newly made. "You did well today."

"I know."

"I think what you found out fleshes out what happened to Shayla, if you're interested."

"More thinking out loud?" Reheema sat back down on the chair, in resignation, if not approval.

"Well, you said that Mar was killed last summer. That's about when Jackson's mother told me she decided to change her life. That would make sense, right?"

"Right."

"Okay, so let's assume Jackson dabbles in crack, and—"

"You don't *dabble* in crack. It dabbles in you."

"What I mean is that Jackson is running with a druggie crowd, and her boyfriend is Browning, ace crack dealer. He moves her into a nice place and sets her up."

"Knocks her up, too."

"I hate that expression."

"Sorry, Miss Vicki."

Vicki smiled. "Okay, anyway. Then she gets pregnant and realizes that she has to keep her body clean and change her life. Or she'll end up like her friend Mar, or her baby will."

"People wake up." Reheema nodded. "Not often enough, but they do. Some do."

"So? So what? We learned more about Jackson, but not enough. Or enough to know why she'd frame you, as part of her rehab. Her calling our office would have happened about the same time." Vicki sighed, her fatigue catching up with her, as well as nagging thoughts about Dan. "The problem is, what do we do now? We're at a dead end."

"Not necessarily. I still got people to canvass. Lots of people weren't home today. I'll go back again tomorrow and talk to the ones I missed. They'll be home because I heard it's gonna snow again tomorrow, so everybody'll be hunkering down."

"Were they nearby neighbors?"

"Not really, but you never know. I never quit a race, and I won't start now."

Vicki smiled. "Okay, good. Because I have to go back to work."

"No problem, I'll keep the car and the phone. If you call, leave a message. I got the code."

"Done."

Reheema scratched the top of Zoe's multicolored head. "Did Dan the Man say anything about my mother?"

"He already talked to the U.S. Attorney, who's gonna talk to the commissioner himself."

"When's that gonna happen?"

"I think today or tomorrow."

"Thanks." Reheema paused. "I didn't bother Bethave today, as much as I wanted to."

"Good restraint."

"Not at all. I figured it'd only make her run. She has to think we let it go." Reheema half-smiled. "I'll take the couch."

"No, I will."

"What if Dan the Man comes home and finds me in your bed?"

"He won't." Vicki gave a short laugh, and Reheema cocked her head.

"Uh-oh. Trouble in paradise?"

"Not really. Well, maybe a little."

"Like what?"

Vicki couldn't decide how much to tell her. "He wants me to behave myself, is all."

"Ha! Then he better come get his damn cat," Reheema said, and burst into laughter.

A minute later, so did Vicki.

Even though she knew it was completely lame, Vicki got up early the next morning and spent way too long trying to look hot for her estranged boyfriend, blow-drying her hair and putting on her best jeans and blue cashmere sweater. Reheema dropped her off at work on her way to canvassing, and Vicki stepped off the elevator at eight o'clock into an empty elevator bank; by the time she got to reception, she realized that the media, staff, and curiosity-seekers wouldn't be in today, only the hardworking, fully committed, blown-dry AUSAs. *Like me!*

Vicki waved to the one receptionist, who buzzed her in without a thumbs-up, and she went down the hall-way, which was also empty. She braced herself and popped her head into Dan's office, but he wasn't at his desk, though his light was on. *Fine. Be that way.*

She had work to do and couldn't mope around forever. She went to her office with a cup of fresh Starbucks, took off her coat, pushed up her sweater sleeves, and closed her door so she wouldn't be tempted to look up and see if Dan was there. The night's sleep had brought no change in perspective on their fight; in other words, she still knew she was right and he was wrong. But she missed him.

She sat down at her desk, finished her grand jury script, then started on the other witnesses. The medical examiner, Dr. Soresh, would have to testify, and Vicki looked through her mound of mail for his report, which had come in last week. She found a thick brown envelope with the familiar seal and braced herself. Autopsy reports were always awful to read; she'd start with Jackson's and move on to Morty's only when she felt strong enough. All she had to do was get the basics from each: official cause of death, number and location of entrance and exit wounds, to sketch the case for the grand jury.

Vicki slid out the papers. POSTMORTEM REPORT: JACKSON, SHAYLA read the boldface line at the top. She scanned the first page, containing the grim details about Jackson: "Pregnant Black Female, Age 23; Height 5'4"; Weight, 145." After that, it stated Cause of Death—exsanguination and internal injury due to gunshot wounds—and Manner of Death—Homicide. Vicki made a note of the Manner of Death for her script and turned the page. EXTERNAL EXAMINATION read the top of the page, and the description of the external examination of the body began at the top: "The head is normocephalic. The scalp hair is black and is up to six inches in length. The irrides are brown and the sclerae showed petechiae . . ."

Vicki skipped ahead, then was sorry she had. The cold, typed detail of the chest wounds, in old-fashioned Courier font, were gruesome, and she skimmed them quickly to get to the facts she needed and finish this awful job. She skimmed down to abdomen, which described in medical detail the gunshot wounds to Jackson's abdomen and her uterus beneath, which were all the more horrifying because of the level of medical detail. Just when Vicki thought she couldn't take any more she noticed something in the detail:

The fetus, approximately eight months and one week in gestation, was a female of mixed race, apparently African American and Caucasian.

She blinked, surprised. Vicki had assumed Shayla Jackson's baby was Browning's, but the report meant that it couldn't have been. What did it mean, if anything? Could that have been why they broke up? She skimmed the rest of the report for another reference, but didn't find any.

Suddenly her phone rang and she jumped. "Allegretti," she said, hoping it was Dan.

"Vicki, it's Jane, in reception? There's a buncha boxes just got delivered for you from ATF, Special Agent Pizer. Label says the matter is Kalahut."

"My new case. I'll be right there." Vicki got up, almost relieved to leave the grisly postmortem report behind for a minute. She opened her door and checked Dan's office on the fly, but it was still empty. She went to the reception room, which was dominated by fifteen cardboard boxes with ATF stickers, stacked in the center. "You weren't kidding."

"They delivered a few boxes last night, too," Jane said from behind her bulletproof window. "They're in the file room."

"There's too many to put in my office. Do we have a spare conference room, at least for a few days? I got a meeting with Agent Pizer today." Vicki checked her watch. 11:05. "At noon."

"Hold on." Jane checked the conference room log. "C is free until Friday. It's the little one, with no windows."

"I'll take it. Where's the dolly?"

"In the closet."

"Thanks." Vicki retrieved the orange dolly, loaded the boxes, and wheeled them into the conference room, making three trips, then she headed to the file room for the remainder. The file room smelled vaguely of dust and was empty, large, and windowless. Four cardboard boxes with ATF stickers sat stacked on the counter. Vicki loaded two boxes on the dolly and was about to leave when she remembered the missing transcript from Shayla Jackson's grand jury testimony. It would only take a second to look for it.

She checked her watch: 11:15.

She'd have to get it done fast.

FORTY-THREE

VICKI PUSHED THE DOLLY ASIDE AND WENT around the counter to the case files, which were kept in cabinets arranged alphabetically by the defendant's last name. She stopped at the Be–Bu drawer, pulled it out, and went through the files for *United States v. Bristow*. No luck. Just in case the transcript had been misfiled, she pulled out Branigan, Brest, Bristol, and Bruster, and thumbed through them, but it wasn't there. She thought a minute. It wasn't that old a file, less than a year, and it would still be active. Maybe it was misfiled under Jackson, which would have been an easy mistake to make. She went to the Ja–Jo cabinet and found the Jackson files; there were at least fifty of them.

Argh. Vicki didn't have much time. She pulled out each Jackson file, one defendant at a time—Alvin, Adam, Boston, Calvin—and checked every one for Shayla Jackson's transcript. Still no luck. She closed the cabinet with a final *click*, but she couldn't stop thinking about that transcript. It would be Jackson's own words and the details of what she knew about Reheema. It had been convincing enough to get a grand jury to indict. Where the hell was it? Vicki thought back to her walk with Cavanaugh and tried to remember what he had said about the transcript:

"I admit it, I wasn't into filing. Maybe it got misfiled."

Vicki reasoned it out. If Cavanaugh hadn't filed the transcript in Reheema's case file before he left the office, then, after he left, it would float around and somebody would most likely send it to the file room. What would the file clerks do with it? It would be a transcript, clearly from a grand jury proceeding. They'd be too diligent, or too scared, to throw it away, so they'd stick it somewhere. Where? Vicki realized the answer as soon as she'd asked the question:

The To Be Filed bin! It was a paper version of a homeless shelter. All sorts of stray legal documents were stuck in To Be Filed; papers that nobody could throw away without guilt, or fear of termination. The file clerks were supposed to file the documents from the To Be Filed bin when they got free time, which was never. Vicki looked around for the To Be Filed bin and on top of the first panel of cabinets sat not one but three overflowing bins, all labeled TO BE FILED. *Maybe they reproduce?*

Vicki went up on tiptoe, slid the first bin off the top of the cabinet, then set it on the floor and sat down in front of it, crossing her legs. She started skimming the papers and setting them aside on the rug; she felt energized by the thought of finding the transcript and by

Mocha Java, grande size. The first document was a proffer letter in *United States v. Streat,* the second was a trial transcript in *United States v. Gola,* the third was a motion to suppress in *United States v. Washington,* and so on. Each case caption listed a litany of aliases and nicknames: "Psycho Chris," "Ant," "Shakey," "Baby Al," and "Boxing Bob." The bin was truly a miscellany, documents thrown into a stack, with the only common thread being that nobody knew what else to do with them. Vicki kept reading and in time finished the first bin. No Jackson transcript.

She got up and traded the first bin for the second, then sat back down and got to work. More stray documents, the mundane and the fascinating, all heaped together. By the end of the second bin and still no Jackson transcript, Vicki was telling herself to keep going because the oldest stuff would logically be in the third bin and Cavanaugh had left the office some time ago. She got up, traded bins, then sat down and kept looking, setting the papers to the side as she read. She slowed as she neared the end of the third pile, like a reader making a good book last. But when she finished, there was no transcript.

Damn it to hell! Vicki sighed and checked her watch. 11:45. The ATF agent would be here in fifteen minutes, if the snow didn't slow her down. It had started this morning, and by the time Vicki had gotten into work, there'd been two inches' accumulation. She hurried to put the stacks of miscellaneous papers back in the bin, then stopped at one of the documents when something caught her eye. She picked it up. It was a standard plea agreement in a drug case, *United States v. David "Kermit" Montgomery.* But it wasn't the caption that caught her eye, it was the address of the defendant: 2356 Pergola Street, Apt. 2.

Vicki paused. How did she know that street name? Then she remembered, because it was such an unusual name. Pergola was the Bethaves' street. She flipped through the plea agreement, curious. The indictment was against Montgomery for conspiracy to distribute, and the guilty plea had been entered for a lesser included offense and jail time of six months.

Vicki raised an eyebrow. *Merry Christmas, Mr. Montgomery.* It was a sweet deal for conspiracy to distribute, especially in this climate. Whose case had this been? She turned to the last page and checked the signatures. Strauss and Bale, who signed every plea agreement, and underneath them, the AUSA who had worked the case: Dan Malloy.

Vicki blinked. Odd. It wasn't like Dan to let anybody off so easy. Still, so what? She had to get ready for that Kalahut meeting. She stuck the plea agreement on top of the other papers, stood up with the To Be Filed bin, and replaced it on the top of the file cabinet. She had to get out of here. The Jackson transcript was gone. She went over to the dolly to leave, then stopped. *Pergola Street.* Looking would take only another second, and she'd come this far.

Vicki went back to the file cabinets, took the plea agreement out of the bin, and double-checked the name. David Montgomery. She went to the M's, opened the drawer, and thumbed through the files to see if there was a case file for David Montgomery. She flipped through Martin, Michelson, then, Montgomery. In fact, there were three David Montgomerys, aka, respectively, "Meenie," "Holy Man," and finally, the one she'd seen on the agreement, "Kermit." *Bingo*.

She pulled out the third Montgomery file, which was fairly thick, and opened it. It was a typical legal-size manila folder, and on the left side, attached by a steel fastener, a copy of Montgomery's mug shot was attached to his criminal record. He had narrow, almost slitted eyes, and a small mouth, unsmiling. Next to his mug shot, it read: "Black Male, D/O/B 1/2/72, Height, 6'2", Weight, 210 lbs." Vicki skimmed down the record of offenses: assault with a deadly (knife), aggravated assault, attempted murder for hire.

She felt her heart stop. Knife assaults. A murder for hire. A hired killer, on Mrs. Bethave's street? Could Montgomery be the man who had knifed Reheema's mother to death? The man Mrs. Bethave had been so afraid of? It was too great a coincidence, wasn't it? How many hired killers could there be on Pergola Street?

Vicki suppressed her emotion, so she wasn't jumping to conclusions. She checked the date of the plea agreement. Eight months ago. So Montgomery would be out of prison by now, having served only six months. He'd be free. Living on Pergola Street. Her mouth went dry. She checked Montgomery's house number, 2356. What had Bethave's house number been? Vicki couldn't remember, but it was in the 2000s; she remembered because she had driven across Twentieth Street to get there. So they lived on the same block of Pergola.

Her thoughts raced ahead. Mrs. Bethave had freaked out when Albertus had signed her the killer's name, as if Montgomery could see Vicki and Reheema at the house if they didn't leave fast enough. She could imagine how it would have happened, if Montgomery was the one: Saturday had been the day of the snowstorm, and Albertus could have been playing on the street, as the Holloway kids had been, on Vicki's block. Albertus could have run into Montgomery on the street, and Montgomery could have handed Albertus the cell phone he'd taken from the woman he killed the night before. Arissa Bristow.

Vicki put it together, with a start. David "Kermit" Montgomery. Kermit. The frog. The man who had answered her cell phone that night had spoken in a gravelly voice. Dan had noticed it, too. Was that why Montgomery's nickname was Kermit? Because of his froggy voice? *My God.*

Abruptly, the door to the file room opened, and Vicki almost jumped out of her skin. She turned, and in the threshold stood Jane, the receptionist. "Vicki, oops, sorry, I didn't mean to scare you. That ATF agent has been waiting outside, for your meeting."

"Oh, jeez. Thanks." It was all Vicki could do to slip the file behind her and to collect herself. "Please, tell her I'm sorry, I'll be right there."

"Okay." Jane closed the door.

Vicki's thoughts were a jumble, but she didn't have time to process anything now. She went to the dolly, tore open the top cardboard box, and shoved the Montgomery file inside. Then she wheeled the boxes out of the file room, dumped them in the conference room, and ran to her office with the Montgomery file, which she hid in a drawer. Then she picked up the phone and pressed in the numbers to her cell phone. Snow fell steadily from a gray sky while the phone rang and rang, then her voicemail picked up. She felt herself tense. Reheema had insisted on turning off the phone during her interviews, and Vicki hoped she wasn't answering because she was with one of Jackson's neighbors.

The beep sounded, and Vicki said, "Reheema, I think I have an ID on the man who killed your mother and I'm worried about you. Watch out for a big black guy." She winced when she realized how it sounded. "I'm not kidding or being suburban. He has slitty eyes, age thirty-three, he's about six two, two hundred pounds. His name is David Montgomery, but don't you dare do anything to track him down. I'm going to the cops with this as soon as I can. Call me when you get this message." She hung up, then hit the buttons to forward her calls to the conference room, for when Reheema called back. Then she arranged her face into a professional mask and went to reception to meet Agent Pizer.

Ten minutes later, Vicki was sitting in the shoe box of a conference room with the very able ATF agent, taking notes when it seemed like she should be, asking questions on autopilot, and organizing papers into more piles of papers. Her thoughts were elsewhere. Not only was it weird enough to work with an ATF agent who wasn't Morty, but she sensed she was right about Montgomery. She'd have to talk with Dan and Bale, then get to the Philly detectives so they could pick Montgomery up. Looking in the Bethaves' neighborhood for suspects with a record of murder-for-hire would have been among the first things the detectives would commonly have done, but she wasn't taking the chance that they'd done it yet.

Vicki wondered how it would make Dan feel to learn that someone he'd given a deal to had killed somebody, or even how it would make him look, but she couldn't think about that now. Bale would feel worse for approving it, whether he had reviewed it with any care at all or even if he'd just signed it on Dan's say-so. She didn't know Strauss that well, but she gave him the benefit of the doubt that he'd feel terrible, or at least unhappy that he'd gotten egg on his face. It wouldn't be enough to upset his appointment to the bench or the other promotions, already in the works.

Vicki couldn't begin to answer the harder question of why anybody would hire Montgomery to kill Reheema's mother, or if she weren't the intended victim, Reheema. There were too many missing pieces. She kept looking over at the telephone on the small credenza, expecting Reheema to call, but she didn't. Had she gotten the message? Was she safe? Was Montgomery after her?

Vicki excused herself, saying she had to go to the bathroom, but instead ran to her office and called Reheema again. Still no answer, and she left another message. She hurried back to the conference room, checking her watch on the run. 3:50. At least it was still light out. Montgomery wouldn't attack in broad daylight, would he? He hadn't before. She returned to the conference room, her thoughts going around and around, and allegedly got back to work. She glanced at her watch at 4:01, 4:20, and five more times until 5:01. It had to be getting dark outside, but she couldn't tell without windows. The ATF agent was working away, but Vicki couldn't take it another minute.

She stood up and stretched, theatrically. "Well, we made a lot of progress today," she said, though she had no idea if they'd made progress or not. "I guess it's closing time."

"I thought we were scheduled until six o'clock, and we're in the middle of this—"

"I'm sorry, I thought five o'clock, and with the snow, we should end a little early, don't you think? It was great meeting you." Vicki extended a firm hand across the table, focusing on Agent Pizer for the first time. She was attractive, with her brunette hair cut chin length, and a warm smile. It would've been great meeting her. "Next time, let's have lunch."

"Sure, and I guess we can knock off now." Agent Pizer seemed relieved to slide her jacket from the chair next to her. "You're right about the snow, and it is Sunday, after all."

"Yes, day of rest and all that. And look at the conference table." Vicki gestured to the clutter. "It's a mess, which means we worked very hard."

Agent Pizer laughed. "I knew you'd be funny. Morty really thought the world of you."

"Really?" Vicki asked, surprised. Neither of them had mentioned him until this minute. "He wasn't the type to get mushy."

"I know, it wasn't his style. But he told all of us about you, and he seemed so happy since you two were working together, this past year."

"Thanks." Vicki swallowed the lump in her throat. "Let me walk you out." They left the conference room and went down the hall to reception, and Vicki looked back as they passed Dan's office. He was on the phone, but perked up and caught her eye.

"Vicki?" he called out, covering the receiver with a hand.

"Gimme five minutes," she called back, almost like the old days.

But she knew those days could be gone forever, after they had their next conversation.

FORTY-FOUR

VICKI WENT BACK TO DAN'S OFFICE, WALKED in, and closed the door behind her, just as he was hanging up. He stood up at his desk, his expression soft and a little sheepish. He looked handsome, unshaven, and regretful in his jeans and navy crewneck, which had to be fusing with his skin by now.

Vicki tabled her feelings. She didn't have time for them. "We have to talk."

Dan put up a hand. "I know, I'm sorry. I'm sorry. I'm sorry." He smiled crookedly. "Did I mention I was sorry?"

Vicki felt a tug. "It's not about us. It's more important than us."

"Nothing is more important than us." Dan smiled, cautiously. "Except maybe giving Zoe her meds in the morning."

"I remembered."

"God, I do love you," Dan said, with meaning, and

as touched as she felt, she set the plea agreement on top of the papers on his desk.

"What's this?"

"You tell me." Vicki sat down as he slid the plea agreement toward him and took his seat, reading it. She wished he would hurry. Night was falling outside the window to his left, a transparent wash of blue, too thin to mirror his office, which was neat, as usual. Books and treatises stood at attention on shelves, and accordion files sat in alphabetical order on the credenza, next to a Nerf football spray-painted gold, a worn baseball glove, and the Leaning Tower of Baseball Caps, standard-issue for every boy AUSA.

"It looks like a plea agreement in *U.S. v. Montgomery*," Dan answered, glancing at the papers.

"Your case."

"No, it's not."

"Yes, it is."

"No, it isn't." Dan smiled. "Is this a game?"

"You signed the plea agreement."

"No, I didn't."

Vicki blinked. "Look at the signature page."

Dan turned to the back of the agreement and read the signature page. "Huh. I didn't sign this."

"It's not your signature? It looks like it."

"I know." Dan shook his head, mystified. "I see what you mean. It does look like my signature, but I didn't sign it. I don't remember this case."

"It's only eight months ago, or so."

"Yes, so I would remember it, and I don't. David Montgomery? Don't know the name, and I'd never give him that easy a deal." Dan eyed the signature again. "Somebody must have forged my name."

"A *forgery*?" Vicki felt her mouth drop open. She just assumed a signature in this office was a valid signature, but maybe she was being naïve. The only alternative was that Dan was lying, and she couldn't bring herself to conclude that, not yet.

"It has to be a forgery, because I didn't sign it."

Vicki considered the possibility. "If it's a forgery, it explains a lot. But who would forge your name, and why?"

"I don't know." Dan looked at the agreement again, then held it up to the lamp on his desk, a halogen light with a black metal shade.

"What are you doing?"

"I don't know, trying to see something. A watermark, a fingerprint, I don't know. This is weird." Dan lowered the document, still examining the last page. "Strauss and Bale signed it, too. This looks like their signatures, but maybe they're forged, too."

"*Three* forged signatures?"

"If you'll forge one, you'll forge three."

"But that's crazy," Vicki said, nonplussed. "Who would do that?"

"I don't know. I can't explain this, babe."

Vicki couldn't either. "Maybe it was your case, and you've forgotten? You were on trial at the time, in Morales, the heroin distribution case." She had figured this out during her ATF meeting. "Maybe you were so preoccupied, you don't remember the deal, or signing it."

"Let me think a minute." Dan frowned deeply. "No, I swear, I don't remember this case at all. I didn't work this case. You have the file?"

Vicki slid it across the table, and Dan thumbed through it, reading.

"This is old CP stuff. Common Pleas. Nothing from the federal case."

"I know. I assumed you had the rest of it, the indictment and the grand jury transcripts."

"I don't. It's not my case. Where'd you get this?"

"The To Be Filed bin, on the very bottom. Buried."

Dan returned to reading the file. "Hmmm. Looks like Mr. Montgomery's been a bad boy. He lucked out with this deal, big-time. Who's his lawyer, Clarence Darrow?"

Vicki felt too confused to laugh, and Dan kept reading and commenting.

"A public defender. Uh-oh, they're gaining on us."

"Dan, it's not funny."

"Tell me about it. It's my name on those papers, and I'm a better prosecutor than that."

Vicki didn't know what to think, and Dan met her eyes with his usual blue frankness.

"What do you want me to say, babe?"

"The truth. I want you to tell me the truth."

"I'll ignore the insult. I'm telling you the truth." Dan stiffened, hurt. "Now what's going on?"

"I think that Montgomery killed Reheema's mother. He lives on the same block as the Bethave family, he's a hired killer who was free when she was murdered, and his nickname's Kermit, I bet because his voice is froggy."

Dan's expression grew as serious as she had ever seen him.

"What?" Vicki asked.

"I should've known, this is about Reheema. I thought it was something from your meeting with the ATF agent, but it's not." Dan looked suddenly sad, his strong shoulders sloping. "I should have known."

"If what you're saying is true, someone forged your

name, and Bale's and Strauss's, unless they signed it. Aren't you concerned about that?" Vicki leaned forward. "A minute ago, before you knew why I was asking, you looked very concerned."

"Yes, it's a bad thing. I was concerned, I *am* concerned. Somebody signed my name on some papers, and we'll look into it tomorrow." Dan sighed. "But that doesn't mean that Montgomery killed Reheema's mother. You didn't find any killer, just because somebody forged my name on papers about his case. It's not logical. It doesn't follow."

"How can you be certain he's not the killer?"

"How can you be certain he is?" Dan raised his voice, and Vicki stood up, taking the file and plea agreement from his desk.

"I don't want to fight anymore, I don't have time. I'm going to ask Bale why he signed this, or if he signed this, and—"

"Don't, Vick. He's not in, anyway."

"Is Strauss?"

"No."

"Where are they?"

"Over at Angelo's, I was just about to tell you. We're all going out to dinner tonight, to celebrate the bust. Plus everybody knows about the promotions, so we're partying before the official announcement. Of course, you're invited. I was hanging around, waiting for you."

"I don't feel like a party. I'm going to the Philly detectives with this."

"Those detectives, Melvin and the other one? They'll be at Angelo's, too." Dan stood up with a final sigh, regarding her as if from a distance. He slipped his hands into the pockets of his jeans. "So now what, babe? You gonna come to the dinner and make a big scene? Wave a plea agreement around and scream about forgery?"

"Why not, Dan?" Vicki gestured at the dark window. "Reheema's out there and this guy is loose. What if he tries to finish the job and kill her? Am I supposed to forget about that? Go out and have a few drinks?"

"There's a time and a place for everything, and the dinner tonight would be neither the time nor the place."

"Is everything about politics with you?"

"I'll ignore that, too, because I know you're upset." Dan bore down, his voice calm and steady. "But please, I'm asking you, don't do this tonight, not there. They'll never forget it. You'll end your career. It's suicide."

"No, Dan. It's murder." Vicki turned on her heel, with the file.

Before she left for the restaurant, Vicki stopped by her office to call Reheema. Her cell rang and rang, then her voicemail picked up again and she left another message: "Reheema, it's getting dark and I'm worried about you. Call me as soon as you get this." Vicki stopped herself. Reheema had her cell, so where could she call her? Angelo's was the office's go-to restaurant, around the corner. "In five minutes, I'll be at a restaurant, Angelo's." Vicki gave Reheema the address and phone number, which she knew from ordering takeout all the time. "Call me there and we'll—"

Beep, the voicemail stopped. Her message box must be full. Vicki hung up, frustrated. She had to get going. She grabbed the plea agreement, folded it, and stuck it in her purse; there was plenty of room now that she'd left the gun at home. Then she went to the door, plucked her down coat from the hook, and hurried out of the office.

FORTY-FIVE

BY THE TIME VICKI HIT THE SIDEWALK, THE sky was dark and the new snow reached almost the top of her boots. The air wasn't as bitter cold as it had been before the storm, and snow fell steadily, more bits of ice than cornflake flurries, visible only under the streetlights, shaken from the sky like common salt. She hustled down Chestnut Street, which sat under a foot of newfallen snow and was deserted except for an empty SEPTA bus churning past, its tires dropping caked white zigzags formed by its treads.

Everybody was staying home tonight, waiting to see what the storm would bring, and Vicki felt approximately the same way. She didn't have any choice but to do what she was going to do. If it ended her career, so be it. If she lost the man she loved, then that would have to be, too. Hurrying along in the cold, kicking snow sparkling in the streetlight, she reflected that she'd never taken a stand with so much on the line.

Even fighting with her father over her job didn't qualify. In the end, Strauss and Bale had been right; this *was* the bigs. Vicki bent her head against the storm and hurried ahead.

The sidewalk in front of Angelo's had been shoveled, but with two feet of snowbank lying around the entrance, the place seemed more bunker than restaurant. Vicki wiped wet hair from her face, pulled on the heavy door, and went inside, where she was greeted by the smells of Rolling Rock on tap, slow-cooked tomato sauce, and filthy red rug. Angelo's Ristorante was an Olive Garden without the health code compliance, and Vicki could never understand why the U.S. Attorney's Office had adopted the dump. Not that it mattered tonight. At least it was warm.

She walked into the small entrance room, actually a dark bar with a greasy counter, which was empty tonight except for the bartender watching ice hockey on the TV. Vicki nodded hello to him and followed the noise level to the back, which was hopping. Three long, red-checkered tables had been set up and the seats filled by everyone who had been at the meeting the other day, but now they were wearing casual dress and mixed drinks. Strauss sat happily at the head of the center table, talking with the mayor on his right, their animated expressions illuminated by candles flickering in thick yellow bowls. Bale sat next to him, chatting up the deputy mayor, and lawyers from the city solicitors, joking around with the office's public relations lady. Filling out the rest of the long table were other AUSAs and some recent alums, including Jim Cavanaugh, who caught Vicki's eye and winked.

The table on the far left was ATF and FBI; Chief

Saxon raised a glass beer mug, along with the top tier of FBI and ATF agents, and a group of federal marshals, all laughing and talking. The table on the right was headed by the police commissioner, in shirt and tie, and the seats occupied by his deputies, a few favored beat cops in uniform, and at the far end, Detective Melvin and his taciturn partner with the golf windbreaker, whose name Vicki kept forgetting. A civilian couple sat at a red-checkered table along the paneled wall, but the smallish, square room was otherwise dominated by law enforcement. Dan was nowhere in sight, and she tried not to care. Her mission was to get Bale's ear in this crowd, then Detective Melvin's.

"Allegretti!" Strauss called out, gesturing to her. "Siddown and dry off! Have a drink!"

"The Vickster!" Bale waved at her with a broad smile, then resumed his conversation with the deputy mayor.

Vicki wiped her hair back again and dripped her way to the table, where the only seat was at the near end, so she took it, sliding out of her coat and purse and hanging them on the back of her chair. She would have to wait to make her move because dinner had just been served. Sheets of eggplant parmigiana, oval plates of fried calamari, huge bowls of meatballs and penne pasta covered the table, and a young waitress materialized and plunked an empty dinner plate in front of Vicki.

"What'd ya want ta drink?" she asked.

"'Course she wants a drink!" Bale shouted down the table, hoisting his glass. "Give her what I'm having, rum and Coke!"

"May I have a Diet Coke?" Vicki asked, turning to the waitress, but she was already gone. Instead, leaning over her, close enough to kiss, was Dan Malloy. He was whispering something when the room erupted with shouting.

"Malloy! Malloy! Where the hell you been?" Strauss yelled, and Bale joined in:

"You workin' late again? Tryin' make me look bad?"

"Malloy, you SUCK!" shouted a federal marshal whom Vicki recognized from the intramural football championship. "They can promote you, but you still SUCK!" The other marshals burst into laughter, then started chanting. "YOU SUCK! YOU SUCK! YOU SUCK!"

"Thank you, thank you!" Dan laughed, straightened up, and waved like a presidential candidate, as Vicki tried to figure out why he was standing there.

"Get your hairy ass over here, Malloy!" Saxon shouted, making a megaphone of his big hands. "I wanna hear that punch line!"

"Gimme a minute!" Dan shouted back, then leaned down again and slipped her his cell phone. "Reheema called. She's fine and she wants you to call her back. Press one." He straightened again quickly and wedged his way toward Saxon.

Surprised, Vicki got up with the cell phone and hurried toward the bar where she could hear, pressing one on the way. The call connected instantly; her new cell phone had been Dan's number one speed dial. "Reheema?" she asked.

"Yo, you there?"

"Yes." Vicki pressed her hand over her free ear. The

noise from the dining room intensified as the chanting turned profane. The civilian couple left, laughing as they walked past Vicki on their way to the exit.

"I'm okay, I'm fine. Good work on Montgomery. Later, you have to tell me how you found out."

"Sure. Why did you call Dan?" Vicki asked, confused.

"I had to. I couldn't reach you at the office, and he was on your speed dial. Number one."

Modern love. We used to be on each other's speed dials.

"Listen, I have news, big news, but you need to be where I can talk to you."

"I can talk here." Vicki was watching Strauss and Bale, laughing. The marshals clustered around Dan and they were laughing, too, their entrees untouched in the revelry.

"Where are you? It sounds noisy."

"It is. I'm at this dinner for work. It's a little hard to hear."

"Who's there, at the dinner?"

"Everybody from work, the detectives, the mayor. What's the difference?"

"Damn, girl! Hurry up and get yourself where you can hear me."

"Okay." Vicki walked farther away from the dining room into the empty bar. The bartender watched the Flyers on TV, but it was quieter. "Now it's fine. What?"

"What I'm going to tell you, you have to stay calm. Don't let it show. Keep a poker face."

"What?" Vicki's gut tensed. Through the doorway she could see Strauss still laughing with Bale, their heads bent together, and the marshals joking around with Dan. She looked away, to concentrate on what Reheema was saying.

"I found this neighbor who knew something, an old lady. Black. Her name is Dolores Cooper, and she lives alone, way down at the end of the block, across the street from Jackson. She doesn't know Jackson, but here's what happened." Reheema was almost breathless with excitement. "Cooper loses her dog one night about a month ago, so she goes knockin' on the neighbors' doors, up and down the street, and she knocks on Jackson's."

"And?"

"It was late at night, around eleven o'clock. Cooper knocks and knocks on the door. Nobody answers it. But she sees the lights on and she hears people, so she keeps knockin'. Still no answer, but she sees the lights on and she's buggin' about her little Taco Bell dog."

"Taco Bell dog?"

"The dog with the Spanish accent. The Taco Bell dog."

"A Chihuahua?"

"Whatever. So she goes to the front window and looks inside the house, through an opening in the curtain."

"Whoa."

"I know, right? She looks inside the living room, and who does she see sitting there on the couch, inside Jackson's house?"

"Who?"

"Chief Bale, from your office, and a white guy."

What? Vicki couldn't have heard Reheema right.

She pressed the cell close enough to her ear to give herself a brain tumor.

"You there?"

"Say again, please," Vicki said, her mouth dry.

"Cooper sees your *boss*! The black one, Chief Bale, and a white guy with him."

No. "That's not possible."

"She's sure of it."

"How does she know it was him?"

"I showed her the front page of today's paper, like you did yesterday. I was showing her Browning, and all of a sudden she points *beside* his picture to Bale. She knows Chief Bale. He was in Jackson's house last month!"

"Couldn't be. Who else's picture is on the front page?"

"Wait a minute." There was the sound of a newspaper rustling. "It's today's paper, Sunday. The page I showed her has Toner, the white van guy, and Browning and his driver, Cole. And Strauss and your boyfriend, Dan the Man. But she didn't identify them. Only Bale."

It couldn't be. Not Bale. "Who is the white guy she saw?"

"She couldn't see his face. She only could see the face of the black guy, Bale. He was closer to the window. They were both sitting on the couch."

"She must be wrong. He would have said something the night Morty and Jackson were shot."

"Vicki, Cooper *identified* the man. Didn't even stop to think about it. Knew Bale right off. Said she remembered him because he was a very nice dresser.

Fancy suit and tie. Mustache. Handsome. Looked like a rich man. Like a lawyer, she said."

My God. It sounded exactly like Bale. Could it have been him? Did Bale know Jackson? Why hadn't he said anything?

Vicki asked, "How good are her eyes? You said she was old."

"Not that old. Sixty."

"She wear glasses?"

"No."

"Is she nuts?"

"No, she's cranky."

"Does she drink or do drugs?"

"Vicki, give it up. She saw Bale and a white guy, and she never got her Taco Bell dog back. She'll never forget that night, she says. She loved the dog. She cried when she told me the story. I spent all afternoon with her."

"What were they doing in the room, Jackson and the two men?"

"Talking."

Something was very wrong at the office. Bale. The forgeries. Montgomery and Jackson. Were they connected? How?

Vicki asked, "Then what happened?"

"Cooper left. She felt all guilty when she found out Jackson was murdered. I think she feels worse about the dog, though."

"Why didn't she tell this to the cops?" Vicki asked, but she knew the reason.

"They didn't interview her, and she was ashamed to admit she spied on the girl, anyway."

"You have her address?"

"Sure." ·

"I'll have to talk to her. I want to verify it."

Reheema scoffed. "Whatever, she'll tell you the same thing."

"Where are you?"

"On Jackson's street, in your car."

"Come home now. Keep moving. Montgomery's out there somewhere."

"It'll take me two hours to get back to Center City, in this snow."

"Good, call me when you're close to the restaurant and you can pick me up. I'll keep Dan's phone with me, or try the restaurant."

"Got it."

"Reheema? Good work," Vicki said, then hung up. She flipped the phone closed, her thoughts and emotions in a tumult, and looked up. In the dining room, they were all laughing, joking, and launching into a chorus of "Danny Boy," with Dan singing loudest of all:

"'From glen to glen, and down the mountain side, The summer's gone, and all the flowers are dying, 'Tis you, 'tis you must go and I must bide.'"

Vicki couldn't go back into the room yet. She couldn't believe it. She had always trusted Bale; she liked him the best of all the brass, and now he was going to be U.S. Attorney. What had he been doing in Jackson's house? Who was the white guy? What, if anything, did any of it have to do with Montgomery? Had Bale forged those signatures, and why? Vicki didn't have any answers, but she couldn't get them standing here. She steeled herself and went back into the party, with Chief Bale and a roomful of white guys.

They were all singing with Dan, "'But come ye back

when summer's in the meadow, Or when the valley's hushed and white with snow, 'Tis I'll be here in sunshine or in shadow, Oh Danny boy, oh Danny boy, I love you so.'"

Ouch. Vicki met Dan's eye, then looked away.

So be it.

FORTY-SIX

VICKI TOOK HER SEAT AND FAKED A SMILE AS
Bale rose and started singing "When Irish Eyes Are
Smiling," which brought more laughter from the
crowd. Beer and wine flowed freely, and the entrees
were forgotten. The waitresses arrived with acute tri-
angles of cherry cheesecake and set the desserts in
front of each seat, whether occupied or not; obviously
the staff wanted to end this meal quickly and close the
restaurant because of the storm. Vicki wished them
luck; she had seen this floor show at the Christmas
party. It started in Ireland and ended in Motown.

Bale led the singing, into a knife microphone,
"'Sure 'tis like the morn in Spring, In the lilt of Irish
laughter, you can hear the angels sing.'"

Vicki plastered her smile in place and sipped the
Coke that had been put beside her plate. Rum. Ugh.
She sipped it because she felt thirsty and watched the
action, thinking. She couldn't bring herself to accept

that Bale knew Jackson, but she couldn't imagine why else he'd be there, only a month ago. Did Bale have something to do with framing Reheema? And who was the white guy? Could it be someone else from the office? The thought stunned her. But what was the connection to Montgomery and the forgeries?

While Bale sang, Vicki reasoned it out, thinking aloud to herself, if such a thing were possible. Bale could have been the one who gave Montgomery the sweet plea deal and forged the other signatures. He still handled some cases himself, so it was at least possible. That would mean that he knew Montgomery. But it didn't mean that he had anything to do with Montgomery killing Reheema's mother, or Reheema, did it? Of course not. But why forge the signatures? Why hide the plea agreement in the To Be Filed bin? Why lose the rest of the federal file on Montgomery?

At the front of the room, Strauss looped an arm around Bale, and they segued into their Motown medley, though instead of "Ooh Baby Baby," they went with "My Guy," to surging laughter.

Vicki analyzed the events separately, to determine if they were connected. One, a month ago, Bale was meeting with the only witness against Reheema, who would frame her on the straw purchase case, and two, almost a year ago, he gave a plea deal to a man who would eventually kill Reheema's mother and maybe Reheema.

Vicki blinked. The nexus could be Reheema. Did Bale have something against Reheema? Some reason to want her convicted for a straw purchase, and later, even dead? What was going on? Vicki resisted the conclusion. What was she thinking? That Bale put Jackson up to framing Reheema and he hired Montgomery to kill her?

Am I nuts? Vicki felt suddenly light-headed and sipped her watery rum and Coke, watching the crowd get rowdier and sing their way through the entire Motown catalog. They tried to get her to join in, but she waved them off, aware that Dan was watching her from the front of the room. She had his cell phone in her purse; she'd give it to him later. She picked at the cheesecake, but it didn't help. She shouldn't have had the rum, and pushed the drink away.

She tried to plan, despite her attack of nausea and/or disillusionment. The most prudent thing would be to wait until she interviewed Cooper, then after she had all the facts, to approach Bale to see if he lied, then trap him. A typical cross-examination. What was it Justice Holmes had said? Cross-examination was the engine of truth. But she couldn't think of Justice Holmes, Bale, or Mystery White Guy right now. Her stomach was iffy. She needed to wash her face, to feel better.

She got up, left the room, and went to the bar. On TV, the Flyers were losing and the bartender wasn't there, and Vicki walked past the barstools and downstairs to the ladies' room, which was a grimy single bathroom in the basement. She washed her face and dried it with toilet paper, because Angelo's had only those stupid air hand driers, then she assessed herself in the mirror. Her eyes were a tired blue, her hair was finally dry but hung in black waves, and her lip gloss was long gone. But her stomach felt a little better. She went back upstairs and crossed the bar area. The bartender was still gone and the TV was on, and Vicki glanced back at the screen. And gasped.

On the TV, the familiar red banner read LIVE—
BREAKING NEWS, under a dark shot of a snowy city
backstreet and a white Cabrio, cordoned off with yellow crime scene tape. The Cabrio's driver's-side door
hung open, and dark stains splattered the beige interior
of the door. Blood. The screen switched to a view from
the back of the Cabrio. In the back window was a crimson H and an Avalon bumper sticker. Vicki felt as if her
heart stopped. It was her car.

Reheema.

The voice-over said, "An attempted carjacking
leaves one dead on a side street in the Greater Northeast tonight. Chopper Six was first on the scene with
this exclusive footage."

*No. Reheema. Montgomery had killed her and
made it look like a carjacking.* Vicki gripped the bar
for support.

The voice-over continued, "The dead man has been
identified as David Montgomery of West Philadelphia."

What? Montgomery, dead?

"An eyewitness told police that the carjacking victim
was the driver of the VW Cabrio, an unidentified
woman, who was stopped at a stop sign when the man
allegedly jumped from a car behind her, opened her car
door, and attempted to forcibly remove her from her
car, ultimately shooting her."

Reheema.

"The victim fired back, killing Montgomery with
one shot. She has been taken to University of Pennsylvania Hospital, and police report that she suffered gunshot wounds to the stomach and is in critical
condition."

Reheema, in critical condition.

The TV screen switched to a weather story, and Vicki watched numbly as a male announcer in a station-logo windbreaker stuck the clichéd yardstick into a snowbank. She felt stunned. Disoriented. Unhinged. The news seemed almost surreal, but the attack on Reheema was proof positive. The killer was Montgomery. Reheema had been shot and could die. Vicki should go to the hospital but she couldn't leave here, not the way she felt right now. She had something to do. She wasn't waiting another minute. Damn prudence, politics, and even Justice Holmes.

FORTY-SEVEN

BALE WAS TALKING TO THE OFFICE'S PR LADY,
standing near the edge of the singing group, now led
by Strauss, who was warbling "Tracks of My Tears"
with the police commissioner and the mayor himself.
The federal marshals formed a separate group, segue-
ing into "Uncle John's Band," for an impromptu battle
of the bands. Dan must have been somewhere in the
center of the marshals group, because Vicki didn't see
him. She made a beeline for Bale.

"I need to talk to you right now," Vicki whispered in
his ear, curling her fingers around the sleeve of his tailored jacket.

"I didn't know you cared," Bale joked, liquor on his
breath. He permitted Vicki to lead him out of the dining room and into the bar, which was still empty, and
they stopped near the front door. Bale wavered
slightly, clearly the result of rum and Coke. His brown
eyes looked shiny, his skin greasy, and his white cut-

away collar was uncharacteristically unbuttoned, with his silk tie hanging.

"Reheema Bristow was just shot by David Montgomery. She killed him."

"I don't understand." Bale blinked slowly, the effects of alcohol or bad acting.

"You're not that drunk, Chief. You know who David Montgomery is. You handed him the deal of the century. You forged Dan's and Strauss's names on the agreement to make it look kosher. And I can't believe this, even as I say it, but you sent Montgomery to kill Reheema. To finish the job he started with her mother."

"I don't know what you're talking about." Bale's gaze shifted nervously to the dining room, but he didn't seem outraged or even confused, which confirmed Vicki's worst suspicions.

"You were in Shayla Jackson's house a month ago. I have an eyewitness. It was late at night, in her living room, you and a white guy."

Bale's face fell abruptly, his forehead creased. He met Vicki's eye and his lips parted slightly; for the first time since Vicki had known him, he wasn't controlling the situation.

"Tell me what's going on, right now, Chief. The truth, or I'm taking you to the commissioner this minute."

"Hold on, it's not what you think, Vick. Come with me, I'll explain everything." Bale took her arm and, before she knew it, he was tugging her outside the restaurant and under the tiny roof over the entrance. Snow fell softly, and the back street was deserted, all the shops closed. Vicki worried for a minute that she wasn't safe, but the entire law enforcement community was on the other side of the door. Bale touched her arm gently. "Relax, Vick, it isn't what it looks like. Calm down."

"I can't calm down. Reheema was *shot*, Chief. Did you—"

"Okay, let me explain." Bale's expression was soft, his brown eyes urgent in the yellowish lights over the restaurant entrance. "I'm trusting you to keep this to yourself. It can all blow over, it's almost blown over already."

"What is? What are you saying?"

"Project Clean Sweep, remember? Strauss's push to get guns off the street. Started last year, before you came. Big success. I had a lotta pressure on me to get convictions. Pressure from Strauss, pressure from the media." Bale stepped closer, lowering his voice needlessly, and Vicki smelled the rum that was undoubtedly loosening his tongue. "You know the reports the gun dealers make, of the multiple purchasers. I took a little shortcut, paid some folks to say they knew the people on the reports and that they resold the guns. Reheema was on the list."

"You *paid* Jackson to frame Reheema?"

"Yeah," Bale admitted, his voice low.

"*Chief.*" It was all Vicki could say.

"Oh come on, get real. You know they resold the guns. Why else they buying eight or nine semiautomatic weapons? Glock, Taurus, Ruger, Smith and Wesson? We knew they did it. We just couldn't prove it without the witness."

"Reheema didn't do it. She didn't—"

"She's the only one, and you know it. With the rest, it was going through the motions."

"The motions are *due process*." Vicki felt sickened and angry. "And where'd you get the money for this?"

"Don't ask too many questions, Vick. Take it from me, it's the government, there's money around."

"How many people did you do this to?"

"Let it lie, Vick, they're in prison now, and I'm about to get the big job. Play ball and it'll go away. It was a one-shot deal, I won't do it again." Bale's tone turned almost plaintive, as if the tables were turned, and Vicki were the chief and he the AUSA. "I learned my lesson, believe me, I did. This thing got way outta control."

Vicki couldn't believe her ears. "Chief, did you really send Montgomery to kill Reheema?"

"Look, I had to. I was exposed, with Bristow. She's got an attitude problem, that one, I heard from the way she mouthed off at the detention hearing. When Jackson got killed and the case against Bristow fell apart, I knew she wouldn't shut up."

"Chief, that's conspiracy to murder!"

"It wasn't all my fault. *You* got into it and you wouldn't let it go! This whole thing woulda gone away if you—"

"Murder doesn't go away!" Vicki interrupted, incredulous. "Montgomery murdered Reheema's mother! He tried to murder her! You can't get away with that!"

"Don't think of it that way, Vick. Just let it go. Montgomery's dead and gone, so I have no exposure. Let it go, and I'll take care of you."

"*Let it go?*" Vicki repeated, horrified.

Suddenly, the wooden door opened, and Angelo's bartender came out in a black knit cap and a Flyers jacket. He nodded to them both and walked up the street in the storm. Bale gestured her away from the entrance, and Vicki followed him to the next little overhang that covered the entrance of a low-rent jewelry store. The lights were off inside the store, and in the front window, a blue neon sign glowed, DIAMONDS BOUGHT AND SOLD. Velveteen display stands in the window stood empty, the diamonds gone.

Vicki tried to gather her thoughts, but they wouldn't gather, she was so appalled. "Chief, how can I just let it go? How can *you*?"

"Look, Montgomery was just insurance, in case another one blackmailed me. Everybody in the neighborhood knew him, he kept everyone in line. I swear, I didn't really think I'd have to use him."

"*Another* one?"

Bale ignored the question. "Come on, when I made the deal with Montgomery, I didn't know the case against Reheema would fall apart. I didn't know those kids would kill Jackson and Morty that night. How would I know that Browning didn't pay his bills? Like I say, it just got outta control."

"It's wrong, Chief, all wrong. You have to turn yourself in."

"Oh, please!" Bale snorted, the neon blue outlining the contours of his cheekbone. "Are you kidding? Right now, when I'm *this* close? When I finally got *over*? Are you *nuts*?"

"You have no other choice!"

"You want me to do time with the clowns I convicted, Vick? Ruin my wife and family?"

"No, I don't, but it's the only way."

Bale stepped back in anger, as if pushed. "You're

pretty high and mighty for a kid, you know. So full of yourself. So naïve, so *gullible*. You think I'm the only one who cuts a corner or two? You're a rich kid, you don't know *jack* about how things get done."

"Chief—"

"You think I worked alone?" Bale's eyes flashed in the blue darkness. "You know I didn't. You know I was in it with a white man. Don't you want to know who he is?"

The white guy.

"Guess. We'll play a little game. Guess the white man who worked with me to set Bristow up. Guess the white man who found Jackson in the first place."

"It's not Dan, is it?" Vicki blurted out, before she realized she'd even suspected him.

And Bale smiled.

FORTY-EIGHT

"THAT ALTAR BOY?" BALE SAID. "MALLOY? No way."

"Not Strauss."

"The boss?" Bale snorted. "Nah, he didn't know a thing. He turns his head away. He only knows what he wants to know. He doesn't like to get his hands dirty."

"Then who?"

"Morty."

Vicki felt stunned, as if from a blow.

"Yes, it was Morty."

No. "Chief, you're lying."

"The hell I am! Your great Morty, your beloved Morty, *everybody's* beloved Morty." Bale looked almost gleeful. "It was Morty who knew Jackson, not me. He found her for me. He was the white man with me that night, when we went to her house, to get her ready for Bristow's trial."

Morty. "That can't be. He would never—"

"Yes, he would. He *did*. He was dedicated, all right. He wanted the guns off the street and he did what it took. Ha!" Bale seemed to draw strength from revealing the secret, a seasoned prosecutor saving his best argument for last. "Your case, Bristow, was the last case, the *last one*, and we woulda made it happen if those kids hadn't broken in that night! Morty didn't see that one comin,' poor guy."

"But why would he—"

"Morty wanted the guns off the street, Vick! You know that! You heard at the wake, nobody worked harder. He was happy to do whatever he could do, and you should be, too. You know, you and him were a lot alike."

Vicki felt too heartsick to ask what he meant.

"You and Malloy, you think I don't know about you two? The way you look at each other? Mixing business with pleasure. Morty was, too. Had to go and fall in love with the CI, with Jackson. She was twenty years younger than him." Bale leaned over. "And it was his baby she was carrying."

The baby in the postmortem report. She was mixed race.

"He was gonna marry the bitch! That's Morty for you! That's the *real* Morty! Married to the job, for real! Surprised?"

Vicki couldn't speak. She flashed to the night Morty was killed. Him lying there, blood bubbling on his lips. The first thing he'd asked: *"How's the CI?"*

"See, that's my point, Vick. Morty was in on it because it was the right thing to do. It got us what we wanted, what we're all working for."

Vicki remembered Mrs. Tillie Bott, telling her that

Shayla had said she was going to change her life. She'd been planning a future with Morty.

"If it was good enough for Morty, isn't it good enough for you?"

Vicki couldn't answer. Agent Thompson, just today, had said, *"He seemed so happy since you two have been working together, this past year."* But it was Shayla Jackson whom Morty had been with this past year. He'd fallen in love and was going to be a father.

"You should've let it go, Vick. I told you to get off it, I *warned* you to get off it! I even assigned you to another case, but you wouldn't let it go."

"How can I, Chief?" Vicki asked, aching.

"You have to."

"I can't. I won't."

"Come on, kid. What're you doin' here? What're you doin' to me?" Bale's gaze shifted, suddenly jittery. "You're backin' me into a corner here, you know that?"

"You backed yourself into it, Chief. I know about you and so does Reheema. Dan will know, too, when he finds out Montgomery shot Reheema. Nobody's gonna let it go, Chief. It's over."

"I thought we were friends! We got along pretty good, didn't we? I didn't fire you when I could have, I knew you would never let go then. Keep your friends close and your enemies closer, right?" Bale's eyes looked suddenly wet, and Vicki felt a twinge of sympathy.

"I'm not your enemy, Chief."

"Sure you are, you're gonna turn me in!"

"I have to turn you in, if you don't turn yourself in."

"You and Malloy! You're gonna ruin my career, my life!" Bale's voice went higher and he grew panicky, desperate. "You want to ruin my life? My kids' lives? That what you want?"

"No, but—"

"I'm not goin' in, Vick. I can't. I know I did wrong, but I can't go in. Sorry." Suddenly Bale slipped his hand into his jacket and pulled out a dark Beretta. His pained eyes locked with Vicki's over the gun, and she knew from his tears what he was going to do. She had faced a loaded gun before, and this bullet wasn't meant for her.

"Chief, no!" Vicki shouted. She lunged for Bale's wrist just as he started to turn the gun on himself.

Crak! the Beretta fired, and Bale fell backward, knocked off balance. They both tumbled back and fell hard on the snowy sidewalk, the gun flying from Bale's open palm.

"CHIEF!" Vicki screamed, terrified that Bale had been hit, but behind her, the glass window of the jewelry store shattered. A security alarm went off in the next minute, earsplitting in the quiet night.

"No!" Bale moaned, lying still and beginning to sob, and Vicki held him close as a shout came from the entrance of Angelo's.

"VICK! VICK!" It was Dan. Then there was another shout from someone else, then another, closer. The cops and AUSAs were coming, running to them. They would arrest Bale, who was wracked with sobs, and take him away.

Vicki felt like crying, too, but she couldn't give in to emotion just yet.

Reheema.

FORTY-NINE

VICKI AND DAN SAT TOGETHER IN THE WAIT-
ing room of the hospital's emergency department, which
was empty except for a couple waiting to see an ER
doctor about a flu. Fluorescent lights shone harshly in
the allegedly comforting room, with its pastel-blue
walls, hotel watercolors, and pink pamphlets about
wellness and the importance of dietary fiber. Newspapers and magazines, their covers curled, made a peri-
odical pile on the wooden coffee table, and the place
smelled vaguely of McDonald's French fries from a
bag left in the waste can. An old TV mounted in the
corner was on low volume, but Vicki couldn't bear to
watch again the footage of her Cabrio with Reheema's
blood on the door. She had left her parents a phone
message, so they didn't freak when they saw the TV.

She rested her head on Dan's shoulder, but she
couldn't stop thinking about Reheema, who was still in
surgery after three hours. Vicki was going crazy with-

out an update on her condition; the doctors were working on her, and the nurses and other emergency staff were busy. She had cried all the tears she could cry and sat in the chair, still in her down coat, feeling exhausted, tense, and guilty.

"I should've been with her, Dan."

"No, you couldn't. You did everything you could."

Vicki didn't reply, but she would never believe that. She could never have predicted where this long road would lead her. Now that she'd reached the end, she didn't want to be here. Not if it cost Reheema her life.

She couldn't stop the mental images of what else was to come. The indictment against Bale. His wife and kids heartbroken. Her office and ATF disgraced. Strauss and Saxon before microphones, reminding the public of the overwhelming majority of hardworking, dedicated AUSAs and agents. Lawsuits by those wrongly imprisoned, costing the federal government millions of dollars. Every penny won would be deserved, and even so, couldn't make anyone whole. And some of those released would surely have been found guilty, if the government had been given the chance to prove its case; now they'd be freed, even well-compensated. So they could buy more guns for resale.

"If justice is good, why does it feel so bad?" Vicki asked.

"Lot of things that are good feel genuinely lousy."

"Like what?"

"Apologies, for example. I owed you a major apology and I gave it to you. I was wrong, down the line, and you were right." Dan smiled, tired and still wearing his North Face coat, too. "You know, I love you."

"I love you, too." Vicki liked the new tone in his

voice, but neither of them felt like kissing. "So when you gonna dump me?"

"After I sleep with you a few more times."

"Hey!" Vicki shoved him, and Dan laughed softly, defending himself with his hands.

"Stop. I'm not dumping you."

"What about work?"

"We can handle it."

"What about what people will say?"

"They don't like it, they can kiss my Irish ass." Dan smiled. "I'm sorry I said you had to choose. I was being stupid."

"I'm sorry I said you were political."

"I am. At least, I was."

"I can't believe Morty," Vicki said, disgusted. "He turned out to be such a fraud. A liar. His whole life was phony."

"You're just angry."

"Damn right I am. Look what he did."

"You and me, we don't see Morty the same way."

Vicki frowned. "Since when did you start talking like Dr. Phil?"

"Since about an hour ago, when my girlfriend almost got killed, *again*, and my professional life turned upside down. It makes you think."

"How do you see him?"

"I'll tell you, if you can listen with an open mind." Dan's smile vanished, and his eyes looked dead-level at Vicki. "It's something I learned from my father, and from Zoe."

"The cat?" Vicki smiled. "Okay."

"As you know, Miss Zoe is loving, smart, and loyal. She has many wonderful qualities. Plus, she loves you."

"I'm her landlord."

"That's beside the point. She hated my evil ex-wife."

"So did I."

Dan smiled. "But to my point. She's wonderful but she's not perfect. She has a heart murmur."

"Yeah, so?"

"I love her anyway."

"So?"

"Think about Morty. He was smart and dedicated and able, but he had something wrong with his heart. And so did Bale. You're angry because you think you can't love them anymore, especially Morty. But you can." Dan nodded. "My father is in the same category, but I love him anyway, too."

"You forgive him?"

"No, I mean I love him. It's a direct line."

"Is that possible?" Vicki didn't get it.

"Yes. Listen to me. I'm older, I'm taller, and I know." Dan reached over and moved a stray tendril from Vicki's face. "You're looking for the perfect man, babe, and all there is is me, and your father."

Vicki blinked, and suddenly there was a rustling at the threshold to the waiting room. They both turned. Reheema's surgeon, an older man in wrinkled blue scrubs and a puffy patterned hat, came bustling in, his face drawn with concern.

"Doc?" Vicki said, alarmed, sitting up.

FIFTY

BY EARLY MORNING, THE SNOW HAD FINALLY
stopped falling outside the hospital room window, leaving the sky a pure sapphire-blue that appeared only in
the coldest winters, as heaven's own reward. Vicki sat in
the high-backed chair while Reheema slept, a transparent green oxygen tube looped under her nose, and her
hair black and fuzzy on the thin white pillow. A thermal
blanket was pulled up to her neck, covering the band-
ages from her surgery. The doctor had said that she was
going to live, but her recovery was going to be slow, so
Vicki had sent Dan home.

In time Reheema stirred and her large eyes fluttered
open, and Vicki got up and crossed to the bed, feeling
a rush of relief. It was one thing to have a doctor say
she was going to live, and another to see her finally
wake up. Vicki eased onto the edge of the bed, near
Reheema. A splint had been taped to the top of her
hand where the IV went into the vein, and her long,

dark fingers bent slightly, with the residuum of dried blood under her fingernails.

Reheema opened her eyes and managed a weak smile. "Back off," she said, her voice hoarse. "Last time you got this close . . . you tried to strangle me."

Vicki smiled. "That was before."

"Before what?"

"Before I knew you'd sue me for it."

Reheema smiled again, then it faded quickly. The spirit was willing, but the body was definitely weak. She looked as if she could barely keep her eyes open, but when she did, they flashed with attitude. "I'll drop that suit . . . you treat me right."

"Now don't get fresh. I've been here all night and we haven't fought once."

"I was asleep."

"I'll take it. How do you feel?"

"Fine."

"Congratulations, you're out of intensive care."

"Dumb . . . to stay in here too long. I feel . . . fine."

"Oh yeah, you look fine. You know, I bet Dan you wouldn't make it. The minute you woke up, I lost fifty bucks."

Reheema smiled again. "Montgomery dead?"

"Yes."

"Good."

Vicki couldn't deny it. "And Bale's going to prison. I'll give you the details when you feel better."

Reheema smiled contentedly.

"Oh yeah, where'd you get the gun?"

"Where'd you . . . think?"

"My top drawer?"

"You hid it under your panties . . . bein' all badass.

Oooh." Reheema smiled again, then ran a dry tongue over her lips. "Yo, got some water?"

"Sure." Vicki picked up the beige plastic pitcher on the rolling bed table, poured water into a Styrofoam cup, and held it to Reheema's lips. "The doc said you'd be thirsty after the surgery, because they had to put a tube down your throat. I asked them, hey, can I put the tube down her throat? But they said no."

"Sorry I messed up your car." Reheema sipped some water, then eased back onto the pillow.

"It's okay." Vicki flashed on the bloodstained door on the TV news. She wasn't sure she wanted the Cabrio back, even if they could clean it up. "Lucky for me I already own an Intrepid."

"I get the Intrepid." Reheema eased back onto the pillow. "You take the Sunbird."

"I can't drive a stick."

"Then I got something . . . to teach *you*, Harvard."

"I could've told you that," Vicki said, and smiled. She set the cup on the bedside table, reached for Reheema's hand, and cradled it, which they both pretended wasn't happening until Reheema started to drift back to sleep.

And only then did Reheema's hand close around hers.

FIFTY-ONE

IT WAS AN AUGUST AFTERNOON, AND A NEC-
tarine sun shone on tall, leggy cosmos, their flowers
neon orange, chrome yellow, and vivid magenta. Next
to them sprouted a bunchy row of zinnias, in dusty
pinks and lemony hues, their heads like pom-poms.
Honeybees landed on the flowers, then buzzed along.
A young mother in jeans shorts and a red Sixers T-shirt
stood with a toddler, picking black-eyed Susans with
breakaway yellow petals and an unlikely black button at
the center. The air felt humid as a hothouse, but it
smelled sweet, earthy, and clean.

"This is amazing!" Vicki said, delighted.

"Nice, huh?" Reheema beamed. She looked relaxed
and healthy in a white cotton T-shirt and khaki shorts
that showed long, muscular legs. Bits of soil caked her
knees and covered the beat-up toes of her white Nikes,
and only an occasional stiffness in her movements suggested that her healing process wasn't yet complete.

"*Very* nice! It's great!"

"We're proud of it." Reheema tugged a curled brown leaf from a mass of tiger lilies, which formed an exotic backdrop to a grouping of lovely golden flowers, each one shaped like a sunny star.

"What are those yellow cuties?" Vicki asked, pointing.

"Coreopsis."

"Listen to you! Coreopsis! You *feelin'* the coreopsis?"

"I know, right? I'm a black girl with a green thumb."

Vicki laughed. "But no gardening gloves."

"Please. I'm not *crazy*."

Vicki laughed again. They were standing in the new community garden on Cater Street, which was located in the vacant lot that used to be the crack store. The neighbors had cleared the lot, built raised beds out of railroad ties, and created a garden on the right side of the lot, which got full sun almost all day. The left side was cleared, too, though beds had yet to be constructed. Vicki was thrilled to finally see the garden in bloom; she'd stopped by on her way to Devon, since it was time for an obligatory Sunday dinner with her parents.

"Now which plot is yours?" she asked.

"We don't do it that way. The way we do, the people like me who want to grow flowers, we sign up and plant the flowers together. We planted 'em in May, and now we all pick the ones we want."

"Sounds good."

"I made the rules, of course."

"Of course. You're the Block Captain."

"I'm the Block *Diva*," Reheema corrected, and they both laughed. "People who want to do vegetables, they sign up for vegetables. The vegetables are behind the flowers, over there."

Vicki shielded her eyes from the sun and looked against the brick wall, in the back bed. Tomato plants stood in neat green lines, tied to stakes by brown string, and an older woman in a sleeveless housedress and orange flip-flops picked ripe beefsteak tomatoes. A row of red and green pepper plants lined up in front, and on a patch of tilled soil lay thick furry vines with large, light green leaves and striped clubs of zucchini, one as big as a Louisville Slugger.

"That zucchini's a lethal weapon," Vicki said.

"Mrs. Walter's pride and joy. She grows so much damn zucchini, she's making bread every day, then relish. You ever eat zucchini relish?" Reheema wrinkled her nose. "S'nasty."

"Now you got suburban problems. You thought it was easy, being rich?"

"Ha! Be careful what you wish, right?"

Vicki laughed, and Reheema did, too, at the ridiculous notion. The neighborhood had begun a comeback, in only two seasons. The town watch patrolled regularly, rarely wanting for volunteers. Neighbors repainted the trim on their houses, replaced asphalt shingles that had fallen off, and put new Astroturf on the porch floors. Trash was stored in cans, not strewn on the street anymore, and the sidewalks had been swept. Best of all, people were outside without fear. This afternoon, mothers hung out on front stoops, talking while little girls jumped rope and boys practiced break-dancing on a flattened refrigerator box. The sight taught Vicki that, however hard-won, justice wasn't an end in itself. Instead, it was a beginning, enabling people to be safe, happy, and free. The rest was up to them.

Reheema cocked her head. "So how's work?"

"Way too busy. With Steptoe cooperating and Bale pleading, I got a boatload of new cases."

"But you love it," Reheema said, and Vicki nodded happily.

"And Dan says hi. And how about you? Did you get that coaching gig you wanted?"

"Yeah, a traveling team, a nice group of girls." Reheema smiled broadly. "Now I'm at city services by day and a track coach on the weekends."

"Take it easy, with the running so soon."

"I'm fine." Reheema waved her off.

Ring! Rring! Vicki's cell phone rang in her shorts pocket and she pulled it out and checked the display. MOM CELL, it read. "Excuse me, I should get this." She opened the phone and said, "Hey, Mom. Are we still on for dinner?"

"Yes, of course."

"What's up?"

"There's been a slight change of plans. We're here."

"What? Where?"

"Your father and I. We're parked in front of your father's old house."

"You and Dad? *Here?*" Vicki's eyes flared in horror, and Reheema stifled a laugh.

"Yes, dear. You left a message that you were stopping by a community garden in Devil's Corner before you came home, so we thought we'd take a ride down and meet you here. Where are you, exactly?"

In shock. "Wait there. I'll come to you."

FIFTY-TWO

"MOM, DAD, IT'S GREAT TO SEE YOU," VICKI said, as she walked over to her parents.

"Isn't this fun, dear?" Her mother came toward her smiling, chic in white Capri pants and a turquoise knit shell, with tan Tod loafers.

"Really fun." Vicki hugged her scented mother, whose sleek hair and skin felt refrigerated from the car's air-conditioning. Her father was standing on the sidewalk and frowning up at his old house, his hands resting on his hips. He wore a white Lacoste shirt and khaki pants, and hovered protectively near the front bumper of their silver Mercedes. The sedan gleamed like a flying saucer, and the Allegrettis looked as out of place as aliens, or at least, lawyers.

"I wanted to see the community garden," her mother said, looking around. Two little girls on their bicycles, their stiff braids flying, stared as they rode past.

"It's around the block, on Cater. I was just there with Reheema."

"Oh, your friend? I'd like to meet her. Is it far?"

"Not really."

"Wonderful, I'll take a little walk. It's good exercise."

NO! DON'T LEAVE ME HERE WITH THIS MAN! "Mom, why don't you wait? We can walk over together."

"But your father wants to look at his old house."

"He'll want to meet Reheema, too."

"Then he will, later. He wants to look at his house now. This trip was his idea. Go talk to him, go through the house with him, then walk over to the community garden." Her mother gave her a discreet shove toward her father, but Vicki had faced loaded Glocks with more enthusiasm.

"Mom—"

"Go!" Her mother turned on her expensive heel and walked away.

"It's on the left, down the middle of the block," Vicki called after her, and her mother waved, though she didn't turn back.

"Where's your mother going?" her father asked, coming over, as lost as Vicki, as if they were two baby birds.

SHE LEFT US ALONE! "To see the community garden."

"Where is it? I thought it was on Lincoln."

"No, it's on Cater. Right around the block." Vicki had grown so used to filling the air with words, she did it reflexively. "I'm sure we can catch up with her. She can't go fast on foot."

"She's a great gardener." Her father kept frowning, but maybe the sun was in his eyes. "She's been talking about that garden all week. This drive was her idea."

Really. "Mom said you wanted to go inside your old house."

"No."

No? "We could." Vicki gestured at the front door, which had been repaired. "A new family moved in, I heard from Reheema. We could just knock and ask, I'm sure they'd let us. Everybody knows Reheema."

"No, it was my father's house, not mine. I don't have any happy memories here. Let's go find your mother."

Ouch. "Okay."

Her father walked back to the Mercedes.

"You'll never get a space on Cater, Dad."

He turned. "I can't leave it here."

"Yes, you can. It's safe."

"It's an S class."

Vicki smiled. "It'll be fine."

"You'll indemnify me?"

"Up to thirty-seven bucks."

Her father pulled out his car keys and chirped the car locked, twice. Vicki turned and they fell into step, walking around the corner, where her father stopped, examining a brick wall. "Funny. I used to play stickball here, against this wall, with a broom and a pimple ball."

"A pimple ball?"

"They were white rubber balls with little raised dots. A pimple ball. We'd play for hours, with a half ball."

"Why half?"

"After the ball was dead, we didn't throw it away. We were too poor to throw it away. We cut it in half." Her father ran his fingers over the wall's soft bricks and came away with soot on his fingerpads that surprisingly, he didn't seem to mind. "We'd mark the wall with chalk for a single, a double, a triple."

"Sounds like fun."

"It was." Her father resumed their walk. "Played with the kids from the block. Mimmy. Squirrel. Lips. Tommy G."

Vicki looked over again, and her father was smiling. "Nicknames," he explained, needlessly.

"Your friends."

"Right. We didn't play on Lincoln as much, because of the traffic." They turned onto Cater and walked two doors down, where he slowed his pace in front of a row house. An African-American man stood on a metal ladder, hanging new red shutters on the windows. Her father stopped in front of the house. "My buddy Lips lived here. Leon DiGiacomo. We used to shoot craps in front of this house."

"That's illegal."

"Tell me about it. I got picked up once, by the cops."

"*You?*"

"Yes, me." Her father sounded almost proud. "They picked us all up for, what they'd call"—he thought a minute, his head cocked—"'gambling on the highway,' that was it. Must've been an old ordinance. They took us into the station and they made us buy tickets to the thrill show."

"What's a thrill show?"

"Like a circus. The PAL put it on, I think. Motorcycles and dancing bears." Her father laughed, and so did Vicki, surprised. She had never heard him talk about his childhood, and now she couldn't shut him up. He was walking again, pointing across the narrow street to the other side. "And we used to play knuckles in the street, right there."

"Knuckles?"

"A card game. And over there we played Pig and Dog. Basketball. We nailed a trash can to the telephone pole for a hoop." He mused as they walked, the sun shining on his head and shoulders. "I played outside all the time. We all did."

"Sounds like you have some happy memories, after all."

"Nah." Her father stiffened, suddenly. "You can't go home again, Victoria."

"I know people say that, but I disagree. I think you never really leave."

"What?"

"I'm Devon, Dad. I'm Devon, wherever I go. Some people are pure South Philly, and a New Yorker is always a New Yorker." Vicki never thought out loud in front of her father, but didn't stop. It was time to stop editing herself, even with him. "Think about it, Dad. There's Jersey girls and Valley girls. Chicagoans and San Franciscans, Texans and Bostonians. Steel magnolias and Southern gentlemen. And Reheema is so West Philly, when you meet her, you'll see it. She's great."

Her father was frowning, but maybe the sun was in his eyes again. Maybe the sun was always in his eyes, even indoors. Someday he would realize they had therapy for that, but Vicki wasn't going to be the one to tell him.

They reached the garden, where her mother was talking with Reheema. More neighbors were hard at work, weeding the pepper beds, restaking the tomato plants, and cutting cosmos for their dinner tables. Vicki introduced Reheema to her father, who shook her hand stiffly.

"So this is the community garden," he said, eyeing the lot. "Very pretty." His gaze fell on the unfinished left side, in the shade. "What are you going to plant there?"

Vicki cringed. It never failed, his always seeing the negative. She'd bring home four A's and a B, and he'd ask, *Why the B?*

"We're not planting anything there," Reheema answered. "We voted to make a place for the little kids. Put in one of those nice wooden playground sets and some wood chips underneath, so they don't get hurt if they fall."

"When are you going to install it?"

"When we get the money. Those wooden sets, they cost like two grand. The neighborhood's tapped out, after the dirt and the railroad ties, but we'll get it." Reheema nodded. "You know, this garden wouldn't have come about without your daughter, Mr. Allegretti. I was just telling your wife, Vicki's the one who got the crack dealers out of here."

"Please," Vicki said, reddening, but Reheema ignored her.

"Vicki saved this block, this whole neighborhood. She should get all the credit."

Her mother smiled, tightly. "We were so worried about her, we didn't appreciate the good she was doing. Maybe we were too worried."

"No, you *shoulda* been worried!" Reheema laughed. "If she were my daughter, I woulda been worried *sick*! You wouldn't believe the trouble we got ourselves into, the newspapers only had half the story. She's a real badass, your daughter!"

Hoo boy.

"She gets it from me," her mother said, her smile relaxing, and Vicki laughed, surprised.

But her father didn't reply and kept looking at the garden. Reheema seemed to run out of steam, uncharacteristically speechless. The moment was so awkward that Vicki stepped in to fill the silence.

"Thanks for the tour," she said. "We should probably get going. Congratulations on the garden."

"Thanks, take care."

"Yes, congratulations," her mother said, hugging Reheema briefly. Then she looped an arm around Vicki and they walked onto the sidewalk.

Her father didn't join them but lingered at the entrance to the garden.

"Dear?" her mother asked, and Vicki turned.

"In a minute," her father said quietly, then looked at Reheema. "I'd like to help you with the playground."

"I don't understand," Reheema said, and neither did Vicki.

"I'd like to send you a check, for the playground. I'll make it out for three thousand dollars, to cover the cost of the playset and the mulch. If you need more, you'll let me know."

"You don't have to do that, Mr. Allegretti," Reheema said, with a puzzled smile. "You don't have any responsibility for the garden. You don't even live here."

"I did once, and Victoria's right, part of me always will."

Whoa! Vicki thought, astounded. She would have hugged him but she wasn't sure he'd taken his Pravachol.

"Well. Okay." Reheema broke into a grin. "Mr. Allegretti, thank you so much, from the whole neighborhood."

"You're welcome," her father said, turning to Vicki with a new smile. "Come on, Devon. I'm taking my girls out to dinner."

"You got it," Vicki said, happily surprised, and the three of them turned to walk up Cater Street.

"That was a wonderful gesture, Victor," her mother whispered, taking her father's hand, and he gave her a quick kiss on the cheek.

Vicki felt her spirits lift, walking behind the two of them. Maybe Dan had been right that night in the hospital. Maybe she just had to accept her father the way he was. And think out loud at every opportunity. Like now:

"Dad, I can't get over it. You said I was right. In front of witnesses."

Her father turned, smiling. "I won't make a habit of it."

"I hope not." Then Vicki got an idea. "Hey, now that we're all in the love mood, can we go to an Olive Garden for dinner?"

"No," her parents answered, in unison.

And Vicki laughed.

AUTHOR'S NOTE
AND ACKNOWLEDGMENTS

I DON'T KNOW WHAT OTHER AUTHORS DO FOR fun, but I eat saturated fats, ride Buddy the Pony, and watch trials at the federal courthouse, where, in my ex-life, I worked as a lawyer. Not long ago I wandered into a courtroom and found myself watching a jury trial for crack-cocaine trafficking against members of one of the most violent gangs in Philadelphia history. I had seen only five minutes of the testimony before ideas and characters started to flow, and I knew I had a novel. In fact, the next morning I woke up with the first line of *Devil's Corner*. That has never happened before, and I'm hoping it happens again. Every year for the next ten years.

The case was *United States v. Williams,* and it was a piece of a much larger prosecution, *United States v. Carter, et al.* The 135-count indictment in *United States v. Carter, et al.,* is almost as thick as this book, and names thirty-seven defendants, charging, inter alia, conspiracy to distribute crack cocaine, use of a firearm during commission of a drug crime, and employing children to distribute drugs near schools and playgrounds. For the next few weeks at trial, I had an eye-opening lesson in crime and justice in a major American city, which happens to be my hometown.

You may recall that the crack cocaine trade reached peak levels in cities in the late 1980s, when it got more media attention than any narcotic deserves. But now that the spotlight has departed, crack trafficking has become business as usual, and unfortunately for all of us, stabilized at very high levels in major American cities, becoming a fixture in the urban landscape and bringing with it a continuous supply of crime and violence, tearing apart neighborhoods and families. As part of its Pulse Check program, the Office of National Drug Control Policy monitors crack cocaine trafficking and its effects in twenty-five major American cities: Atlanta, Baltimore, Boston, Chicago, Cincinnati, Cleveland, Dallas, Denver, Detroit, Houston, Los Angeles, Miami, Minneapolis/St. Paul, New York, Philadelphia, Phoenix, Pittsburgh, Portland, Sacramento, St. Louis, San Diego, San Francisco, Seattle, Tampa/St. Petersburg, and Washington, D.C. According to the most recent Pulse Check, of January 2004, crack abuse and trafficking are now infecting formerly "nice" neighborhoods in these cities and, inevitably, moving beyond the city into the suburbs. Also, crack is more frequently being traded for guns, stolen merchandise, drug-buying services, and sex than during the past ten years, though cash remains eternal. The effects on the quality of life, and of death, are profound, and they affect our country as a whole.

I wanted to deal with those themes in *Devil's Corner*, and I picked the brains of many experts, most of them involved in some way with *U.S. v. Williams*, to give this story its verisimilitude. Of course, any and all mistakes or misinterpretations are mine. The prosecution in *U.S. v. Williams* was steered by the experienced, able, and remarkably kind Rich Lloret Esq., of the U.S. Attorney's Office, working with his colleague AUSA Kathy Stark Esq., and super-dedicated agents from the Bureau of Alcohol, Tobacco, Firearms, and Explosives, among them Special Agent Anthony Tropea, Special Agent Steve Bartholomew, and as luck would have it, Special Agent Mike Morrone, whose wife, Marcelle, is an old friend of mine. I should make the obvious clear before I go further: I admire these people, not only for their intelligence and skill, but for their dedication and service to the public. I don't think we know enough about the amazing job they do, or the many sacrifices they make for all of us. But the characters in this book are not them, or "real" in any sense whatsoever, and this story isn't based on *U.S. v. Williams* or *U.S. v. Carter*. No truly original novel duplicates court cases or is "ripped from" today's headlines. Any fiction worth reading (or writing) comes from the imagination, and heart.

Having said that, this is me thanking every one of the people named above, who took the time to answer my endless questions, permitted me to watch them in action, and took me on office tours. Special thanks to Special Agent Mike Morrone, who lent encouragement, read a draft of the manuscript, and made corrections. Likewise, I am indebted to Nancy Beam Winter of the U.S. Attorney's Office, a brilliant and gorgeous prosecutor who read *two* early drafts of this novel; I owe you forever, girl, and admire you more than I can say.

Thanks, too, to my old friend Joan Markman Esq., of the U.S. Attorney's Office, who put me on to the right track at the outset. For background information about criminal defense lawyering, many thanks to Joe Mancano Esq., who was court-appointed in *U.S. v. Williams* and was equally generous with his time and expertise to help me, and to David Nenner Esq. And a special thanks to Judge Stewart Dalzell, of the Eastern District of Pennsylvania, who is one of the smartest, fairest, and finest jurists ever to serve on our local, or any other, bench. His integrity, literacy, and humanity epitomize what a judge should be.

Thanks again to Glenn Gilman Esq., public defender extraordinaire, and Art Mee, retired detective extraordinaire.

And thanks to another special group. As is my custom, character names in this novel have been auctioned off to wonderful people who supported a number of worthwhile causes, and thanks are due to those generous people; first to the Durham family, who contributed to the Literacy Council of Miami Valley, Ohio, in honor of their beloved mother, Marilyn Durham. Marilyn was a book lover and a devoted reader of mine, but sadly, she passed away before she could see her name in print. I think of Marilyn and her daughters often, and this book is in her memory.

Thank you to Ben and Illy Strauss, for their generous contribution to Key to the Cure, which raises money for breast cancer research, to Susan Schwartz, for her contribution to the Free Library of Philadelphia, Gail Graves and Lynne Graves Stephenson (donated to Chester County Library), Maureen Thompson (donated to Montgomery County Community College), Debbie

Hodill (donated to the Carrie Martin Fund), Janet and Harry Knowles of Metrologic Instruments, Inc. (donated to Goodwill Industries of southern New Jersey), and Karan Abdalla-Oliver (donated to Riddle Memorial Hospital). For various contributions, Lee Ann and David Donato, Phyllis Banks, the lovely Mama Jean Brightcliffe, and Barbara Pizer, for her many efforts to find a cure for breast cancer.

Thanks to the wonderful and hardworking booksellers like my local pals Joe Drabyak, Kelly Gartner, and Kathy Siciliano, to name only a few, who continue to support me and my books; I appreciate your friendship and loyalty so much, and am forever grateful. Joe always reads my early manuscripts, and I thank him so much for that. And to my readers, of course, this is a major hug. I think of you with every line.

Thank you to HarperCollins Publishers, my home for over twelve books now, and special thanks to the brilliant Jane Friedman, Brian Murray, Michael Morrison, Susan Weinberg, and Carrie Kania, for all of their support and very hard work. Thanks to Christine Boyd and Ana Maria Alessi, and to the wonderful, hardworking, and extremely gorgeous Marie Elena Martinez. Last but hardly least, a huge hug to my invaluable editor since page one, Carolyn Marino, a dear friend. And thanks to Jennifer Civiletto, who keeps both Carolyn and me on track.

Another huge hug to Molly Friedrich, Aaron Priest, and Paul Cirone, who have guided me for so many years. And to Laura Leonard, without whom nothing is possible.

And to my great kid, which is exactly when words fail.

A THANK-YOU NOTE
TO BOOK CLUBS, FROM LISA

THANKS TO BOOK CLUBS! I'M THRILLED AND honored that so many book clubs are reading my books and discussing issues like love, family, and justice. I thought I would help by proposing a list of questions about *Devil's Corner,* which book clubs can use as a starting point for discussion. And if you're not in a book club, you can play along, too:

Devil's Corner: Questions for Book Clubs

1. Do you like Vicki? Why? Are you happy or disappointed that the book features a new character instead of the regular women at Rosato & Associates?

2. Did you like the girlfriend connection between Reheema and Vicki? Do you think that two people from very different backgrounds can find a commonality for a friendship?

3. Do you think Dan and Vicki make a good couple? Do you think that people who work together should date? Do you think that Vicki crossed the line with Dan while he was married, even though they didn't have sexual contact before his wife left? Do you have a "work spouse"? Are they inevitable?

4. Do you think that Vicki has finally earned her father's respect? Why, even as adults, do we strive for our parents' approval? Do you think that Vicki owed it to her father to join his law firm, or did she owe it to herself to follow her own path?

5. Do you think that drugs are a major factor in the

decline of American cities? Do you think we are doing enough to control drugs? Are we doing enough drug education, and does it work? Did you understand what a "straw purchase" is? Did I do a good or lousy job making it clear? (Answer: In case I didn't make it clear, a "straw purchase" is when someone buys guns for the sole purpose of reselling them for drugs or cash.)

6. How strong do you think is the correlation between drugs and crime? Do you believe in legalizing drugs? Do you think it would have a negative or positive impact on the crime rate?

7. Is it fair to sacrifice a few innocent people to stop many crimes with projects such as Clean Sweep? Do we owe restitution to those who are unjustly accused?

8. Do you think that one or two people can make a difference and actually change a neighborhood? Do you think there will ever again be a day when we can just send our children out to play, even in the "safest" neighborhoods, in the same carefree way our parents could?

9. Were you surprised by the ending?

If your book club chooses to read *Devil's Corner*, I'd be happy to have a phone visit with you to discuss the book. Just go to the special page for book clubs on www.scottoline.com and sign up. And if you want a live, in-person visit from me, enter the annual contest—all you have to do is send in your book club photo, holding the book! If you win, I'll come and give you all the answers to the questions, so we can get right to the wine and saturated fats.

With thanks and lotsa love,

Lisa

Here is a sneak preview of
Lisa Scottoline's novel

DIRTY BLONDE

Now available from
HarperCollins Publishers

CATE FANTE WAS THE GUEST OF HONOR AT this celebration, which was drawing to a liquefied close. She raised a final snifter of cognac, joining the judges toasting her appointment to the district court. Tomorrow would be a slow day on the bench. The wheels of justice weren't lubricated by Remy Martin.

"To Judge Cate Fante, our new colleague!" Chief Judge Sherman shouted, and the judges clinked glasses with a costly chime. Wrinkled cheeks draped their tipsy smiles, and their bifocals reflected the flickering candlelight. Their average age was sixty-two, and an appointment to the federal bench was for life. At thirty-nine, Cate felt like she was joining the world's most exclusive retirement village.

"Speech, speech!" the judges called out, their encouragement echoing in the private room. Golden light glowed from brass sconces, and coffee cooled next to scalloped half-moons of crême brulee and bread pudding veined with cinnamon. "Speech, Judge Fante!"

"Order in the court, you crazy kids," Cate called back, rising with her glass and only apparent bravado. She managed a smile that masked her panic about what to say. She couldn't tell the truth: namely, that she was secretly intimidated by a job described in the Constitution of the United States. Or that she only looked the part, in a Chanel suit of butterscotch tweed, donned like overpriced armor.

"Keep it short, Cate." Judge William Sasso formed a megaphone with his hands. "It's past my bedtime."

Judge Gloria Sullivan chuckled. "Give her a break, Bill. We listen to you, and God knows what a trial that can be."

"No, he's right." Cate gathered her nerve. "Thank you for this lovely dinner, everyone. You said a lot of nice things about me tonight, and I just want you to know—I *deserve* every single word."

"At last, an honest judge!" Chief Judge Sherman burst into laughter, as did the others. The young waiter smiled, hovering by the wall. The judges clapped, shouting, "Way to go!" "Well done!"

"Thank you and good night." Cate mock-bowed and caught the waiter's eye, then looked away. She accepted the congratulations and good-byes as the judges rose to leave, collecting their briefcases and bags. She grabbed her purse and they all walked to the door, filing out of the Four Seasons restaurant. On the way out, Cate felt a soft touch on her arm and turned to see Chief Judge Sherman, tall and stooped at her shoulder, his sterling silver hair slightly frizzy.

"Don't look so happy, kiddo. You're taking a major pay cut."

Cate laughed. "Chief, you give fixed income a good name."

Chief Judge Sherman laughed, as did Judge Jonathan Meriden, who fell into stride. Meriden was fifty-something, conventionally handsome, with sandy hair going to gray and a fit, if short, stature. Cate had legal history with Meriden. When they were both in practice, he'd tried a securities case against her and ended up losing the jury verdict and the client. Tonight he'd acted as if all was forgotten, so he'd sucked it up or warmed to her, with Glenlivet's help. They walked out of the lobby into the humid summer night, and Cate played the good hostess, waiting, until everyone had dispersed, to grab the last cab.

Inside, she leaned against the black vinyl as the cab lurched into light traffic. Its tires rumbled on the gritty streets, wet from an earlier thunderstorm. The air conditioning blew only faintly, and Cate eyed the rain-slick buildings like a stranger to the city. She'd lived in Philadelphia since law school, but her heart wasn't in the city. She'd grown up in the mountains, in a small town erased from the map. Cate still felt a twinge at the thought, even though she knew she wasn't supposed to care about her hometown anymore. She was pretty sure the official cutoff was fourth grade.

Cate's head began to ache. Today she'd presided over opening arguments in her first major trial, a construction contract case with damages of fifty million dollars. Fleets of pricey lawyers from New York had filed special appearances, and the witness lists contained more PhDs than most colleges. It was a bench trial, with no jury to make the decision, but at least it was a civil case. Cate already sentenced four men to federal prison, which was four too many.

The cab was stifling, and Cate lowered the window. A breeze blew in, too sticky to offer any relief, and she unbuttoned the top of her silk blouse. She felt the weight of her pearls like a noose. The night sky was black and starless, and the full moon a spotlight. She leaned back against the seat but her chignon got in the way, so she loosened it with her fingers.

She looked idly out the window. Couples walked together, their arms wrapped around each other, their hips bumping. A handsome man in a white oxford shirt dashed across the street, his tie flying. The cab turned onto one of the skinny backstreets that scored Center City, no more than an alley with rusted blue Dumpsters lining the curb. Cate caught a whiff of the rotting smell. "The scenic route, huh?"

"It's faster than South," the driver said, and the cab slowed to a stop sign, waiting for someone to cross the street.

Cate eyed a rundown tavern on the corner. DEL & ROY'S flickered a failing neon sign, and graffiti blanketed its brick. Its side window was covered with plywood, though an amber glow emanated from yellow Plexiglas in the front door, which was the only indication the bar wasn't abandoned.

It's Miller time, Cate thought. The line from an old TV commercial. Her mother used to drink Miller. *The champagne of bottled beer.*

"I'll get out here," she said suddenly, digging in her purse for the fare.

"Here?" The driver twisted around on his side of the smudged plastic divider. "Lady, this ain't the best block. I thought we were going to Society Hill."

"Change of plans." Cate slid a twenty from her wallet and handed it to him. Ten minutes later, she was perched on a wobbly barstool behind a glass of Miller. Lipstick stained the rim of her glass, a sticky red kiss slashed with lines, like vanity's own fingerprint. It wasn't her color, but she drank anyway.

The bar reeked of stale draft and Marlboros, and dusty liquor bottles cluttered its back underneath a cardboard cutout of Donovan McNabb, set askew. The bar area doubled as a hallway to a closed dining room, its darkened doorway marked by an old-fashioned sign that read LADIES ENTRANCE. Cate looked away.

The bar was half-empty, and a man with dark hair hunched over a beer two seats from her, smoking a cigarette. He wore a white T-shirt that said C&C TOWING, stretching in block letters across a muscular back. Three men sat beyond him, silently watching the baseball game, the Phillies playing San Francisco, on a TV mounted above the bar. They watched with their heads tilted back, their bald spots an ellipsis.

Cate crossed her legs, bare in her brown pumps, and took a sip of warm beer. She hated herself for being here, and at the same time, wondered how long it would take. It wasn't that she wanted to get home to sleep. She could function on almost none, from a childhood interrupted by nighttime alarms. She'd be pulled from bed and dressed in a winter coat with an embroidered penguin, worn over a thin nightgown. The coat was turquoise and the penguin of raised black fuzz, she remembered now, for some reason. She had loved that coat.

"Hey," said a voice beside her, and Cate looked over. It was the man in the T-shirt, with his beer and Marlboro. Up close, he had blood-shot blue eyes, heavy stubble, and hair that shone in greasy strands. He smiled drunkenly and asked, "How're you, beautiful?"

Cate turned to him and smiled. "Evidently, beautiful."

The man chuckled and set his beer on the bar, his cigarette trailing a snake of smoke. "I think I know you from somewhere," he said, putting his hand on Cate's bare knee. "Whas' your name again?"

"Karen," Cate told him, then moved his hand up onto her thigh.

Feeling thrilled and miserable, both at once.

*　*　*

Six months later, Cate sat in her high-backed chair atop the dais, waiting to start the day's session. The courtroom was packed, and she hid her anticipation behind a professional mask, which was turning out to be a job requirement. The jury trial had taken all last week, but today was the only day that counted, like the final two minutes in a basketball game.

Sixers-Hornets. It was on at the bar last night. Wonder who won.

Cate shifted behind the slippery wall of stacked pleadings in front of her. She hadn't slept well last night and was relying on her concealer, but was otherwise in full costume: synthetic black robes, dark blond hair in a judicial chignon, a swipe of pink gloss on her lips, and neutral makeup on largish, blue eyes. Finally the courtroom deputy flashed Cate a wink.

Showtime. Cate gestured to plaintiff's counsel. "Mr. Temin, let's begin. I assume that plaintiff continues his testimony this morning."

"Yes, Your Honor." Nathan Temin was a roly-poly lawyer with the paunch of a much older man and a dark suit that begged to be ironed, worn with equally unruly black hair. Still, Cate knew better than to judge a trial lawyer by his cover. She had dressed down for court many times. Prada didn't win jury verdicts.

"Excellent." Cate nodded. "Fire when ready."

"Thank you, Your Honor." Temin hustled to the podium with a Bic pen and a legal pad, then pressed down his suit with a pudgy hand. He greeted the jury and turned to his client, already rising from counsel table. "Mr. Marz, please take the stand."

Richard Marz walked to the witness stand, and necks craned from the gallery. Reporters scribbled away, and sketch artists switched to their flesh-toned chalk. The Eastern District of Pennsylvania didn't allow cameras in the courtroom, for which Cate thanked God and Chief Judge Sherman.

"Good morning, Your Honor," Marz said in his soft-spoken way, sitting down after he was sworn in. He was barely thirty years old, and his baby-blue eyes showed litigation strain. He smiled tightly, his lips taut as a rubber band, and he ran a finger-rake through muddy-brown curls that sprouted from under a cro-cheted yarmulke. A dark suit jacket popped open over his white shirt, and his striped tie hung unevenly. Everybody knew that people looked like their dogs, but Cate thought they looked like their lawyers.

"Good morning, Mr. Marz." She smiled at Marz in a professional way, feeling subterranean sympathy for his position. He was claiming that a powerful TV pro-ducer had stolen his idea for a series about Philadel-phia lawyers and developed it into the cable blockbuster

Attorneys@Law. In this battle between David and Goliath, Marz held the slingshot.

At the lectern, Temin tugged the black bud of a microphone down to his height. "Now, Mr. Marz, you testified last week that you had two meetings with Mr. Simone, leading up to the critical meeting. Please remind the jury of what took place at the first meeting, on June 10."

"Objection, Your Honor," said George Hartford, defense counsel. Hartford had gray eyes behind slightly tinted bifocals and was prematurely bald. He had to be about fifty, and stood tall and fit in a slim Italian suit with a yellow silk tie. "Asked and answered. Plaintiff's counsel is wasting the jury's time."

Temin said, "Your Honor, it's appropriate to review this proof because the weekend intervened."

"Overruled." Cate shot both lawyers her sternest look. "Let's not let the objections get out of hand today, boys. Play nice."

"Thank you, Your Honor." Temin nodded, but a cranky Hartford eased back in his chair next to his client, producer Art Simone. Even seated, Simone looked tall and trim, in his prime at a prosperous forty-something. His reddish hair had been shorn fashionably close to his scalp, and his tortoiseshell glasses paired with a caramel-colored silk tie and tan houndstooth suit. If Marz and Temin were the mutts in this dogfight, Simone and Hartford were purebred afghans.

"Mr. Marz," Temin began again, "tell us briefly what happened at the June meeting with Mr. Simone."

"Well, my background is from the DA's office, handling cases concerning computer fraud and Internet crime. I always liked computers." Marz sounded almost apologetic. "But I wanted to be a writer, so I started writing a screenplay for a TV show about four lawyers and how they use computer skills to solve murders. I called it *Hard Drive*. It was my wife who said, 'Why don't you do something about it?'" Marz smiled at his wife in the front row of the gallery, a sweet-faced brunette wearing a long skirt and sensible shoes. "So I called Art—Mr. Simone—and told him what I was doing and asked if he would meet with me about it, and he agreed to fly out to Philly to take the meeting." Marz turned to the jury in an earnest way. "That's what they call it in L.A., 'taking a meeting.' When they say no, they call it 'taking a hard pass.' A 'soft pass' is a maybe. I thought a soft pass was about sex, but what do I know?"

The jurors chuckled with evident warmth. Nobody loved underdogs like Philly.

Temin asked, "Had you known Mr. Simone, prior?"

"Yes, I knew him from summer camp from when I was, like, ten years old. Camp Willowbark, Unit A. He was my senior counselor, and I looked up to him like a big brother. I heard he was doing TV in Hollywood, so I hoped he'd help me out."

"And what happened at the meeting, briefly?"

"We met at Le Bec Fin and I told him all the details about my idea and asked him would he consider it for his production company. The lead lawyer in my series is a former detective, an Italian guy from South Philly who dresses great and is, like, a tie freak—"

"You needn't repeat the details," Temin interjected, preempting Hartford's objection.

"Okay, right, sorry. All that's important is that the four lawyers I told Mr. Simone about ended up being exactly like the four lawyers on *Attorneys@Law*."

"Objection, opinion!" Hartford said, and Cate waved him off.

"Overruled. The jury knows it's his opinion."

Temin paused. "By the way, Mr. Marz, were you surprised that Mr. Simone flew here to see you, as opposed to you flying out to California to see him?"

"I was, but he said he wanted to visit his mom anyway. She lives in a nursing home in Jersey." Marz's expression darkened. "Now I think he said to meet in Philly because Pennsylvania law is tougher than California law on—"

"Objection!" Hartford shouted, next to a stiffening client, and Cate raised a hand.

"Granted. That's enough opinion, Mr. Marz. Don't make me sorry."

The jury smiled, and Temin asked, "Did Mr. Simone take notes during this meeting?"

"No."

"Now, Mr. Marz, let's jump to the second meeting on September 15 and 16, also in Philadelphia. Who was present?"

"Myself, Detective Russo, and Mr. Simone and his assistant, Micah Gilbert."

"Is that Ms. Gilbert, seated in the gallery behind Mr. Simone?"

"Yes." Marz gestured to a pretty young woman in the front row. Micah Gilbert had attended the trial since day one, sitting next to an attractive jury consultant whose chin-length hair was an optimistic shade of red.

"What happened at that meeting?"

"Mr. Simone came to Philly to meet with me and a friend from the Homicide Division, Detective Frank Russo. Russo was the role model for the main character in my show, the South Philly guy. On the first day, we met at Liberties in Northern Liberties. I picked the place because real detectives hang there."

The jurors' eyes had lit up with recognition. The restaurant in *Attorneys@Law* was also called Liberties, and most of them had seen the show. It was impossible to find anyone in America who hadn't, despite Hartford's best efforts. The defense lawyer had used his three preemptory strikes to eliminate as many viewers as possible, with the help of his redheaded jury consultant. Cate never used a consultant. Picking a jury was Trial Lawyer 101.

"Now, what took place at Liberties?"

"Detective Russo and I told Mr. Simone about our characters and storylines. Also, I gave him some info on computers." Marz's gaze slid sideways to Simone. "Because he doesn't know anything about them."

"Did Mr. Simone or Ms. Gilbert take notes while you were talking?"

"No."

"Did you think that was strange?"

"I didn't then but now I think he didn't want a record of—"

"Objection! That's speculation again, Your Honor. Move that the irrelevant evidence be stricken." Hartford rose, but Cate waved him into his seat.

"Granted." Cate turned to Marz, on the stand. "Please refrain from editorializing."

Temin continued, "And what happened after lunch at Liberties?"

"Detective Russo and I took Mr. Simone and Ms. Gilbert to the Roundhouse, the police administration building, and we told him how things really work in

Homicide. We showed him some details about the squad room, like how the detectives prop the door open with an old trashcan and they never notice that the trashcan stinks, only visitors do." Marz turned again to the jury. "The trashcan matters, because it tells you about the characters. How they get so used to bad stuff, like the ugliness they see every day on the job."

Several of the jurors nodded soberly and one cast a cold eye at defense table. If the jury got the case now, they'd vote for Marz and his symbolic trashcan.

"And what did you do the second day?"

"Detective Russo and I drove Mr. Simone and Ms. Gilbert around the neighborhoods where the stories took place. It's called 'scouting locations.'"

Temin turned a page on his legal pad. "Finally, we come to your critical meeting with Mr. Simone, on November 9, also at Le Bec Fin. Who was present at the meeting?"

"Me and Mr. Simone."

"And what took place at this lunch meeting?"

"Mr. Simone said we were celebrating. He ordered champagne, two bottles, even though I'm not a big drinker." Marz shot a resentful glance at defense table. "Anyway I told him I had the treatment ready ahead of schedule and I gave it to him."

"Please explain to the jury what a treatment is."

"A treatment is a detailed outline of who the characters are and what the storylines would be. I had told Mr. Simone I'd get the treatment done by August, but I couldn't do it and my job at the DA's office, so I quit my job."

"Your Honor, may I approach?" Temin asked, and Cate nodded. He took from counsel table three thick black binders labeled HARD DRIVE and gave one to Hartford, one to the court clerk, and walked to the witness stand, handing the third to Marz. "Mr. Marz, is this the treatment that you wrote and gave to Mr. Simone?"

"Yes," Marz answered, examining the notebook, which was admitted into evidence. Temin turned again to his witness.

"Did Mr. Simone take notes at the luncheon?"

"No."

Temin let the implication sink in. "And then what happened?"

"Then Mr. Simone said—"

"Objection, hearsay," Hartford called out, his shiny Mont Blanc poised in midair, and Temin stiffened.

"It's not hearsay, Your Honor."

"Overruled." Cate turned to Marz. "Please. Go ahead."

"He said he was going to get the show ready to be produced and when he got it together, he'd call me. He was very excited, and we made a deal."

"Objection to the characterization, Your Honor!" Hartford called out louder, rising. "There was no deal in this matter!"

"Yes, there was!" Temin matched him decibel for decibel, and Cate raised her hand, like a stop sign.

"Gentlemen, enough. The objection is overruled. Mr. Hartford, the plaintiff can give his side of the story in his testimony, and your client can give his side. It has a nice symmetry, yes?" Cate gestured at Temin. "Proceed."

"Mr. Marz, what was the deal between you and Mr. Simone?"

"The deal was that he would produce my idea as a TV series, and he said, 'If I make money, you'll make money.'"

"He said those words?" Temin asked, and back at defense table, Hartford shook his head in mute frustration. Simone remained stoic.

Marz answered, "Verbatim."

"Is it possible that you misheard him? You testified that you had been drinking champagne. Maybe he said, 'Pass the salt?'"

"No, I heard him perfectly. Plus he already had the salt."

The jury laughed, and so did the gallery. Temin was trying to take the sting out of the cross-examination to come, but Cate didn't think it would do any good. She disguised her concern, resting her chin on her fist.

"Mr. Marz, seriously, how can you be so sure?"

"Because I had been wondering about when we were going to discuss money. My wife kept wanting me to ask him, but it was never the right time." Marz reddened, and his wife looked down. "So when he said that, I knew we had a real deal."

"Did you and Mr. Simone put this deal into writing?"

"We didn't need to, at least I didn't think we needed to." Marz scowled. "We're friends, *were* friends. He was my senior counselor. I trusted him to take care of me." Marz pursed his lips, and his disillusionment hung in the air between him and the jurors.

On the bench, Cate was about to burst, but instead wrote on her pad, DIDN'T LAW SCHOOL CURE YOU OF TRUSTING OTHERS?

Temin said, "Mr. Marz, some jurors might not understand that you, as a lawyer, would go so far without a written contract. What would you say to that?"

"I'd say they were right, but lawyers are people, too." Marz turned again to the jury. "I admit, I got carried away with the whole Hollywood thing. He has a jet. A limo. He knows all these famous people. I felt cool for the first time in my life. I may have been naïve, but that doesn't change the fact that Art Simone stole my show."

"No further questions," Temin said, but Hartford was already on his feet.